THE VIEW FROM DELPHI
A NOVEL BY JONATHAN ODELL

MacAdam/Cage
155 Sansome Street, Suite 550
San Francisco, CA 94104
www.macadamcage.com
Copyright © 2004 by Jonathan Odell
ALL RIGHTS RESERVED.

Library of Congress Cataloging-in-Publication Data

Odell, Jonathan, 1951 —
The view from Delphi / by Jonathan Odell.
    p. cm.
ISBN 1-931561-68-0 (hardcover: alk. paper)
    1. Loss (Psychology)–Fiction. 2. Children–Death–Fiction 3. Race
Relations–Fiction. 4. Mississippi–Fiction. 5. Young women–fiction. 6.
Hate–Fiction. I. Title.

PS3615.D454V54   2004
813'.6–dc22

                                                                2004000674

Paperback edition: July 2005
ISBN 1-59692-144-7

Manufactured in the United States of America.
10 9 8 7 6 5 4 3 2 1

Jacket and book design by Dorothy Carico Smith

THE VIEW FROM DELPHI

A NOVEL BY JONATHAN ODELL

MacAdam/Cage

My parents, Faye and Odell Johnson.

Your stories have mattered.

Many brave men lived before Agamemnon, but all unwept and unknown,
they sleep in endless night, for they had not poets to sound their praises.

— Horace

1944

Chapter 1
THE PICTURE TAKER

Through all her chores, Hazel kept a steady eye on the horizon, watching for her father's cloud to drift over the ridge, hoping against hope that today he would have it. So even before the guineas began their squawking "pot-a-rack, pot-a-rack, pot-a-rack," she knew it was him, rising with the dust above the last hill, his body weaving from side to side on the nut-brown mule named Jawbone. He must have it with him this time. The last two months had tested Hazel's capacity to keep hope at a simmer.

Her eyes still on his approach, she crammed an ear of corn into the mouth of the sheller and furiously spun the crank. Iron teeth ripped the kernels from the cob, pinging the hard pellets against the sides of the zinc bucket, alerting every chicken in the barnyard. They swarmed at her like pond minnows to a crumb of biscuit. Hazel shook her head. Some of God's creatures just didn't know how to handle it when things hoped for finally came into view. But Hazel did. At twelve, Hazel Ishee was a serious student of hope.

Impatient for the first handful of corn, a Rhode Island red scratched the dirt at her bare feet. Hazel scowled at the chicken. "Greedy feather duster. Don't you know how good things come to them that wait on it?" The hen pecked her big toe.

Hazel reared back her leg and let go with a fast kick to the tail feathers, sending the chicken squawking across the yard. "I hope Momma lets me pick Sunday dinner!" she yelled after it. That chicken didn't know the first thing about what Hazel knew. If she did, she would know that the most dangerous time of all was when hope gets close enough to touch. If you grab too quickly, you are likely to come back with a handful of nothing. Hope had to be coaxed within sure snatching distance.

Hazel raced to meet her father, flinging corn as she ran. When she got to the chinaberry tree, her bucket empty, she stopped abruptly, waiting for him to come the rest of the distance. She watched as the old mule poked like Christmas into the yard, as if he hated for his day in town to be done. Two bulging croaker sacks hung down from his broad neck. Not yet, Hazel told herself. It's not safe. Let it come closer.

A rapid series of bangs of the screen door brought eight blue-eyed, mostly towheaded children to gather around Hazel, all watching intently as Jawbone bore their father to the solid shade of the great tree. The littlest ones, nervously digging their toes in the dirt, whispered among themselves. Hazel heard names of candy rise up from them like prayers—"root beer barrels," "lemon drops," "peppermint sticks." Hazel was silent. The hope of candy didn't make her heart pound and cause her lungs to parcel out her breath one thin gasp at a time.

Major General Ishee slid to the ground and stood for a moment, wobbly kneed, before catching his balance against Jawbone. Steadied, he removed his floppy brimmed hat and slapped it across his leg, raising up a dry cloud of dust into his face. He coughed and spat.

Holding back with the others in a hot, tight knot just beyond the shady reach of the tree, Hazel tried her best to keep calm and steady. She knew you had to let him come on at his own gait. You couldn't rush him. If you tried, you were liable to get nothing at all.

A lone cloud passed over the blazing afternoon sun, casting a shadow over the entire yard. With the darkening came a rapid swell in the chirring of locusts from the woods across the road. A dominecker rooster clucked his way over to the darkened spot in the dirt where her father had spat and pecked at it. Breaking loose from the cloud, the sun retook the yard with a scorching vengeance. Not a child moved.

The screen door banged again, and Hazel's mother, Baby Ishee, drying her hands on a flour-sack apron, limped out onto the porch with twin boys who looked nothing alike, one angelic and the other wormy, clinging to the folds of her unbleached cotton shift cut deep at the breast for nursing. Gray and tired, hunchbacked from the weight of babies and time, she was not yet forty. At her feet, little Jewel, who had been laid out earlier in a potato crate lined with burlap in the shade of the porch, woke from her afternoon nap. Three months old and perilously puny, she began to squirm and cry, fussy at having been awakened by all the racket. Her mother looked down on the girl, like for all the world she wished she had the strength to lift up one more baby one more time. Instead she turned toward her husband and studied him warily as he lifted the sacks from the mule.

Major General, feeling his wife's keen eye trying to judge him innocent or guilty, held himself straight and steady. He nodded his head at her and smiled sheepishly, like one of her children situating himself for forgiveness. "I got you everthing you wonted, Baby," he called up to the porch, articulating too carefully.

When she glanced back up at her mother, Hazel wondered if her look was one more of disgust or of dread. Whichever it was, they all knew Major General's tender manners would not survive daylight.

Holding out the sacks to the two oldest girls, Onareen and Lurleen, he tilted forward and almost stumbled. The girls quickly retrieved the heavy sacks, saving their daddy from toppling over, but not before Baby Ishee had caught sight of the false step. She shook her head hopelessly at her husband and backed into the house, slapping the door behind her.

Major General looked up after his wife and frowned. "Y'all take them store goods on in to Baby," he grumbled to the kids. "Reckon that's all I'm good for anyways."

Hazel kept her eyes on her father in his sulk, but could hear her sisters giggling on their way to the house. They had found something in the sacks besides the usual flour and sugar and coffee and snuff for her mother. Most likely there was cloth and thread for making dresses, but not for her—for Onareen and Lurleen. By the time a dress worked its way down to Hazel, there wasn't anything left but a lot of patch and faded memory. Her older sisters were lucky in all things. They stayed in the house during the day to cook and clean and tend the younger children, while Hazel got sent to the fields dressed like one of the boys. Normally, she'd be jealous. But today, none of this concerned her. Hazel was waiting for something better than calico or even dotted swiss.

Her father held out the reins to a tall shirtless boy in overalls. "Dub, you and Aaron take Jawbone to the water trough, and then get him hitched up. Y'all still got daylight for plowing."

The older boys silently led the mule away as the smaller children, joined now by the twins, looked wide-eyed at their father, almost afraid to breathe. "What y'all looking at? Think I got money to spend on foolishness?"

The sharp smell of corn liquor attended his words. Somewhere between the farm and Bear Creek, he had already hidden the jug in a place easy for him to locate once the sun had gone down. Soon, he would find a reason to leave the house mad, storming off into the woods, and would stay until well after dark. But that was forever from now. Maybe by then he would have given Hazel what she had been hoping for. She could already feel the magic transforming her, lifting her above the petty concerns that worried the old Hazel. She might never be the same again.

The children's eyes followed his hand as it reached into a side pocket and then came out again, palm open and empty. He watched their expressions cloud up and only just before tears appeared did he reach in again and pull out a crumpled paper sack. He handed it to one of the boys.

"Georgie, you make sure everybody shares. No fighting, do you hear?"

They raced across the yard toward the barn and scrambled up into the hayloft to divide the loot. Hazel alone waited with her father.

"Did it come, Daddy?" she finally asked.

"Did what come, girl?"

"You know." She drew a circle in the dirt with her big toe. "The pichure. The pichure of me."

"Of you? They ain't just of you. I had them pictures took of all of us."

He pulled a can of Prince Albert from the bib pocket of his overalls and began to roll himself a cigarette. "You beat all," he said, missing the paper completely and spilling tobacco into the dirt. "Only other person you think about over you is you again."

Her father squatted down on his haunches, steadying his elbows on the tops of his legs, and started on his cigarette once more. In the pocket where the tin of tobacco had been, Hazel spied the envelope. Twisting her wrist behind her back, she anxiously hoisted herself up and down on tiptoes.

Once he had his cigarette lit, he pulled out the packet and held it just shy of Hazel's reach. "Gimme some sugar and I'll let you see em."

Hazel looked into her father's eyes. They were bleary, but still good-natured enough. Puckering her lips and slowly leaning down to him, she watched for his lids to close. When they did, she snatched the photographs from his grasp and fled.

Her father reached out for her, lost his balance, and with no one left to catch him, fell forward on his knees. Struggling to right himself, he called after her. "Come back here! You ain't the only one wonts to see em."

There was no stopping Hazel. Clinging tightly to her treasure, she headed straight for the storm pit.

When she pulled back the rough plank door of the earthen hole dug into the side of the high road bank, she was greeted by the smell of damp rot and bad dreams. Her father had dug the room for a shelter against tornadoes and summer storms, but so far the only storms were the ones her daddy brought home with him from town every Saturday in the jug.

Hazel picked up a heavy stick and, reaching through the doorway, beat the dirt floor three times, hard. She stood back, listening closely for the sounds of skittering in the dark, giving any snake that lay cooling itself in the pit a chance to be on its way. Hearing nothing, she entered.

Once her eyes had adjusted a bit to the dark, Hazel found the coal oil lamp and lit it. She pulled the door closed behind her and settled herself on the plank bench. For now, she had the pit all to herself. In a few hours, after her father finished off the rest of his jug, her mother would send all the kids down into the pit to join Hazel. It was the same thing each week. The children would huddle together and sing church songs to drown out their mother's screaming. At first light, they would sneak back to the house and into their beds, and neither the storm that passed in the night nor the injury it had done to their mother would ever be mentioned by anyone.

Hazel laid her hands on the envelope in her lap and closed her eyes, trying to imagine the miracle awaiting her. This would be the first photograph of herself she had ever seen, and she breathed deeply, savoring the excitement. Hazel was known to stretch good feelings out as far as they could go, anticipation being one of the best feelings she knew of. After everyone else had gobbled down treats or ripped open their presents,

Hazel always had something left to gloat with.

Once, when Hazel's father had taken her into town and bought her ice cream for the very first time, she took so long trying to imagine what the taste would be like, the whole thing melted to nothing but a puddle in the bottom of her Dixie cup. Her daddy got mad at her, not for the wasted ice cream, but for trying to cultivate the habit of hope. "Faith is fine," he said, "but hope is a luxury folks like us can't well afford. Hope does the plowing in Misery's field."

But Hazel didn't know if she could live without thinking something good was about to happen, not in the sweet by and by, but tomorrow, if not today.

Her eyes shut tight, sitting alone in the pit, Hazel imagined how beautiful that mysterious black box would have made her. The handsome traveling photographer from Memphis had promised his camera would make her look as pretty as anybody she had ever seen in the movies. She told him she had only been to one, but remembered every bit of it. He teased her and said she could ride along with him and show everyone just what pretty was. With a green-eyed wink, he said, "I reckon most people would order a dozen pictures on the chance one of them would come back looking like you."

She flirted with him, too. She tossed back her hair and licked her lips like she had seen Jean Harlow do. Her skin burned hot thinking about escaping from the Tombigbee Hills with a pearly toothed man wearing a seersucker suit and driving a red Ford coupe.

Hazel opened her eyes and saw her shadow flickering in the lamplight against the earthen wall. She stood and curtsied to the dirt screen. "Why, I would love to have this dance, Mister Pichure Taker," she said aloud.

Imagining she wore dainty silver slippers, she tiptoed barefoot across the cool dirt floor. She spun full circle with her eyes half shut, making believe she was a beautiful gypsy dancer immodestly twirling her silken skirts to a scandalized audience of hardshell Baptists. Basking in their disapproval, she took her bows and threw her final kiss before settling down once more on the plank. Her hands trembled as she opened the envelope and removed the photographs.

The first was of her momma and daddy sitting stiffly next to each other like strangers sharing a bench at the dentist's office. The next was of her daddy with his arm around Jawbone's neck. It struck her how much more at ease her father appeared posing with the mule.

Finally there was the family portrait. On one end was her daddy in his white starched shirt and overalls, and on the other end was her momma, holding little Jewel. Bunched between them was the brood of wooden-faced children, not a size missing between knee high and full grown, with two spaces left empty for the boys still off to war in the Pacific.

Something was wrong. She studied the picture again. Hazel could identify each brother and sister, but her own face was missing. Had the camera skipped over her completely?

Hazel gasped. That photographer had played an awful joke on her! In her place he had put in some half-starved orphan girl, neglected and bound to die soon. The poor little girl was stoop-shouldered and had hair the texture of broom straw. A dingy, hand-me-down dress swallowed the rail-thin body. The face was gaunt and hollow-eyed. She had the haggard look of a woman of fifty, not of a girl of twelve.

Gradually, her shock gave way to tears. The photographer had played no trick on Hazel. She should have known. Her older sisters had told her often enough. The wavy looking glass in her parents' bedroom had no reason to lie. Hazel Ishee was as homely as a wartheaded chicken. No fancy man with a magic black box or a head full of hope was going to change that fact of life.

Chapter 2
HOPE IN A BOTTLE

Baby Ishee tried to comfort her daughter by telling her that she was pretty enough, but Hazel was doubtful and pulled her mother by the hand to the mirror.

"You say pretty, but where do you see pretty? Point to me where I'm pretty."

Baby quickly grew impatient with her daughter's vanity and turned away from their reflections. "I said you're pretty enough."

"Enough for what?"

"Enough for any man from these parts. They ain't all that choosy bout looks."

"Were you ever pretty, Momma?" Hazel asked, not meaning to offend and biting her lip when she noticed the quick tensing of her mother's face.

For the first time, Hazel beheld her mother clearly, instead of through the clouded lens of a child's familiarity. She saw the hump that rose from her mother's back. She saw the tiny foot that had not grown since her mother was a child and had turned inward, causing the hobble Hazel had accepted as being as natural as hair color. Before she asked the question, Hazel hadn't thought of her mother in terms of "pretty" or "not pretty." But now the hump became freakish and the crippled foot grotesque.

She became aware of other things, too. Her mother's own nickname, Baby, had not been given to her out of affection or devotion, but because of a deformed baby foot, like one would call a person Stump or Gimp. With Hazel's question about prettiness came the understanding of why beauty was a topic that had been silently banned from their home. Suddenly, Hazel was ashamed for her mother.

As if reading her daughter's thoughts, Baby scowled at herself in the mirror. "Pretty don't mean much. Men are like hawgs," she said. "Ever seen an ol' hawg wearing spectacles?"

"No ma'am," Hazel answered, running her toe along a crack in the floor.

"Course not. Old hawg don't care what he gobbling up. Pretty ain't worth doodly-squat to no hawg." With that, her mother left the room, the baby foot sweeping the floor as she walked.

Hazel resigned herself to her ugliness. She took to her fate like a Christian martyr, wrenching all the nobility she could from her destined lot in life. She would become the wife of some man who didn't care what she looked like and who was more flattered at having his picture taken with a mule than with her. Like her mother, she would have a brood of children, each year pushing the last baby out of her lap to make room for the next one. She would live hidden away in hills so rugged and brutal that people might eventually compliment her ugliness as a sign of endurance, or even sainthood. In old age she would succumb to the surrounding landscape completely, doubling herself over like a mountain and watching time erode her face with gullies you could drive a truck into. Through it all she would never complain once. One day there would be a movie made of her life to inspire other ugly people. The thought moved her.

Hazel went about trying to nurture her father's brand of faith—faith that things would work out the way they were supposed to, in God's own time. It was a crushing, suffocating kind of faith that said, even though God struck hard bargains, He always paid off in the end. You might be dead when He got around to it, but nevertheless, He still paid off.

On one particularly fretful Sunday, after the preacher delivered an angry sermon about the vanity of human desire, Hazel made a sacred promise to renounce joy wherever it lurked. That very afternoon, when she came across her little brothers squatting under the chinaberry tree, lost in a game of marbles, she rebuked them with the fervor of a missionary. "Life ain't gonna be nothing but working from can to can't," she proclaimed.

"And y'all better get used to it."

She overheard Onareen and Lurleen in the kitchen giggling over some cute boy they'd seen at church. "One day we all gonna be deader than stumps," she reminded them. They were quite taken back by the pronouncement.

But in the end, it was hope that Hazel couldn't do without, that tingling anticipation of something bright and shiny and new and far beyond the hemmed-in horizon of the Tombigbee Hills, conjured up by little phrases she read on the magazine pages her momma pasted over the holes in the walls like "Fit for a Queen" and "Showroom New" and "Super Deluxe Model."

Late one afternoon, while wandering among some outcroppings, wrestling with her rebellious desires, she perched herself on a sandstone shelf that overlooked Bear Creek, and swung her legs fitfully over the edge, praying to Jesus to give her peace from all the nameless passions that mocked her faith. On the inswing, her bare foot grazed something cool and smooth under the ledge. Letting out a surprised little yelp, Hazel sprang off the rock, sure she had been snake-bit. When her imagined demise didn't commence, she examined her foot but found no wounds. She took a stick and waved it under the shelf. The stick found something and sounded with a clink. Reaching into the dark cavity, she pulled out a jug, partially filled with what looked like water. But it wasn't water. She had discovered one of her father's hiding places.

Hazel unscrewed the top and brought the bottle up to her nose. It cut her breath and made her eyes burn. She took a drink. The clear liquid breathed its fiery breath deep down into her and caused her to tear up and cough. She took another.

The sensation was like nothing she had expected, like two warm, loving hands clasping her face. Her spirits soared higher than the chinquapin oaks before her, higher than the Appalachian foothills that surrounded her. She now understood why her father drank. He missed hope, too.

Hazel stumbled home to find her prettiest sister, Onareen, sweeping the yard with a black gum branch. Noticing that Hazel's step was unsteady and her eyes wild, Onareen stopped sweeping and watched from the eye of the dust storm she had stirred up.

"Where you been? Look like you got the blind staggers."

Hazel only glowered at her sister, daring her to say the wrong thing.

"What's the matter with you?" Onareen asked.

"I'm ugly! Ain't you noticed?" she snapped. The magic liquid had transformed Hazel's despair into a giddy kind of anger, not at all unpleasant.

Feeling sorry for Hazel, Onareen told her that having beauty to lose was much worse of a burden than never having it to start with. "God was looking out for you by making you plain."

"So, you saying He did it on purpose?" she slurred. "You saying me being homely is God's will?"

"That's right, Hazel. Take it as a blessing."

Hazel pushed Onareen into the water trough. Right then and there she decided she was coming down whole-hog on the side of hope. Hazel was going to be pretty if it killed her.

She began with her hair. At the risk of getting whipped with her daddy's shaving strop, she snatched eggs out from under the laying hens and concocted a hair remedy made from the fresh yolks and mineral oil. Each night, after everyone had gone to bed, she boiled a flour sack towel and wrapped it around her treated hair. In a few weeks the texture began to improve. It was a good start, but after studying the photograph again, she knew she had long way to go.

Hazel tried to recall Jean Harlow's face up on the screen. On those close-ups, her lips and lashes and eyes all shone like distinct islands of beauty floating on a milk-white sea. In her own picture, Hazel's features appeared raw and fuzzy, blurring indifferently one into another. She decided she just had to get some cosmetic assistance. Knowing of only one person who used makeup, she cornered the undertaker at church and privately begged a supply of lipstick and rouge and powder. For her arms, which were as spotted as turkey eggs, she sent away for sample jars of freckle cream from ads in the back of the almanac.

The biggest challenge was her stooped shoulders. The effects of dragging a cotton sack from the time she was six, and years of hunching so as not to tower over the boys at school, could not be fixed with cosmetics.

After much deliberation, Hazel hit upon the solution. Salvaging a discard-ed mule harness from the barn, she constructed herself a halter to wear. Though the leather bit into her skin, it made her straighten up by forcing her shoulders back. For hours she practiced walking like Jean Harlow, one foot directly in front of the other.

It took a few weeks of clandestine experimentation before Hazel was ready for her grand debut. One Sunday before church, she secretly made herself up in the wash-shed and stayed hidden until everybody was on the wagon, impatient and calling for her to hurry up. Then, when Hazel judged the anticipation to be at its peak, she came waltzing out of the shed, painted like royalty.

The reaction was immediate. She was met soundly with a round of hoots. Her brothers called her Little Miss Sow's Ear. Her sisters called her worse. Her father made her go wash her face in the mule trough. She might have given up out of pure humiliation if not for the dark brooding look she saw on her mother's face. That's when Hazel knew she was on to some-thing good.

Then and there Hazel made herself a promise. Unlike her mother, she wasn't going to end up marrying somebody who couldn't tell the differ-ence between his wife and a mule, a man who was liable to beat the two-legged one and have his picture taken with the other, somebody so hope-less he couldn't see any other way to make a living than by breaking not only his own back but his wife's spirit to boot.

When I do take a man, she swore, I'm going to find me one who thinks I'm too deluxe of a woman to live and die behind a damned field animal.

1947

Chapter 3

MEN WITH ROUTES

Hazel eased carefully out of bed before first light, so as not to awaken her sisters, and slipped into Onareen's newest dress. Then she headed out to the wash-shed where her funereal cosmetics were stashed in a baking powder can under a loose board in the slatted floor.

Twenty minutes later, with a touch of sun breaking over the ridge and the roosters crowing, she was on her way. The morning light filtered through the trees and dappled the twisty dirt track as Hazel almost sprinted the two miles down to the big road. The day was perfectly suited to Hazel's high spirits. The early spring sky was so crystal blue she believed if she threw a pebble into it, it just might ripple. The hour was early yet and she had the whole day in front of her.

Once at the crossroads, she brushed the dust off her feet and slipped into her shoes. After smoothing the skirt of the stolen dotted swiss, she stood with perfect posture, awaiting her ride like a roadside princess under the bough of a flowering red bud. The blossoms were only a few shades lighter than her lips.

If Hazel had it timed right, the Watkins Flavoring man would be along before too long, and she was sure she could talk him into breaking off his route and driving her on into Iuka. He might even take the Natchez Trace down to Tupelo if she promised to go to the movies with him sometime and let him tell her during the newsreels how pretty she was, which was now a widely known fact.

It had taken a few years of shoring herself up and straightening herself out, but when she was fifteen, Hazel's looks took a sharp turn for the better. Her hair was a lustrous auburn, her eyes blued brighter than robins' eggs, and she had grown lovely, round breasts, finer even than Onareen's.

Or so she was told by her many new admirers, for Hazel was unable to stand before a mirror and judge her own looks. She could see her reflection clearly enough to fix her hair and apply makeup, but for the life of her, she still couldn't point confidently to the mirror and say, "This is where I am pretty." When she closed her eyes and tried to picture herself, the blurry image that came to mind most resembled the wretched little girl in the family portrait. So instead, she had to look for her reflection in the eyes of others. Sometimes, when there was no one around to reassure her, she would go to one of her father's hiding places where, after a few sips, she could feel loveliness radiating about her like foxfire.

Hazel heard the low grumble of an engine from off in the near distance, down below the hill. Just before the truck took the rise, Hazel recognized what sounded like the chiming of bells, but she knew it to be the tinkling of flavoring bottles and salves and cough syrups and shampoos tapping happily one against another. Her ride was here!

Hazel waved at the large driver jostling behind the wheel of the black paneled truck. She straightened her dress once more, smoothed down her hair, and prepared a cherry-lipped smile for Mr. Willis.

To her family's dismay, Hazel had discovered there were other types of men in the world besides farmers and sons of farmers. There were men with routes—men who drove automobiles from farm to farm, never getting their hands dirty on any of them, who looked at you directly in the eyes and weren't afraid to laugh at nothing at all. These were men who talked for the same reason other people sang, just for the pure, simple sound of it.

Hazel thought nothing of skipping school to make day trips into Tupelo with the insurance man and into Corinth with the Standard Coffee man and into Iuka with the man who had the rolling store. Hazel would catch a ride from any man with a route going her way. They looked at her with smiling eyes and told her she belonged in California. Or Jackson, maybe.

They would drop her off and she would spend the day at the soda fountain counter studying the fashions and poses of those picture-perfect women in the movie magazines. Poring over the color photographs, enveloped by the smells emanating from the cosmetic displays, she felt more at home in those drugstores than she ever did on the farm. There was something uplifting about being surrounded by beauty and beauty aids.

"Why, Hazel!" Rayford Willis called out from the window of the truck. "What's yore pleasure today? Vanilla? Black walnut? Rum? Lemon? I got it all. Yore wish is my command."

Hazel batted her lashes. Rayford Willis was terribly overweight, but Hazel loved his soft, doe-like eyes he never took off her. "You got anything that tastes like Cape jasmine smells?" she asked. "If you did, I believe I could eat it for dessert everday."

"Seems like I remember you saying that last time." Mr. Willis gave her a heavy-lidded wink. "I got a surprise for you, Hazel."

He reached down next to him. "Just happen to have a little bottle of gardenia perfume. That's another word for Cape jasmine. Want a sample sniff?" He unscrewed the top with his pudgy fingers and held the bottle out the window for her to smell, tempting her closer.

Instead, she reached out and snatched the bottle from his hand. The liquid was the color of gold. Then she smelled it. "Well, I swan! It's wonderful, Mr. Willis."

"Rayford."

Hazel noticed him blushing. "Rayford," she said. She looked again at the bottle. "It says here it's called Gardenia Paradise. What a pretty name. That's where Eve was, waddent it? Paradise? I'm gonna save up for me a bottle. Can I borry a dab of this?"

"It's yores, Hazel. A present."

"Ain't you sweet!" She wasted no time wetting a finger and touching it behind both ears.

"What you doing standing out on the road for, Hazel?"

"Oh, nothing mostly," she said, gently prying the bottle cap from his fingers, all the while looking up at him sweetly. "I was just hoping somebody might come by on their way to Tupelo. I sure could use me some ice cream. You don't know anybody heading that way, do you, Mr. Willis?" She dropped her eyes. "I mean, Rayford."

He checked his gas gauge and frowned. It was nearly full. "I reckon I need to go to the filling station anyways. Come on around and get in the truck."

In all these little roadside transactions, Hazel half understood that she was making promises, and was likely running up some kind of tab, but she didn't quite know yet what it was she owed. Then again, men like Rayford seemed happy enough just hearing their first names spoken and getting a soft good-bye kiss on the lips. Maybe, she told herself, that's really all there was to it.

An hour later, Hazel had already selected a magazine from the rack and was settling herself in at the counter. This was not the first time she had sneaked away from home in a dress not yet hers to wear, ready to pass the day sitting perfectly erect on a padded backless stool at Tupelo City Drug. She had become an expert at making her ice cream last for the longest possible time, while flipping through the pages of *Photoplay*.

Mr. Denton, the drugstore owner, was a middle-aged man with a full moon face and sad gray eyes that always seemed to lighten a bit when Hazel walked into his store. She got the impression she could stay perched at his fountain twenty-four hours a day and it would be just fine by him.

"This one's on the house, Hazel," he said as he set a bowl of her favorite in front of her. She noticed that his clean, scalded-pink hands were not much lighter than the strawberry swirl in the ice cream.

Watching her out of the corner of his eye, he slid the bowl a few places further down the counter toward the door. He grinned. "You know, I think my walk-in trade goes up on the days you sit closest to the window."

Giggling, Hazel got up and moved.

Mr. Denton was all the time saying nice things to Hazel, complimenting her on how pleasant she was to be around and telling her how impressed he was at the way she carried herself. Through their conversations, she had learned that he lived in a big rambling house with a childless wife. Hazel could tell he was lonely.

For a while he stood there watching Hazel as she carefully spooned her ice cream. Out of the blue he asked, "How old are you, Hazel?"

Even though she didn't know why he was asking, she sensed fifteen would be far too young. "Eighteen," she lied, a little surprised at how easy it was.

"How would you like to work for me? Tending the fountain here?"

"You want me?"

"Sure. I could start you out tomorrow. And after a while, I could even teach you how to keep the books." Mr. Denton lowered his eyes about to the level of her breasts. "Hazel, I can give you a future here." He stopped talking and stared silently for a moment, like he had forgotten he was in the middle of a job offer.

"Mr. Denton?"

He looked up quickly, his blush spreading through his thinning hair like a brush fire. Then he coughed and stammered, "Maybe it's because I never had a child of my own. But I'd sure like to help you get a leg up in life."

The more excited she became, the more excited he became and the more things he offered "Hazel, you could even stay with me and Mrs. Denton. We got rooms galore and I'm sure we can find you one you'd care to call your own."

"Why, that's one name I ain't never called a room before—my own."

"I won't even charge you rent. All you have to do is check in on my wife from time to time. How about it, Hazel? Will you move in with me...us?" His eyes were a lighter gray than she had ever noticed before, almost like a little blue was trying to peek through.

Mr. Denton didn't need to ask twice. That very day Hazel caught a ride back home with a Bible salesman to gather up her things. With the car idling under the chinaberry tree, Hazel informed her family that she was quitting school, moving out of the house, and taking a town job.

Her father turned his face to the wall. She was surprised to see her mother smile. "Done traded em off, ain't you?" she asked.

"Traded off what, Momma?"

"Yore purty ways." The smile soured.

"Ma'am?" she asked.

Her mother waved her off like a stray. "Go ahead on. You been bought and paid for. I can see it plain as day."

Onareen and Lurleen surveyed her with squinted eyes, as if they were trying to figure out who it was their mother was disgracing.

But Hazel could not be shamed. At long last, her family was no longer laughing at her. Appearing severely wounded, they acted as if Hazel had betrayed them by breaking with the family faith. With dark suspicious scowls they studied Hazel as she stood before them, gripping a fertilizer sack filled with all her hand-me-down possessions, burning with an alien hunger that wasn't from the want of food or clothes or shelter or anything else they could give or take away. They were powerless over her. It was obvious this strange girl nurtured a longing that looked right past them and into horizons that none of them could name.

Though Hazel could not explain her mysterious hunger, she knew it was either go now or let that unnamed longing suffocate in her breast. Whatever it was, this strange sensation taking her away from her family, she was sure of one thing: it was hers. Deluxe and Brand New. Never before used by nobody.

While the Bible salesman's Packard idled out in the yard, Hazel said good-bye to her parents and their grind-yourself-into-dust faith and headed out the door for her new life

The car had begun to pull away when Onareen, barefoot and wearing only her slip, ran across the porch and down the steps, signaling for Hazel to wait up. In one hand she carried a paper sack. When she reached the car she grabbed her sister's neck through the window and cried, "Go get it, Hazel! Go get whatever it is you been lookin for." As the Packard picked up speed, Hazel opened the bag to find Onareen's brand-new dress, the one she had been wearing only minutes before, still exuding the warmth of her sister's body.

That evening Hazel got dropped off at the large Victorian on Goodlett Street. Mr. Denton greeted her at the door with such a contrite look, Hazel suspected the deal was off. She held her breath, waiting for him to explain.

He reached out and took her sack. "Well, I think the first order of business is for you to meet Mrs. Denton. Don't be scared," which she hadn't been until he told her not to be. Exuding an air of dread, he turned and led Hazel upstairs to meet the bedridden Mrs. Denton.

It was obvious Miss Ellen had been expecting her. She sat upright against the massive oak headboard, her arms crossed, scowling. The woman's hair snaked down her neck in greasy black ropes, and from her pallor it was evident, even in the dimness of the room, Miss Ellen had not seen the light of day for quite some time. Scores of dirty dishes and medicine bottles were strewn about the room, littering every inch of furniture surface.

Miss Ellen gave Hazel the once-over, sniffed, and then turned to her husband. "Put her in the room across the hall from me. And tomorrow get some niggers and move my bed so I have a full-time view of her door. Do you understand me, Harold?"

Mr. Denton nodded. The woman might be ailing, but it was obvious to Hazel who was in charge of this household.

Miss Ellen reached over and picked out a marble from several she kept in a crystal dish on her nightstand. She stared hard at Hazel. "That way, Miss Ishee, if I need anything during the night and can't call out, I can throw one of these marbles at your door." Looking at her husband once more, she said, "I want a clean shot, if you know what I mean, Harold."

From the way Mr. Denton pinked up, Hazel could tell there was more to that story than marbles.

Surprisingly, Mr. Denton was decent to Hazel. Before she had put in her first full month, he kept his promise and tried to teach her bookkeeping. He seemed to enjoy standing close checking her columns, and occasionally commenting on the fragrance of her hair. Even though she wasn't skilled with the numbers, she did have nice handwriting, and he said that was almost just as important and gave her a dollar-a-week raise.

Hazel might not have been good with numbers, but she still had the sneaking suspicion that some invisible hand, better with arithmetic than she, was busy totaling all those unearned kindnesses cast her way, and one day the bill collector was going to come a-calling. She could deal firmly with a wayward pinch or a stray touch or an overheated embrace. That did not worry her. It was something else she felt but could not name that was on the table. Something more serious than the taking of her sex. It had to do with what she would be expected to give up willingly to the custody of some man.

Miss Ellen's suspicions, however, were strictly carnal in nature. Whenever Mr. Denton and Hazel were in the house at the same time, Miss Ellen made sure she had at least one of them in her sights. If both got out of range she was sure to call out for a glass of tea or an extra pillow.

But Hazel couldn't help thinking how nice it would be to make friends with an older woman. In her brand-new life, Hazel was in bad need of advice on matters she could never discuss with her own mother. Like men, for instance. They were beginning to drop by the drugstore, flirting and asking her out. But their hungry eyes and grinning, greedy mouths wanted too much, frightening her. Anyway, she had been doing just fine without a man. She liked working in the drugstore and greeting customers and learning about cosmetics. Already she had gotten off the farm without a man. Maybe she should just leave well enough alone until she was sure the right one had shown up.

That was just it. How do you know, she wondered, when you meet the right one? She needed guidance from a woman with experience in such matters, even if the only one she knew of was a sickly old thing with a dirty imagination. Miss Ellen, however, showed no signs of softening.

The day arrived when Hazel's need for counsel grew urgent. She was arranging a display of Tangee beauty products when a tall handsome man right off the bus, fresh from the Navy and still wearing his summer whites, strode confidently into the drugstore. He had eyes like two dark stars. Hazel could tell by his high cheekbones, wide jaw and straight black hair he probably had a little Choctaw or Chickasaw in him, but not too much. Just enough for shading.

He grinned at her and tilted his head in a way that set the butterflies in her stomach to fluttering. "Is the druggist in? I need to get me a prescription filled for a root beer float." He spoke in a voice that was confident and at the same time lilted sweetly like a country love song. At first Hazel couldn't answer, she just stared wide-mouthed at him like she was waiting for the second verse.

"Now you wouldn't happen to know the formula for one, would you?" he asked, still grinning, tilting his head.

Blushing, she could only stammer, "I sure do…can…will." By the time she got behind the fountain, she had calmed herself a bit and thought to say, "I won't even ask to see your doctor's note."

That made him laugh. It was a good laugh, gentle, seemingly incapable of meanness. It was unlike other men's laughter, which seemed to ask for things she was not ready to give. She noticed feeling excited but at the same time strangely at ease with this man. Setting the ice cream before him, she warned with a wink, "Don't eat this too fast or you'll freeze your goozle."

He gave her an openmouthed smile, flashing those ivory teeth of his, and said, "I'm sure not in any hurry now."

It was his eyes that really got her attention. Like dark mirrors of polished iron, they were beautiful to look at, but they wouldn't let Hazel in. His eyes seemed to push back on her, making her want to come all the closer. She told him, "I bet you could stare a buzzard out of a tree."

He blushed and said, "You got the best posture of any girl I've ever met."

Hazel could tell he wanted to say more, but he didn't need to. In his mirrored eyes, she saw herself as pretty, as pretty as she felt the day that traveling photographer had snapped her picture.

It was sure nice, all right, but Hazel had more questions than ever. Was this how true love shows itself? Can a complete stranger walk into your life on a fine Indian summer afternoon while you are stacking tubes of lipstick, and then, just like that—in the twinkle of a mirrored eye and the flash of a toothy smile—all your hoping suddenly pays off and life is never the same? Is that the way it's supposed to work? Can something that happens so quickly be counted on to last a lifetime?

From all the true romance stories she had been reading, Hazel gathered that finding the right man and living off true love was the key to everlasting happiness. But she was not foolish enough to believe just any man would do. You needed one you could lay your best hopes on, one who would love you enough to see you got everything you wanted, even before you knew you wanted it yourself. That part was important. If you had to ask, it didn't count. She knew that much about love for sure.

But what worried Hazel the most was the impermanence of good feelings in general. From what she could tell, they tended to melt away like ice cream in the bottom of a Dixie cup or fade like the heart-pounding thrill she got from her father's jug. Was love going to be the same way? Breathtaking but brief?

Hazel just had to talk to somebody about her feelings, so she doubled her efforts at making Miss Ellen like her, bringing her ice cream from her husband's drugstore, and cosmetic samples the salesmen left behind, and even offered to do her hair and makeup. Even though she ate the ice cream and let Hazel wash her greasy hair and set it, Miss Ellen remained unmoved, still convinced Hazel was up to no good. She only barked out orders, dismissing Hazel once she had what she wanted.

Late one night while Hazel was tossing and turning in her bed trying to figure the ins and outs of love, she heard what sounded like a rifle going off in her room. After her heart began beating again, she decided that it had not been an explosion but the crack of a marble striking her door.

Hazel emerged from her room, squinching her eyes against the light, her hair littered with bobby pins and rollers. Miss Ellen was waiting, sitting up in bed, arms crossed, her scowl lit by the bedside lamp. "I'm sorry to wake you, Hazel," she said, not acting very sorry at all. "I was just wondering where Harold was. He hasn't come in to say goodnight."

Hazel reminded Miss Ellen that her husband was attending an evening-till-dawn church sing of gospel quartets. What'd she think? Hazel wondered. That she had Mr. Denton tucked up under her bed?

Miss Ellen apologized again for waking Hazel, this time appearing a little guilty.

"Oh, you didn't wake me," Hazel said, pretty sure Miss Ellen would not be interested in her problem now that her husband was accounted for. "I was just laying there running things over in my mind."

But Miss Ellen was interested. She narrowed her gaze and asked,

"Something you need to get off your chest?" She blushed and looked away, adding, "In a manner of speaking, I mean."

"Well," Hazel said hesitantly, wondering if now was the time to seek the woman's advice. "Something has been worrying at me, and I don't know who else to talk to about it."

A shadow passed over Miss Ellen's face. "Is it about Harold?" she asked bluntly.

"Oh, no ma'am! Not Mr. Denton."

The muscles in Miss Ellen's face softened a bit and she patted the bed-spread. "Come here and tell me about it, child."

Sitting on the edge of Miss Ellen's bed, Hazel asked, "Miss Ellen, how do you know when you found the right man?"

The older woman's eyebrows vaulted. "You met somebody, girl?"

"Yes, ma'am. His name's Floyd Graham," Hazel answered, watching Miss Ellen's face light up. "But I been wondering, when you fall in love, how do you know them feelings is going to last?"

Miss Ellen drew a deep breath, causing her poor lungs to whistle. She got very serious. "Well, child," she said, as if this could be the only piece of motherly advice she might ever be asked to render, "feelings come and go like morning dew on a pasture. They aren't anything to build a future on."

Miss Ellen noticed her disappointment and reached out to pat Hazel's hand. She leaned her head toward her, close enough for Hazel to smell the medicines on the woman's breath. "Girl," she said, "I've found there are two kinds of men in the world. Them that take care of their own and them that don't. You see, young love, sure as the day is long, dries up like that morning dew. Now the first kind of man will stay on out of duty. No matter how long the drought. The other?" Miss Ellen flicked her hand like she was shooing a noisome insect. "Why as soon as there's a dry spell, the other kind has jumped the fence and is looking for fresh dew. If you know what I mean."

Hazel lay awake in her bed pondering the advice. Even though she didn't like the dewy part, she did like the part about a man taking care of his own. That sure sounded right enough.

1948

Chapter 4
FIRE-SCARRED HANDS

Hazel and Floyd had been seeing each other for several months now. Saturday nights he drove to Tupelo in his daddy's old Dodge truck, picked Hazel up and took her to the movies, usually a double feature. Afterwards they went to Donna's Dairy Bar and gazed starry-eyed at each other over their shiny metal bowls of ice cream. Floyd was a wonder to Hazel.

She discovered he had grown up just a few ridges over from her, but acted like he was from another world. He was so cocksure of himself, and at the same time friendly and outgoing like the route men she admired so. Still, there was something about him she couldn't quite put her finger on. She suspected that behind those dark mirrored eyes that pushed back on her, there was a part of himself he kept protected and out of view. As much as she loved his bold smile and his easy talk, sometimes she knew they also served to nudge her away from something frailer, something living beneath his confident manner. She began to wonder if it didn't have something to do with his family, whom he was always reluctant to talk about.

One night over ice cream she got up the nerve to ask about his mother. Without blinking, he said, "Died when I was six months old."

Hazel didn't know what to say, but she must have looked sad because Floyd quickly tried to reassure her. "I never knew her so I don't miss her none."

"How'd she die?" Hazel asked, sounding a lot more sorrowful about the loss than he.

Floyd looked down at his hands and began to rub the little purple blotches on his fingers that Hazel had always assumed were birthmarks. "Well, what they tell me is Momma was holding me in her arms, warming herself in front of the fireplace, when she had a stroke and fell out." He held out his hands for her to see. "Daddy said I got these burn marks when I grabbed aholt of the burning logs."

Hazel swallowed hard, again not knowing how to respond.

Floyd continued talking in a singsong voice devoid of any emotion. He told her how around his eighth birthday his daddy married a widowed country schoolteacher with four boys of her own and made Floyd move out to the barn with the cow and mules.

Hazel's eyes welled up with tears, but Floyd, now obviously in a mood to talk, told her next about how when he was in the service, he had scrimped and saved and even signed up for another tour of duty so he could have enough to go to veterinary school. Every month he sent all his pay to his daddy for safekeeping. But Floyd said when he got home, his stepmother, Momma Maud he called her, had spent it all on her own boys.

His stories made Hazel cry, but Floyd told them like they had happened to somebody else, a person he had little patience or feeling for. Wiping her eyes, Hazel guessed it had something to do with a person reaching out for his mother and touching fire instead.

The thing she had the hardest time understanding was why in the world, after his family had treated him so badly, was he back there now, putting off his own future to help his shiftless father and his spiteful stepmother and her worthless sons get that broken-down farm ready for spring planting? What kept him from taking off like she had? She knew he wasn't the type to be scared. She found herself wishing she could save him from the clutches of his kin.

Floyd fell silent, watching Hazel as she dabbed at her eyes. "They ain't all that bad, you know," he said carefully, "once you get to know em." He smiled bashfully. "Maybe it's time I took you home. To meet them. My family. Will you go?" He tilted his head to the side.

Hazel froze. Did this mean what she thought it did? Was she ready to be a wife? Even to a handsome man who could break her heart with his stories? She began stammering, "OK. Sure. Yes, I do…I mean…I will…when?"

The next Sunday they headed back up into the hills in his daddy's truck to Floyd's home-place to pay a visit to his family.

She hadn't been in their tumbledown house two minutes when his father, Mr. Graham, winked at her. Then he patted the chair next to him, inviting her to sit. On her way down he pinched her on the behind in broad view of his own wife, who acted like it was Hazel's fault and actually accused her out loud of putting on airs. Momma Maud said Hazel was just asking for trouble by the way she held herself all proper and flaunted herself in that bought dress.

Even though Maud was supposed to have been a schoolteacher, Hazel figured from the way she talked and the hateful way she acted, it was back in the days when they let anybody teach who could say their ABC's and count their toes.

With a disgusted look, Momma Maud turned to Floyd. "La dee da," she said, as if Hazel hadn't been sitting there, "she sure acts like something on a stick, don't she now?"

While Maud was glowering at Hazel over the tops of her steel-rimmed glasses, Floyd's daddy whispered to Hazel, "Wont to see how a horse bites an apple?"

"Yes sir," Hazel said, just to be polite. The old geezer grabbed a handful of her leg well above the knee and squeezed as hard as he could, whinnying like a pony. Hazel yelped in pain.

She could have crawled up under the house with the dogs and died of shame, but Maud scowled at her anyway, like Hazel had provoked her husband into doing it. She looked over at Floyd for help. He just sat there, tight-jawed and red-faced, staring off out the window, saying absolutely nothing.

Neither did his good-for-nothing stepbrothers. The whole time she was there, all they did was sit slouched in their chairs, looking mean and surly, like they were envious of Floyd's good fortune to have found him a woman pretty enough to make their old man act so crazy and turn their mother green with envy.

On the way back, they wouldn't look at each other, and for a long time sat in awkward silence. Hazel had never seen such a circus and made a vow to herself never to return.

At last Floyd took a deep breath and said sheepishly, "I think they liked you."

"Well," Hazel said, staring out the window, "They seem like good people, Floyd. Thanks for bringing me." What she was really thankful for was getting out of there alive with only a few bruises. What in the world kept Floyd going back for more?

That's when it struck her. This was exactly what Miss Ellen had been talking about. Even after having to grow up in his daddy's barn, and even after they stole his money, and humiliated his girlfriend, even after all that, Floyd was still determined to do for his family. Hadn't Miss Ellen said that was a good thing to look for in a man?

Hazel looked at Floyd with new eyes. Here was a fella who would take care of his own no matter how rough it got. Loving Floyd more than ever, she scooted across the seat and sidled up next to him. He looked a little surprised, but then put his arm around her, smiling like it made him proud.

Anyway, she thought, Floyd was too full of ambition to hang around Tishomingo County for long. Hazel could tell he wanted out of the hills just as much as she had. She only hoped before he left to seek out his fortune, he would make her one of his own, too.

By the time Saturday rolled around again and she was dressing for her date, Hazel had convinced herself a proposal was in the offing. Why else would he risk letting her see his deranged family in action?

With her makeup almost done, she peeked out into the hallway to check the hall clock. Seeing that it was only a few minutes before six, she rushed over to her dresser to finish readying herself for Floyd's arrival. He was more punctual than a summer cold and twice as demanding, expecting her to be on time, too. But she didn't mind much. He was always so good-natured about having his way. With just a grin and a tilt of the head, that man could ask for the world tied up in a pretty bow. And get it.

She inspected herself closely in the mirror, powder puff in hand, on the lookout for an untended freckle. If Hazel knew how to do nothing else in the world, she knew how to make herself up, having come a long way from the days of funeral parlor cosmetics and homemade dresses. Countless hours of studying California movie stars and New York models in the drugstore magazines and talking with the sales girls at Peltz's Department Store had refined her skills in what they called the sly art of fashion. She liked the sound of that. It acknowledged what she understood about hope—that sometimes what you hoped for needed a little encouragement to come your way.

Hazel was dabbing Gardenia Paradise on her pulse points when the clock in the hallway struck six. She pulled back the curtain in time to see Floyd pulling up to the curb. She quickly removed the jumbo roller from the curl over her forehead, grabbed a pink chiffon wrap, tiptoed past Miss Ellen's room, and because it was important to her to be there before the first knock, flew down the stairs with pumps in hand. When she got to the front door, she slipped into her shoes, then took a moment to catch her breath.

At this point every Saturday night, she liked to play a little game with herself to build her excitement to a peak. With her eyes closed, she placed her hand over her stomach, feeling the delicious anticipation bubbling up into her chest. She pretended it was Christmas and opening the door was like unwrapping her present. She told herself there was no telling what she would end up with. Was it going to be a sack of oranges again? Or would she get that pretty doll she had hoped for?

Then came the confident knock. She cracked the door, carefully peering out onto the porch. Right there stood exactly what she had always wanted!

She flung open the door the rest of the way, beaming. Finding Floyd at her door was like a wonderful surprise every time. From the open-eyed way he beamed back at her, it was obvious he had never been greeted with so much high regard by anybody in all his life.

As Floyd walked her to the truck, she let him put his arm around her waist. But when he did, he used it as leverage to steer her over to his side of the walk. Thinking it might be some kind of game he was playing, she in turn tried reining him over to her side.

All at once he stopped walking and turned to her, cocking his head and grinning. "You outdid yourself this evening, Hazel. You're prettier ever time I see you. How do you manage that?" He leaned his head in close to hers.

Forgetting completely about the foolish little tug of war, she smiled.

"You're the most sugar-mouthed man I ever met, Floyd Graham. If I was as pretty as you make me feel, I'd run off to Hollywood."

He chucked her playfully under the chin. "Well, I wouldn't want to lose you to the pictures. From now on I'm going to keep you *and* my compliments to myself." He gave her waist a tight squeeze and they continued to the truck on his side of the walk.

Floyd got Hazel's door open and he firmly guided her into her seat, almost like she might not be able to figure out such a complicated maneuver on her own. Did he think she was half-witted, or was he just looking out for her?

Hazel studied Floyd as he drove her through downtown Tupelo, confidently handling the old cantankerous Dodge like a horse broke to saddle. "You sure know how to show a truck who's boss," she joked.

He laughed and reached over and gave her hand a squeeze. "A thing will behave itself if it feels the grip of a sure hand." His touch was so gentle, and at the same time firm. That was something else she had never seen in a man.

He angle parked in front of the Lyric Theater, and without saying a word, sprang out of the truck, ran around to the other side to get her door. She had to smile when he offered his arm so Hazel could lift herself out of her seat down to the pavement. Didn't he realize she grew up being dragged behind a mule and just might be able to manage a three-foot drop to firm ground? But she took hold of his arm nonetheless. Because it seemed important to him, she also allowed Floyd to gallantly point out the curb step to the sidewalk.

Yep, she thought, Floyd Graham was a man who would certainly take care of his own, and from the china doll way he was treating her this evening, she prayed she wasn't mishoping by thinking tonight she would be his.

Floyd couldn't sit still during the movie, and even though it was a good one about the son of Zorro, Hazel didn't think it was all the shooting and whipcracking that was giving Floyd the fidgets. Before the second feature began, and without saying a word, he grabbed Hazel's hand and rushed her up the aisle, heading for the exit. Once outside the theater, he cut across the square in the direction of Donna's Dairy Bar with Hazel stumbling on behind him, wondering what had happened to the delicate approach.

Once they were seated in their usual booth and served two bowls of ice cream, Floyd attacked his butter pecan like it was a chore to be got out of the way. Hazel could tell something serious was on his mind that he was trying to shovel his way to. She hoped it was a proposal he was tunneling toward.

Floyd pushed his bowl aside. He took a deep breath and began speaking in a tone that sounded strange to Hazel's ear. "Ain't no reason to go on doing something just cause it was done before us," he firmly asserted. "There's plenty of other ways for a man to make a living than farming. Don't you agree, Hazel?"

Hazel was taken aback, not at what he said, but the way he had said it, like he had rehearsed the words beforehand in a mirror, and now he was acting out his little speech just for her. While she studied him curiously, he tilted his head to the side and smiled the way he did when he wanted her to answer a certain way. The idea that her response was so important caused Hazel's heart to pound like the drum in the homecoming parade. She said, "You right about that, Floyd. Why, they's many a man who get themselves a good route and never look back."

Floyd's face lit up like a bulb, and Hazel knew she had said the right thing.

"Selling!" he exclaimed, slapping his hand on the table. "You reading my mind. That's exactly what I'm talking about." Floyd was as excited as a schoolboy. "Selling is where the country's future is at. Like they say, 'In America, nothing happens till somebody sells something.'"

"Well," she said, "I'll have to think on that one." Hazel had no idea what he meant, but figured it would help if she had a saying to swap. She could only think of one about selling and before she had thought it through, she came out with it. "My daddy says, 'A man who makes a living with his mouth is a sorry excuse for a man.' Why, Daddy wouldn't even go hear a preacher less he knew he worked his own farm during the week."

As she brought another spoon of ice cream up to her mouth, it hit her that that was exactly the wrong thing to say. What got into her? She didn't even believe her daddy's stupid saying. But it was the only one she knew of off the top of her head. She watched for his reaction to see if she had bruised his feelings. But Floyd kept looking at her like she was the most interesting person in Mississippi.

"Now me personally," she continued, very much relieved to be getting a second chance, "I think it's a gift to be able to set people at ease and make them glad to see you coming down the road. That's worth paying for. And you got that way about you for sure, Floyd Graham. Why, I bet you could sell manners to a Yankee." Hoping that had put her on the right side of the argument, she waited for Floyd to say something.

He didn't speak at first. Instead he studied Hazel for a moment, and then nodded his head, like she had passed some kind of test. His expression serious, he leaned in over the table, and let her in on his secret. "You see, I read a book while I was off in the Pacific," he said in a hushed, reverential tone. "It was called *There's No Future in Looking Back: The Science of Controlled Thinking.* Writ by a preacher who figured out this hidden code in the Bible. The 'knock and ye shall receive' part. He went on to make a fortune selling soap door to door."

"I swan," Hazel whispered back.

"I'll let you read it one day, but it all comes down to this. You are what you think. And your mind can be trained like ever other muscle. Like your leg or your arm muscle."

Floyd's eyes were shining and he was speaking with such authority, Hazel felt chill bumps on her arms.

"Hazel, an untrained mind spends all its time looking back on things it can't do nothing about. This preacher says if you keep your mind focused on what you want and think positive thoughts, you bound to get what you after. He says it's right from the Savior's own mouth. To cut the tail off the dog, it's changed my life."

"Already?"

He smiled shyly. "Met you, didn't I?"

"Floyd."

"Plus, I just got a letter from this ol' boy that was on my ship. He said he could get me a job selling these mechanical cotton pickers to the big Delta planters."

"The Delta? I heard of that."

"Shore. That's where all the money is. Clear on the other side of the state from here. Cotton as high as a man and stretching as far as the eye can see. All being handpicked by a million niggers. A man with a good product to sell and a positive attitude could make something of hisself."

"A million niggers? I swan."

"Yep. In Hopalachie County alone. And as soon as I get Daddy's crop put in, I'm buying my bus passage to Delphi, the county seat. I already told him I'm good as gone. You never gonna catch me looking at the south end of a mule again."

"Nothing I hate worse than seeing a man married to a mule." Then she blushed, afraid she may have mentioned marriage too soon, even if it was in reference to a mule.

"Hazel, it's like you think just like me." Floyd reached for her hand. "When I go on out to the Delta, would you wait on me till I got some money saved up?"

He tilted his head to the side and grinned, but he didn't need to coax. Floyd's plan was so big with hope, Hazel believed she could live off the anticipation for years. By the time he sent for her, maybe she would be ready to give whatever it was a wife was supposed to give.

"Hazel…" he said, and she felt the squeeze of his hand, "Would you…I mean…"

She looked into his eyes to find herself, and she liked what she saw. "Floyd Graham, I ain't budging till you come and get me."

For a week of Saturdays they met over ice cream like conspirators, plotting their escape, planning for the day Floyd would take off to a place called Delphi, seeking a brand-new future, never before lived by anybody.

Mentally, they packed and repacked their suitcases, imagining cozy rooms and grassy front yards and evenings filled with fireflies, until Hazel dared to believe that in the end, maybe there was no debt to be paid, no balance due on this man's love.

1948

Chapter 5

A DEAL WITH THE DEVIL

Billy Dean was gaining the rise on Redeemer's Hill, and he wanted clear sailing on the downslope. After honking twice, he butted the front fenders of his uncle's rattletrap Ford into the tailgate of the gin wagon that hogged the middle of the gravel road. The colored driver swung about, but when he saw the two white men, he smiled weakly, touched his hat, and popped his mules sharply with the ends of the reins.

Nothing could hold him back now. If there was any such animal as a sure thing, Billy Dean had treed him one this time. Blind to what might be coming at him from over the hill, Billy Dean swerved the car to the opposite ditch and held his ground, leaving no room for oncoming traffic.

"Wait on it, you hear?" his uncle said. "They ain't enough road for you to pass."

Billy Dean grinned. He drove the left side of the truck into the ditch. Now they were straddling the road ledge.

"Dammit to hell," his uncle muttered.

No doubt about it, good luck had come over to Billy Dean's side to stay. Come fall, Hopalachie County would be his for the taking and nobody could keep him from grabbing ahold of it with both hands and a knee to the throat. No matter if he did have to make a deal with the devil to get it. With two tires on the road and two in the ditch, dirt and rock slinging out from the rear, Billy Dean drowned the wagon, its colored driver, and his two brown mules in a storm of dust.

Victorious, he took off his Stetson, waved it out the window, and yelled "Hi-Yo, Silver!" He now had Redeemer's Hill all to himself. Knowing what was coming next, his uncle scooted down in his seat and closed his eyes.

Billy Dean jammed the Stetson tight on his head, reared back in his seat, and mashed the accelerator flat to the floor. The truck, propelled as much by gravity as gasoline, sailed down Redeemer's Hill, the final roller-coaster drop from the bluffs to the flatter-than-flat Delta. There was nothing ahead now but miles and miles of cotton plants studded with pink and white blossoms as far as the eye could see, the horizon a streak of green nuzzling up to a blue summer sky.

The old man held his stomach with both hands. "Damned, Billy Dean! Slow down, son. You nearly floated up my grits that time."

Billy Dean's uncle pulled up in his seat again. Furman was a big man with a nose like raw hamburger. "You drivin like a blue-assed fly," he said, "Ain't gone live long enough to win no lection." He reached down to the floorboard for the fruit jar.

Billy Dean tipped back his Stetson with his thumb. He knew better. The bargain had already been struck. That primary was his for the taking. "Where's the next stop at?"

With two fingers pressed against his lips, the old man turned to the window and spit, finessing a brown trail of tobacco juice clear of the rear fender. "You gone take a right bout a mile up ahead." Furman unscrewed the top of the jar, took a sip, and swallowed hard. "Hodamighty!" He handed the jar to his nephew.

Billy Dean took his turn at the jar while keeping an eye on a horizon that never seemed to get any closer, no matter how fast he went. He didn't know just how big Hopalachie County was until he decided he was going to be sheriff over all of it. Then it got mighty big.

There was this, the Delta part, with its thousands of lookalike acres of nothing but cotton, hiding tiny crossroad settlements built around gins and country stores. Farther west there were the swamps and bayous with little clusters of cabins and fishing shacks raised up on stilts. To their backs, where Billy Dean and his uncle had just come from, were the bluffs.

Perched up there in those bluffs was the uppity little town of Delphi, looking down like an old powdered woman on the whole shebang. That's where Billy Dean was going to settle when the devil paid him his due. He was going to be high sheriff and move to town and live in a big white house with the rich folks. All he had to do to make that happen was to marry the ugliest girl in Hopalachie County. Billy Dean took another drink.

His uncle had tried to tell him Miss Hertha wasn't all that ugly, but Billy Dean knew from the way his face got all screwed up when he got to "...all that ugly," that he didn't believe it himself. His uncle had looked away and said, "Well, shit, you know what I mean."

The gravel had nearly given out and the road became like a ribbed washboard. They were coming up on the Hopalachie River. Shaking wildly, the truck began to drift off in a sideways direction. Uncle Furman reached down for where the door handle used to be and then crossed his arms over his face instead.

"Get a holt, boy," he shouted with a mouth full of chambray. "You gone dump us in the river!"

The truck continued to shimmy across the road toward the ravine. "Slow down!" he yelled louder.

Billy Dean stomped on the gas and swerved back sharply, bringing the truck to true center just before reaching the bridge. Hearing the loose planks rumble beneath the tires, Furman peeked out from behind his arms and commenced to breathing again. "Boy, what's got into you? You temptin the devil?"

Maybe he was. But at that moment, Billy Dean's future seemed to be laid out before him as sure and straight as one of these Delta plantation roads. Nothing could change that now. He and the Senator had shook on it. Sitting there in the mahogany-paneled study off the chandeliered hallway, they had come to terms.

The Senator was leaned back in his fat leather chair, summoning and dismissing nigger servants like he was King Tut himself. "Pour me some bourbon. Light my seegar. Shut that door. Wipe my goddam ass." All the time the Senator acting like he could care less about Billy Dean Brister. Acting as if his older daughter had a wide selection of men to choose from. Like all she had to do was to open up the Sears Roebuck catalogue and point.

Billy Dean knew different. Miss Hertha had settled on him and she was in a hurry. Her baby sister Delia had hoarded all the good looks in the family and already had suitors lining up at the door. Hertha was bound and

determined not to be picked over and left hanging on the vine like bad
fruit. Seeing as how Hertha was as headstrong as she was ugly, Billy Dean
figured she could out-filibuster the Senator any day.

"Boy," the Senator said, "Far's I'm concerned, your kind is as common
as pig tracks. Nothing but a Good Time Charley. You ought to be *begging*
me for my girl's hand."

That made Billy Dean mad but he held himself back from saying
something stupid and storming out. For once in his life he was going to
sit a minute and think before he blew up. So, somewhere between the
Senator telling one of his niggers to drop ice in his drink and then cussing
him for sloshing bourbon on his silk tie, Billy Dean thought of something
smart to say.

"*You* the one trying to sell me goods I ain't even said I wanted yet."

The Senator's turkey jowls pinked up and his dull gray eyes smoldered
a deep blue. He was trying to act like he didn't care one way or the other,
but Billy Dean knew better.

Holding his cigar up close to his catfish mouth and rolling it between
his fat fingers, the Senator cast a sidelong glance at Billy Dean. "What's
your price?" he asked, and he added disdainfully, "*Mister* Brister." As cool
as the Senator tried to act, he couldn't say "Mister" and "Brister" in the
same sentence without looking like it soured his mouth.

It didn't bother Billy Dean any. His mind was winter morning, bell-
ringing clear, and he asked for the first thing that came to his head. The
thing he didn't know he had wanted until he said it, and when he said it, it
was like he had wanted it all his life.

"Make me the sheriff."

The Senator had laughed. "I don't make the sheriff. The citizenry elect
the sheriff. It's called democracy. Civilization. Your people ever heard of it?"

Again, Billy Dean decided not to go off on the Senator. In that
moment, Billy Dean was fighting off generations of Bristers who would
have gladly set themselves afire on the chance of singeing their enemies.
Like his own daddy who had torched their house because the bank had
refused to extend the mortgage on the home-place. Billy Dean knew good
and well he had inherited the Brister family habit of shooting his last

chance right between the eyes if it looked at him crossways.

So it was not without considerable strain that he decided to try some-thing new. Easing back into his chair, he let up on his anger, not gunning it all at once, allowing the heat of the Senator's insult to idle a moment, savoring it. Then he fed it just enough gas to keep it revved up but still under control. His thoughts were hitting on all eight cylinders.

Billy Dean surprised himself by half-smiling at the Senator, which made the old man's color heat up from pink to purple. Fishing out a ciga-rette from his shirt pocket and lighting it, Billy Dean played it slow and deliberate, again in opposition to everything his nature was telling him. It was like doing the two-step with a grizzly bear. He was damned near giddy.

There he was, sitting across from the most powerful man in the coun-ty. Mississippi, maybe. A used-to-be senator. Owned more land than Adam. And poor ol' Billy Dean Brister, "common as pig tracks," was hold-ing his own, acting uppity enough to take his eyes off the big man and let them trespass around the study, boldly getting the lay of the land.

Lining the wall he saw paintings of the Senator's ancient kin as well as pictures of the Senator himself shaking hands with presidents and movie stars and college football coaches and people so famous Billy Dean didn't even recognize them. He eyed the silver candlestick holders and the fine old carpets and burnished woods so shiny a fella could see to put a part in his hair.

And there it was, right before him, as clear as the cut crystal in the Senator's hand. What it was that had set his father on fire. It was nothing but shame. Pure-dee, plain as mud, white trash shame.

Exhaling a blue cloud, Billy Dean looked straight into the Senator's aristocratic eyes and with a bald face said, "The *citizenry* will do exactly like you tell em, I reckon." Then he kind of half-smiled. "Yes sir. I'll marry Miss Hertha as soon the vote is counted my way."

From watching how mule traders did their business, Billy Dean knew the next one to speak would come out with the short end of the stick. So he clamped down on his cigarette and counted to twenty.

The next day Billy Dean went to Delphi and bought himself a Stetson and a pair of hand-tooled cowboy boots.

Pointing on down the road, Uncle Furman shouted over the rattle of the truck. "Get ready to take a right down here just a piece. Slow down, do you hear?"

Billy Dean sped up. He took the turn in a long slide of gravel and dust. When the rusty tin roof of the store came into view, the old man began to relax a little, but his relief was short-lived.

His nephew swung the car into the yard at a sideways tilt, and then gunned it. The truck barreled straight for the gallery on the front of the store. A few feet from the building, Billy Dean stomped on the brakes and went into a skid, with Furman pushing as hard as he could against the dash, trying to keep his head from going through the hole where the windshield used to be.

Furman remained stock-still for a full minute until he was convinced the truck was stopped for good, then fell back into his seat. He pulled out a tobacco-stained bandanna from his Big Mac overalls, wiped the sweat off his face, and blew the dust out of his big bruised nose. Billy Dean reached for the jar.

The world had gone dead quiet. The store sat on a bare island of packed dirt surrounded by cotton plants that lapped right up to the back door. According to the little boy wearing the bottle cap on the thermometer nailed to the front of the store, the temperature had already hit ninety-three in the shade.

As the dust settled around the truck, Billy Dean opened his door and turned himself sideways in the seat, giving his legs an extra-long stretch. Looking around, he began to recollect the place. He had bought shine here one time. After dark. It had been a couple of years, but now he was starting to remember it good.

He took another drink. The store appeared deserted. Even the bench up on the shaded gallery was unoccupied. Looking up into the July morning sky Billy Dean figured the sun was at eleven or past. Almost dinnertime. The place would be swarming with niggers soon enough, counting out pennies for sardines and crackers. Billy Dean lit a Lucky and looked back toward the road.

Off in the distance a silent cloud of dust was rising above the green horizon, heading their way. As it neared, Billy Dean could make out the deep-throated hum of a car with a substantial engine. Finally, a dark green Buick, old but well tended to, came into sight, drawing the cloud behind it. The car turned off into the yard and rolled to a careful stop.

It was a colored man who got out. He was taller than even Billy Dean, and all dressed up in an old-fashioned baggy suit with a gold watch chained across his stomach. Bending down to his open window, he said a word to the three children who remained in the car, two in the front and one in the back. Then he slumped his shoulders and headed toward the store.

Coming up on Billy Dean and his uncle, the colored man removed his felt hat, nodded respectfully, and said, "How do, sirs?"

Billy Dean didn't bother to answer. He was more interested in two little gold hands, pressed together in prayer, hanging from the man's watch chain like a charm. His uncle just glowered.

After the man had gone into the store, Uncle Furman got out of the truck and shambled over to the Buick. "Boy that just chaps my ass!" he said. "How many white folks you know got a car this good?" He aimed a stream of tobacco juice at a shiny hubcap with expert precision.

The boy sitting in the backseat was glaring at Furman through the open window with all the ferocity he could muster. He wore a red straw cowboy hat with a yellow star painted on the crown, the drawstring pulled tight under his chin.

Billy Dean clenched his cigarette in one side of his mouth and spoke out the other. "Them nigger preachers sure know how to spend the Lord's money."

"Sho!" Furman said. "That's what he was, awright. Wearin a tie as wide as your Aunt Beula's butt. And did you see that chain on his belly? Looked a hunnurd percent karat gold."

The girl in the front seat was studying Billy Dean's face hard, and when she saw him looking back, her eyes got big as cabbages. She swung her head toward the store again, whipping her plaits over her shoulder. Even though sweat beaded up and ran down her face, she reached her arm around the light-skinned baby boy sitting next to her and pulled him closer.

Furman noticed the girl, too. With his hands on his back, he crouched down and peered through the front window at her. She was dressed in white from head to toe—a white ruffled dress, white shiny shoes and cotton socks, white satin ribbons tied to the end of her plaits. "Hey, Billy Dean, looks like we got the Cotton Queen in here!"

The girl didn't flinch. Instead she kept looking straight ahead, into the smug face painted on the new screen door. Little Miss Sally Sunbeam, with her corn-silk hair and baby-doll blue eyes, seemed to be smiling back at her, all the time holding a slice of light bread up to her mouth. Miss Sally didn't appear to be worried about a thing.

Gripping the back of the front seat, the boy in the straw hat pulled himself forward. He gave Furman a steely look that defied the old man to touch his sister. Even though he couldn't be any older than ten, it was enough to give Furman pause. The boy had a certain disregard that said he would bet everything on a dare and nothing any white man could do would scare him out of it.

"Lookie here, Billy Dean." Furman pointed to the star on the boy's hat. "This'n wants to be sheriff too. Think you can beat a nigger boy come the primary?"

Billy Dean grinned, but looked down. "Might be close." He lifted his boot and smoothed over a scrape on the toe with the pad of his thumb.

Furman's gaze shifted to the baby boy in the front seat, who was holding tight to one of the girl's plaits. "Girl, who's that baby belong to? Ain't yores, is it?"

"Yessuh," the girl answered, squinting hard at the screen door as if willing her father's return.

Furman studied the baby for a moment. "That don't look like no nigger baby to me. I reckon some white boy been sneaking around her wood pile late at night." Turning back to his nephew, Furman asked, "Who you think he takes after?"

Billy Dean examined his other boot, but sneaked a look at the baby boy when his uncle had turned back to the car.

"How old are you, girl?" asked Furman.

"Fo'teen, suh."

"You hear that, Billy Dean? Her baby can't be but a year. Maybe even two. Jesus! They born to breed, ain't they?"

Billy Dean did the math. Shit, he thought, surely there was others. He jumped down from the truck, but kept his eyes fixed on the girl. "Get me that ball-peen hammer out of the back of the truck," he told Furman.

The girl's eyes grew big again. She put her hand on the window crank, thought better of it, and tightened her grip on her baby instead.

While Furman rattled around in the truck bed, Billy Dean pushed back his Stetson and leaned into the girl's window. "You—" was all he said before she blurted in a dry whisper, "I ain't said nothin! Ain't never gone say nothin. Just like you tole me."

"Shut up!" Billy Dean spat, low and harsh. He studied the child next to her. She wouldn't have to tell nobody. The boy's face would tell the deed.

Billy Dean took the cigarette from his mouth and flicked it into the car, landing it on the driver's seat. The girl sat stock-still, clutching the boy, while the smell of scorched cloth filled the car. In the back seat, her brother made a move for the cigarette, but without turning around, the girl said in a panicked voice, "Willie! Leave it be. Don't do nothin."

He slowly eased back in the seat, his eyes not breaking from Billy Dean's.

When Furman came with the hammer, Billy Dean took it and slapped the head into the palm of his hand. The child in the front seat started to whimper, but his mother resisted looking down at him.

Suddenly the screen creaked open and the girl's father stepped onto the gallery carrying his sack of groceries. Seeing the two white men over by his daughter, he stooped his shoulders and moved hurriedly toward the car. "Yes, Lord! Gone be a hot one, ain't it?" he said. "How are you sirs today? I hope you all be keepin out from under this heat."

The colored man opened the rear door and put the groceries in the backseat. "Too hot to be out of the shade for long," he went on. "Nossuh. Maybe the good Lord gone send a little shower this a way. Look like it's comin up a cloud down off yonder." He nodded toward the distant north, but didn't take his eyes off the ball-peen hammer.

The men watched without expression as the preacher carried on with his foolishness.

"Yessuh. Be nice to get a little rain to cool things down. Maybe settle the dust some." He opened the door on the driver's side and casually brushed the smoldering cigarette onto the ground. Then he removed his handkerchief from his coat pocket and laid it out over the burn.

"Well, I best be gettin on to home. You sirs have a fine day now." Tipping his hat to the men, the preacher cranked the Buick, backed it up, and pulled out into the road, departing faster than he had come.

"Crazy preacher," Furman said and then spit. "Wouldn't mind getting a crack at that poontang, though." He laughed a laugh so dry it triggered a quick coughing spell.

Wiping the tears from his eyes, Furman grabbed a handful of fliers from off the truck seat and joined his nephew up on the gallery. He held one of the fliers flat against the gray weathered wood, right between a faded War Bonds poster and the Garrett Snuff sign. Billy Dean hammered a nail into each of the four corners.

Furman took a step back and said, "Looks just like you."

Billy Dean spun around. "Who looks just like me?"

His uncle nodded at the flier, "Yore picture there. Good likeness, don't you think?"

He studied Furman for a moment and then turned back toward the flier. "Yeah," he said. "Reckon they caught me."

"Odds say you gone win that primary easy, Billy Dean."

"Better," Billy Dean said darkly. "The Senator done had all my competition paid off or scared off, one."

"Aw, hit's OK," Furman reassured him. "The Senator just doin what's best for his little girl. She gone be the wife of the next high sheriff if it costs him half his plantation." Furman spit over the railing. "Boy, howdy, are you a lucky shit."

"Yeah, well," Billy Dean said. "Everthing's got its price."

Furman put his hand on his nephew's shoulder. "Don't worry, son. You and Hertha's younguns probly take after our side of the family. Brister blood always wins out when it comes to looks."

"Seems to," Billy Dean said under his breath, staring down the road to where the Buick had vanished. Billy Dean wondered for a moment if there was such an animal as a sure thing after all.

Chapter 6

SNOWFLAKE BABY

The baby played on the parlor rug with his collection of wooden spools, as the preacher and his daughter, sitting on opposite sides of the room, worked hard to avoid each other's eyes: Vida, on the sofa, by staring down at the satin bows on the toes of her baby-doll shoes, and her father, in his armchair, by studying his light-skinned grandson as he stacked one spool on top of another, toppled them over, and began again.

They often found themselves stiff and awkward and embarrassed in each other's presence, like students expecting to be called on to explain themselves. It had not always been this way between them.

Before Nate was born, her father had doted on Vida. It was obvious to everybody who knew them Vida was the apple of the widowed preacher's eye. His face brimming with pride, he would call Vida his Snowflake Baby. Not because her last name was Snow, which it was. And not because her skin was white, which it wasn't. Vida had the same light coffee-with-cream complexion as her father. She was his Snowflake Baby because he always dressed her in white.

For her eleventh birthday, Levi even sent off to Memphis for a parasol of white satin, which he said would keep his Snowflake Baby from melting in the Delta sun. The day it arrived, Vida had excitedly snatched the package from the mail rider and tore away the brown paper wrapping. She twirled the pretty parasol over her head in the bright noonday sun, thrilled that she could now throw a shadow over herself whenever she wanted.

Her father had laughed with delight and proclaimed, "Now my Snowflake Baby can carry shade ever where she goes." He raised her up in his strong arms. "No sir! Nothing never gone hurt my Snowflake Baby. Not even that bad ol' sun up in the sky." Levi proudly pranced Vida around the yard, twirling her in half circles, while she giggled and kicked her feet gaily in the air, holding the parasol over them both.

Later there were the music lessons. Vida was the only colored girl in all of Hopalachie County able to take piano. Her father personally had gone to Miss Josephine Folks, the white lady music teacher, and arranged it. That's how important her father was. He could get things other colored people couldn't even think about. Of course, Miss Josephine charged Levi a dollar a lesson, twice as much as her white students, and she insisted that Vida only come after last dark. But even that didn't spoil it for Vida. She greedily hoarded rhythms and scales and choruses straight from the *Broadman Baptist Hymnal* to serenade her father with when he picked her up in the Buick.

Except for one night when he didn't. Her father was conferencing late with his deacons, and Vida had to walk the two miles to her house, alone in the dark. But she wasn't scared. Vida had walked the road hundreds of times with Willie.

Mr. Bobber's general store sat midway between Miss Josephine's and Vida's house, and when she passed, she saw the lights were still on. She had often gone inside the store by herself, but her father had solemnly warned her to never venture in there after dark, refusing to say more. But tonight she put the warning aside. With a robust Baptist refrain coursing through her blood, Vida marched right in and got herself an Orange Crush.

The screen door slapped behind her, and the music fled from Vida's head. The light was dim and smoke floated thick and eerie. Through it, from the back of the store, came the sounds of laughter, not at all like the free and easy daytime laughter. This laughter was hard and coarse.

Even the odors were different. No longer the clean bright scents of hoop cheese and mule feed and honey-cured hams and yard goods. The night smells were stale and rancid and clotted at the back of her throat when she tried to swallow. Everything had an unsteady weave to it, like a dream that was about to go bad.

Leaning with one arm against the counter, holding himself at a tipsy angle, stood the man. His dark eyes, swimming drunkenly in pools shot with red, trying to focus in on her. He smiled. But it wasn't at her. His sideways grin was meant for the squat white man behind the counter who was placing a Mason jar into a brown paper bag.

Mr. Bobber frowned at his customer and said, "Boy, next time come around to the back, you hear?" He pushed the bag across the countertop.

Several men sitting in ladder-back chairs in the rear of the store under a swirling haze of smoke made coughing sounds and moved about uneasily in their seats, but kept their eyes cut toward the business up front.

"That'll be three bits," Mr. Bobber said to the man.

Eyeing Vida, the man sniggered. "And I bet she's worth ever cent."

More laughing, hoarse and ragged, came from the back of the store.

Mr. Bobber wasn't laughing. "You got it or you don't, boy?" Then he looked down at Vida and said, not unkindly, maybe even like her father would have done, with a firm warning in his voice, "You better get on home, now, Vida. You know better than to come round here past dark." He looked warily at the customer, and then at Vida again. "Now git, do you hear?"

Vida found her legs and took two steps backward, bumped the screen, and fled the store, running through the yard for the dark of the roadbed. Her stomach had gone queasy from the way the man had looked at her and from the worry that had been in Mr. Bobber's voice. She must have done something very bad.

Vida raced down the road toward home. She needed her father to tell her she was still his Snowflake Baby and promise that nobody would ever dare hurt Levi Snow's little girl. Then the headlights fell upon her.

Nate toppled the spools a final time and pointed to his grandfather, but looked at Vida with his eyes narrowed and his bottom lip pooched out. She knew what he wanted. Nate was telling her to get up and fetch the chain from Levi so he could hold it up before him and watch the two little hands dangle and glint in the sunlight. It was his favorite thing. He couldn't get to sleep at night unless he was gripping tightly to that gold chain.

"Hands, Momma. Hands," he pleaded.

Vida didn't move. She was waiting for her father to speak his mind. Waiting for him to say his first word since they had left the store.

Why was it so hard for them to talk anymore? Why couldn't it be like the days before the white man when every problem she told her father brought forth a story with a happy ending? Stories where God saved the day like the movie cowboys in Greenwood.

These days her father mostly talked to her in his sermons, when he was filled with the Holy Ghost and couldn't keep his disappointment locked up. When he got to shouting about Jezebel's wantonness or Delilah's betrayal or Eve's fall and that snake's getting everybody thrown out of the garden, his eyes would fall upon her for the briefest moment. Just long enough for Vida to understand that it was she he had in mind.

Her father broke the silence. "That was the one who got you bigged. That white man at the store be Nate's daddy." Levi Snow wasn't asking, he was telling, speaking with the same certitude as when he told his congregations that Jesus was coming to total up their books and they best settle their accounts today. "You can't cross over into Bright Glory with a balance due," he would warn them in his stern voice, just before his elders passed the plate.

These were not the words she wanted from her father, harsh and accusing. Trying to pretend she hadn't heard him, Vida stretched out her legs so that the white baby-doll shoes caught the late-afternoon light streaming through the open window. The patent leather finish shone like the icing on a coconut cake.

"I said, that be the man. He be Nate's daddy," her father repeated.

Hearing his name mentioned again, Nate's eyes darted back and forth between his mother and his grandfather.

Sweat had darkened the top of Levi's white collar. Taking a handkerchief from his back pocket, he mopped his face. "Look a-here, girl, and tell me the truth."

Tears welled up in Vida's eyes. Why was he asking her to say the truth, now that he knew what the truth was? When it happened, the night her father came home to find her crying and her dress torn, he had gotten quiet when she told him it was a white man who had done it. That had been enough truth for him then. He hadn't even asked which white man it was.

She wouldn't have told him anyway. The man said he would kill her whole family if she told. For a while she had comforted herself by making believe her daddy was protecting her by not asking, and that she was protecting them all by not telling.

"Yessuh," Vida finally answered without looking up from her baby-doll shoes. "He be the one."

"Oh, my sweet Jesus!" he said like she knew he would. "And now that man runnin for high sheriff. You know what that means?"

Vida wouldn't look up, but from how angry his voice was, she figured it meant something about his standing as the Reach Out Man. That's what they called him and what he was most proud of. If you needed something from the white man, they said that Levi Snow was the one to go to. People bragged that he sure enough knew how to tickle the white man's ear. Colored folks were always coming to her father with some favor for him to carry to their bosses. Like mothers who wanted to visit their sons in jail, or sharecroppers who got cheated at settlement time, or families who lost their credit at the plantation commissary. Very seldom did Levi get what he asked for, but sometimes he got something, and in the coloreds' eyes that was a pretty good record. Two years ago he even got the Senator to let Statia Collins put a little pea patch on her place to help feed her ten children, the first time the Senator had let any sharecropper raise something besides cotton and field corn for the mules.

"I'll tell you what it means." Levi struck the tops of his legs with his fists. "If that peckerwood get voted high sheriff, it be the end of everthing."

He bolted to his feet. "Let's go. We got to go warn the Senator." Calling to the back of the house, he cried, "Willie! Get out here."

Vida's brother bounded into the parlor and did a march-step up to where his father stood. Giving his father what he called his Texas Ranger salute, Willie called out, "Yes! Sir!"

"Stop actin a fool. Get out front and wipe down the car. I got to conference with the Senator."

"Can I go too, Daddy?" Willie begged, no longer a Texas Ranger. "Let me drive y'all out there. I can drive good. I can reach the pedals now. You let Vida drive."

"This me and yo sister's business. Now hurry on up. I need to get there fore the Senator sits down to his supper." He turned to Vida. "Get my hat and brush it off. Need to look my best for the conference."

Vida finally looked up at her father, her expression pleading. Since she was a child she had heard stories about the Senator and how bad niggers disappeared into secret dungeons and how he ate colored babies for breakfast. "Daddy, don't make me go," she begged. "I ain't got nothin to say to the Senator." Even though her daddy was known for being able to handle the Senator, she was still afraid.

The boy toddled over to Vida and looked up at her with searching eyes. When she picked him up and held him close, he grabbed hold of her plait, and with his other arm reached out toward Levi, opening and closing his fist, signaling for the gold chain. "Momma! Hands!" he cried.

"You my baby," she whispered to him. "You my baby and that's the onliest thing anybody need to know."

Forgetting about the chain, Nate placed the palm of his hand flat against his mother's face and gently patted her, as if trying to soothe her thoughts. She turned and kissed his hand and then closed her lips around his little fingers.

Levi turned his back to both of them and straightened his tie in the looking glass. He talked at his reflection. "You got to tell the Senator how that white man took you and got you bigged. When he hear that, he'll show that cracker the fastest road out the county."

"He say he kill us all, Daddy," she cried. "He say he burn us up alive!"

Levi didn't turn from the glass. "Hush up, now. The Senator always done the right thing by us. You just explain it to him how it waddent yo fault."

Without thinking, and still holding Nate, Vida ran across the room and flung her loose arm around her father. She began sobbing into his boiled white shirt.

"What's got into you, girl? What you carrying on for?"

"Cause you say it waddent my fault," she sobbed.

Levi tenderly patted the back of Vida's head until his eyes fell down upon his light-colored grandson.

"I spect you better bring the baby on to the conference, too," her father said with a sigh, watching the boy cram the golden hands into his mouth. "He can tell the story without speaking nary a word."

Chapter 7
THE COLUMNS

The sun was setting scarlet by the time Levi drove past the last cluster of tenant shacks and turned onto the generously graveled lane leading up to the Columns. Like emerald-suited soldiers, house-tall cedars lined both sides of the quarter-mile entrance. The Buick slipped between the last pair of trees and Levi slowed, proceeding at a crawl as if in reverence to the white mansion that rose up before them.

This was as close as Vida had been to the Columns. Once, before Nate, she and Willie had sneaked up the lane, him on one side and her on the other, each crouching down low behind a cedar, where on Willie's secret owl hoot from the other side, they scurried from one tree to the next until they made their way unseen to the very last pair of evergreen sentinels. There they stood, peeking out through the lattice-like foliage, gazing in silent wonderment at the storybook house, in awe that something that bright and gleaming had been plopped down in a heat-distorted world of mules and shanties and sweating fieldhands.

Of course, if someone had spotted Vida and her brother peering through the trees, it wouldn't have mattered. Just two more colored children on the grounds. But the lengths to which Vida and Willie went to remain hidden transformed the sight into a forbidden one, which was all the better.

They would stand there gawking while the Senator's visitors came calling. The tires of the approaching cars crunching gravel announced their arrivals in time for Willie and Vida to wheel themselves behind a cedar to avoid detection. Slowly they twined around the trees like stringing a top, staying out of sight as the sleek automobiles made their way up the lane and stopped in front of the house.

They watched as the white men in their summer-weight suits climbed out of their shiny cars and scurried around to open the doors for their passengers. That's when Vida heard it—the shrill, mindless chatter of white women. It was a noise so disagreeable, it assured her that regardless of how her father dressed her, and called her his Snowflake Baby, and no matter how much he loved the white man, there was no way he could ever really want her to be one of *those* creatures. She silently cursed them as they emerged from the sedans, in flimsy dresses, giggling and fanning their ghostly faces and patting their curls, limp and frail.

Tonight, as Levi neared the house, Vida counted half a dozen cars already parked in the circular drive. Instead of joining them, Levi pulled off the lane onto a rough track used by mules and tractors, and drove carefully around to the rear of the house, bringing the Buick to a stop at the back gate. He got out and walked over to the cast-iron bell that sat atop a cedar post. He pulled the rope three times, clanging the bell noisily.

The kitchen door flung open and Vida was relieved to see that it was Lillie Dee Prophet, the Senator's cook, who came out, limping across the yard up to the fence.

"Zat you, Brother Pastor?" she asked, squinting hard into his face.

"Hello, Sister Prophet." He formally tipped his hat to the wizened woman. "How you this evenin?"

"I ain't jumpin no stumps, Rev'rund."

"Ain't that the truth!" Vida's father laughed and shook his head in the way that made you feel like you were really something for saying what you said.

Lillie Dee bent her head down and strained to make out the shadows inside the car, her toothless gums working without pause. "But it's like I tole my last boy over there," Lillie Dee said, nodding her head toward the wood shed in back of the house, "like I tole Rezel, ever day I can get out of bed, I count it as a blessing from the Lord."

Hearing Rezel's name, Vida crooked her head to see around Lillie Dee. She spied him standing in the shadows, gathering an armload of stove wood, and wearing overalls and a ripped cotton shirt. Tall and hard-muscled and sullen, he stubbornly kept his eyes away from the place where people were bandying his name about. Vida heard stories about him singing the blues at the jook joints in a way that could turn sisters one against the other.

Her father said to the old cook. "Well, Lillie Dee, you certainly blessed to have your boy stayin on with you. That bound to be a comfort."

"Rezel?" Lillie Dee shook her head sadly. She looked back at the boy, throwing her voice loud enough for him to hear. "He like all the rest of em. Goin up North. Say people up there pay him money to sing that debbil's music. Pardon my snuff, Rev'rund." Lillie Dee spit juice on the ground and continued. "Why, you think it be the Promised Land the way they all headin off up thataway."

"I'm sorry to hear bout it, Sister Prophet. They still plenty of good life left in Mis'sippi for the upright colored man. Cause of you, Rezel got him good work here with the Senator. Too bad he don't know that."

"That's the truth, Rev'rund." Lillie Dee looked at Levi through the tops of her eyes and grinned slyly. "Carryin my wood never did you no harm, did it?"

Vida saw that Lillie Dee's comment brought a rare expression of shyness to her father's face, and for a moment, Lillie Dee was no longer a member of his flock, but the woman who had overseen his chores when he was the houseboy for the Senator's father.

He cleared his throat and removed his hat. "Lillie, will you tell the Senator that I need to conference with him on something weighty?"

"Senator's got comp'ny tonight, Rev'rund. Why don't you come back in the morning after breakfast?"

"It can't wait. Tell him it's about the election. He gone wont to see me and my girl."

The old woman worked her gums thoughtfully for a moment. "Well," she said, "Y'all drive on up in the yard and I'll tell 'im." But as she unlatched the gate, she warned, "I'm telling you, now, he ain't gone like it. They just commenced they supper."

While Vida, Nate, and Levi waited in the car, the Senator's bird dogs sniffed around the Buick and, one by one, hiked their legs and relieved themselves on the tires. They watched as fieldhands drove tractors and led mules in through the gate and put them away in the barn for the evening.

White people's laughter, cold and brittle, broke over the darkening yard. For over an hour, Levi sat sweating behind the wheel, mopping his face and jumping in his seat every time the door opened. But each time the screen swung back, it was only Lillie Dee announcing the start of another course.

This was not how Vida had imagined the "conferences" her father talked about so proudly. She had expected the Senator to welcome her father on the front gallery under those grand columns and make him comfortable in a room fit for Solomon where her daddy would advise the Senator on important matters.

The smells from the Senator's supper drifted into the car, and Nate began to whimper and fidget and tug on Vida's braids. She tried to comfort him by stroking his soft black hair, but her own fingers trembled.

"It's a ways past Nate's suppertime, Daddy. Maybe we ought to do like Lillie Dee says and come back again."

Her father was gripping the steering wheel tightly, staring through the windshield into a grove of pecan trees rapidly disappearing in the dark. "Caint. The Senator know we out here. Anyways, he be glad we come with a warning. He gone thank us. You wait and see."

There was something missing from her father's words. They had a lonely, far-off sound to them, like a single bobwhite quail calling out unanswered in the distance.

"He'll show that peckerwood which road leads out the county. I know he will. You wait and see if he don't."

At last Lillie Dee poked her head out of the door and called, "I just served em they cake and coffee. Won't be too long now."

Levi turned to Vida, his eyes pleading through the darkness. She had never seen her father fearful before and the sight jerked at her stomach.

"Now, Vida, you pay respect to the Senator. Say 'Yessuh' and 'Nossuh.' Don't look him in his eyes. Don't shame me, girl."

"I'm scared, Daddy. What he gone do to Nate?"

Her father didn't seem to hear Vida's question. "The Senator been good to me. He raised up my first church. He believed in me when I tole him about seein the shinin face of God in a mighty whirlpool of churnin water, callin me to be the preacher of the Word. He believe me then. He believe me now, too."

Like a canon, the voice of the Senator came booming from the kitchen. "All right now, Lillie Dee. Tell Levi to come on in."

They came through the back door, and Vida saw the Senator up close for the first time. His frame rose before her like a cypress trunk, dense and broad. He had one massive arm propped against a marble biscuit block while the other held out an empty whiskey glass to Lillie Dee, who took it and left the room. Other colored servants scurried in and out of the kitchen carrying silver trays of tinkling china.

"Now what's so important that it can't wait, Levi? And why you got the young'uns with you?" The Senator wiped his hand on the coat of his linen suit. "Hurry up, now, I got company."

Levi kneaded the brim of his hat with both hands. "Yessuh. I know you do. I just thought, see'n as you and me go way back…Well, suh…What I got's to say…"

Vida's heart dipped down past her stomach. This was not how it was supposed to be at all! This was her father, the man whose words made people shout with joy and dance in the aisles. The man who stood up with authority to the white man. She found herself taking a step backward toward the door.

The Senator's face colored. "Stop beatin the devil around the stump, Levi. Just spit it out."

"Yessuh. Just that my girl here…. Well, she got somethin to say."

Vida could feel the Senator's bleary gaze fall upon her, but no words would come. The only sound was the pulsing of her own blood pounding in her ears. She took yet another step backward.

When things didn't seem like they could get any worse, she saw her father's shoulders fall as if a cord of wood had been dropped on his back. Looking up, she saw that the man from the store had stepped into the room. His eyes, as dark and cold as the iron pots that hung on the wall behind him, bored into Vida through mean little slits.

"Go on ahead, girl," he said. "What you got to tell the Senator?"

Vida's knees went soft as Nate grew impossibly heavy in her arms. She backed against the warming oven to keep from crumpling to the floor. Even though she wasn't supposed to look a white man in the eyes, in his, she clearly had seen murder.

"Billy Dean," the Senator said, not bothering to turn around. "I'm glad you were able to tear yourself away from my daughters." His voice was full of scorn. "It's getting hard to tell which one it was you got engaged to. I hope I don't have to point Hertha out to you."

"Just being sociable, Senator. Don't you worry bout me none. I ain't letting Miss Hertha out of my sights." Then Billy Dean stepped up beside the Senator and smiled a sideways grin. He slapped the Senator on the back. "I'm a man of my word. Just like you." He winked at the Senator.

The Senator wasn't amused. Billy Dean quickly removed his hand and then waved his drink at the callers. "You having yourself some kind of high-level meeting back here with all these fancy-dressed niggers?"

The Senator scowled at Billy Dean. "For your information, this here's the colored preacher I was telling you about. You take care of ol' Levi and he'll tell you what the nigruhs are up to."

The Senator smiled fondly at the preacher. "Ain't that right, Levi?"

"Yessuh. That sho is right," Levi mumbled, looking at his shoes.

"Why do I care what the niggers are up to?" Billy Dean scoffed.

The Senator spun toward Billy Dean. "I'll tell you why you *better* care. If you going to be *my* sheriff, looking out for *my* five thousand acres, you sure as hell better know what the nigruhs and everbody else is up to. I want to know about Yankee labor agents trying to steal my tenants and croppers lying about my gin weights and the federal government trying to stir up trouble. And I better know about trouble a day before trouble happens. You got that, Billy Dean?" The Senator kept up his glare until Billy Dean dropped his eyes.

He focused on Levi's chain, glowering at the folded hands. "Whatever you say," Billy Dean grumbled, looking like he had more to add, but jiggling the ice in his drink instead.

The Senator turned back to Levi. "Now what you got to tell me bout the election?"

Vida prayed for her father to say something, but he just stood there motionless, bent like a willow after an ice storm. There was only silence. Finally Lillie Dee returned with a tray of fresh drinks for the Senator and Billy Dean.

Billy Dean tossed back half his drink and wiped his mouth. He sniggered. "I bet I know what Levi wants. He wants to vote for me come the election. That right, boy?"

Levi looked as if he had been slapped. "Nossuh!" he said quickly, the sound of alarm ringing in his voice. "Votin is the white man's business. You won't catch me messin with none a that."

"I don't know," Billy Dean said. "Could be I heard talk about you and that secret nigger club. What y'all call it? *N double A and CP?*"

The Senator looked at Billy Dean like he was an idiot. "Levi?" he said with a sharp laugh. "Levi cares as much about voting as a horse cares about Christmas. Besides, he knows which side his bread is buttered on." This time it was the Senator who slapped Billy Dean on the back and sneered, "Just like you, boy."

Billy Dean's face reddened again, but his angry scowl was directed toward Levi.

The inside kitchen door swung open and a plump, well-dressed woman about the Senator's age poked her head through. "What are you men doing in here?" she asked, holding a lacey handkerchief up to a neck whiter than the china on the countertops. "You have guests in your house, Hugh. Did you forget?"

When her brother didn't answer at once, she looked carefully around the kitchen filled with tense expressions. Without speaking another word, she touched the handkerchief to her lips and eased back through the door.

Straightening his jacket, the Senator started after his sister. "Billy Dean," he said on his way through the door, "you find out what Levi there wants. Then come tell me. Get some practice at being my sheriff."

Left alone in the kitchen with the preacher and his family, and his face still flushed from having been told off, Billy Dean motioned toward the back door. Through clenched teeth, he said, "Let's go outside and have us a little powwow."

Vida hurried Nate down the steps first, but before her father could take the first step, Billy Dean shoved him hard, causing him to topple down from the porch and land sprawled on the ground at Vida's feet.

Looking up, she saw the crazy smile on Billy Dean's face. His eyes cut toward the boy in her arms and at last Vida found her voice. "Lillie Dee!" she screamed.

The old cook was at the door in a flash. "Merciful Jesus! What's goin on out here? Levi, whachoo doin spraddled out in the dirt? You hurt yoself?" Without waiting for an answer she yelled out into the yard. "Rezel! Where you? Ge'cheer and hep the Rev'rund on his feet."

Her boy emerged out of the dark of the yard. From his shamed-faced expression Vida could tell Rezel must have been watching the whole thing from the shadows. He got Levi to his feet.

Vida saw that the Senator's younger daughter, Delia, the one they called "the pretty one," had joined Lillie Dee on the back porch. "Billy Dean," she cooed, "what on earth are you all doing out here? You were in the middle of telling me an amusing story, remember?"

Upon making out that it was Levi brushing himself, Delia's voice, much to Vida's surprise, filled with concern. "Levi! My goodness, are you all right?" She shot Billy Dean a hard look. "What have you done to Levi?"

"The old man fell down's all," Billy Dean said gruffly. "I'll take care of it. Everbody get on back in the house."

Lillie Dee and Rezel did as they were told, but Delia didn't move. "Levi, that all right with you? You tell me to stay and I will. I won't let anything happen to you."

Levi was adamant. "No, ma'am, Miss Delia. Nothin goin on out here to worry you bout. I was just givin my best to Mr. Billy Dean on his lection."

She looked back at Billy Dean. "You!" she teased. "Our next sheriff. How low has our democracy sunk!" Delia shook her head, teasingly. "Hurry on back in, Billy Dean. Your fiancée—oops!" she said, covering her mouth in mock embarrassment, "I mean, your food is getting cold." She gave out a giggle and went back into the kitchen.

The screen door shut behind her and Vida felt their last hope had left with her. She could hear Billy Dean's breathing, fast and furious. In a voice bled dry of emotion, he said, "This ain't over," and then stomped back into the house.

During the ride home, the car was thick with things not said. Vida could tell from her father's shallow breaths and clenched jaw and from the way he leaned rigidly over the wheel that he was figuring hard, considering and then discarding one option after another. As for herself, she could only come up with one and she was doing it, holding tight to her baby until the nightmare passed.

Levi parked the car next to their house, switched off the motor, but left the lights burning. He sat there motionless, looking off into the distance where the headlights cut a ghostly path across the field. His breathing was slow and steady. Vida knew that he had settled on a plan.

Without looking at Vida, he said, "The boy ain't safe here with us. And we ain't safe with the boy."

Nate was trying to tickle Vida's neck with her plait. She stilled his hand, struggling with what her father had said. "What that mean, Daddy?"

"You heard the man. He say it ain't over. Nate make that man crazy." Then he said, almost to himself, "Your momma had kin in Alabama."

Grasping his meaning, Vida cried, "I ain't lettin go of Nate, Daddy. You can't make me do that."

Turning off the headlights, Levi said only, "We got to take it to the Lord. He will show us a way."

Chapter 8
BABY MOSES

If Levi Snow had known that this would be his final sermon, he might have chosen a different text. If he, the most revered colored preacher in Hopalachie County, a man favored by God with not one but three churches, had known that before the day was out he would be pleading for his own life, he might have chosen to preach on Daniel in the lion's den. Or Jesus being tempted in the desert. Or God's taking everything away from Job for no other reason than to show Satan what a righteous man he was. A story that would move his people to see how the good and the upright suffer for their faith and need to be stood by in dangerous times. If he had, maybe his people would not have been deaf to his cries in his time of desolation. Perhaps then someone would have been there when he himself needed saving.

But Levi Snow, the Reach Out Man, didn't know any of this when the choir fell back breathless in their seats and he strode majestically up to the pulpit, on his way glancing down at the gold watch cupped in the palm of his hand and then slipping it back into its pocket. Like time was nobody's business but his.

Towering over the congregation, Levi searched every sweating face in the church, letting the tension mount as a hundred hand-held funeral fans flashed the face of Jesus back at him.

The rigid benches were jam-packed with fieldhands, transformed for the day into baggy-suited deacons and white-clad mothers of the church and royally robed choristers. Fine white cotton gloves kept their secrets, disguising the field-wrecked hands of men as well as women.

Except for Vida's, of course, who sat clutching her gloves, revealing smooth, delicate fingers that had never picked a boll of cotton in all her privileged life as the daughter of Reverend Snow.

Every eye was now riveted upon Levi, watching for him to cut loose and tear up the pulpit. Every eye including Vida's, who awaited more anxiously than most.

What message would her father send her today? What story could he possibly preach to put everything back in its place? She prayed he would be able to create a story with a happy ending big enough to hold them all. That he would pull some loose threads from his raggedy Bible, knit up a new meaning and put the world right again, like he had done so many times before. With the right story she had heard her father turn losses into victories, slaves into masters, pain and suffering into glory.

What about her boy, wanted dead by a white man? How would her father weave Nate safely into their lives again?

Levi Snow's silence began weighing heavy on the congregation, and they began to stir.

"Tell it, brother!" a bald-headed deacon called out in a voice frail with age.

"Feed us the holy word, Preacher!" sang out a breasty church mother.

Hooking his thumbs up under his arms and rocking back and forth on his heels, Levi Snow stared up into the rafters and shook his head, like he was conferencing with God Himself about whether or not to go ahead and preach today. Reverend Snow nodded solemnly, as if the Lord had whispered something that the preacher couldn't argue with, and then glared down again on the congregation.

He began. "Next to God's love there is no love like a mother's love."

Heads nodded. A few said "Amen," and others, "That's right."

He said it again, this time chanting the words in his profound bass. "Next to God's love...There is no love...Like a mother's love."

More scattered shouts cried out.

"The Lord said, even though a mother's love is mighty, His is mightier. Ain't that right?"

Everybody was agreed. "Sho is!"

"That's the truth."

"Isaiah say, even if a mother forgets the babe at her breast, God will never forget you. Ain't that right, too?"

"That's right!"

"Preach it!"

"But a mother ain't likely to forget the babe at her breast, is she?"

"No, lawd!"

"Because...Next to God's love...There is no love...Like a mother's love. A mother's love is mighty love."

Then he looked down at his own daughter and smiled, as if to put flesh and blood on his story.

Vida swelled with pride. Her father was bragging on her in front of the whole church. Putting her arm around the boy, she pulled him close. She should have known her father would find a way.

Levi Snow continued. "You all know bout Moses, don't you?"

"A good man!"

"A righteous man!"

"A man of God!"

"We likes to hear bout how he stood up to ol' Pharaoh and said 'Let my people go.' Ain't that right?"

"That's God's truth!"

"About how he marched the slaves out of Egypt and split the Red Sea wide open and then led the people to the Promised Land. Yes, Lord! We all know the story bout Moses. Moses indeed was a great man. God surely loved Moses."

"Sho did!"

"But there was somebody else who loved Moses."

Levi let this new information settle in between the benches before he sang out again. "Next to God's love...There is no love...Like a mother's love. Moses had a momma. How mighty was his mother's love?"

"Tell it, preacher!"

"When Moses was a baby at his momma's breast, the Pharaoh wanted to snatch him up and drown him in the River Nile. How mighty was his mother's love?"

"Go on!"

"Did his momma forget about that baby at her breast?"

"No, Lord."

"Did she want to keep her baby close at her breast? Like any momma would?"

"Yes, Lord!"

"Course she did. But...How mighty was his mother's love?"

"How mighty?"

"The love she had for her baby was bigger than her own selfishness. She had a love so mighty she laid her baby in a basket and put him in the bullrushes and let the river take him. Now I ask you, how mighty was his mother's love?" His eyes burned hot and bright. "How mighty, Lord?"

He dropped his gaze onto Vida, like the question was for her, but then he answered it himself in a loud crackling whisper, "Mighty enough to let him go."

At first she wasn't sure she had heard him right. Holding onto Nate, she kept her eyes glued to her father, struggling with the divine revelation.

Levi turned back to his congregation. "Next to God's love...There is no love...Like a mother's love. Before Moses could grow up and tell the Pharaoh, 'You got to let my people go,' his momma had to pull her own child from her breast and say, 'I got to let my baby go.' Now, I ask you again. How mighty was his mother's love?"

The shouting increased and some rose to their feet.

"Her love was mighty!" a deacon called at the top of his voice.

Levi looked down at his daughter again, as if giving her this final chance to give her answer, and then he raised his arms over his head and sang out to the rafters, "Mighty enough to let that baby go!"

Her father's words had whipped up a sea of motion across the church. All around Vida, people were standing with their palms toward heaven, others rocking side to side on their benches and clapping their hands. It was as if she were caught up in a mighty current threatening to pull her and her son under. She gasped for air and gripped Nate's shoulder tightly. So tightly he cried out and tried to squirm loose, but Vida held on.

Chapter 9
LATE NIGHT VISITATION

Billy Dean slewed the truck backward out of the churchyard and into the road, and then stopped. He watched, mesmerized, as the blazing church lit up the late-night sky. Sweat beaded on his face, not from flame but from memory. His dad, fallen down drunk in the dirt-yard. The kerosene lantern crashing through the window of the shack. The fiery explosion followed by his mother's screams. Her running off the porch like a lit torch, dropping dead to the side of her husband, who scrambled on all fours to get away from her. Billy Dean, watching it all, unable to go to either of them.

He shook the memory from his head and threw the truck into first gear, pulling off so hard his uncle bumped his head against the back window.

Billy Dean was bad drunk and his eyes wouldn't focus, which wouldn't have been any big deal if he weren't racing down washed-out roads in the dead of night. He tried covering up one of his eyes with the palm of his hand, which seemed to help, but it didn't make Furman any more comfortable.

"Boy, pull this truck over and let me drive. You all over the road." Furman's foot had been pumping vainly at the floorboard ever since they left the burning church.

"You listnin to me? You ain't even goin in the right direction. I got to get on back to the house or Beula have my hide. She'll think I'm runnin around with another woman."

Billy Dean switched eyes. "We ain't goin back to the house yet. Got one more piece a business needs tendin to."

Off in the distance, something dark and dog-high, with a tail like frayed rope, leaped out of a ditch and into the path of the truck.

"Hell, boy. Don't you reckon we took care of enough bidness for one night? You aimin to torch all his churches the same time?" Furman reached his hand toward the wheel, guessing his nephew wouldn't spot the creature in time.

A pair of unblinking eyes set aflame by the headlights stared back at the truck from the middle of the road. Billy Dean pulled the wheel sharply to the left, sending the thing scrambling into the opposite ditch.

"We goin to burn his house. Gone smoke me out a rat."

"What you talkin about a rat?"

Furman's foot hit the floorboard, hard. "You ain't meanin—"

"That little nigger rat." Billy Dean slowed, looking for the turnoff. "It's either him or me. Burn him up. Shit. Burn em all. Nothin but ashes. Ashes to ashes."

Reckoning the turn too late, he jumped the ditch and the truck came to a lurching stop in a turn row.

"Billy Dean, that's drunk talk. You done scared the pee-diddle out of that preacher. He ain't gone be no bother." Furman put his hand on his nephew's shoulder. "Let's get turned around out of this field and go on to the house. Tomorrow's another day."

"Tole you ain't goin to the house. Ain't over." Billy Dean tossed his head in his uncle's direction. "Gone smoke me out a rat. If Senator see that boy…all she wrote. No Sheriff Billy Dean Brister. No big white house in Delphi. No nothin. Tired of nothin. Ashes to ashes like my daddy said."

"You don't want to kill nobody, son. Specially not no little baby. Specially not yore—" Furman stopped short.

"Shut your mouth! He ain't my nothin. You hear? Little rat's all he is. Smoke him out. Tonight."

Billy Dean took out several rows of cotton but got the truck turned around. Gunning the engine and aiming for the road, he jumped the truck back over the ditch.

As dark as the night was, and as drunk as Billy Dean was, it still wasn't hard to find Levi's place. The truck rounded the curve and its headlights washed over a newly painted house, nice as a white man's, sitting proudly among a cluster of falling-down shacks.

Everybody in the quarter was asleep.

Billy Dean pulled alongside a row of neatly trimmed ligustrum bushes that made a hedgerow on one side of the house. He cut his lights.

"Boy, I'm tellin you. This ain't right. I don't mind burnin down a church or two. You know I ain't no nigger lover, but you takin this thing too far. Let's wait on it, you hear?"

"Get the can."

The uncle hesitated and then went around to the back of the truck. He lifted out the can of kerosene, and while Billy Dean was watching the porch, he stuck the can behind a ligustrum bush.

Getting back in the truck and closing the door, he said in a shaky voice. "Ain't got no kerosene. Must of left the can back at the church. Billy Dean, let's go on home now, please boy. Fore anybody wakes up."

"Shit!" Billy Dean said. "You old fool."

He cut on his headlights. Stepping on the gas, he ran the truck straight for the house, braking hard just a few feet shy of the porch, his headlights aimed through the front room window. Revving the engine, he said, "Let's see if we can shine a coon out its tree."

Lights came on throughout the quarter. Furman frantically rubbed the back of his neck.

The door of the house eased open and the preacher stepped out in his nightshirt, shielding his eyes against the glare with his upraised palm.

"Who that?" he called into the light. "What business you got here?"

Billy Dean stumbled out of the truck, weaved around to the rear, and pulled out his shotgun. He staggered back again and propped himself against the hood, between the glaring headlights. "Get that little rat out here," he slurred. "That little albino piece of shit."

"Mr. Billy Dean, sir," Levi stammered, falling back toward the door. "We don't mean you no harm. I sho didn't know bout you and Miss Hertha." He took another step back, his arm reaching behind him for the door. "I hope you two be real happy," he said. "And I sho sorry for that little misunderstandin."

With one arm Billy Dean steadied himself against the hood of the truck and with the other he raised the shotgun to his hip. It was aimed at the preacher's midsection. "Not as sorry as you gonna be. I tole you what I wanted. Get that boy out here. Now!"

Suddenly the door flew open and Willie came charging out past his father. He took the porch in two leaps and was halfway down the steps before Billy Dean got both barrels aimed at the boy's head.

"Stop right there, nigger! I'll blow it off. I swear I will."

Willie came to a dead stop. His face threw off more heat than fear.

As Billy Dean watched Willie's blurry figure weave in and out of his sights, he heard the screen door slam shut in the back of the house. Moving across the field was the ghost-like silhouette of a young girl dressed in white carrying a large bundle, fading deeper into the darkness. Beyond was the bayou and the swampy safety of a dark stand of cypress.

Billy Dean staggered back to the truck and took off, plowing through the hedge and into the field behind the house. Cotton plants half as tall as men scraped the bottom of the truck. He was almost up on the girl.

Furman was close to tears. "Dammit, Billy Dean! Pull up and let me out. We splittin the sheets right cheer. Find somebody else to make yore deputy. I ain't got the stomach for it."

All at once the girl disappeared from sight. Billy Dean pulled to a stop. "She's dropped down between the rows. Come on!"

They both got out of the truck, but then stood silent, listening to the night, the headlights throwing the men's shadows long across the field. From several yards beyond, they heard a child's whimpering. Billy Dean stumbled off in the direction of the sound.

Furman lurched after his nephew. "No!" he shouted.

Almost on his nephew now, Furman yelled again, "Gal! Stay down. You hear me? Don't raise up." He reached out to grab Billy Dean by the arm.

Suddenly, Vida leaped up and started off again. A second later there came a blast from the shotgun. As the explosion echoed throughout the quarter, the lanterns in the shanties dimmed as quickly as they had come on.

Chapter 10
THE PROMISED LAND

Vida stood at the parlor window, holding open the lace curtains, gazing out into the clouded sky. It was nearly dusk and time to begin her nightly trek to Lillie Dee's cabin. It had rained most of the day and the low-hanging clouds threatened more, but there would be no stopping her.

"You gone get wet," her little brother warned. "Ask Daddy to carry you."

Vida glanced over at their father, who sat in his chair in a darkened corner, fingering the links of his gold chain, the one Nate used to cling so tightly to. She looked out the window again.

"It might be lightenin up some," she said, studying the paler shade of gray on the horizon. "I bet it be faired off by mornin."

Of course that would make tomorrow, hers and Willie's first day to ever pick cotton, a hot and steamy one. But Vida would pick two hundred pounds and not grumble once if Lillie Dee had good news tonight.

"Wont me to walk with you?" Willie asked. "You always come back lookin sad."

"I be all right." Then she whispered, "Willie, I got a good feelin bout tonight."

Willie smiled, not saying she always had a good feeling, when she left.

As she walked past his chair, Levi took no notice of Vida. Anyway, it wouldn't do any good to ask him to drive her the five miles to Lillie Dee's. He refused to leave the house anymore, afraid he would be absent when the Senator finally sent for him. Any hour now, any minute, word might arrive and Levi would be called into conference with the Senator, his oldest friend, the man he used to be boys with. All Levi needed was that one conference and the world would be set right again.

Vida knew the truth. Levi had been out to the Columns so many times in the past two months, the Senator had sent word through Lillie Dee that if he wanted to speak to Levi, he would send for him and to stop coming around and bothering the help. Even though Vida didn't think that was much to hang your hopes on, Levi was certain that with Nate gone, the lies would die down and soon the Senator would get around to setting the record straight.

The day after the fire, when nothing remained of his biggest church but a pile of ashes smoldering behind a kerosene cross, rumors began to spread about how Levi must have been working with the NAACP trying to get the vote. His deacons were quick to turn him out, forever marking him as a troublemaker bound to draw the white man's fire wherever he showed up to preach. He didn't dare tell them the real reason the church had been burned—or by whom. It wasn't necessary. Levi believed that as soon as the Senator said the word, the deacons would give Levi his churches back and the collections would start coming in again and all would be as it was.

They had long since used up the staples the Senator's daughter Delia had brought over, and Levi had been acting so sure of his story, she and Willie were afraid to tell him that they had decided to hire on as fieldhands so they could at least bring in some grocery money. As for the car and the house, they had no idea how he planned on keeping up the payments to the Senator, and they dared not ask.

Vida reached for her parasol hanging by the door and was suddenly taken by the memory of the day it arrived, and how she and her father danced around the sun-drenched yard in a shade brought from Memphis. She turned back toward him, and almost called out that she loved him, wanting only to draw the same from him.

But when she saw him sitting there in his make-believe world, the words caught in her throat. Things would never be the same between them. She knew that now. Had known it for sure that day in the graveyard, when he acted the way he did.

The funeral had been a small, pitiful affair. Most people were just too afraid to be seen in public with Levi. A preacher from Holmes County, an old friend of Levi's, had traveled in by night to hold the service. Nobody cried except for Vida. Everybody else, including her father, just sat dry-eyed before the little pine coffin, as the preacher intoned mournfully about how the innocence of children was a sure ticket to the Promised Land.

As the preacher droned on with his eulogy, Vida thought about the Promised Land. She never noticed before how often her people spoke of it. That made three the number of times that very week she had heard about the Promised Land. Once was from Lillie Dee. She had complained that Rezel was following the rest of her sons up North, to the Promised Land. Another time was from her father's pulpit. It was where Moses headed after he grew up.

Now this preacher was praying for Nate's departed soul, saying Nate was gone off to the Promised Land, like it might even be a good thing she had lost her baby. But Vida couldn't believe that Moses' momma would agree.

Sitting at the graveside next to her father, looking at the coffin, she thought she knew how Moses' momma must have felt when she laid her baby in the basket. She wanted to tell her father that she knew. And she wanted her father to tell her once more how blessed Moses' momma was for doing the right thing. But when she looked up at him through her tears, she realized she would get nothing. He sat there proud and aloof, like this funeral should have been for his own pain and trouble. Trouble he wouldn't have had without her.

Reaching for the door, she opened her mouth to say something to her father and once more she choked off her words. Her father turned his face in her direction and she froze inside. This time it was Vida who looked away. She left the house and walked out into the light drizzle.

Vida trudged down the muddied road into the gathering darkness, trying her best to sidestep water-filled ruts as deep as washtubs. Her feet began to feel like cinder blocks. When the moon peeked out from behind a veil of black clouds she looked down to see her baby-doll shoes caked with mud. Standing on one foot at a time, balancing her weight on the parasol, she removed her shoes and socks. Then she beat the soles together to knock off the mud, splattering her dress. She walked the rest of the way barefoot.

Lillie Dee's cabin sat out in the darkness, back off in the field her boys had worked before they one at a time left her and headed up North. There were no lights on in the house, but Vida knew Lillie Dee was there nevertheless. She always ate her supper in the Senator's kitchen and later he had one of the tractor drivers take her home where she would sit outside, rocking on her porch until it was time for sleep.

Vida approached the shack and heard the sound of the rocker creaking like a rain frog in the night. She made out Lillie Dee's silhouette on the porch. When the rocking stopped, she knew that Lillie Dee had spotted her.

Vida sucked in her breath, braving herself against the old woman's first words. Would it be the usual discouraging greeting: "Baby, I ain't heard one lonely word." Or would tonight be different?

Lillie Dee called out brightly, "I bet you a fat man that be Vida comin down my path! Seen you shinin like an angel the minute you turned off the big road."

Vida's heart leaped to her throat. For the first night in two months, Lillie Dee sounded like she was glad to see her. "Say it, Miss Lillie Dee!" Vida shouted, running the rest of the way, splashing puddles as she went. "Say you got word. You did! I can tell."

Vida was nearly breathless as she climbed the steps to the porch. "Don't fool me, please! Tell me straight out."

Through the dark Vida could see Lillie Dee lift her hand. It held a white envelope. Vida dropped her shoes and parasol on the porch and grabbed at the letter, letting out a shriek. Then she started stamping her muddy feet on the porch with excitement.

"Light the lan'ern there behind you and read it out loud. I couldn't hardly tell one word from t'other. Cept I'm sho it be from my boy. I knows the writin for Rezel's name."

Vida's hands shook so badly she almost dropped the globe. It took three matches but she got the lamp lit. As the kerosene sputtered, she fumbled with the envelope but her hands were shaking so violently she couldn't get it open. So she held it to her chest and shut her eyes tight. Vida was sick with fright. For the millionth time, she prayed she had done the right thing. The decision had had to be made so quickly.

It was the only choice, she told herself yet again. Her father had sworn to her it was for the best. He had said it was God's will that the man had missed point blank with his shotgun and then passed out flat on his face in the cotton. It had been God working on the old uncle's heart, had made him walk right up to Vida and tell her to get her baby out of the county.

"Better yet," he had said, "get him out of the State of Mis'sippi."

Vida remembered the sound of panic in his voice. "Bury an empty grave box," he said. "I'll vouch that the boy's dead." He glanced down at where his nephew lay grumbling in his sleep. "I know Billy Dean. It's the only way he ain't gone hunt the boy down. Once he gets a hold of somethin, he's like a snappin turtle. Won't let go till lightenin strikes him in the ass."

Vida stood there in the darkness trembling, with Nate crying in her arms, trying to read the old man's face in the moonlight.

"But girl, if you do it," he had said, shaking bad as she was, "you can't never tell it. Be the end of me and you both. The boy, too."

That night her father told Vida it meant God was giving her a second chance. Before the man had shown up with his gun, she refused to send her baby away. Now he said they didn't have a choice. They had to act fast. He reminded her about Lillie Dee's boy going up North. It would be a simple thing for Rezel to sneak Nate away on the train. It would fool the man.

"It's the only way we can save the child," her father had said. "Lillie Dee's oldest boy got a family in Memphis. Rezel can drop Nate off with them. They take good care of him. He be safe there."

"No," she cried. "I can't let go of my baby."

"Just for a while," her father had pleaded. "We can go get him soon as I conference with the Senator. I promise."

Vida would never forget how her father had looked at her in that moment. With desperation in his face, he had pleaded, "Snowflake Baby, God's givin us a chance to set things right. To put things back the way they was before." In his tears Vida believed she saw the way to his forgiveness.

She clutched the envelope over her heart and whispered, "Oh, God, please show me the way to Nate."

Trembling, Vida opened the letter and then held the paper to the light. First thing she did was drop her eyes to the bottom of the page.

Sure enough, there was Rezel's name. He had finally written. The night he caught the Memphis train with Nate, Rezel had promised he would write as soon as they got to his brother Toby's. That was two months ago.

Taking a deep breath, Vida began to decipher the wild scribble. As the words piled up, she began shaking her head in disbelief. Then she read the letter again.

Lillie Dee leaned forward in her rocker. "What's it say, baby?" She waved her hand in front of her face, swooshing the night insects drawn by the light.

"Rezel say he got to Memphis."

"Praise the Lamb!" Lillie Dee clapped her hands together. "They made it live out of Mis'sippi."

Vida was not as relieved. The writing was in such a tangle, she was still struggling with the meaning.

"But, Lillie Dee," she said with panic rising in her voice, "they ain't there no more." Vida turned the envelope over and checked the postmark. It was true.

"They ain't? Where is they?"

"They in Chicargo."

"Chicargo," Lillie Dee said to herself.

Vida went through the letter yet again.

"Rezel found Toby's wife livin with another man. Toby done left her."

"My sweet grandbabies!" Lillie Dee cried. "What become of them? They stay in Memphis with they momma?"

"I reckon so," Vida answered, but her words were halting. "She say Toby left his family and took hisself off to that Chicargo."

"Cold-soundin word." Lillie Dee said it slower. "Chicarrr-go."

"She said she don't wont to take on no more chil'ren. So Rezel took Nate to Chicargo. And they lookin for Toby."

"Chicargo," Lillie Dee said again. "Where that be at, zactly?"

Like a stone falling through water, Vida slid down against the wall to the porch floor. She was overwhelmed with exhaustion. Closing her eyes, she tried to recall the map that hung in the front of her classroom. The one with greens and blues and yellows she ignored year after year, when it was not important to know where anyplace in the world was except home. Until tonight she thought everybody knew where home was.

She shook her head hopelessly. "I don't know where it be at. Maybe on the other end of the river. Maybe clear on the other side of the Promised Land."

In one moment the world became impossibly big to Vida, capable of gobbling up grown men, and more so little boys. How would Nate ever find his way home in such a flung-out world? Who would show him on a map the place where somebody needed him so bad tonight?

Lifting her head she saw that the moon had broke loose again. The sooty blanket of clouds was moving toward some other land. One she probably couldn't name if her life depended on it. If Nate's life depended on it.

Chapter 11
WATCHING FOR THE FACE OF GOD

Word finally arrived from the Senator. As the sun rose, streaking the sky an early-morning pink, Bester Simmons, one of the Senator's tractor drivers as well as one of Levi's old deacons, showed up with a flatbed truck. Bester, a giant of a man with coal-black skin, wept when he informed his old reverend that today Levi was the Senator's newest sharecropper and the house was to be emptied immediately. He said he had been told to move Levi and his family into a tenant's shack sitting all by itself on seventeen acres on the other side of the bayou. The crop had already been planted and was ready for picking. Next spring, Bester said, two mules, seed, fertilizer, and supplies would be charged to Levi's account, along with everything else he owed the Senator, and then Levi could make his own crop.

Vida was stunned silent. Her father was *told* he would do it. No choice about it except to leave the county in the dead of night, in debt to the most powerful man in the Delta. The Senator had spoken. Conference over. As she stood there, listening to the news, she waited for her father to react, but he just stood there looking off into the distance toward the bayou.

"He can't make us move into no shack," Vida blurted. "Can't just up and tell us to make him a crop."

"Can, too. And mo'," said Bester, climbing down out of the cab. He had the contract in his hand. "If y'all make a fuss, he can sell yo debt to some other plantation. Make me haul y'all clear to another county if he wont to. End up with some boss twiced as bad. The kind that chain you in the crib till you work off what you owe. Yessum. He can sho nuf do it. I seed him done it."

Her father took the contract and signed it without protest, without asking a single question. Levi saw her staring at him in disbelief, all he said was, "The Senator knows what best. It's gone work itself out."

⚜

They left behind the car and all their household goods—the feather-soft beds and the horsehide sofa and stuffed chairs and floor rugs—to pay down on Levi's debt to the Senator, and moved into the two-room shotgun shack, sparsely furnished with two iron beds, a rickety dresser, a cookstove, and a wobbly table and four mismatched chairs.

Vida found no running water on the place, not a single pane of glass or window screen. The former tenants left fertilizer sacks hanging down over the window openings for curtains. Still her father said nothing. He moved around the place in a daze.

The next day, in September's seething heat, they began picking cotton, sharecropping their own plot, trying to remember what they had seen done around them all their lives.

The week began hot and got even worse. It got so bad Vida and Willie saw heat devils dancing in front of their eyes. After a few days, Levi began acting odd. When the sun dipped to the level of the cypress in the bayou off in the distance, he would drop his sack and head toward the sinking sun. Vida would holler after him, but he would act like he didn't hear her and just keep walking straight away. He wouldn't get back until well after supper, his voice ragged and hoarse, never bothering to explain his absence.

Then came one particularly miserable afternoon in late September. It had rained hard earlier in the day, turning the fields to mud, and when the sun came back out, it was so hot that steam rose up from between the rows. Vida's fingers stung from the bolls, and mosquitoes and buffalo gnats swarmed her face. Rising up to stretch her back, she saw her father drop his sack and walk off toward the bayou. It made her so mad she decided to go after him and find out for herself what was important enough to abandon her and Willie to all the work.

She followed him down the rows, but he never looked back once, keeping his face pointed toward the west until he reached the bayou and disappeared inside the swampy growth. Vida kept after him. She traced his footsteps like an Indian, down a footpath and to the edge of the black water, and she ducked behind a cottonwood tree.

From her hiding place she could see her father, standing motionless on the bank beside a giant bald cypress. For a moment all she heard was the plunking of turtles slipping into the water until she noticed a rushing sound from around the bend, where she knew the water ran fast and made the deadly whirlpools.

She understood. This was the place her father called his praying ground, the secret place where as a young man he had prayed day after day, night after night, to see the shining face of God. Finally God called out to him from a whirlpool of churning water. This was the very spot where Levi received the calling to become a preacher of the Word.

The frogs, now accustomed to human presence, resumed their chorus. Then came the dry rattle of the kingfisher that sat perched on a dead cypress stump. Next it was her father she heard. At first he spoke so soft and low she couldn't make out the words. But she soon recognized the slow, singsong chant he used when he preached, just before launching into his sermon. He would take a phrase and repeat it over and over in his deepest bass until he got the people's blood to stirring.

Vida listened, and his voice became fervent and full, larger than the swamp itself, groaning with emotion.

"Let this cup pass," he called out. "Lift up this yoke. Let this cup pass me by, oh Lord."

Over and over he called, louder and louder each time, until she was sure his voice resonated beyond this swampy place and thundered at the very door of Heaven. He pleaded with God not to hide His face any longer, begging Him not to desert His good and faithful servant. He asked God to send him a sign that he was still favored by the Father. He prayed that God still had a mighty purpose for him and please, please, to show His face one more time. "Send me a righteous story to live out," he shouted.

His words became angry, like he was mad at God, offended that He would keep hidden from him, reducing Levi to a common field worker and plunging him into darkness. He cried out with fury until a sudden upsurge of emotion strangled off his words and dropped him to his knees. For a while he sobbed bitterly, his shoulders heaving up and down. Then he began sputtering, "I'm sorry, I'm sorry, I'm sorry."

Through his choked tears she heard him say, "I wouldn't never have gone against you. Never. Please, please forgive me."

Vida's father was now only a shadow against the late bayou dusk, a vanishing man crying out to his white-faced God. Fireflies began their twinkling throughout the swamp. As her father's image was being stolen by the darkness, she strained again to hear his words. His tone had softened and was as tender as a comforting embrace. It was the same velvety voice he once used to soothe away her bad dreams.

"It's all right now," he said to someone Vida could not see. "Everthing gone be all right. Like the Good Book say, Whoso harkeneth unto me shall dwell safely, and shall be quiet from fear of evil."

Vida imagined her father gathering around him everyone and everything that had been taken. All his glory moments. The church before it burned. The flock he once tended. His old friend the Senator. A long-dead wife. Pampered children. Even Nate.

"Ain't gone be no more suffering. No more sorrow," he said to the shadows and silent shapes. "I got you all now. Come closer to me."

Right there in the bayou, on what Levi called his praying ground, Vida saw her father slip like one of those turtles under the surface into another world, one which she could not enter. She slumped behind the cottonwood, listening to her father and holding herself, wishing she too could slip into that place where he now granted his comfort so freely.

"Snowflake Baby," she whispered softly. Then she covered her face with her hands so that there would be no sound to her weeping.

1949

Chapter 12
DELPHI

Floyd's letters brought only good news from Hopalachie County. The mechanical cotton pickers were just catching on and Floyd proved to be real good at showing the planters how much better off they would be with one giant green machine rather than fifty colored fieldhands to keep up with. Instead of talking about horsepower, he told Hazel how he converted everything to nigger power. He would say, "This here is a fifty nigger-power machine and you don't have to bail it out of jail Monday morning." The planters loved it.

Floyd said everybody won on the deal because the coloreds wanted free of the fields as much as the planters wanted shed of the coloreds. He wrote to Hazel that he felt like a modern-day Abraham Lincoln.

Finally one of the letters ended with a PS. *Will you marry me? Please say yes.* She could just imagine Floyd as he wrote it cocking his head and smiling.

Not long after, on a coolish day in March, Hazel said good-bye to the druggist and his wife, one looking very sad and the other fairly relieved, and stepped out onto their broad green porch, a cardboard suitcase in her hand. Her makeup was careful, and she wore bright red earbobs and a cotton print dress splashed with roses so big they threatened to bloom right off the cloth. Her toenails, which were on view for the world to see from a pair of fancy strapped shoes, were like ten rose petals fallen from her dress.

A dark-haired, handsome man with an easy smile and a firm grip took her arm and guided her down the steps to his shiny sedan. Hazel noticed he squeezed her arm a little tighter than what seemed necessary, seeing as how she wasn't the least bit inclined to go anyplace but where he led.

Once in the car, Hazel said, "Now you got to ask me out loud."

"Ask you what?"

"You know. So far you just writ it. I ain't no mail-order bride."

"Oh," Floyd said, now understanding. "Hazel Ishee, will you marry me this very day?" He raised his eyebrows expectantly. Hazel guessed he had sold many a picker that way.

She didn't answer at once, putting a little anticipation into the moment and then, like a woman who had narrowed down a long list of choices, said "All right. I will."

The justice of the peace was a kindly old man and his wife as sweet as could be. Right there in his own cozy home with his wife at the piano, looking lovingly to him for her cues, he said Hazel and Floyd were a couple blessed in the sight of God. After the vows, the old man's wife kissed Hazel gently on the cheek and whispered some motherly advice in her ear.

Hazel didn't quite get the gist of it, but it made her feel almost holy, seeing as how it must have been from the Bible. It went something like, "A woman who submits to her husband in all things is sure to bring glory to God."

Anyway, the sweet old lady said it like it was a blessing and made Hazel feel warm inside, even if she didn't know what submit meant.

As a wedding gift, in addition to the hand-stitched sampler that read, FAITH, HOPE, CHARITY. BUT THE GREATEST OF THESE IS CHARITY, Miss Ellen had presented Hazel and Floyd with one night's paid lodging at the Jeff Davis Hotel on the courthouse square in Tupelo. Floyd, obviously anxious to redeem his gift, rushed Hazel into the car and they sped to downtown Tupelo.

Up to then, married life had been just fine with Hazel. But all those good feelings would begin to evaporate before first dark. While Floyd was signing into the hotel, Hazel noticed the sly look on the clerk's face, and she got the feeling she might be in over her head. Her daddy's warnings about hoping for too much began to ring in her ears like the tardy bell at school.

"Chickens come home to roost," she remembered him saying, and "Ain't no such a thing as a free lunch." "Every good deed has a handle on it." "Favors come due like everthing else."

She thought of all the free rides into town with the route men, the courtesies she got from the druggist, the attention from other men, all those countless flirtations. She reluctantly admitted the truth to herself. It was more than smiles and winks she had been giving those men. She was giving them ideas, too. The difference was she had been able to pull away just at the last second. But the mighty-pleased-with-myself grin on Floyd's face told Hazel it was payback time at last.

It wasn't so much the upcoming sex part that was scaring her. Onareen, who was married and had been pregnant twice, told her pretty much what to expect. No, it was something else that had her spooked.

That word came back to her again. The one the sweet old lady at the wedding had used. "Submit," she had advised Hazel with a tender smile. But now the word seemed heavy and wore a scowl like her mother's.

When they got to their room on the third floor, Floyd shut the door behind them. Eager to get out of his range, Hazel quickly hurried over to the window. "I swan. Look down there at all them cars. Just a-coming and a-going. Going and a-coming. Where you think they all heading for? Look a-there! They's a mule wagon right in the middle of the street."

She spun around toward Floyd, her face flushed, talking a mile a minute. "You hungry? I sure am. You ever had one of them grilled cheese sandwiches over at Woolsworth? I could eat four just about now."

"You seem a little wound up, Hazel. You OK?"

"Sure I'm OK! Never been better. I'm just hungry's all. Is there a crime in that? Can't a woman be hungry and everything still be OK?"

Hazel knew she was talking out of her head, she just couldn't help it. But if a ramble of words could buy some time, then so be it. "Ain't it all right to want a grilled cheese sandwich? And maybe a double scoop of strawberry ice cream?" She weakly stamped her foot on the floor. "Is that the wrong thing to be asking for right now, Floyd Graham?"

Hazel crossed her arms and her breathing became rushed. "I just don't know what you want is all." Hazel could feel the tears well in her eyes.

"What I want is if you would calm down a bit, sugar," Floyd said as he slowly walked over to Hazel. He carefully laid his hands on her shoulders. "You shaking like a little pup in a cold rain. Ain't nobody gonna hurt you,

Hazel. I promise."

"Maybe this is all a mistake, Floyd. A bad mistake. Maybe we should of waited a while longer. I'm just not ready," she sniffled. "I'm sorry."

Floyd smiled at her, and she began to cry full bore, relieved he had not hit her.

Gently, Floyd pulled her to him. "You just got a bad case of the second-guesses is all. Happens all the time. Even to men."

He patted her gently on the back of her head. "Why, last week I sold a picker to a planter and two days later he wanted to cancel the order. You know what I told him?"

"What you tell him, Floyd?" Hazel asked, her tears moistening his shirt.

"I told him to take his time. Ride around on the thing for a few days. And if he still didn't like it, I would take 'er back. No questions asked."

"You are a good man, Floyd Graham," Hazel sniffled. "That was a nice thing to do."

"No, it waddent. It was smart. I knew he'd keep it once he didn't think he had to. He just needed some time to make that machine his was all."

"And he kept it?"

"Sure. And ordered another to boot. So, what I'm saying is we can eat all the grilled cheese sandwiches you want till you feel easy about this thing."

Hazel pulled back and looked up into Floyd's face. "For true?"

"Yep," Floyd said, smiling easily. "For true."

Gazing into Floyd's eyes, Hazel believed every word he said. She put her arms around him again and laid her head flat against his chest. It was like all of creation, the scary parts as well as the familiar, melted in their embrace, until Hazel felt there was no geography standing between them at all. In that moment, Floyd became the safe center of her new world.

Her appetite for food vanished and all she wanted was to be close to Floyd. She relaxed to his gentle touch, accepted his confident lead, and then, intoxicated by the sweet urgency gathering between them, she opened herself completely to Floyd. He asked for nothing but what she wanted to give him. Here was one man who could be trusted with the secret parts of herself.

That night, for the first time in her life, Hazel's body made sense to her—all the curves and the crevices and sticking-out places. Startling colors that had remained hidden at the bottom of some deep inner well erupted at his bidding, exploding like fireworks before her very eyes. In that one night, it was as if Floyd defined for Hazel all the mysterious inturns and out-turns of her entire being. It left her wondering how many other natural wonders her mother had neglected to tell her about.

The next day Hazel and Floyd were heading across state, with the Tombigbee Hills to their backs and the Delta in their sights. They were man and wife, muleless, betting their futures on an easy smile and an irresistible tilt of the head.

The early spring woods were mostly bare of leaves, and from the car, Hazel could see dogwoods blooming deep among the oak and sycamore and sweet gum, and from the road the delicate white flowers resembled clouds of butterflies wafting through the woods.

Hazel took everything in, becoming more excited by the moment, and though the whole trip would take her less than two hundred miles from home, and would leave her in the same State of Mississippi, anything new or different—a change in the color of pavement or the sudden preponderance of pine trees or the darkening or reddening of the soil in a freshly plowed field—all were weighted in her mind with heavy significance, portending great events to come.

The farther they drove, the more the geography began to straighten out and lose its rocky ruggedness. "Is this the Delta?" she asked every time she believed things couldn't get any flatter.

"Not by a long shot," Floyd kept saying. "Just wait till we get to Hopalachie County. That's where God invented flat."

As the terrain began to lift once more, Hazel became confused. "Looks like the hills are taking over again." There was disappointment in her voice. "Did we miss the Delta?"

This time Floyd didn't say anything. He didn't tell her that the hills they were entering were unlike what she had grown up with, nothing at all like the rugged Appalachian foothills, where sandstone outcroppings grew northward into mountains. No, this was something she wouldn't be able to comprehend if he told it to her in words—that what they were entering was actually a narrow band of bluffs, and instead of steadily climbing into the clouds like her mountains, these suddenly drop to their knees on a floor so level a marble wouldn't roll.

No way he could explain that what they were driving on was nothing more than a gigantic rim of river silt, wind-blown and piled over millions of years, and that these fragile bluffs contained the great flood plain like the cliffs contain the ocean. So instead of telling her, Floyd waited for her to see it for herself.

Finally drawing the car into a shallow curve, Floyd cut the engine. "Let's go for a little walk. I got something to show you."

Hazel followed Floyd across a shallow ditch to a locust post fence, entwined with Carolina jasmine. After pulling up on one wire strand with his hand and stepping on the bottom with his foot, Floyd waited patiently for Hazel to gather her skirt and squeeze through. He led her up a rise crowded with oak and hickory, and then turned and told her to shut her eyes. When she did, he reached for her arm and guided her to the top of the bluff. Again, Hazel noticed how tight his grip was. Did he think she was going to bolt down the hill without him?

"Now open," he said.

The sight made Hazel shudder. Spread out before her was the Delta, miles and miles of flatness stretching relentlessly into some foreign horizon, China perhaps. Nothing was hidden from sight. She saw vast open fields of black earth ready for planting and green ribbons of cypress swamps snaking through the terrain and lakes strewn about like pieces of a giant's broken mirror and not a single rising or falling to ease the unyielding openness of it all.

The spectacle drew Hazel forward, and she momentarily leaned into it, like someone tempted to step into a painting. Catching herself, she pulled back, leaning against Floyd instead.

To Hazel, home was a place where nature provided plenty of places to hide. Ridges and hollows and bends. But out there the world was laid bare for all to see. Hazel wrapped her arms around herself, like someone who has been sleeping soundly and has the blanket snatched off.

Floyd reached for Hazel and pulled her close. "You're shivering. Somebody step on your grave?"

"What a wondrous thing," she whispered reverently, as if God had just finished making it. "You can see everything at once." Had that revival preacher been right when he said the earth was really as flat as somebody's front porch? If he was, then the falling-off place must be out there on that very horizon. "How far does this Delta reach, Floyd?"

He pointed. "See where the sun is sinking?"

Hazel shaded her eyes with her hand and looked into the sunset.

"That's where the mighty Mississippi runs. The sun beds down in the river for the night. In a few minutes, when the sun slips between the levees, you can hear the river sizzle."

Hazel looked up at Floyd, half-believing. "Don't fun me."

"For true. At sundown, the river water gets so hot, catfish jump out on the banks already fried and ready to eat. All you need is the hushpuppies."

"Floyd, you could make me believe about anything." Hazel reached her arm around her husband. "We gonna have us a house down there somewhere and live off catfish and hushpuppies?"

"Nope. We gonna live up here in the bluffs with the rich people." Waving his arm over the vast river basin, he said, "Down there is where the money is made. Nothing but cotton and mules and niggers. More niggers than you can shake a stick at. They outnumber white people four to one."

"I ain't never heard of such a thing," Hazel said, thinking it a foreign country after all.

"Most everbody with planting interests hire overseers to run their places and work their niggers, so they can live up here in the bluffs. In houses older than the levees. Built when the river used to flood everything from Missouri to the Gulf Coast."

Hazel's gaze swept once more over the landscape. "I swan," was all she could say, still trying to imagine such a thing as a whole world of niggers, living on the flatbed bottom of the earth.

Winding back through the bluffs, Floyd topped a ridge and there, nestled below, in the soft rolling terrain, was Delphi. The town was old even by Mississippi standards, settled long before the giant flood plain below had been tamed from bears and Indians and malaria.

Gallatin, the main street and the only straight road in town, was cut vertically into the hilly terrain and was five blocks long. It began at the top of a hill with the Baptist Church and sloped downward to the feet of the Confederate soldier who stood guard in front of the courthouse, and then took another downward pitch to the bridge that passed over the Hopalachie River. Wedged between the church and the bridge was a pretty collection of wooden and brick storefronts. Meandering out from Gallatin, the residential streets were more accommodating to the landscape, wrapping themselves lazily around the contours of the surrounding hills, resulting in a tangle of lanes and alleys.

Hazel was speechless. Stately homes with expansive lawns and ancient live oaks crowned the hills of Delphi. Home sites were laid out without rhyme or reason, each fine house oriented without consideration to any other. Houses stood like individual monuments, sovereign and aloof. To Hazel each house gleamed brighter than the next. Until she was eight, she hadn't known you could put paint on a house. About that time she saw a picture in her history book of Mount Vernon.

"My Lord," she gasped. "If it don't look like George Washington went on a tear and built hisself a town."

Floyd turned onto a down-sloping gravel lane that led up to a little house sitting in the shadow of one of the grander homes above. After turning off the car, he got real quiet for a moment. He looked up at the cottage and said almost apologetically, "It used to be a slave cabin to the house up on the hill. A dependency they called it. But it's been fixed up real nice."

Hazel beamed, and without waiting for Floyd to get her door, hurried out of the car and ran up to the house. The front door was unlocked. Before Floyd was even up the walk, Hazel was running from room to room. He was right. It had been fixed up nice, and already furnished to boot. There was an indoor bathroom, floors that were smoothed and varnished, and had rugs throughout. A ringer washing machine sat right out on the back porch. There were two bedrooms and brown iron beds with roses painted on the posts. It even had a little parlor with a couch and two stuffed chairs.

Then Floyd took her into the kitchen. "Look, Hazel, a stove that don't need wood." He turned a knob and a blue flame snapped to attention. As soon as she saw it she began to cry.

Floyd's face fell. "Don't worry, Hazel. One day, I'll put you in one of them houses up on a hill. I promise."

"Oh! No! It ain't that. I love the house." She sobbed even louder.

"Then what is it?"

"Oh, Floyd." She blew her nose into a tissue. "I ain't been honest with you. I can't cook. I can't sew. I don't even know how to change a diaper or burp a baby. All I can do is pick cotton and strip cane and dig taters. I ain't no good to you!"

Floyd smiled at her. "It don't matter, don't you see? We're starting fresh. You and me are through with them old-timey ways. I don't care if you can't cook. You're my wife. You don't have to earn your keep. And we gonna have children cause we want children, not farmhands. I'll take care of my family."

Hazel looked up to find herself reflected in his eyes. My God, she thought, he still thinks I'm beautiful. She leaned her head against his chest and started to cry again. Today she was a brand-new wife to a new kind of man, living in a storybook town overlooking a mysterious flattened-out world. Her future was like that view from the bluffs, wide open, without a single familiar landmark. She felt lost and found all at the same time.

As she cried, Floyd wrapped his arms around her, and she found her brand-new center again. It was like taking cover under a rock ledge during a summer storm. Even Miss Ellen would have to agree; Hazel had definitely found a man who was bound to take care of his own.

Chapter 13
THE WAY OF THE MULE

It was a warm morning in July and Hazel served her husband a late Saturday breakfast. She eased the plate down in front of Floyd and took a step back. She was pretty sure what his response was going to be.

Floyd stared silent and unblinking at his fried eggs, goopy with the uncooked whites shimmering in the morning light, the bacon in ashes, and the toast, soggy with butter in the center and burnt black around the edges.

Hazel said dejectedly, "You don't have to eat it." Then, forcing a laugh, she said, "I'll just bury it in the backyard with last night's supper."

"No, honey," he stammered, "There might be something here I can—"

"Just let me fix you anothern." What she didn't say was this was already her second half-hearted attempt this morning. The first had even made her own stomach queasy, which was happening almost every time she cooked now.

Floyd managed a weak smile and pushed the plate away. "Don't worry bout it, sugar. Slept too late. I'm in a hurry."

Her face clouded up. "On a Saturday? I thought you were going to take me driving today."

"Can't. Big customer out in the Delta." He looked at her hopefully. "Maybe you can have something fixed for me by supper time."

She squeezed out a smile, but inside Hazel bridled at the suggestion. Not that she would ever say it, but she just couldn't bear another minute in front of that stove. It was like somebody trying to hitch her up to a mule again. If she got good at it, she might never break out of her harness. She knew she should be ashamed of herself for thinking such thoughts.

As she was wrestling with her conscience, she noticed her husband casually turn away from her and cast his gaze out the window, staring off into space again. Look at him, she thought. Already he was a million miles away from this kitchen and his bumbling housewife. Probably thinking about his meeting in the Delta, and already forgotten about the ruined breakfast. Right there was another vote for staying out of the kitchen. Floyd really didn't seem to care one way or the other. Not once had he held Hazel's failures against her, even though they were legion. She got the impression he thought her ineptness was kind of cute, like he was proud of being able to afford a wife who couldn't keep a house.

"Floyd? Sure I can't fix you something?" she asked him reluctantly, his face still turned toward the window. "Maybe some Cheerios or…Floyd!"

Finally hearing his name, he beamed a surprised smile and then rose up from the table to give Hazel a hug. "You sure are pretty. Takes my hunger for food clean away."

She sighed in his arms. Exactly what she thought he would say. But she remembered what her mother had said about pretty the day Hazel promenaded out of the wash-shed in a full coat of makeup. "Forget about pretty," she had told her daughter flatly. "Pretty can't keep no husband. Cause pretty can't cook and pretty can't clean and pretty can't raise children. And girl, the biggest thing pretty can't do is last."

"Floyd, what kind of wife am I to send you off to work without a decent breakfast?" she said, waiting for him to ease her guilt a bit more.

"It don't matter," he assured. "I love you, anyway."

She knew he would say that, too. There had been a lot of those "anyways" lately. Like when she got up the courage to use the washing machine and then cracked most of his buttons feeding his shirts through the ringer. And when she thought she had broken the oven and spent all day crying, until Floyd came home and told her about the pilot light. As he held her, she asked, "Floyd, how many 'anyways' reckon you got left in you?"

Drawing back and looking down on her doubting face, he promised, "As many as the stars you got left in your eyes."

With all her heart she wanted to believe him, that he loved her no matter what and his love would be enough to get them through a lifetime of bad cooking. But it still left her wondering, what was it he *did* want from her?

After kissing her on the cheek, Floyd walked over to a kitchen drawer and fished out a safety pin to fasten the cuff of his shirt. The button had popped off again, the one she had spent an hour sewing on yesterday. Hazel shook her head at her own ineptitude.

"Besides," Floyd said, not looking up from his sleeve, "It ain't important."

As she watched him fumble with the safety pin, she asked anxiously, "But what is important to you, Floyd?"

But Floyd was still at work on his shirt. Having got the safety pin fastened, he discovered that the button on the other cuff was missing, too. Without saying a word, he patiently commenced to unfasten the safety pin from the first cuff.

How could he put up with her? she wondered. God! she thought to herself. I hope it ain't a head of children he's waiting for. No way was she ready to be a momma. But Floyd, having given up on the cuffs and now rolling up both sleeves, was still quiet on her question about what he wanted from her.

"Are you listening, Floyd? I'm saying I just don't know what good I am to you."

Looking up to see her sulky little pout, he put his mind on her again. "Stop fretting about it," he said. "What I *don't* want is no farm wife who works herself to a ugly, wore out nubbin of a woman. Anyhow, you don't see any other white women around here doing for themselves. Just study on how to keep yourself the pretty and pampered wife of Delphi's next rich man."

"We going to be rich?" Hazel asked, again knowing what he would say next, word for word.

"If you can see it, you can be it," Floyd said, reciting his favorite saying from the success book he kept by his side of the bed. "The way things are going, won't be long before I can get you some regular colored help. It's about time we took a step up."

She smiled sadly. "Floyd, you stepping so high now, I get a nosebleed looking up at you."

"Well, get used to it," he grinned. "You know where I'm off to this morning?"

"Where to?" she asked. "Where you going without me?"

"To talk face-to-face with one of the biggest men in the Delta. You heard me tell about him. They call him the Senator. He asked me to come by this morning to look over his place on my own. To get the lay of the land."

"That's real nice, Floyd," her voice resigned.

"But listen to this part, Hazel. Later, after he gets back from some funeral, probably royalty or the like, this successful, rich-as-Midas pillar of the community is going to sit down with *me* and get *my* advice on what he should do with his acreage. What do you say to that?"

"It ain't that I'm not proud to be your wife, Floyd. It's just that I don't know how I figure into—"

"But don't you see, Hazel?" he interrupted. "*He* asked specially for *me*. Floyd Graham. Can you believe that?"

"Course I can. But—"

"He's a real old-time planter. Lives down in the Delta amongst his tenants and the skeeters. Everbody swore he would be the last to buy machinery to replace his niggers with. Why, the first time I called on him he tole me I was wasting my breath and his time. Remember what I tole you I said to turn him around?"

"It's just that if you and me could spend some time—"

"What got him was when I tole him, 'Senator, do you want to spend your time studying the mysterious habits of niggers or do you want to make money?' " Floyd shook his head at himself for saying such a thing. "Then I tole him, 'Are you a planter or a dad-blamed anthropologist?' You should have heard him laughing at that one."

Again, Hazel smiled weakly, ashamed to ask him what an anthropologist was, even though this was the third time she had heard the story. "Floyd, it's just that I've been feeling—"

"You just wait," he said. "By the end of next season, I'll have four mechanical harvesters and a fleet of new tractors on his place. Drop his cost from fifty-nine dollars a bale by hand to four dollars and some change with a mechanical picker. Less depreciation and reconditioning, of course."

"Of course," Hazel said, latching on to the only two words she understood.

"If he sticks with me he'll go from messing with 600 niggers to just a handful of drivers."

"Where they all going to go to?" she asked with a sudden pang of sympathy for the displaced.

"Where's who gonna go?"

"The niggers," she said, beginning to feel slightly foolish for asking. "You know, if nobody needs em no more, where they all going to go to?"

Floyd shrugged. "Oh. Somewhere I reckon. Anyways, I bet I'll make his Jim Beam Christmas list this year."

"His what?"

"Ever year the Senator sends out a bottle of whiskey to all the hotshots in Hopalachie County. I can see it coming. Ain't no stopping us, Hazel. We done put the mule behind us for good." He playfully patted her on the rear on his way to the door.

"Nope. You right about that," she said with a sigh and then turned to the sink to scrape out her husband's breakfast. "Not a mule in sight nowhere."

Floyd pushed open the screen and turned to say good-bye, but he just stood there for a long moment, staring at Hazel with a curious look on his face.

"What!" she yelped, afraid she had gone ugly in his eyes.

He rushed back to Hazel and laid the flat of his hand on her stomach. "If I'm not wrong, looks like you might better go see the doctor."

Hazel's heart sank. "You want me to go to the doctor cause I'm getting fat?"

"Don't you know?" he asked. "Think about it. You been queasy in the mornings. And your skin has been kinda splotchy. Anything else happening to you that's been different?"

Hazel thought for a moment and then her face burned. "You think I'm going to have a baby!" she said. "That's what you're saying! Ain't it?"

Floyd backed up a little and held his hands out in front of him. "Now don't fly hot, Hazel." He gave her a few seconds and then asked carefully,

"Well, what do you think, honey? You the one it's happening to."

She should have known. Her sister Onareen told her the only way not to get pregnant was to do it standing up, and she sure wasn't going to suggest that to Floyd. "I thought all I had was the weak trembles from the sight of my cooking."

Hazel sat down, all of a sudden feeling woozy. Oh, Lord, she thought, the only thing worse than being pregnant would be Floyd knowing about it before me. "No, I can't be preg…You got to be wrong about it."

Floyd knelt down by Hazel and slipped his arm around her, placing his hand on her belly again. As if knowing her thoughts, he said, "Don't worry. You gonna be a good mother. Remember, if you can see it, you can be it."

Her smile was pained. Well, that was just it, Hazel was thinking, I can't see it. Just what was a "good mother" supposed to look like? she wanted to know. Where Hazel came from, there wasn't talk about good ones or bad ones—only live ones and dead ones, sturdy ones and sickly ones, fertile ones and ones who had dried up early. But now with this good-bad difference, she was convinced she would end up being a naturally bad one. Another thing Floyd would have to love her anyway for.

She looked into his face. Her husband's eyes were gazing at her with so much faith and hope, it made her heart ache. "But, Floyd, I'm scared. I don't know how to care for a baby. I seen it done, but I ain't never done it myself."

His smile dismissed her concerns. "Oh, that ain't no problem. We can ask some of the women from the church to help. You can even write your momma. Get her to come stay a spell."

"Momma," she whimpered, for the first time in years finding a kind of comfort in the word. She couldn't help saying it again. "Momma. I want my momma."

"Well then," he said with a snappy nod of his head, "you can have her."

Hazel warmed at the thought of her mother coming all the way to the Delta to be on her side. Yes, she needed her mother now. She needed somebody who knew her, somebody who wouldn't expect too much from her. She raised her eyes and looked into Floyd's face again. He was so confident, counting on her for so much. The sense of dread returned.

Why should that be? she wondered. Why should her own husband's rock-hard certainty scare her so, making her feel so little and lost? What had happened to her own feelings of hope? She remembered the day Floyd had come home and found her sitting by the oven, crying. Somehow, it was as if the rush of Floyd's success had blown out her own little pilot light.

"Momma," she said again, laying her head against his shoulder. "I want my momma."

Chapter 14
LILLIE DEE'S FUNERAL

Down the bluffs and out in the Delta, a multitude of mourners dressed in their finest were on their way to pay their last respects to the most sainted church mother in the county. Lillie Dee Prophet had passed on the stroke of six, sitting alone in the Senator's kitchen having her supper. The Senator himself had heard the platter of cornbread shatter against the floor and found his cook, the woman who had raised him and his sister Pearl, and after them his own daughters, slumped over the kitchen table.

The road to the church was dry and unshaded, and after half an hour, the morning sun was bearing down on Vida as she walked, setting like a weight on her shoulders. Every now and then a car or a wagon would pull up, the driver offering a ride, but each time she refused, wanting to be left alone with her thoughts. This morning there was so much to think about.

Her father had stayed back at the cabin with Willie, having long quit being seen in public. After his congregations had shunned him, he swore he was through with the coloreds of Hopalachie County, and he had been as good as his word, staying away from the places where sharecroppers and farmhands customarily gather—the plantation commissary, the Saturday streets of Delphi, the gin at picking time—instead sending Vida and Willie to handle whatever business needed tending to. He especially stayed away from the church, restricting his own preaching to down in the bayou among the testifying of frogs and crickets.

"Vipers," he had called out to a pretend congregation on the banks of the bayou, with Vida hiding behind the cottonwood. "Yours is a generation of vipers."

But Vida wouldn't miss the funeral today for the world, even if she did have to go alone. She had been so impatient for daylight, she rolled from pillar to post the whole night through. The biggest part of it had nothing to do with mourning Lillie Dee.

Another car approached from behind. Vida closed her eyes and lowered her chin, waiting for the cloud of dust to billow over her. With her head bowed, a breath of air locked tightly in her chest, she prayed that by the end of this day there would be another link, that the funeral would bring her one step closer to Nate.

The white frame structure recently arisen from the ashes of her father's old church was twin-spired with large glass windows painted in shades of blues and greens and was considerably bigger than his had been. Walking inside, she saw that sturdy oak-backed pews had replaced the old rickety benches. They were already filled with mourners.

Most of the people paid Vida no mind, pretending they didn't know this common fieldhand wearing lye-scrubbed gingham. But a few stared at her, almost embarrassed, certainly remembering another girl, a year's growth smaller, who used to come to the church dressed in white organdy, her plaits tied with satin bows. Avoiding their pitying looks, Vida sidled over to the side of the church where ladder-back chairs from half the porches in the county had been carted in for the overflow crowd and lined up against the wall. There, off to the side and unobserved, she could focus on her business.

Quickly, she scanned the church, trying to take in all the faces at once. Where was he? she wondered anxiously. Surely he would come home for his own mother's funeral. But not able to pick him out on first glance, she started with those at the back and methodically surveyed the crowd, one face at a time.

She worked her way to the front of the church, but there was still no Rezel. Disappointed, but refusing to give up hope, she tried to recollect the faces of his brothers. Maybe the one who left his wife in Memphis had come. Toby was his name. Vida recalled him being lighter colored than Rezel. Or maybe the oldest boy had come home; Pinetop, they called him because he was so tall and lean. Was he here? There were seven boys in all.

If God was good, at least one was bound to show up and with him some news of Nate.

Since the one letter the year before, there had not been another word from Rezel, nor from any of Lillie Dee's sons for that matter. Probably ashamed, Vida guessed. They all moved to and from cities with cold, iron-hard names that scraped the back of your throat to say them. Like Akron and Scranton and Chicar-go. In and out of jail so many times, they probably just didn't have the heart to tell their mother nothing but the same ol' bad news. But surely they would come to her funeral.

But no, she saw not a one. To keep her tears at bay, she told herself maybe later, at the graveside. That's it. Maybe one of those Prophet boys would dare show his hangdog face when they lowered their mother into the ground.

The whispering around her hushed. Levi's successor had risen from his chair and was striding up to the pulpit. He was a soft-looking man with raised brows, lids that seemed to never blink and rimless spectacles that magnified his eyes, all working together to grant him a frozen look of surprise. As he mopped his forehead with a handkerchief, he opened his mouth to speak. But before he could utter his first words, the back doors flung open and heads whipped to the rear of the church.

In streamed a procession of white people, marching down the aisle as if they owned the building. The sight of that many whites in a colored church was so off-putting to her, it took a moment for Vida to recognize who they were. When she did, her insides shivered. The large man with the shock of white hair and thundering footsteps leading the group was the Senator. On his arm was his sister, Pearl, who breathed through a lace handkerchief pressed against her powdered white nose. Just behind the two of them was Delia, the Senator's pretty daughter, whose cobalt blue eyes flitted recklessly from the face of one young man to another. Right there was a woman bound to get some colored man lynched, Vida confidently predicted.

Bringing up the rear was Hertha, the Senator's older daughter, as dark and scary as any midnight visitation. She seemed to be fuming mad, casting menacing looks back toward the rear of the church. As Vida and Hertha watched the door together, a cold dread settled on Vida's chest. She knew the procession had not ended. There was one member of the family unaccounted for. Sure enough, it was the sheriff who finally sauntered in.

The man didn't even bother to remove his Stetson, which he wore at a swaggering angle. His hands were crammed in his pockets like a child in a sulk. With what appeared to be much reluctance, he joined his wife where she had halted midway down the aisle, her stone-hard stare telling him she refused to take another step without him.

Farther down the aisle, the Senator had stopped beside one of the pews, causing the people seated there to begin shifting uncomfortably about, but he didn't glance to the left or right, and instead kept his red-rimmed, watery eyes straight ahead on the dove-gray coffin draped with gladiolas. As the entire pew stood up and emptied to make room for the white people, the preacher stumbled over his words. "Ain't this an honor, now? Such a great honor…an honor to us all…that is to Sister Prophet…." He paused to wipe his brow and then continued. "The Senator and all his kin comin to pay they respects. I know we all happy to have them among us today as we praise the life of our dear departed sister." He paused again, allowing a murmur of agreement to course through the church.

While the preacher continued praising the white people, Vida studied them one by one. First, the Senator, looking like God without the beard, all-powerful, but now weeping like a baby for his old colored cook. Lillie Dee always said he would mourn her like a mother once she was gone. She said she only wished she didn't have to be dead to see it.

Next Vida eyed the three white women. Their skin as slick and sallow as a slab of fatback. Haughty and pampered. Dressed like queens in silks and satins and looping chains of gold and pearls. Vida ran her hand over her own dress, and felt the rough scratch of the fabric.

But the one Vida was most curious about was blocked from her view by a large church mother's white-scarved head. Building her nerve, Vida edged over in her chair and furtively crooked her neck to steal a look.

She saw him. His arms were crossed and he glowered down at his boots. He had changed little over the past year, a little thinner maybe, more hard-bitten. But it was still there, in the almond shape of the eyes, in the uplifted corners of the mouth, in the fine-boned cheeks—the beginnings of Nate. Vida trembled inside. Something so innocent peering through a countenance so evil. How was it possible to fully hate the man when Nate's goodness shone through like foxfire?

The sheriff, as if sensing her gaze upon him, looked up at Vida. The man still had the eyes of burned-out cinders. At first his expression revealed no sign he even knew who she was. But then Vida thought she saw the trace of a taunting smile. She quickly pulled back from the sheriff's line of sight.

The preacher was still paying homage to the Senator. "We would name it an honor if you was to say some words to us today, Senator."

Slowly the Senator rose to his feet, brushed his nose with his handkerchief and then cleared his throat. "No nigruh has been held in greater esteem than Lillie Dee," he began. "She was, at all times, loyal and devoted to me and mine. She was a member of our family. Y'all know that."

The congregation nodded their heads and murmured agreeably to let him know that indeed they were well aware of that special bond.

Tears streamed down the Senator's face. "I'm not embarrassed in telling you that me and my sister, Pearl, both were nursed from her very own black breast."

Pearl's face flushed bright red, and she gave her brother a horrified look, making Vida grin for the first time that week. And somebody else obviously enjoyed the comment. Coming from behind the church mother's head, Vida heard a snicker. From the wounded expression on the Senator's face, it was evident he had heard it too.

The big man looked down in the direction of the sheriff and said pointedly, "*Some* might say that makes me a nigger lover. Well, so be it. I indeed loved Lillie Dee and I'm not too big a man to admit it."

The congregation became even more aggressive in their agreement. There were some "amen's" this time.

"And I've sent all the way to Memphis for a gravestone that will say as much. It will be the biggest stone in the nigruh cemetery." The Senator's words were now charged with emotion. "Lillie Dee represented the best of what we can achieve between our two peoples. And if believing in harmony and devotion between the races makes me a nigger lover, then so be it.

Harmony and devotion is what I stand for." As tears dripped down from his jowls, he continued gazing forlornly at the coffin and he said again, "Harmony and devotion. Just like Lillie Dee." The Senator put a hand over his face and his voice began to break in anguish. "Harmony and devotion. Harmony and devotion." He dropped down to his bench in a sobbing heap.

A voice rang out from the pulpit, "Isn't that the truth, people! Isn't that the Lord's truth!"

The preacher's words inspired the response of one foot tapping against the plank floor, soon joined by another and then another, until an electric gallop vibrated though the church, rocking the structure to its foundation. But the Senator, still hunkered down in tears, never looked up

The preacher called out, "Let that be a testimony to us all! By carrying her corner for Jesus, Lillie Dee touched many important lives." Then, shaking his head sadly, he said, "It is a piteous thing that Lillie Dee's own chilren won't be with us here today. They done scattered to the four winds. Only God knows where they are. Only our prayers can reach them."

Vida bit her lip. The words had cut across her heart like a razor.

As the mourners muttered about the shame of it, Vida heard a high thin voice say what sounded like Rezel's name and then giggle. She frantically scanned the church trying to find the face of somebody likely to be so irreverent at a funeral and finally settled on a high-toned man toward the back. It had to be him. She memorized his face. But in his green pongee shirt and sharkskin suit, he would be hard to lose. When he noticed Vida staring, he winked.

After the preacher was done with the service, and Lillie Dee had been carried from the church, he asked everybody to show respect and let the Senator and his kin pass first. However, Vida stood anyway, trying to catch the man's eye again. He wasn't looking.

When the last white person was gone and the rest of the church rose up to leave, Vida struck out like a hound on his trail. Once outside she spied him under a pecan tree, alone, studying the crowd moiling about in the churchyard. Vida sidled over next to him, and he smiled, obviously pleased to have her company. Looking around to make sure no one was listening, Vida said very softly, "I heared you say somethin bout Rezel. You know Lillie Dee's boy?"

The man pulled an ivory toothpick from a tiny pocket in his satin vest and eyed Vida wickedly. "Sho. I know Rezel."

Vida's heart began to race. Excitedly she asked, "How you know him?"

Grinning, he said, "What's it to you, sweetness? He yo boyfriend?" He worked the toothpick between his long white teeth, not taking his eyes off Vida for a second, but she remained silent, tortured by the suspense.

"What I'm sayin is, if he *is* yo boyfriend, you might better find you another man to tide you over." He winked again. "How bout checking me out," the man suggested. He flicked the toothpick from one side of his mouth to the other.

Vida gasped. "Whachoo mean I better look for anothern? What happened to Rezel?"

"You his girl and you don't know?"

Vida had no patience for this. "Tell me," she demanded.

"Well," he said, dropping his gaze, "he got out a month ahead of me."

"Got out of what?"

"Joliet," he said. "You sure y'all was tight?"

Not remembering that name from her map at school, she asked, "Where's Joliet?"

"It ain't a 'where' zactly. More like a 'what.' Rezel and me did time together. But don't look for him back here. He say he ain't never comin back to Mis'sippi no more." The man must have noticed the stricken look on Vida's face. "That's all right, baby. How bout lettin me soothe yo broken heart." He reached out to stroke Vida's face with the back of his well-tended hand. She pushed it away.

"He never said nothin bout Vida Snow? Bout a little boy?"

The smile caved on the man's face. "Rezel was a daddy? Sho nuf?" He took a step backward. "Rezel never said a word bout being no daddy. How many chilren y'all got?"

Vida moved a step closer. "Where he go off to?"

Returning the toothpick to his pocket, he said, without the flirty lilt in his voice, "Look a-here. Me and him wasn't best buddies or nothin. Rezel mostly kept to hisself. Just sit around makin up songs and beatin em out on any damn thang that sounded back. Rezel did his talkin in his songs, not to me."

"So what he sang bout?" Vida asked, moving closer still.

The man wasn't even looking at Vida anymore. His eyes were scanning the yard again. "Let me see," he said absently. "Hmmm."

"What!" she snapped.

His attention shifted back to Vida. "Oh, yeah! Rezel always singing bout how he done with Mis'sippi. Singin bout a sweet deal waitin on him when he got out of the pen. A meal ticket he called it."

"A meal ticket?"

"Yeah," he said, waving to someone across the yard. "'Drivin a big black car for a big white man.' That's how it went. Sang it over and over." The man took another step back. "Now, I got to go see somebody bout a dog."

Vida moved in again. She now had him wedged between her and the tree. "What man?" she badgered, glaring up into his face. "Why that man givin Rezel a meal ticket for?"

"I don't know, girl. It was just a song's all." He flapped his hands in front of him. "Shoo!" But seeing that wasn't going to send her away, he said, "Maybe it was a fella he turned out a favor for. Mob man maybe. Might a been the warden, for all I know. Hell! You got me makin up shit now."

Vida opened her mouth to speak, but the man held up the flat of his hand to her. "Befo' you even ask it, I don't know what the favor was. But don't you reckon Rezel gave a fella somethin a fella wonted? Ain't that the way favors work usually?"

"You don't know nothin else? Must be somethin you ain't told." She grabbed him by the collar of his coat. "Sing me that song!" she demanded, almost shouting. Heads in the yard were beginning to turn in their direction.

"You loony, girl?" the man hissed, his eyes cutting back and forth, embarrassed by the audience they were attracting. He grabbed her hands and wrenched them from his coat. "I ain't gone sing you no blues song standing in no goddamned churchyard. Now go on and let me alone. You *is* crazy!" With that he made a mad dash out of the yard.

※

Later that evening, without having commented on the day to her family, Vida put away her gingham dress and changed into a plain cotton shift and a flour sack apron, both of which she kept hanging on a nail between her bed and the cookstove. It was time to think about supper.

After lighting a fire in the stove, she got down on her knees and felt around under the bed until she located her old parasol. Using the handle to hook the edge of a wooden crate, she drew it out from under the bed and carried it to the eating table. There she ferreted through the contents—white satin ribbons, her mother's cotton gloves, empty thread spools. She quickly leafed through photographs and yellowed sheets of piano music, crayon-scribbled pages in a child's hand. As she searched she kept repeating the verse the man had told her.

Drivin a big black car
For a big white man.

What was the music that went to that song? she wondered. What were the rest of the words? Probably something that went with car or man. *Hand. Can. Land. Promised Land.*

At last she came upon what she had been looking for. After carefully removing Rezel's letter from the ink-smudged envelope, she smoothed the page out flat on the table. Bits of the oilcloth showed through creases from all the folding and unfolding over the past year. Reading the letter she knew by heart, she tried to weave its contents with the information she had received today, hoping it would add up to something new.

Rezel no longer had Nate. So maybe Nate had a new home. Did that mean he had a new mother, too? Or did it only mean that Nate was as lost to Rezel as he was to Vida? Why wouldn't Rezel tell her, either way? Why wouldn't he write? He must be ashamed of what he had done.

The thought was like a cold wind whipping through Vida's chest. What was it Rezel done for the white man? Was the answer in the rest of that song? *Car. Star. Far. So far.*

Vida folded the letter and dropped it back in the box. There were no new answers. Only more questions. She was no closer to Nate. Maybe even one step further away. Feeling the tears well up in her eyes, she rose from the table and walked over to the stove. With a stick of kindling, she furiously poked at the embers.

She lifted her skirt to mid-thigh and stepped closer to the stove. She let the fire in its black belly scorch her legs. As the heat bit into her skin, with her jaw clenched, she swore a silent oath to Nate. Next time he needed her, he wouldn't find his momma weak and pitiful, letting others tell her what was best for her own flesh and blood. She swore if only he would give her a second chance, Nate would find his mother tough-minded and strong, fierce enough to strike anybody dead that tried to take him away from her again.

Tears rolled down Vida's cheeks, not from sadness but from the blistering pain steeling her will. There would be no more tears of sadness from her. She was ready now. If only he would give her one more chance.

1950

Chapter 15
MOTHER AND CHILD

Hazel was getting the feeling her baby might be having second thoughts about this arrangement as well. She was two weeks overdue and to induce delivery the doctor had her on a program that involved hopping up and down, standing on one leg and then the other, lying on her back while puffing and pushing, and drinking orange juice mixed with castor oil until she swore her insides had to be as slick as a greased pole. What was that baby using for traction? she wondered. But then, finally, about two o'clock on a cold February morning the labor pains began in earnest.

Before waking Floyd, Hazel took a moment to calm her nerves, reminding herself that she was a grown woman of eighteen and she had a job to do. Nobody could do it for her. It was up to her.

She elbowed Floyd and told him the little joke she been practicing for this occasion, to show him what a trooper she was. "Floyd, honey. This baby's finally figured out it's a one-way ticket he's holding. I think he's ready to get off the bus." She got it out but her voice was shaky.

"Bus?" Floyd said sleepily, not getting the joke.

"Floyd, he's ready to meet his momma and daddy."

Floyd shot up out of bed like a rocket and announced, "This is it!" like that made it official. Fumbling in the dark trying to lace up his shoes, he asked, "'He'? You said 'he.' You got a feeling it might be a boy?"

"Oooh," Hazel moaned as she dropped her legs over the side of the bed. Trying hard again to be funny in a courageous sort of way, she said, "No doubt in my mind it's a boy. Reminds me of a bobcat scratching his way out of a burlap sack."

Hazel clicked on the bedside lamp and noticed that Floyd was now removing his shoes so he could slip on his pants. Only then did it occur to

her how goosey he was acting. Floyd Graham was scared! Strangely, the
more anxious he became, the more her own nervousness subsided. She felt
out in front of things for the first time in a very long while. Maybe I really can do this, she thought. All by myself.

"Calm down, honey," she found herself saying with immense satisfaction. "Everything's going to be just fine. Remember, if you can see it, you
can be it." She couldn't help but giggle.

With Hazel assuring Floyd along the way, he raced the car down
Redeemer's Hill, out of the darkened bluffs, and sped across the moon-
drenched Delta toward Greenwood. All the time, Hazel noticed feeling
closer to Floyd than she had in some time. She didn't know why, but she
found herself remembering their conversations over ice cream when he
told her the sad stories about his childhood and growing up in a barn,
those very precious moments when she was able to cry his tears for him.

Floyd made it to the hospital emergency entrance in less than thirty
minutes, and by the time they had put Hazel on the gurney, things had
flip-flopped again. "Now everything is going to be OK," Floyd said, striding confidently beside Hazel as they rolled her down the corridor. "All you
got to do is lay back and let nature take its course. Do everything the doctor says, do you hear?"

"Yes," she said, feeling a spark of anger.

"And remember to push. That's always a good thing."

"Yes, I will," she said. But what she wanted to say was, "How do you
know? How many babies have you birthed between cotton picker deals?"

Mercifully, the nurse told Floyd he had to stop at the delivery room
door. Hazel was more than relieved when she heard the sound of his footsteps retreating toward the waiting room.

With or without Floyd, Hazel could never have been ready for what
came next. The pain was unlike anything she had ever imagined. Nothing
anybody could possibly live through. But that wasn't the scariest part. As

she lay spread open and vulnerable on that table, pinned down and surrounded by the doctor and nurses who were demanding so much of her, her own body turning on her, with only her elbows to support her, the worst part was that this time there was no escape. No back door. No place to run. It had been put squarely on her shoulders. She alone was expected to see it through.

The screaming bright lights that caromed off the sterile white walls were indifferent to her pain. The faceless doctor yelled at her, telling her to bear down. She didn't think she could. Hazel shut her eyes against it and prayed to die.

"She's crowning!" the doctor shouted. His tone was now jubilant, conveying to Hazel that she was doing something right. No, that *they* were doing it right—her and her baby, together. With the doctor's words, from the center of her pitch-black world of hurt, flashed the most glorious realization. She could read it like lightning across the night sky. This baby was coming to help her, not to harm her.

Hazel gave in to the pain, no longer afraid, and thrilled by the prospect that somebody was arriving who, no matter what, would always be on her side. She welcomed her son into the world with a cry of joy.

Back in her room, Hazel held her baby, whispering softly to the newcomer in her arms, "*My* baby. My *baby*," over and over, trying to get her ears used to the words. The nurse who had attended patted Hazel's hand and said right there in front of Floyd, "You did a real good job, honey. Your son is healthy, whole and one of the best looking things ever to come out of the Greenwood Leflore Hospital."

Hazel smiled at the baby. "He knew what he was doing all right. I couldn't a done it without him."

There was a short silence while the nurse and Floyd looked at each other curiously.

"Well, little momma," the nurse said, "I guess I never looked at it that way. What y'all going to name him?"

Without batting an eye, Floyd announced his decision. "Johnny Earl

Graham."

"After who?" asked the nurse.

"After nobody," he said proudly. "From neither side. Our boy ain't gonna owe his future to nobody's past."

Hazel smiled, liking the sound of that. Maybe it was true. She hoped it was—that she and Floyd and Johnny Earl had been cut loose and were traveling free, floating high above all the doubts and fears that prowled the past. Like maybe there was nothing ahead of them but blue-sky future.

Five days later, as Floyd drove, neither he nor Hazel could take their eyes off the baby, which put Floyd all over the road. Peeking at the little bundle in his wife's arms for about the hundredth time, Floyd asked. "How's my little monkey doing?"

"Floyd," Hazel said, "I hate it when you call him that. He don't look anything like a monkey."

He patted Hazel on the knee. "That's not what I mean by it. He's just so cute and all."

Narrowing her eyes at the baby, she said, "Floyd, he's got your black hair. Your dark eyes. He even got them wide moccasin jaws. I swan, I don't see me anywhere. Looks like you did the whole thing without me."

Floyd laughed and without even looking this time he said, "He's got your cute pug nose. Don't you see?"

Hazel didn't, but she figured Floyd was giving her the nose to be nice, which was just fine. Right now she needed him to be real nice. Without a whole hospital of nurses backing her up, she was desperately struggling to keep on top of her fears. She was returning to Floyd's world, and she was not going alone. She had a baby to keep alive. Here was this living, squirming, kicking, crying, puking, peeing, wordless ball of needs. Everything depended on her being able to decipher what he wanted quick enough to keep him from dying, so that he would grow up to love her and be on her side in all things. Until then, she hoped he gave good directions.

At least she had help coming. "I'm so glad you went to get Momma," she said. "I got a million questions to ask her about babies."

Floyd half smiled and then bit his lip as he turned onto Gallatin Street.

"What's wrong?" she gasped. "Ain't she there yet? Didn't you go get Momma like you said you would?" She was doing her best not to cry. "I need my momma," she said, sounding smaller than she had intended. "When's my momma coming?"

"Hazel, now honey," Floyd said carefully. "I went to get her all right. But as soon as I got her in the truck your daddy came out the door raising sand. Said with all the women gone, there wouldn't be nobody left to cook. He made her get out right then and start dinner."

"So you went and got Onareen?" she said with a whimper creeping into her voice, but Floyd only shook his head.

"Lurleen?"

"No, sweetnin," he said. "There waddent time to head off to Alabama." Floyd turned down their little lane and pulled up in the front of the house. He cut off the engine and just sat there, staring out the windshield, taking little shallow breaths.

"Well, who then?" she asked, the panic rising in her voice. She feared she knew the answer, but she asked again, "Who's gonna help me?"

"Well." With a broken grin, Floyd tilted his head toward the house.

Hazel looked up and saw his Momma Maud step out onto the porch, looking out over the tops of her steel-rimmed glasses. "Floyd!" she cried. "How could you?" But he didn't hear her. He was already out of the truck, hurrying around to get her door.

As they got Hazel settled into bed, it was clear from how efficient and tasky Floyd was being, he wanted to remove himself from the field of battle as quickly as possible. First he listed out for Maud the numbers to the drugstore and the doctor and the fire department and for grocery delivery and his office at the implement company. He made another list of feeding times and formulas and blood types. Finally, he kissed Hazel briskly and the baby, like it was something he had written down on his own list.

Easing out of the room, he turned and grinned sheepishly at the both of them. "Now y'all be nice to each other. I know y'all can do it if you try."

Maud gave her stepson a motherly smile. "Now you don't worry about a thing here. We women know what we're doing. Right, Hazel?"

But Hazel didn't answer She only eyed Maud coldly.

The back door slammed shut, and Maud remained standing at Hazel's bedside, not speaking a word. She wore her long, steel-gray hair roped, coiled, and bobby-pinned in a pile sitting atop her head, in a fashion which Hazel always called a cow paddy perm. The corners of her tight little mouth were stained brown with snuff juice, as was the front of her cheap print dress, giving Hazel an idea why the woman got run off from her teaching job. She must have been a real terror to look at in front of a class. The woman had features as sharp as a face card.

Maud stared over the tops of her glasses at the baby boy lying next to Hazel. She said, "You know, Hazel, that's a retarded baby you got there."

Hazel gasped. "Wha...?"

"I can tell by the way his eyes cross. Yore womb was probably poisoned. All this high living and all." Maud shook her head pitifully. "Yore milk's probably gone bad, too."

It was as if Hazel had been knocked senseless. Maud's comments only confirmed her worst fears. Already she believed herself liable for a multitude of imaginary ills destined to beset her child. Even so, Hazel marshaled enough deep-seated hatred for Maud to say, "Get out of my room, old woman. Before I knock you in the head with a flat iron." Her voice may have trembled a bit, but she meant it. Nobody was going to come between her and her baby.

Maud grinned, spit into the Calumet can she toted everywhere, and turned on her half-block heels. She left Hazel alone to stare at Johnny's eyes in horror, wondering what had she done to her own baby.

By the time Floyd got home that evening, Hazel was nearly hysterical. He found her sitting up in bed holding on to Johnny for dear life, and they were both crying up a storm. He flew into a panic. "What's wrong? What happened? Is the doctor on his way?"

Hazel glared through her tears and pointed at the doorway. "No!" she almost screamed, "but *she* better be. And before dark!"

Floyd turned to see his stepmother standing there nodding her old head like somebody who had seen it all before. "First-time mothers," she said, smiling sweetly at Floyd. "Some can get a might over-wrought. We just have to be patient with em, don't we?"

No matter how many times Floyd asked Hazel to tell him what Maud had said, she refused to repeat it, only that he better get the old witch out of the house. Not knowing what else to do, he relented. He left early the next morning with Maud and returned late that evening with Onareen.

Her sister spent most of her week there trying to convince Hazel the baby was just fine. She told her a baby's eyes sometimes don't focus too good for the first few days. "You got to relax about it, Hazel," she said. "There ain't that much a mother can do wrong. It'll come natural."

Hazel didn't buy it. "If he was a little tater, I would know what to do," she told Onareen. "Or a shoot of corn. Anything that come up out of the ground. Ain't it strange that something that sprouted from my own self could be such a puzzlement?"

Onareen took Hazel's hand and patted it. "It's only your first. I've had three. And I promise, it's damned near impossible to break one in two. You going to be a good mother. Give it time."

After Onareen left, Hazel spent one sleepless night after the other, repeatedly getting up out of bed to check on Johnny in his crib. In the beginning she was afraid to touch him. Later, she was afraid to set him down. She studied him desperately for signs of intelligence, of hunger, of thirst, of infestation and blight, trying to read him like she would a field of corn, pleading with him to tell her what it was he wanted of her.

"What would a good mother be doing now?" she asked him over and over. He stared back silently with those big, dark Indian eyes, not so much looking at her, she thought, as considering her, like he was sizing her up.

She became more exhausted and found herself looking back longing-ly on that time spent in the delivery room. It was so full of urgency, and there was only one way to proceed, with the baby there pointing the way, and the doctor rooting her on, and her finally letting go and giving in to something bigger and wiser and more ancient than anything she had ever

known. It had been like falling toward home, a home she never knew existed but felt deep in her bones. Out there somewhere, she had the sense that
loving arms were waiting to catch her. But all that had vanished and it was
just her again, hanging on to the edge of a cliff for dear life.

Floyd watched anxiously from the sidelines, hoping Hazel would find
her gait and come around to the job. "Hazel," he called to her one night,
gently shaking her arm. "Honey, you're doing it again. Wake up."

Awake now, she continued to cry. "Oh, Floyd! It was awful," she
sobbed. "I was trapped in Daddy's storm pit and I couldn't find the door.
I knew it was there somewhere and it was so dark and I heard Johnny crying on the other side and I couldn't get a match lit and he...and..."

Floyd pulled her to him and soothed her with his words, letting her cry
until she was all cried out. He said all the right things. That they were in it
together. He would always be there for her. They had come a long way and
had a wonderful life still ahead. He said even he had his doubts sometimes.

"You, Floyd?" she asked, feeling an immense comfort in his confession.

"Uh-huh. Everbody does."

"Tell em to me, Floyd." She anxiously waited to hear what they were.
Maybe she could even comfort him for a change.

Floyd switched on the light and smiled at her sympathetically. At first
she thought he was going to say that he loved her. Maybe without the anyway. His expression was just that tender.

"Hazel, honey?" he said,

"Yes, sweetheart," she answered, feeling comforted. "I'm listening." She
nuzzled up to his neck.

"Hazel, honey," he said again, "I think it's time you learned about the
Science of Controlled Thinking."

"Wha—?"

"Now hear me out," Floyd said, taking her hand. "Controlled Thinking
is the way to get rid of all the second-guessing you been doing. It's the reason why I'm selling more equipment than any John Deere salesman in the
Delta."

"But Floyd, what has that—"

"Now I've been considering it for a while, and I don't think raising a baby is no different. Sure, you're having a little problem adjusting to it all," Floyd said. "Any change is hard. But change is also opportunity. If you let me help, I promise you'll come around."

Floyd reached beside him on the nightstand and brought his book into bed with them. "Like I was reading last night, 'Enthusiasm is contagious.' And Hazel," he grinned, "probly nobody around is more catching than me."

He began flipping through the pages and pointing out his favorite little sayings. "Just listen to this," he said excitedly, "'…to a controlled thinker, every problem is an opportunity.'"

"And here's a good 'un. 'If you get lemons, make lemonade.' And, 'if life serves you a bum steer, eat steaks.' How about this one, 'if you get a raw deal—'"

By then she had stopped listening. Those things didn't make any sense to her at all, and she sure didn't see what they had to do with Johnny Earl. So instead of looking at the book as he pointed out the words, she stared at the old purple burn scars on his hands, where as a baby he had grabbed a log afire. She wondered why he didn't have nightmares, too. What was wrong with her that she couldn't get past it all?

Over the next few months, the more fearful she became, the more Floyd preached his religion of success at her. He told her that in every failure there is the seed for the next victory. It's all in a person's thinking. Then he began to write the sayings down on tablet paper and hung them around the house for her to find.

"Don't spend a second of today fretting tomorrow or regretting yesterday," the bathroom mirror warned her. The Philco greeted her with, "It's a matter of mental magnetism: what are your thoughts attracting today?" "Be a controlled thinker!" the hall closet door hollered.

The last words she heard at night were from the lamp by her bed. The paper taped to its shade chided, "How fast you travel on the track to success is determined by your train of thought," and to hear Floyd tell it, they were still in only slow motion. He had big plans for his family and was keeping a positive mind on the future and she needed to be there with him. Rooting him on along the way.

Hazel tried to live by his words, wanting desperately to be a good wife and a good mother, but couldn't gain that Floyd-Graham-rock-solid certainty. She watched with a mixture of wonderment and trepidation as Johnny ate regular, never got sick, learned to walk, and grew like he was supposed to. Best of all, he loved his mother and knew how to show it. That especially was a comfort. Of course Hazel loved him, too, but love took its toll. Hazel's stabbing anxiety dulled to a constant dread. She knew there were things she was missing. There had to be.

Not long after Johnny's first birthday, Floyd talked her into getting pregnant again. He figured with two children she wouldn't have time to fret over things that didn't matter. Another child would help prioritize her thinking, he advised.

Hazel did as Floyd asked. She got pregnant. She memorized more sayings. She even recited them to her children like nursery rhymes. But as much as she tried changing her thinking, she couldn't get that old feeling of hope back. Giddy anticipation seemed to have flown the coop and left a nest of dread. Hazel felt she had only the loosest of handholds on the caboose of Floyd's speeding train of success.

1955

Chapter 16

THE SLAUGHTER HOUSE

Even though she couldn't find her voice to say it, Hazel figured their entire cottage could easily fit into this one room, and she was not alone in reverential silence. She and Floyd turned slowly in the middle of the empty parlor and neither spoke, as if a house this grand might not want to carry voices as common as their own. That the house was now theirs may have been a reality on paper, but this minute, as they gawked openmouthed, that truth felt as hollow as the cavernous rooms themselves.

Everybody in town called the place the old Slaughter house, and it had a history that echoed the up and down fortunes of Hopalachie County itself. Built by an early cotton baron, the house was lost in a poker game to a professional rogue turned Civil War colonel, foreclosed on by a Memphis bank, then bought for nothing by a carpetbagger from New Jersey. It rapidly passed down through that lineage propelled by a family disposition toward suicide, until the last one terminated the tradition by hanging himself in the attic without having the forethought to marry and beget an heir. That's when Floyd snapped it up for a song.

"Well, punkin," Floyd said, whispering for a reason unknown to him, "it took me six years to keep my promise. But I did it. I got you out of that slave cabin and put you up on the hill."

He looked at her with that sweet expression she remembered from before they married. It was the way he looked at her over ice cream, during that magical month of planning their escape.

"You proud of me?" he asked.

The question comforted Hazel. He still cared what she thought. "I'm real proud, Floyd," she whispered back. "It's like a dream come true."

Floyd stood a little straighter. "Like I always say," his voice stronger now, "success is a dream with sweat on it." He spoke the last part loud enough to send the saying echoing lightly off the walls. He must have liked the way it sounded because he said it again, even louder. "Success is a dream with sweat on it," he shouted and smiled at Hazel proudly as his voice rang throughout the house.

Hazel smiled back, but weakly. There was no doubt about it. Floyd had been sweating big time. He broke all records selling farm implements, single-handedly putting enough machinery into operation to free up thousands of fieldhands. Floyd had been such a standout, he convinced the president of the bank, Hayes Alcorn, whose wife was the Senator's sister, to loan him the money to start Delphi Motors. They say the Senator himself pushed the deal through. The old man had taken a liking to Floyd.

Floyd was right about the Christmas whiskey. Every year, along with a few judges and politicians and other assorted big wheels, Floyd received a decanter of Jim Beam. Real collectable bottles in the shape of things like footballs and turkeys and cowboy boots that Floyd had proudly lined up along the kitchen counter like trophies. It was the Senator's way of saying that Floyd was among those who were doing great things for Hopalachie County.

On one occasion, the Senator had slapped Floyd on the back and said that already, with nothing more than a few well-turned phrases and that shit-eating grin of his, Floyd had changed the Delta landscape more than the Yankee army had during the invasion. He had replaced the primitive hollers of the niggers with the smooth hum of machinery. The Senator said there was no telling how far Floyd could go if he was his own boss. Now thanks to the Senator and his brother-in-law at the bank, plus Floyd's positive thinking of course, he was selling Mercurys and Lincolns and Ford trucks out of a business he owned himself.

While the boys scampered through the house, discovering how loud they could make their bare feet screech against the slick hardwood floors, Hazel stood there holding fast to Floyd, the same way she had that late afternoon when he showed her what lay beyond the bluffs, with her struggling to make sense of it all.

The walls around her were the pinkish color of mimosa blossoms, and all along their length were the empty, lighter spaces where portraits of the previous owner's suicidal ancestors had hung. It occurred to Hazel it might be easier living with the ghosts of slaves than of rich people. She suddenly wished she was back there, alone with a bottle of Floyd's Christmas whiskey.

"How we going to fill it up, just the four of us?" she asked, beginning to panic. "This house has more rooms than Carter's got pills. Why, it's got rooms I don't even know the names of."

"That's why I'm taking you to Greenwood. So you can outfit this house with the grandest things you can find. Like I always say, 'If you want to attract money, you got to act like money.'"

Choosing the curtains for the little slave cabin had stretched Hazel's imagination to the limit, but this assignment made her head swim. She had no idea how rich folks went about filling up their homes, never having been inside a house this grand before. In all the time they had lived in Delphi, not once had they been invited into their neighbors' homes. Their little cabin, tucked away on a downslope, even though geographically a part of Delphi, was like a mothhole in the social fabric that surrounded it. The Grahams were not counted among their Episcopalian and Presbyterian neighbors who occupied the brow of Delphi proper. Socially, to Floyd's chagrin, they had been lumped in with the lower-class Baptists and Methodists who lived in tight little clusters of tract homes down in East Delphi, a flattened-out place on the other side of the bridge.

"Now I mean it," Floyd said. "When we go to Greenwood, only buy deluxe. We got an image now." His eyes narrowed. "Oh, that reminds me."

Hazel braced herself. She could feel one of Floyd's "lists for success" coming on.

"You got to stop tussling with Johnny and Davie in the yard right out in plain view. I'll find you a colored girl to watch them. And another thing, don't let the boys go out the house looking like Indians. Put shirts and shoes on em. Even in summertime. We ain't in the hills no more. People are going to be watching us close now."

Stamping like horses, Johnny and Davie, half-naked and already brown as berries, their feet stained green with spring grass, giddy-yupped into the sitting room. Hazel got that old sinking feeling again in her chest. A good mother would have known better. This was supposed to be getting easier, she thought. Lurleen and Onareen turned out children like canned vegetables and never seemed to give being a mother a second thought.

With his arms outstretched, his frail blue eyes pleading, Davie was bouncing up and down at his father's feet, calling out, "Catch me. Catch me."

Floyd lifted his son off the ground and threw him into the air, making Davie gurgle with laughter. At the peak of his rise, Davie yelled out "Catch me!"

Hazel clutched herself. She hated this game. Quickly, she shifted her attention to Johnny. He was already watching her with his black, brooding eyes, as if waiting for a signal to act on her behalf. When she gave him a pained, helpless look, Johnny immediately began fussing at Floyd.

"Daddy, you be careful. Don't drop Davie on his head."

Hazel smiled sadly at Johnny, relieved, but at the same time a little ashamed that he had been the one to speak out. However, he didn't seem to mind. She noticed the set of his mouth, so determined, just like his father's. He was a boy bound to take care of his own.

"We just having some fun. No harm done." Floyd set Davie down on the floor and then turned to Johnny, "Hey, Little Monkey. You wanna go next?" he asked, holding out his arms. But Johnny took two steps backward.

Rebuffed, Floyd turned his attention back to his wife. "Now, like I was saying, you got to help me, Hazel. We're building us up a reputation. This house is only the start of it."

Nodding her agreement, she looked up into his confident face. Floyd was already acting like he had been born and bred in this house, when only a few minutes ago he was asking in a childlike whisper if she was proud of him. It amazed her how things came so natural to him, like raising babies came natural to her sisters.

Continuing with his list for success, Floyd, out of the blue, suggested, "Maybe we should change churches while we're at it."

Hazel gasped. "But we've always been Baptists, Floyd. I don't know nothing about them other religions." Not that Hazel knew much about religion period, but the Baptist church was the only place she got to see people who were most like her, more redneck hill than blue-blood Delta. She had even made a few friends. "Maybe we ought to stay where God knows us, so when we need Him, He'll know how to get a-holt of us."

Floyd seemed to sull up. "All I know is He seems to stay in better touch with the Episcopals."

Hazel didn't even need to look at Johnny this time. From over by the window where he had just pulled Davie down from the ledge, he shouted "I don't wanna go to no 'Pissable church!"

Ganged up on again, Floyd dropped it. Anyway, Hazel could tell by the easy way he let it go that he had only been half-serious. He knew as well as she that Brother Dear would have turned it into a holy stink if they switched. Like he did when the Holifields went Presbyterian. Told the whole congregation they had been tampered with and ruined by money.

Conceding to his wife on the matter of religion, Floyd unveiled the last item on his list. "I think it's time you learnt to drive."

Hazel's mouth dropped open. "You gonna teach me, Floyd?" she asked, not believing her ears. She had always assumed that driving was beyond her. Mainly because Floyd had never suggested it before.

"That and more. I'm going to give you your very own car. Brand-new Lincoln. Columbia blue. Special-ordered it."

"My own car? For me?" Hazel began to tear up.

"Yep. That way you can be a rolling advertisement for Delphi Motors. I'll put the trucks under the men, and you can help me put Lincolns under their wives." He winked at her. "We can be a team."

"A team," she repeated. Yes, she thought, that was it! Exactly what she had wanted and didn't know how to say it until Floyd put it into words. He was so smart. Hazel wanted to be a team with him. The idea thrilled her as nothing had in years. Leave it to Floyd to find a way for her to catch up and travel by his side.

To her delight and Floyd's amazement, Hazel took to driving like a duck to water. Two weeks with her new Lincoln and she was backing up the big car, passing on the left, even parallel parking. Her stops became feather light and her turns as smooth as butter. After all those hours riding around with the route men, she figured something must have rubbed off. Hazel didn't mention that to Floyd. She just let him assume that at long last there was something she took to natural. Others might be good cooks and good mothers, and good salesmen, but driving a car was going to be Hazel's special calling.

In no time at all she was confident enough to do the furniture shopping all by herself. She would get behind the wheel and power the mighty machine west on 84, taking the highway straight on into Greenwood. Once there she negotiated big-city traffic, insisted on her rightful turn at intersections, and competed for parking places with the most aggressive of men drivers. The Lincoln was making her into a new woman.

Floyd was nearly as excited about her success as she was. After the furniture started arriving and they began to get settled into the house, he lost no time in setting the next phase of his team plan into motion. He told Hazel her team goal was to put at least ten miles a day on the Lincoln and to do it in public view. "You can be an inspiration to all the women in Delphi," he told her. "Nowadays ever woman ought to have her own independent means of transportation. It's the way the world is going."

One evening he brought home a brochure and dramatically spread it out on the kitchen table. "Look a-here," he said.

What Hazel saw was the full-color picture of a very happy woman driving down the road in her Lincoln. "Try to look like her," he said reverently. "She's the sign of things to come."

The beautiful woman wore a large off-the-face hat with a mile-long ribbon rippling out the window, a matching scarf and white gloves just to the wrist. At first Hazel felt a little strange about the idea, hoping that Floyd wasn't trying to trade her up into something that she wasn't. But when she saw the look of respect with which he regarded the woman in the picture, she knew she had to do it. Taking the advertisement to Gooseberry Department Store, she suited herself up as close as she could come to the happy woman.

Hazel put shirts and shoes and bowties on the boys, loaded them up, and in her new picture hat with a blue satin ribbon, silk chiffon scarf and white gloves, backed away from their beautiful home, and drove up and down Gallatin Street, from the bridge to the church and around the courthouse, looking happy, six times a day.

Chapter 17

THE TROIS ARTS LEAGUE

Hazel stepped back from the hall mirror and tugged at her skirt, evening up the hemline. The dress was the most beautiful thing she had ever bought, an ice-blue shirtwaist made of silk shantung which the salesman swore set her eyes to dancing like the sunlight on lake water. She took a tissue from the hostess pocket and, leaning in close to the glass, carefully dabbed at the lipstick in the corner of her mouth. Next she fussed expertly with the collar, smoothing the tips down flat.

Well, the clothes and the makeup were certainly up to muster. Everything shaded, highlighted, smoothed down and lined up. But what Hazel couldn't see was the person between the lines. Touching her cheek gently, she longed for Floyd and wished he was there to tell her how beautiful she looked. Just a glimmer in his eye would do. But he wasn't there and she needed to do this on her own. Floyd was counting on her to be a team with him.

At his insistence, she invited some of the neighbor ladies over for punch and to show them what she had done with the house. More than three months had passed since moving in and not a single person had come calling. Floyd had told her, "Hazel, you can't wait for success to come knocking. You have to find out where it lives and then go hunt it down with a stick."

"But I don't know what to say to women like that. What do they talk about?" Whatever it was, she was sure it wasn't mules, heel flies, and ringworm.

The women reigning in the houses around her were formidable-looking creatures, skin untouched by the sun and white as alabaster, with rouged cheeks, severe as Delta sunsets, their shoulders pulled back and chests puffed out, dripping with brooches and breastpins and cameos like decorated generals on inspection. They were proper in ways that were foreign to Hazel, having cultivated curious manners that pushed you away rather than pulled you closer. When met on the street they could use a smile like an extended arm as if to say, "OK, that's near enough."

Hazel heard Johnny yelling from the back yard. "Momma! She's here! She's here!"

At last! The maid Floyd had promised for the day. A day is probably as long as she would last. Maids came and went with such regularity, Hazel barely got to know their names, because usually by the end of their first day on the job, Floyd had found some reason to suspect them of stealing from him.

Hazel waited to hear the confirming slap of the back door and then called out, "Bring her on in here!" She quickly drained the bourbon from the tumbler she kept hidden behind the flour sack, put a peppermint in her mouth, and checked in the mirror for any smudges.

A husky voice sang out "Whoo-ee!" When Hazel turned, the first thing that caught her eye was a stretch of white fabric showcasing a prominent rear end. At that moment the colored woman it was attached to was gazing into the parlor, her hands planted on her well-rounded hips.

"Look at all them pretty colors," the woman said, apparently to the boys who stood on either flank. "More tints than One Wing Hannah's jookbox."

Davie yelped and then took off in the direction of the green vinyl sectional, undoubtedly with the aim of scaling up the back of the couch and falling off. A split second later, Johnny was in hot pursuit.

The woman turned back toward Hazel. She was wearing the snuggest maid's uniform Hazel had ever seen. Her breasts were pooching out the top of her dress reaching for daylight. She beamed a smile that involved at least two gold teeth. "Hiddy. My name Sweet Pea. You Miss Hazel?"

"Glad to know you," Hazel said hesitantly. Where did Floyd find this one? she wondered. He was surely scraping the bottom of the barrel now.

Sweet Pea turned back around and surveyed the room again. "Where you git all them nice things, Miss Hazel? I never seen nothing like it in

Delphi."

That definitely tipped the scales in the maid's favor. She gave Sweet Pea a big grin and crossed the hall to stand next to woman. "And you won't see nothing like it in the whole State of Mis'sippi, neither," she said excitedly, noticing how badly she had been wanting to brag on herself. "I had to order all the way to Chicago. The salesman says this stuff is just catching on. Colors nobody ever even heard of before. Just invented. Parakeet green. Flamingo pink. Peacock blue. I tried to get some of each."

Sweet Pea laughed. "Um-hum! I can see that. Look like a big flock of zoo birds done shedded all over yo company room." She took a moment to admire the yellow Formica coffee table shaped like a prize banana, the plastic end tables with gleaming enameled metal legs, and the aluminum pole lamp with pink, blue, and green bullet shades. "Yo furniture shines like the front end of a Cadillac. And not a stick of wood to be seen."

"You're mighty gracious to say so," Hazel said delightedly. "When that salesman showed me all those pretty pictures, I said to myself, why be old-fashioned when nowadays you can get everything in plastic, chrome, and vinyl?"

Sweet Pea waggled her head appreciatively. "Must be a joy to sit in a room like this when the morning sun hits it. You probly need to put on you some sunglasses to do yo dustin."

The maid's opinion, even though it was a colored one, was doing wonders to boost Hazel's confidence. For the first time since Floyd suggested the party, she almost looked forward to the ladies coming over. If they were only half as struck as Sweet Pea, Hazel would do Floyd proud.

After Johnny had successfully fussed his brother down from the couch, Hazel told him, "Take Davie outside and finish that quiet game y'all were playin, OK honey? We got to get things ready for company."

Johnny led Davie out by the hand and Sweet Pea let out a little squeal. "Them boys is precious! That least one takes after you. Do the other favor his daddy?"

"That's right. Ain't no use denying neither of em."

Getting back to business Sweet Pea asked, "What we going to feed these womens, Miss Hazel?"

Hazel pulled out the newspaper article from her waist pocket. It was titled *Entertaining: Elegant and Easy.* "Now here's some new recipes they say everybody just loves. I thought between the two of us we could figure out how to put it together. I bought all the ingredients."

"Whachoo wont me to do?"

"Well, I ain't much in the kitchen," Hazel said, "So you do the cooking part and I'll do the opening and stirring. And you can serve it, if you don't mind."

This took Sweet Pea back for a moment. "No'm. I don't mind," she said, half smiling, amused at the thought that her minding had something to do with anything.

The doorbell rang just as Sweet Pea finished spooning the crushed pineapple around the chunks of ham. "They's just in time," she said, looking up at Hazel. When she saw the blood drain from Hazel's face, she comforted her, "Don't you fret none, Miss Hazel. Everthing gone come off jest fine." She headed for the door.

Hazel checked herself for a final time in the hall mirror, once more wishing Floyd were there to tell her how pretty she looked. The bourbon didn't seem to be working. She breathed deeply and tried to act like she imagined the happy woman in the Lincoln advertisement would if she had to get out of her car and entertain. Straightening her shoulders, she prepared her smile and followed Sweet Pea airily down the hallway to meet the women.

Sweet Pea flung open the door to see that three women had arrived at once, looking like a posse. "How y'all doin today?" Sweet Pea bawled happily. "Come on in out the heat!"

The women stepped into the entryway and Hazel said the words she had practiced. "How good of y'all to visit me today." Her voice was shaky but the words clearly enunciated.

Miss Pearl, the Senator's sister, smiled warmly and brought her handkerchiefed hand up to her delicately wattled neck. In a rush of breath she said, "Hazel, you are so kind to have us over. When Hayes told me about your new home, I felt terrible that I hadn't stopped by before and properly welcomed you to the neighborhood. And me just living across the lane from y'all. Will you forgive me, dear?"

With all those kind words having been spent on Hazel, and with so much feeling backing them up, Hazel felt her stomach settling a bit. "That's mighty gracious of you to say, but I'm just proud y'all could come today's all."

"Well, better late than never. Isn't that what the sage professed, Hazel?" she smiled sweetly again.

Pearl Alcorn was an older woman with kind, misty blue eyes and an understanding smile. Her silver blue hair looked like it was still warm from the beauty parlor. Hazel thought she was quite lovely, even if she did have a crippled hand. It was said that when Miss Pearl was a little girl living at the Columns, she was out riding and her horse stumbled, threw her off, and then rolled over on her hand, crushing the bones. From that time on, she was never seen without a lace handkerchief carefully arranged among the fingers to make the hand look useful. It gave her an air of tragic elegance Hazel just couldn't help but admire.

Miss Pearl waved her handkerchief at an unpleasant, horsy-looking woman to her side. "Hazel, I want you to meet my nieces. Hertha." The frightful woman she had pointed out emitted a little snort. "She's your next-door neighbor, so to speak. You've undoubted met her husband the sheriff."

"How do you do?" Hazel said, slow and careful.

"And Delia." A beautiful younger woman with lustrous blonde curls and blue eyes that seemed to be laughing at something.

"So you two is sisters?" Hazel blurted. "I swan, you don't look nothin' like each…"

Pearl coughed once and said, "Isn't this nice, Hazel. I hope you will consider us your new best friends."

Realizing she had just been saved from something terrible, Hazel nodded. "Best friends. Oh, yes ma'am. I would like that more than I can say."

The sisters met the suggestion of friendship with blank expressions, but Pearl seemed sincere, and Hazel found herself surprised she had not noticed this kindness when they had occasionally passed on the street. But that was back when they lived in the slave cabin, before she had officially moved up the hill into Delphi proper. Maybe things would be different after all.

Hazel sucked in a deep breath. It was time to show them her new room. Gesturing with a wide sweep of her arm, she said, "Will y'all please come into my company room."

Miss Pearl led the way and the other two followed dutifully behind, but upon entering the parlor, the trio stopped cold, appearing to have been stunned simultaneously. The women put Sweet Pea in mind of a herd of fainting goats her uncle used to have. When startled their joints locked up and they toppled over, rigid as boards. Sweet Pea smiled, picturing all three white ladies dressed in voile and crinoline laying about Miss Hazel's new rubberized floor, stiff as a load of lumber.

As for Hazel, at first she smiled proudly, judging their reaction to be positive, but as the seconds ticked by without a word, Hazel's stomach began to grow queasy again. She didn't know what to say. She would have fled through the door if she were not in her own home.

"Y'all sit yoselves down," Sweet Pea said, taking charge. "Miss Hazel done got some fine eatin planned."

"Yes. Yes," Hazel stammered. "Y'all sit down. Anywhere."

Still standing in a tight little bunch, the women swiveled their heads around the room simultaneously, as if they were determined to find a place to roost as a flock. Finally, Miss Pearl and Miss Hertha chose the Stratoloungers and Delia settled on the vinyl couch. When her guests were seated Hazel eased herself into a plastic shell chair. There was a period of uncomfortable silence while Sweet Pea disappeared into the kitchen.

Hazel's mind raced furiously trying to think of something to say in order to save the moment. But when she looked over at Miss Pearl, the woman smiled pleasantly, dismissing any awkwardness from the room. Pearl leaned in toward Hazel and said tenderly. "I'm so sorry but we can't possibly stay but a few minutes. Our little club meeting went longer than we planned and the rest of the ladies are at this very moment finishing up without us."

"What kind of club y'all got?" Hazel blurted, excited she had thought of something to say.

"Why, we call it the Trois Arts League."

"It's French," Delia explained, her eyes still laughing. "For 'three arts.'"

"I swan."

"Exactly," said Miss Pearl. "Every month we consider the life of a painter, a composer, and an author."

"Ain't that nice! Sounds so smart of y'all."

"Why, thank you, Hazel," Pearl said. "And of course we do our part for the community. Our busiest time is coming up and we have a host of events to plan for." Pearl touched her handkerchief to her heart and whispered, "Charity season you know," as if the poor people might be listening. "So we can only stay for a chat. I hope you don't mind."

"Don't think nothing of it," Hazel said to Pearl. "I'm just glad y'all could show." Hazel knew she should be disappointed, but she wasn't. These three ladies had only been there under five minutes and they had already overloaded her wagon.

Of course Pearl wasn't being bad at all. It was her niece Hertha who sent shivers through Hazel. The sheriff's wife was sitting straight-backed and wooden in her lounger. Hazel couldn't help noticing that her front teeth bucked like a rodeo horse and her brow hung like a fireplace mantel over eyes the color of cold ashes. She may well have been the most disagreeable-looking person Hazel had ever seen. It was she who spoke next. "Well, you certainly have a unique decorating style, Hazel." There was something about the way the word "unique" splintered in Hertha's throat that made Hazel judge the observation not at all complimentary. "What do you call it?" she asked. Even though Hertha was asking Hazel, she was looking sidelong at Delia. There was a slight curl to Hertha's lip.

Thinking of how to answer a question she didn't understand, Hazel noticed how warm it had become in the perpetually cool house. She heard something like the tinkling bells on a faraway hill. Or maybe, she thought, like laughter just before it breaks out into sound.

She looked again to Miss Pearl, who smiled at her sympathetically, encouraging her on. "Well, I don't call it nothing by name," Hazel said haltingly. "Just furniture, I suppose. Things I thought was pretty." She winced at Hertha like something hurt.

The woman nodded and the corners of her mouth twitched and her nose scrunched up, like she could burst into ugly hysterical snorts at any moment. "It's certainly…what's the word? Intense."

The tinkling of the bells grew louder, and Hazel checked Miss Pearl's expression. She was still smiling reassuringly.

Delia spoke up. "It all looks so…new."

"Brand-new. Just been bought," Hazel said hopefully.

"Didn't you bring any family pieces with you from home?" Hertha asked.

"No. My folks is still sitting in em, I reckon," Hazel answered.

Little coughs were exchanged between Hertha and Delia, like a cold was catching. To keep from crying, Hazel bit her lip and again looked over at Miss Pearl, her eyes pleading.

 Pearl nodded agreeably and said, "It must be nice not to have to bother with dusty old hand-me-downs and just start fresh." She raised her lace handkerchief to her creamy throat and lowered her voice, like she was confessing a deep dark secret. "Why, many a day I want to throw out the old and begin anew. Just because we saved them from the Yankees, we feel we have to display our pieces like monuments. Now, *that's* what I call silly. We should all be more sensible like Hazel here."

The other ladies nodded, agreeing that they were the foolish ones after all. The bells were silenced and Hazel breathed easier.

"Where did your ancestors distinguish themselves during the War, Hazel?" It was Hertha asking.

Hazel was confused. She snatched at the collar of her dress and said timidly, "War?"

"Well, for instance, my great-great-uncle served with Lee. And my great-grandfather was the drummer boy at Chickamauga. In fact, all the Trois Arts women belong to the United Daughters of the Confederacy."

"Chicka…Oh that war!" Hazel said, very relieved to be catching on. "We got a funny story bout that."

"Do tell it, Hazel," Miss Pearl urged.

"Well, my great-great-granddaddy didn't own no niggers, so he didn't figure he should have to fight no war to keep em. He spent the whole time up a sycamore tree hiding from both sides. The only general we got in my family is my daddy, Major General Ishee, and that's just because he got to name hisself."

The laughter Hazel evoked from her story was different from what she was aiming for. It was sharp and jagged like broken glass. Miss Pearl shot the two women daggers and the laughter ceased.

Then into the deathly silence clattered Sweet Pea with a large serving tray and bellowing, "Now y'all sholy gone love this here." She set the tray on the banana table next to the punch bowl and backed away to let the women gaze at the feast of potato chips and onion dip, Vienna sausages smothered in barbecue sauce, and boiled ham bits floating in a bowl of crushed pineapple.

No one moved. Figuring the women may not have read the *Hopalachie Courier* and therefore not be up to date on their delicacies, Sweet Pea decided to instruct them, bending down so low over the tray that everyone's eyes went nervously to her tightly bound breasts which looked ready to discharge themselves into the dip like cannon balls.

Sweet Pea held up a toothpick, "You git you a little stick here and poke yoself one of these little veener sausages." She pointed at the dip, "Or you can drag yo tater chip through this here mess. Go on now and get you some." Sweet Pea smiled at them wide, her gold teeth gleaming like the furniture.

Miss Pearl squirmed a little in her vinyl recliner. "It certainly looks delicious, Hazel. But I have to confess the club lunched at my house earlier and I'm sure I forced too much food on them. As inferior as mine was. Just finger sandwiches and such. Nothing as hearty as what you offer." Miss Pearl dabbed the corner of her mouth with her handkerchief.

Sweet Pea shrugged her shoulders as if there was no accounting for taste and ladled the punch, making sure everyone got a marshmallow, except Hazel who got two and a sympathetic wink. Then she made her hip-rolling exit from the room.

There followed another long silence. Her face hot with shame, Hazel seized the opportunity to change the subject away from the food. "What y'all studying in your club?" she asked Miss Pearl desperately. She was the only one Hazel dared look at now.

"Well, we are presently up to the P's. Puccini, Proust, and Picasso. Hertha here has been leading us in an animated discussion of *Remembrance of Things Past*." When Hazel only stared blankly at Miss Pearl, she asked, "Have you ever read it, Hazel?"

"No. It don't sound familiar. I know a good book, though," Hazel ventured. "Have you ever heard of *David Copperfield*?"

"Why yes! By Mister Charles Dickens! Are you familiar with that work?" Miss Pearl asked, pleasantly surprised. But the other women leaned forward greedily, gawking like customers at a sideshow promising a French-speaking pig.

"I sure do!" Hazel said, relieved to be talking about something she knew. "When I was a girl they playacted that story on the radio. We never had a radio before. Just when it got good, Daddy said I had to go milk the cows. Well, I thought when you turned the thing off, and then come back later, you could pick up right where you left it. Lord, was I disappointed to find out my program done went on without me." Hazel shook her head sadly and then looked up at Miss Pearl. "I never did find out how that boy turned out. Do you happen to know?"

Miss Pearl smiled tenderly. "He turned out just fine, Hazel. Just fine." She began to edge herself out of the recliner. "Hazel, I'm afraid I really must be going. Hayes will be back from the bank any time now and I've still got the meeting to adjourn."

Hertha and Delia followed suit and began their ascent. They made little sucking sounds as they peeled themselves from the furniture.

As the other two ladies filed out the front door, Miss Pearl lingered behind for a moment. "Hazel, thank you so much. I think it went very well, don't you dear?"

"Well, I hope it did."

"We'll do it again real soon, all right? Next time Hayes and I will have you and Floyd over."

Miss Pearl left trailing agreeable beauty parlor smells. Even though

Hazel wasn't so sure things had gone as well as Miss Pearl said, she was delighted that she had made at least one new friend. Floyd would be proud.

Sweet Pea looked down at the untouched tray. "It's a shame they done et. Sho is some purty food. Should a sent a plate home with em."

Hazel beamed. "That's a good idea!" she said and wrapped up some Fancy Franks and filled an orange Fiestaware bowl with Hula Ham. She headed off for Miss Pearl's house, thinking maybe she could serve them to Mr. Hayes with his supper.

As she came up the steps, she was met by gales of laughter pouring through the Irish lace curtains and unshuttered windows. The Trois Arts League must not have adjourned yet.

"And did you see the wallpaper?" That was Miss Hertha's voice. "Am I wrong or were those actually birddogs with pheasants in their mouths?"

"You've got to hand it to her," Delia said. "Most people choose their wallpaper as background. Not Hazel. Hers screams out 'Hey, y'all! We got wallpaper!'"

"How could you keep from bursting out laughing on the spot?" someone asked.

"And the colors!" Delia went on. "I couldn't hear myself think, they were in such a riot."

Hazel didn't stand and listen because she wanted to. She stood there because she was too shamed to move.

"Now that's enough!" Miss Pearl was speaking. Hazel waited for her new friend to set them straight about her. Miss Pearl knew who Hazel really was. Hazel had seen it in the woman's kindly eyes.

"You can't blame her, girls," she said in the same sad whisper in which had spoken earlier about charity. "Just put yourself in her place for a moment. Being poor and from the hills, you're probably just thankful to get a new spread for the bed. You can't be terribly concerned if it goes with your curtains. Or if your curtains go with the rug on the floor. It's only natural Hazel missed out on the concept of 'goes with.'" That brought on another burst of laughter.

"I wasn't trying to be humorous. Y'all are just being too hard on her, now." Miss Pearl was sounding flustered. "After all, she has learned to dress nicely. You saw that. Very tasteful. And she's pretty. Maybe interior decorating is her next conquest. Just give her time."

The women stopped to consider Miss Pearl's point for a moment and then sped right past it. Hertha said, "And that sassy colored girl she found. Sweet Pea. A real Saturday-night brawler. She might as well have been serving drinks in a barrel house." Miss Hertha lowered her voice. "Billy Dean has that girl in jail more times than I can say. Why every time I see my husband, he's got her in the back of his cruiser. For soliciting, you know."

There was a chorus of clucks and gasps.

"Thank heavens you didn't touch the food!"

"What did you say she called them? Fancy Franks?"

"Speaking of soliciting," Miss Hertha said, "Hazel seems to have her own route. Have y'all seen her peddling Lincolns for her husband up and down Gallatin? And with those poor children in tow. A sorry spectacle. What *will* become of them with a mother like that?"

"Really!" Miss Pearl said. "That's uncalled for. You are being *much* too hard on that poor woman."

By the time Floyd came home, Hazel had stopped her crying and pulled herself together. When he asked how things had gone, she didn't answer. She went to the sink and began scrubbing a clean pot.

"Do you think they'll invite you to join their club?" he asked. "That sure would be good for business."

"Well, I'm not sure," she said with her eyes closed, keeping her back to him. "I don't think they have any openings."

She dried her hands on her apron. "And besides, I might not be their kind of people, Floyd." Hazel's breathing was becoming labored and she began to feel a little wobbly. It was another one of those "sinking spells" she had been having lately. She leaned against the counter for a moment and then turned to look at her husband, hoping he might reach out and steady her. That would feel real nice about now.

"Nonsense," he said. "You've got to stop thinking like that. If you want something bad enough, you can have it. Ain't I proved that to you? Look how far I brought us already." He said he wished Hazel would read some of his books on Controlled Thinking, because right now she seemed bound and determined to let her attitude get the worst of her. "Quit dwelling on the negative. Some right thinking would do you wonders," he said.

Hazel looked up at the man who stood before her. Sure and certain. She really did wish she could think like him, clear and positive, like the slogans he was always spouting. "Winners never quit and quitters never win." "Can't never could." "Failures find excuses and Controlled Thinkers find a way." To him it was all a matter of knowing where you want to go, setting your jaw, and moving on in a straight line without any time-wasting detours. To Floyd, life ought to be the straightest road between birth and death.

But Hazel felt she was living her life in an ever-widening curve, blind at both ends. Not only had she lost sight of where she had come from, she could no longer see where Floyd was taking her. Back in the hills she had hope. At least she thought it was hope, that vague whispering in her ear that there was something grand up ahead. The whiskey in her daddy's jug always confirmed it when she had any doubts.

Perhaps it was only the prospect of getting out that had excited her. Maybe the only hope she had was a backwards kind of hope, one that had retreated in the rearview mirror as Floyd put distance between them and home. Certainly, the further she traveled from her roots, the dimmer things looked in both directions, coming and going. Her kin resented her for getting above her raising. She could see in their faces that they had been shamed by her husband's success. Now Floyd would be shamed by her failure. Hazel was caught between two worlds, both of which she was bound to disappoint.

Floyd kissed her lightly on the cheek. "Your attitude determines your altitude," he said. Then he fixed a plate of Vienna sausages and pineapple ham and took it with him into his den to read the news. A moment later she heard him call out, "I think that colored girl made off with my paper!"

Hazel reached for the Jim Beam bottle in the shape of a bowling pin and poured a small bit into her special tumbler. After returning an equivalent amount of tap water to the decanter and grabbing a couple of peppermints from the drawer, she went out to the back porch to sit alone and sip her drink.

As the shadows lengthened across the yard, she watched two fat mourning doves wobble like a drunken couple under a nearby oak. It was obvious they belonged together. Staggering around in no particular hurry to get anywhere, not caring one bit if they were traveling in a straight line or not. She envied them their tipsy little dance full of stops and starts and unbalanced strides, and how, in all their separate, uncoordinated motions, they remained together.

The doves suddenly lifted in flight, breaking her reverie. Davie came toddling around the corner of the house, with Johnny screaming after him.

"Get that rock out of your mouth, Davie. You gonna swallow it and die!"

Should I do something, she wondered? No, Johnny could handle it. He could do it better than me.

Down below, at the foot of the stairs, Johnny caught up with Davie and grabbed him by the shoulders. As Hazel watched unobserved, he shook Davie firmly, yelling for him to spit. But Davie just grinned and then swallowed hard. Did he swallow the rock? Seeing the look of panic on Johnny's face, Hazel almost cried out.

Before she could utter a sound, Davie opened his mouth wide, his face beaming. He began to laugh. There was no rock. He had fooled his brother and he was proud of it. Hazel smiled.

Instead of being relieved, Johnny's face darkened with anger and shame. He reared back and slapped his brother. Hazel could hear the sharp whack from where she sat on the porch, stunned.

She opened her mouth to call out, but again she was checked, this time by the look on Davie's face. It was one of pure bewilderment, as if he were still trying to connect the sting of the slap with any action on his brother's part.

Both boys appeared to have suspended their breathing, as if something hung in the balance. It was like they were waiting for the significance of what had just occurred to settle, so they would know how it had changed their world.

By Davie's confused expression, it was obvious this was the first time his brother had ever hit him. But as his eyes brimmed with tears, Hazel could see that reality was slowly setting in, as if something inside Davie was beginning to break. She felt it was perhaps a thing so fragile that when it does break, it crumbles into pieces as fine as powder.

Even though the tears were trickling down Davie's cheeks, he still seemed to be holding his breath, his mouth open in wonder, watching his brother. As if holding on to his unquestioning trust for as long as he could, before he would have to relinquish it forever, seeing it crumble and blow away. It hurt Hazel to watch him.

She knew she should hurry down the steps and comfort Davie. To hold him. To tell him his brother hadn't meant it. Tell him it wasn't important. Lie to him. Anything to keep the pieces together for a little while longer. But still she sat there, her limbs heavy, because she knew the truth. Things do break and there's nothing a person can do about it.

Instead she turned her eyes to Johnny, hoping he would know what needed to be done. But his expression was one of pained horror, and at the same time, he seemed to be pleading with his brother. Davie began to sniffle and Johnny looked at his little brother like he might a favorite toy he had thrown in a fit of anger, frantically hoping it would fix itself and go back to the way it was before.

It was Johnny she pitied now, wanting to comfort him, unable to. She knew he would never be able to take it back. Some things never could be put like they were before. You can disappoint people and they really do lose faith in you and there is not a damned thing in the world you could do about it. Before she could decide which one was in need of comforting the most, Johnny did a strange thing. Still with an expression of fear cast with sorrow, he pushed Davie squarely on the shoulder.

Davie dried his tears. "Stobbit, Bubba," he whined, covering an eye with the back of his hand.

Johnny shoved him again, a little harder this time. "Stobbit!" Davie yelled, now angry.

Johnny shoved Davie harder still. But this time Davie pushed back.

Clumsily and purposefully, Johnny fell to the ground and his brother climbed on top of him and began flailing away with his tiny fists. Johnny let his brother hit him again and again, on the chest, in the face, refusing to make the slightest gesture to defend himself.

Tears streamed down Johnny's face, but Hazel still did not move toward him. She suspected that Johnny's tears were not from the pain of being hit, and that being beaten would be a small price to pay if one could replace all that had been lost.

As the twilight took hold of the world, and her sons vanished from the yard, and the mourning doves called to each other through the dusk, Hazel remained in her chair, weighted down with the belief that anything she did, any movement she made, now, tomorrow, forever, would in the end make no difference at all, would be of significance to no one.

Chapter 18

FISHERS OF MEN

"Look at you," Hazel said. "Natural blonde hair with a little blue ribbon to match your eyes. Good teeth. Probably never knew an ugly day in your life. Everything handed to you on a silver platter, like that slice of light bread you're eating. You the kind everybody wants to have in their club, ain't you little girl?"

The face of Little Miss Sally Sunbeam stared back at Hazel from the battered screen. The girl was doing more up there than selling bread. She was taunting Hazel. Her eyes, still baby blue after years of weather and dust, saying, "Pretty is as pretty does."

"What the hell does that mean anyway?" Hazel said back. "Sounds like something Floyd would come up with. Like, 'Can't never could.' or 'Today's thoughts determine tomorrow's prize,' or 'You can't stand still for success.' Or 'Attitude determines altitude.'"

Floyd's slogans never made much sense to Hazel, but beneath the snappy phrases she could hear his scolding voice. "Catch up! Catch up! You're dragging your end of it." Just where was it they were going in such a hurry? That's what she wanted to know. Hazel drained the last of the bottle.

About a dozen colored men were lolled around on the gallery, filling the bench, leaning against the wall, sitting on the steps. But they acted unaware of the white woman and her two children out in the Lincoln. Their low talk and half-grins were only for one another, and their shifting glances never seemed to rise above the level of the car's hood.

From off in the distance she thought she could hear the gnarling and rumbling of what sounded like a herd of ferocious animals, closing in on her and her boys. When she turned toward the field she saw a single hulking green machine, growling greedily, eating its way through the impossibly white cotton.

Hazel glanced down at her two boys drowsing next to her on the front seat, Johnny leaning against the door and Davie nuzzled under his brother's arm. After riding out in the country with Hazel for hours, they were tuckered out.

Since her humiliation at the hands of her neighbors, Hazel had abandoned her town route and had taken to driving down from the bluffs and out into the Delta. Each morning she drove the endless depression for miles, along desolate dirt roads, where the only people who would see her were fieldhands or work gangs from the state penitentiary. Nobody she expected Floyd was out to impress. Driving the earth's flattened-down places, Hazel could yell and cuss and cry to her heart's content. Nothing could creep up on her. Everything could be seen at once and for what it was. Out here was where the bare-bones truth lived, plain and simple and absolute. No silly childish dreams or false hopes or wishful thinking could survive. It was like looking God square in the eye and speaking your name and daring Him to strike you dead.

Hazel usually drove until her half-pint ran out. Then she went home and spent the rest of the afternoon sobering up for Floyd. But lately, a half-pint hadn't done the trick. Hope couldn't be roused from its sickbed. So Hazel blew her horn twice and a colored boy ran out onto the gallery, saw Hazel, and then ducked back into the store.

Her children had begun to stir with the honking, but Hazel didn't notice. She had locked her eyes on Miss Sally again; the girl was still holding the bread up to her mouth, like she had all the time in the world. No sense in gobbling it down. Sally knew there was more where that slice came from.

"Yeah, little Miss Sunbeam," Hazel said, feeling good and sorry for herself now, "you don't know what life can do to people like me. Make-do people. That's what I am." She hiccuped.

"You don't even know what 'making do' means, do you, you little spoiled brat? Well, just ask me. The gold-plated queen of make-do. I been making do all my life. Make-do clothes. Make-do schooling. Make-do looks. It's a funny saying, ain't it? Make-do. That why you smirking at me?

Well, go on ahead and laugh. Everbody else does. The joke's on me. Told myself if I ever got out of those hills I wouldn't never make do again. Well. I'm driving a Lincoln and living in a rich man's house and still making do. And everbody laughing at the make-do girl."

Hazel's eyes began to tear up, and she gritted her teeth at the same time. "I don't know what it was I hoped for, Sally. Just something else. Something with my name on it. Like you and your screen door there. That door's yours, no doubt about it. Your name is painted all over it."

The screen door swung open and shut again, but otherwise Sally Sunbeam remained unmoved. Hazel let a tear trickle unimpeded down her cheek. "My husband done put me behind the wheel of a Lincoln like Daddy put me behind Jawbone. Looks like I'm a-gonna be plowing somebody else's fields till the day I die."

The door flew open again and the colored boy came running up to Hazel's window with a paper sack in his hand. Hazel began to dig though her purse.

"Momma, I'm hungry." Johnny was awake now and began pushing his little brother away. "Get off me. You're slobbering all over my shirt."

Davie pushed back. "Make him stop, Momma."

"He's been sleeping with his mouth open again, Momma. Look at his spit all over me. When we going to eat dinner?"

While the colored boy waited with his thumbs hooked in the straps of his raggedy overalls, he watched the two white children with matching bow ties, dressed nice enough for Sunday. When Johnny caught him staring and glared back, the boy dropped his eyes and placed one bare foot on top of the other, switched feet, and then shifted again, like he was trying to decide which leg would stand him better.

"Here," Hazel said as she handed the boy a little extra, "go on back in the store and get me a couple of banana Moon Pies and two Nehi grapes."

The boy took off, leaving Hazel to feel Sally's eyes looking disapprovingly at her. "Well, what do you expect, Little Miss Perfect? I'm a make-do-momma, making do the best I can."

⚜

Hazel sped along, the wind in her hair, sipping from her bottle. After a few miles, the seemingly endless sunlit fields were interrupted by a deep green band of trees that followed the Hopalachie River as it snaked through the Delta. When she entered that shadowy world, the temperature immediately cooled. Hazel slowed the Lincoln and edged the car right up to the lip of a rickety one-lane bridge suspended between the two high riverbanks.

Getting out of the car, and weaving slightly, she made her way to the front bumper and stooped down to look underneath, making sure her tires were lined up with the two raised plank tracks that led across the wooden structure. Satisfied the car had a good chance of making it to the other side, she decided to walk out a little farther and get a look at the river below from the vantage of the bridge. When she passed this way earlier she thought she had seen some colored people fishing down on the bank, and she wanted to make sure they were still there.

Her high-heeled pumps tapped hollow against the wood. Hazel tried to decide if the swaying she felt was due to the movement of the bridge or her present condition. Either way, she somehow made it safely halfway across.

Lacking any railing, the bridge offered an unimpeded twenty-foot drop into the dark, snaky water below. Hazel walked right up to the edge, but didn't see the colored people. Leaning forward to get a look underneath, she tottered, frantically thrashed her arms in the air, and, a moment before toppling over the side, caught her balance. She dropped to her hands and knees to view the river through the cracks between the boards.

Just as she had hoped! The people were still up under there. From where she knelt, she could see a man who was standing up to his knees in the water throw a heavy line deep into the river and then drag it back toward the bank. A few other colored people, both men and women, stood by on the bank, watching intently. Never having seen this kind of fishing before, she rushed back to the car and her children and then carefully maneuvered the massive Lincoln over the creaking bridge, off the road, and into the shade of an old beech tree.

This was not unusual for Hazel. When she drove out into the Delta, she often stopped to observe coloreds at work, with the same fascination she had as a child observing a colony of ants or a nest of wasps. She thought there was a sad kind of beauty in the way their motions would blend into a shared dance, transcending their earthly lot. It was like something from the Bible. Or maybe a Carter Family gospel song.

Once she sat for over an hour watching a gang of colored convicts from Parchman work with their scythes in a weedy ditch. Garbed in black-and-white stripes, they moved in unison, their blades glinting like a single instrument under the eye of the fierce white sun. And how they could holler out! The whiskey having shrunk any distinction between a white housewife's melancholy and the woes of a dozen colored convicts, Hazel had hollered with them.

Goin up to Memphis
I'll be able when I die
Load my body on the freight car
Send my soul on by and by.

The boys had joined in the best they could. "Going uptomemphis, Going uptomemphis" they sang over and over again.

There they had been. Two little white boys dressed in their Sunday clothes clutching Moon Pies, and their make-do mother sipping boot-legged whiskey behind the wheel of her Lincoln, tears rolling down her cheeks, sharing with a gang of convicts a song about life's injustice.

These colored people by the riverbank weren't singing, but they did appear very solemn about their fishing, so Hazel hoped for a good show. Maybe, she thought, if they caught something they would burst out into song.

Hazel led the children to a shady place in the trees above the river where they all could sit and observe without being noticed. She then spread out a pallet she kept in the car trunk for such occasions as this. While she busied herself, smoothing out the lumps in the quilt, Johnny called out urgently. Hazel turned to see Davie scurrying up toward the road, no doubt returning to the altitude of the bridge to fall from. When she stood, a heaviness dropped over Hazel like an iron net, and she couldn't move or even speak. It was as if she were caught up in a current pulling her in the opposite direction from her child, away from where she was needed.

Johnny saw the bewildered look on his mother's face and broke after Davie. Just as he reached the bridge Davie stumbled in the road, and before he could right himself, Johnny had him by the ankle. As Hazel stood there paralyzed, her heart pounding, she watched as Johnny led Davie back to safety, on the way inventing for his brother cautionary tales about drowning.

Like a brilliant flare, a single thought shone through the fog that had enveloped Hazel, the thought that all this she was witnessing, the way things were playing out before her that very minute, was how it had to be. The three of them were like trains barreling down separate tracks, and none of them had a voice about direction. They might could slow and they might could speed up. But they could not choose what it was they were bearing down on. Or what was bearing down on them. God had fixed it.

She continued watching her children in stunned amazement, as if seeing them for the very first time. Davie was squirming, already anxious to loose himself again, to make his way to the highest point around and, having found it, fall, to feel the pull of gravity and then to know the salvation of waiting arms just before touching earth. And Hazel thought, that is who he is. That is what he is bound to do. And that is what he will always do. No momma, bad or good, was going to change that.

There was Johnny, always earthbound, gripping Davie by the arm, checking his mother's eyes for his bearings, doing everything he could to keep them all here safely together, firmly planted on the ground. Again the thought resonated in her head. Yes, and that is who Johnny is, and always will be. That is who he will be when he is an old man. Nothing she could do, as a good mother or a bad mother, would change that. There was as much comfort as there was rapture in the thought. Hazel began to weep.

She knelt down and clutched her boys to her chest. She told them she loved them, over and over again. Still in a state of wonder, she distributed the Moon Pies and soft drinks as solemnly as if it were the Last Supper. She tenderly kissed each child on the cheek, and with her mind clouded with whiskey and shadowy revelation, Hazel leaned against a hickory tree with her half-pint firmly clasped to her chest.

Her attention returned to the spectacle unfolding in the river. Down below them, the man standing in the water and doing the fishing had moved a little farther upstream, like he was trying to find the perfect spot. Hazel was a little disappointed in him. A real fisherman would have more patience.

The water was the color of strong tea and very deep by the bridge, and Hazel was unable to see what was tied to the massive fishing line that, now that she studied it, looked more like a rope. As she watched, the fisherman carefully pulled in the line and hauled a shapeless, dark mass up on the bank. A couple of other men gathered around and snatched away what had been grabbed from the river bottom—leaves and branches and snag roots and such. That's when Hazel saw what they were using for a hook. Attached to the rope was what looked like a lead pipe with spurs on the end. No wonder they hadn't caught anything! All they would catch with that contraption was more bottom trash. Amateurs!

Without even bothering to bait his line, the man doing the casting waded to yet another spot in the river and once more threw his rope into the water. This time when the man pulled on the rope he yelled something to the others on the bank. Two more men joined the fisherman in the water and began tugging at what looked like a big haul.

"Look, boys," Hazel said, rising up wobbly to her feet to get a better view, "They done caught em something. Must be a big'un."

After lifting Davie in her arms, Hazel stood and watched as they dragged a giant black catfish onto the shore. She heard one of the women on the bank scream.

Johnny bounced on his tiptoes to see the fish. "Momma, what's that woman yellin for? Did she get bit by the fishy?"

Hazel's eyes tried to focus in on the catch. It was about five or six feet long and was wrapped in barbed wire. There was a big piece of machinery tied around its neck. My, god! she thought, the thing's got a neck! She made out the bloated face, with one eye beaten closed and one hanging from its socket. She heard the woman call the fish by name.

"Hiram! Lawd, lawd!" The woman screamed. "My baby, Hiram!"

Then Hazel heard herself scream.

The Lincoln was all over the road, from ditch to ditch, all three crying their hearts out. Hazel didn't know where she was heading, nor did she care. Speed and distance was all she wanted from the car now.

An hour later, when the black-and-white cruiser with the big star on the door happened upon Hazel and her boys, she had sunk the two left tires deep into a sandy ditch and was hunched over the wheel sobbing. Johnny was patting his mother gently on the arm. Then she heard a man's voice at her ear. "That you, Missus Graham? You all right in there?"

Hazel raised her eyes to see the sheriff. He was watching her with a kind of detached, wary look, like she might be a stray dog with a touch of foam around the mouth. "Oh, Sheriff!" she cried. "I'm so glad you come along. Back there. In the river. They's a dead boy."

His eyes narrowed. For a moment the sheriff seemed concerned. "A white one?"

"No, a colored one. I watched them pull him off the river bottom. He was all bound up and weighted down. Somebody killed him for sure."

The sheriff's eyes warmed a little. He took off his hat and bent down to the window. "Now don't you worry none. I'll check into it, Miss Hazel." His voice was reassuring. "You know how them niggers is always knifin one another. Come Saturday night ever creek in Hopalachie County'll have niggers floatin in it." He shook his head sadly. "I'm just sorry you had to see it, is all."

Hazel thought he really did look sorry. What a kind, thoughtful man. He was treating her with so much politeness. More than she could say for that wife of his. Right then Hazel's heart went out to the sheriff for being saddled with a horse like Hertha. He was such a nice-looking man, too.

"Let's see if we can't get you out of this ditch," he said. "I got a chain in the turtle hull."

When he motioned to his cruiser, Hazel was surprised to see somebody waving at her from the backseat. Why, it was that whore-for-a-maid, Sweet Pea, grinning to beat the band, her gold teeth gleaming in the afternoon light through the sheriff's back window.

The sheriff saw the curious look on Hazel's face. "Got me a prisoner," he said quickly. "Just hauling her in for questioning."

Nodding back at Sweet Pea, Hazel couldn't help but think she seemed mighty happy to be a prisoner.

Chapter 19
ONE WING HANNAH'S

Vida reckoned that if the woman who plopped down uninvited at her table wasn't drunk, she was within hollering distance of it. Her shiny black hair, greased down and hot combed, hugged a plump face glistening with sweat and she grinned at Vida like they were best friends.

"You ought to get out of them fields, honey," the woman lost no time in advising. "You wastin yoself. Girl like you do a lot better in town. The mens like yo type." She smiled brightly at Vida with a mouth full of gold teeth and then winked. Motioning toward Vida's chest with an empty Mason jar, she said, "You young and pretty, even with that head of drawed-up hair. And you probly totin some nice boobies in that sack you wearin."

The whiskey-scarred voice of some old bluesman called out for his woman from the lighted Seeburg smoldering from pink to purple to violet over in one corner of the stifling hot jook joint. Vida knew she shouldn't have come. Shifting self-consciously in her chair, she yanked at her loose calico dress, trying to pull out some of the slack. Then she stuck her ragged hands under the table and out of sight. It vexed her to think a looped-up stranger could tell straight away that she worked in the fields. Especially in a smoke-crowded room lit by two dim bulbs dangling from a tarpaper ceiling.

Vida squinched her brows together in a mean little wad and searched the room, partly to defy the busybody stare of her table companion and partly to locate her brother. Throughout the room, couples were close-dancing in the cigarette haze, wrapped around each other so tightly, Vida thought, they might as well be lying down.

Across the room several young men wearing fedoras and bright-colored shirts, smoking cigarettes and chewing on matchsticks, strutted like roosters around a wobbly pool table, appearing to be doing more posing than shooting. Like her, the patrons of the jook were mostly fieldhands and croppers, but you couldn't tell it by looking at them tonight in their satins and silks. Lord, Vida said to herself, more colors than coal oil on pond water.

She didn't have any business among these people. All this foolish fun-making could only distract a person from what was really important in life. Years of being single-minded in purpose had honed Vida's ability to tamp out any spark of pleasure lest it flare up and blind her to her duty. Nothing else in the world mattered but what she owed her son.

Vida crooked her head around the woman, to see out the door. If she could find Willie, she would fuss at him good. Coming to One Wing Hannah's jook on pay night had been her brother's idea and now he had went and disappeared, saddling her with some looped-up gal whose nature had obviously gone to her head. Knowing Willie, he was probably outside skylarking with the no-account men they had passed on their way in, hang-ing about the yard, smoking rolled cigarettes and passing bottles, their laughter secretive and edged with devilment. She had felt the hard little "heh heh heh's" pelting her backside when she climbed up the wobbly steps.

As she watched the door, Vida saw a tall honey-skinned man with a purplish red shirt and green pointed shoes saunter in the shack. Almost instinctively, the gold-toothed woman spun around and caught his eye. He gave her a wolfish smile and she gave him a sidelong glance and then turned back to Vida and said confidentially. "Look see. Three dollars right there. Five if he was white. How many pounds of cotton you got to pick for five dollars?"

Vida gasped, "You do it with white men!" She couldn't imagine some-body doing it with a white man if they didn't have to. The thought sent a million little bug feet traipsing across her skin.

"Now don't look at me that-a-way. It don't rub off. You tell me which sounds smarter. Pickin the white man's cotton for two dollars a day or layin on it for five? And that's an hour. I'm talkin year-round." She winked at Vida. "I didn't pass through the eighth grade for nothin. I got that deal figgered."

The woman could "figger" all she wanted. White people frightened

Vida, the white man with his face as sharp as the steel head of a hatchet and eyes that cut to the bone like the wind on a wet day in January, swaggering around the countryside, unthinking as a cocked pistol. But it was the white woman that vexed Vida the most. Her nose poked in the air like she was all the time smelling dog doo. Acting all soft and breakable when her man was around and conniving and fish-blooded when he wasn't.

Sure, Vida knew of girls who had gone into town and found them a white woman to work for and bragged that the money was year-round and the work was considerably lighter than field labor. But the thought of being under the same roof with one of those cold-hearted, bloodless haints made Vida's stomach curdle. Wasn't but a few weeks ago a white woman accused Statia Collins's grandnephew of cutting his eyes at her. She said he might have even whistled. The woman told anybody who would listen that a real man would do something about it and went on sniveling until last week they pulled the boy out of the Hopalachie dressed in barbed wire and gin parts.

While Vida was having her thoughts about white people, the jookers around her all at once hushed, and the room went dead still. The only sound left in the place was the voice of the woman in the Seeburg, her lovelorn complaints wafting through the smoke. When Vida looked up toward the door she saw why. There stood Sheriff Billy Dean Brister surveying the shack like he was trying to see if there were any butts that needed kicking tonight. Then he strode directly over to the owner with his hand out.

One Wing Hannah, her hefty bulk propped up on a stool behind the wood plank that passed for a bar, handed him an envelope with her good arm. Vida watched as Hannah turned around, and with the armpit of her stump, got a grip on a bottle from the shelf behind her and swung it around at the sheriff. He gave her a nasty look, but took it anyway.

The sheriff scanned the room again, but when his eyes got to Vida's table, they came to a dead stop. Vida did her best to keep up her stare, wanting him to know she wasn't the least bit afraid, but avoiding the eyes of a white man was a hard habit to break. Years of warnings dropped like weights on her lids. She looked down at the table, but he was still clearly engraved in her mind. For so long he had been a constant presence.

Soon after she lost Nate, he was a regular visitor. He would park his patrol car at a distance from their shack and just stare in their direction. Sometimes late at night, he would pull his car up close to the shack, like he did that other night so long ago, and sit there, his lights illuminating the inside of the house, while she and her father and Willie waited for him to kill them or leave. He was warning her to keep their secret.

When she peeked up again, she saw it wasn't her that the sheriff was studying. He had settled his eyes on her table companion, his face devoid of any expression except the usual contempt. He took his loot and walked out as abruptly as he came in, like a man with a route to make.

The gold-toothed woman nodded at the door. "And girl, there goes seven dollars. And he pay in advance."

Vida let go such a look of disgust it would have sobered the woman up if the light had been better. "You done it with—?"

"Mess a times," she said. "We go to an old burned-out house up in the woods."

Vida's disapproval must have shown even through the dimness of the room. The woman squared her shoulders. "Well, it ain't like we do it all that much," she said defensively. "And some days we don't do it at all. They times he just wonts somebody to drink with and talk to. Then he go to sleep." She shrugged. "On or off, still cost him seven dollars."

"Y'all talk? Both of you?" Vida asked, not able to imagine the sheriff having a conversation with this woman.

"I don't talk, hon. He do the talkin. I just listens. Sometimes."

More curious now than disgusted, Vida leaned in and lifted her brows. "Yeah? Like what he say?"

"Well," the woman said, "one time he got *some* drunk. Give his wife a real badmouthin. Cried bout how ugly she was and how she as cold as an outhouse in a ice storm. And bout his two pishy little girls. How his own fambly don't think he ain't nothing but po white trash. I figger he go out to that old shack just to get apart from em." The woman leaned in toward Vida, so close Vida could smell the rotten sweet smell of shine on her breath. "Girl, then he passes out and he talk *some mo*."

"He talk in his sleep?"

"Yeah, girl! Crazy shit. Can't make no sense from it. Don't wont to. Lot of yellin and cussin. He sho nuf bein rode hard by the devil."

"You don't understand nothin he say?"

"No. And I ain't there to be askin no questions, if you know what I mean. He can have any crazy dream he wont for seven dollars advance money."

The woman eyed Vida suspiciously. "What you care for, anyway? You ain't tryin to steal my trade, is you?"

Vida lowered her eyes, disappointed, and said, "Nothin. I just wondered if sometime he didn't talk about a boy."

"A boy? What boy?"

"Any boy," Vida said.

The woman began tapping the bottom of her empty jar against the tabletop. "Like I done tole you," she said, sounding done with the conversation. "He ain't got no boy. Just them two pishy girls."

Vida nodded and was about to get up when the woman laughed. "Now that you mind me of it, he did ax me the beatinist thing the first time we done it."

Vida looked up. "What? What he ax you?

"He ax if I ever heard tell of a white boy livin mongst the colored." She laughed, "Ain't that crazy? Said he got a call bout one bein' kidnapped! Magine that. Tole me to let him know if I come across such a thing."

The woman was casting her gaze over the room like she was ready for new company, but Vida took no notice. It was as if the woman had taken a stick and poked at a wasp nest in Vida's head. A hundred thoughts swarmed at once. She hadn't fooled the sheriff after all. That's why he had come by the shack all those times, looking for Nate.

Somebody had to have told about the empty coffin. That old uncle. Or the undertaker. Or another somebody looking to be the next Reach Out Man. Oh, Lord, Vida thought, the sheriff's dreams could be telling him to track his son down.

Something grabbed at Vida's chest like an icy fist. Maybe the sheriff had already found Nate. Or was getting close. He was the sheriff and he was white and white people knew everything worth knowing in the world. They could find things out. Track down Rezel. What if it was Nate's little ghost who was haunting the sheriff's dreams now?

Her head buzzed with maybes, but Vida told herself the only thing she knew for sure was that the sheriff was having bad dreams. Could be about anything. Or nothing. She had to be careful. The less she knew, the more she imagined.

She had waited for seven years, afraid to leave the county lest she be gone when Nate finally sent word. It would be just like her father's God to be this heartless. After all her praying, to send a message from her son—alive or dead—through the dreams of the one person she could never get near enough to listen to.

The woman at the table made a great show of raising the empty fruit jar to her lips, throwing back her head and thumping the jar on the bottom to loosen any remaining drops clinging to the sides. She rimmed the mouth of the glass with a long pink tongue.

Before Vida could ask any more questions, the honey-skinned man with the green pointed shoes and a smile like a wolf came over to the table. "You look thirsty tonight, girl! You as hot as me?"

The woman smiled gold at him, but then glanced back at Vida, as if to say, "Watch this."

The man began to rub his thigh into her shoulder to the rhythm of the music. Bending down, he moaned into her ear, loud enough for Vida to hear through the din.

"Umm. Umm. Sweet Pea. You feelin good tonight. How bout you and me doin the drag, sugar? Then I put some mo shinny in yo jar."

Sweet Pea began rubbing on him, gyrating her shoulder into his crotch, but talking to Vida at the same time. "Honey, if you don't wont a white man, then least find you a white woman."

Sweet Pea snapped her fingers. "And Lawd do I have the right one for you! I done a little piece of work for her onced. She live in a big ol' house in Delphi. That lady need somebody bad. She be a piteous mess."

Sweet Pea shook her head sadly. "Heard she just lost her boy. Must sho nuf be a wreck now."

"Lost him?" Vida asked, still thinking about Nate. "Where she lose him at?"

"I don't mean she sat him down and forgot him, girl. You crazy? I mean he be dead."

Vida scowled at Sweet Pea and tried to sound tough. "What that be to me? I ain't got no tears for no white woman."

"Whoo-ee!" Sweet Pea exclaimed and then looked up at the man with a wink. "Ain't she a hard-hearted one?"

The man grinned at Vida.

"All I'm sayin," Sweet Pea confided, "is play yo cards right and you be the boss in that house. She don't know her shit from Shinola."

Vida had a thought. "She live anywheres near the sheriff?"

The woman eyed Vida warily. "Uh-huh. That's right. All them rich people live over there bunched up together like a wad of money. Why you askin?"

The question jolted Vida back to reality. How could she even consider the possibility? Vida shook her head disdainfully. "I ain't studyin on being no maid for no white woman."

Sweet Pea shrugged and then rose from the table in her tight dress of white satin, traveling up the man like a curl of smoke.

Anyway, Vida thought, she was stuck on the plantation. They had made a couple of bad crops and owed the Senator. If she left, she would sure enough get to see the sheriff up close. Through the bars of his jail cell. But maybe, she thought, just maybe she could find a way.

She looked across the room at Sweet Pea and her new acquaintance. Their arms around each other, hers loosely around his muscled neck, his on her big booty, they danced belly to belly, groin to groin, leg to leg to the grinding beat. Vida wasn't sure about her own future, but could see three dollars in the woman's.

All of a sudden One Wing Hannah started cussing like a mule skinner, grabbed her pistol from behind the bar, and hauled her two hundred and fifty pounds toward the door like she was mounted on freshly greased wheels. "Where is that good-for-nothin devilish-eyed scound? That pretty boy bout to have him two assholes to shit out of."

"Willie!" Vida gasped. She watched as Hannah disappeared through the door. A second later a shot rang out.

In a flash Vida was on her feet and flying. She got to the gallery in time to see people in the yard scattering behind trees and diving under cars. The sweet smell of cordite still hung heavy in the thick summer air. In the middle of the yard One Wing Hannah was flapping her stump and pointing the gun with her good arm at Willie.

Vida grabbed a pool stick from one of the gawkers standing next to her, ready to break it on Hannah's head if need be. But Willie seemed unfazed. He stood there grinning like a child caught sneaking candy. That boy had nerves of steel.

"Nigger, I tole you don't you come round my place sellin no hootch."

Hannah had bolted down the steps so fast her wig had slipped over to one side of her head. Her chest was heaving like two pigs crowding a trough.

"Yes, ma'am, Miss Hannah. You shore got a right to be mad." Willie talked like he had a mouth full of butter. Now Vida knew why Willie had insisted on coming tonight. That rascal must have taken up bootlegging! Probably had him a supply stashed close by.

"Boy, you might be fine to look at, but I'm a mean ol' biddy. You see this here stump?" Hannah waved it proudly in the air. "Know how I got it? Got my arm chewed off by one of dem damdable cotton pickers."

"Yes, ma'am." Willie said, his voice smooth with admiration. "And the Senator let you open this here place cause of it."

"You damned right. And I do whatever it takes to keep it. I'll knock heads, bust knees, and pull yo pecker out by the root if you get in my way. No matter how sweet-lookin you be."

"Yes, ma'am. You sholy a rare woman. Rare as one of the blue hen's chickens." Willie gave her his devil's grin. "And you sexy when you riled."

Smiling like a schoolgirl, Hannah straightened her wig with the pistol-toting hand and waved it back in Willie's general direction. Her voice sweetened considerably. "Now, baby, you listen to me. I be the one who pays the sheriff, so I be the one who sells the whiskey—at least in this cotton patch. That be the nub of it. I'd hate to sic Sheriff Billy Dean on you.

Be a waste of some fine-lookin ass. Now, you behave from here on out."

"I sholy will, Miss Hannah. You a generous woman to be so understandable. You sho something special."

Hannah shook her head and chuckled, like she knew she was the kind of woman destined to be done in by a pretty face every time. "Baby, if you bound and determined to sell hootch, you come see me. Maybe we can work something out."

All of a sudden, just as she had with Sweet Pea, Vida could see into Willie's future, and working a plot of land with her and Levi was not part of it.

Chapter 20
JESUS IN THE GRAVEYARD

The graveyard lay on the other side of the bridge from the town, down an unpaved road that tunneled through vegetation so thick that in places it blotted out the early-afternoon sun. There were no houses along the way, and as the procession of cars descended the last hill and rounded the final curve, the road ended like a sigh at the foot of an ancient gate, its elaborate ironwork intertwined with honeysuckle vines.

Beyond was a clearing strewn with weathered black headstones, winged children with dead marble eyes, and green Styrofoam crosses stuck with plastic flowers. Johnny and Davie had ridden down this road many times with their mother. At the graveyard, she would let them take off their shoes, always warning them not to step on the graves lest Jesus grab their feet.

Even though Johnny was pretty sure he had to keep his shoes on today, Jesus was still on his mind. He watched carefully as they lowered his brother down into the hole and as Brother Dear talked to Jesus with tears leaking out from behind his tightly closed lids, and as Johnny's mother sat stone-faced, smelling one minute like Gardenia Paradise and the other like the medicine she had been taking from half-pint bottles.

It seemed everybody around him was crying except his mother. The biggest part of the town was there sitting in rows and rows of straight-back funeral chairs, men sniffling and bashfully brushing their noses with the tops of their knuckles, while offering their pocket handkerchiefs to their wives. Even his father was wiping away tears as big as summer raindrops. Every now and then, from directly behind him, he heard the sobs of his Aunt Onareen, the only one from Hazel's family to attend.

"How long is Jesus going to keep Davie down there in that hole,

Momma?" Johnny whispered.

She acted like she hadn't heard him. Her dry stare was focused on Brother Dear, who shone brighter than the sun on snow in his pure white suit. The preacher was saying something about God's will and Jesus' master plan and about never, never, never asking why.

Johnny nudged his mother. "When's Jesus going to let go of Davie's feet and send him back home?"

Still staring at Brother Dear, Hazel shredded her tissue until there was nothing but a mound of white bits on the lap of her black silk dress. Floyd reached over and brushed her off and then rested his palm over her hands, stilling them.

On an earlier trip to the graveyard, Johnny had asked his mother about the yellow sign that stood where the road began. He was curious about these colored sheets of metal that could make his parents do things without even raising a voice. He knew "Yield" and "Slow" and "Rail Road Crossing Mississippi Law Stop." But this one was different. "What's it tell, Momma?" he had asked.

"Dead End. It means you have to turn back around the way you come."

She said this matter-of-factly, as if there were nothing odd at all about a DEAD END sign on a road that went to a place where dead people slept, as if she were so accustomed to seeing the sign, she never connected it to the graveyard that lay beyond. But Johnny did.

Davie got himself killed and today had been taken to the sleeping place at the end of the road. The yellow sign was a promise to Johnny that his brother would soon be turned around and sent back home after a short visit with Jesus.

As Floyd drove past the sign after the funeral, Johnny asked his momma from the backseat how Davie was going to find his way back to the house. "Will Jesus set him loose at night? Oughten we come back in the car and get him so he don't get lost?"

His mother swung her head around in the seat. "What are you going on about?" she shouted. "Davie ain't coming home. Never! Do you understand me? Jesus don't let nobody go once He gets a-holt of them!"

Johnny sat stone still in the backseat. He was too startled to cry.

Floyd turned to Hazel. "Why are you yelling at the boy? Why are you yelling at all? Why ain't you crying like everbody else? It ain't right you being dry-eyed at your own son's funeral."

Hazel looked accusingly at her husband. "Ain't you the one always saying we can't go back and change the past? That spilt milk ain't worth crying over?"

After taking a deep breath and slowly letting it out, Floyd shifted to his low serious voice, the one he used when he felt he was getting to the nub of a matter. "I'll tell you why you ain't crying, Hazel. It's because you're stinking drunk. It ain't cute no more. You get mean when you drink. Just like your daddy. And I'm sure everybody at the funeral smelt it."

"I ain't drunk and don't you talk about my daddy." Hazel gritted her teeth. "And I'll cry whenever somebody tells me why Davie is gone." She shot Floyd a look that accused him of holding back the answer from her all along.

"Well…" Floyd said. He didn't seem so sure of himself for a second or so, and appeared to be thinking real hard about the problem Hazel had posed to him. Finally he said, "Now Jesus tells us we got to—"

Hazel flew hot again. "I done heard enough about what Jesus tells us! Jesus and His many mansions. Jesus and His big ol' everlasting arms. If His arms is so big and strong, how come they didn't catch Davie? Tell me that!"

Floyd didn't offer an answer. When Davie had died, Floyd and his big ol' arms had been there, too. Floyd had been working on the lawn mower when Davie decided he wanted to play "Catch me!" from the porch. Certain as always his daddy was watching, Davie stepped to the rail edge and stretched out his arms.

Only Johnny had been watching. It was he who had heard his brother's voice call out "catch me," sounding more like a bird chirping or a squirrel barking, and he who saw his brother drop off the man-tall porch. It wasn't until his father heard the soft thud on the grass and then something like the sound of a twig snapping that he glanced up from the broken mower to see Davie lying in front of him, motionless, his arms akimbo, facing up at Floyd with only the slightest look of surprise.

☙

In the autumn that followed the funeral, Hazel's tears still didn't get shed for Davie, but instead hung dark and heavy on the family's horizon like an approaching Delta storm. The drinking continued. Hazel said if she couldn't drink, she would surely suffocate. She said, "Drinking is like breaking open a window to yell out of."

Floyd said he was trying to understand, but all he thought her drinking did was to make her mad. He said every time he looked at her, all he saw in her eyes was a fight ready to happen, and he couldn't afford being around somebody that negative all the time. Not with everything they had riding on his positive attitude. Finally, he moved into a separate bedroom.

They left Davie's bed and toys and clothes untouched, strengthening Johnny's belief that his brother was coming back. Several times a week he would awaken to see his father silhouetted in the doorway, looking toward Davie's bed for minutes at a time. One night, after a particularly loud fight between his parents, Floyd came to the doorway and stood there as usual, staring, but this time, Johnny thought he heard a sniffling sound.

"Hey, Big Monkey," Johnny called out to him.

"Hey, Little Monkey," his father whispered in a way that made Johnny's heart hurt.

"He's not back yet, Daddy," he said, trying to comfort him. "I'll yell at you when he gets home."

Later, after his father had gone to bed, Johnny woke to the touch of a hand running through his hair. As his mother knelt by his bedside, smelling strongly of medicine, she whispered the oddest question in his ear.

"Who do you love the most? Me or your daddy?"

Certain of the answer she wanted, he said, "You, Momma."

She bent over and kissed him on his forehead and said before leaving. "Don't tell your daddy. You're on my side. Do you hear?"

His mother's question tore the world in two for Johnny. It was like the day he had seen the setting sun and the rising moon in the sky at the same time, opposite each other. Until that moment, he believed they were the same entity, the silver moon being the soft evening face of the hot, laboring sun. But when his mother asked him that question, and made him choose between his parents, Johnny grasped how separate his parents really were. They traveled in their own orbits. And most terrifying of all, there could be one without the other.

Chapter 21
FAITH, HOPE AND CHARITY

Johnny and his mother sat at the kitchen table having their usual afternoon drinks—Johnny his grape Nehi and Hazel a large dose of her medicine. Raising the special tumbler she kept hidden in the pantry, Hazel toasted, "Here's mud in your eye!"

"Mud in your eye!" Johnny echoed, but before they had taken their slugs, he cried out, "No, Momma! Let's do it again." Holding out his glass, he grinned and said, "Here's *Maud* in your eye."

They both giggled at that one, Maud being very much on their minds today. Floyd's father had passed three months after they buried Davie, and on the very afternoon of the funeral the unthinkable happened. Floyd insisted that Maud leave the hills and come live with them in Delphi, without even the slightest tilt of the head to Hazel, knowing full well her feelings on the matter.

He couldn't very well use grief for his father as an excuse, because Floyd didn't seem to have an ounce of it. Nobody did. Embarrassment was the only emotion in common currency that day. Little wonder. The deceased had been found two days dead lying up under another woman's bed, dressed only in a sun bonnet and a pair of lady's high-button shoes.

No. It wasn't grief that made him do it. But Hazel knew what it was. Maud had finagled Floyd and had the nerve to use Jesus as bait. Because when Maud lost her husband, she professed to have found the Savior. But not in the spiritual sense. She had walked out on her porch and *really* found Him. Sitting there in her husband's favorite rocker.

Hazel had seen the whole thing. On the afternoon of the funeral, all the relatives had been sitting on the porch of the paintless dogtrot house, balancing plates of food on their knees. The men were talking in low voices about cars and crops and the women louder about children and sickness. From out in the barnyard came the yelps of Johnny's cousins trying their best to batter one another senseless in a corncob war.

Now and then one of Floyd's four stepbrothers would sneak an envious peek out into the front yard filled with old black pickups and rusted-out sedans to glimpse Hazel's shiny new 1956 Columbia blue Lincoln, too ashamed to go out to the yard like they wanted to and rub their hands over the hood, and poke their heads in the window to smell the newness and argue out loud about how fast she would do. Instead, they sat sullen in their ill-fitting suits with their clay-streaked brogans tucked up under their chairs.

Their wives, in shapeless straight-cut cotton dresses of dead, dismal colors, permanently scented with snuff and bacon grease, had acted offended when they saw Hazel wearing her sleek silk dress. One at a time, as they caught wind of her perfume, they would cast sideways glances over at their husbands, as if to reassure themselves that their own men had more appetite for turnip greens and cow peas than for gardenias.

Hazel was determined not to pay any of them any mind today. Even with Johnny about to break her lap, Hazel sat erect as a queen at the end of the broken glider, proudly dressed in the only store-bought dress on the porch. She didn't even get upset when Maud, who that very day had taken to using two hickory walking sticks, clumped up to the glider and told Hazel that Johnny wasn't a porch baby anymore, much less a lap baby.

"Ain't you afraid you going to make a sissy out of him?" she asked.

Hazel couldn't believe Maud used to teach school. Poor children, she thought. The woman's questions were so sharp they could put an eye out. But Hazel was determined not to let the old woman get the best of her. She gave Maud a dry grin. "He's fine right the way he is, thank you."

Shrugging, Maud said she guessed it was up to Hazel how she wanted the boy to turn out, but she thought he should be out in the barnyard with his cousins throwing corncobs like a real boy. With that, Maud turned her back on them and clop-clop-shuffle-shuffled away on her walking sticks.

Johnny had just asked his mother what a real boy was and Hazel was about to tell him he already was one and didn't need a knot on his head to prove it when the miracle happened. Maud was standing over the deceased's fox-skin rocker, left vacant out of respect, and directed a question right to it.

"What are you doing here?" Maud asked in a loud voice.

The porch got dead quiet. All eyes were on Maud as she spoke again to the rocker. "Well, who are you and why are you still in your nightshirt?"

At once, everybody's eyes shifted to the empty chair. There was another silent spell as all the relatives leaned in, trying to hear what the rocker had to say.

"How'm I to know you really are Jesus?" she asked. "Prove it."

At that everybody pulled back from Maud and sat straight up in their seats, saying not a word. It was the charged silence of the sort preceding a cattle stampede. Hazel drew Johnny closer as relatives grabbed their glasses of iced tea and dinner plates and fled through the open dogtrot to the back porch, leaving Floyd to handle this new family development. As envious as his family was of Floyd's success, Hazel noticed whenever there was a problem, they were never too envious to let him fix it. They knew him as the kind of man who took care of his own. Plus, nobody had forgiven Floyd for being the sole beneficiary of his father's will. Hazel feared they might be throwing Maud into the bargain.

Floyd walked over to where Maud was standing. "Momma Maud, who are you talking to?"

She looked at Floyd and then at the chair and then back at Floyd again, like he ought to see for himself. When Floyd just stared blankly at her, she answered. "I was speaking to our Savior Jesus Christ the Lord."

"Um-hmm," Floyd said, as if Maud had just told him she wanted eight cylinders instead of six. "I guess we should all pray to Him at times like this."

"I weren't praying to him," Maud scolded. "I was talking to him. Face to face."

Floyd's expression went slack, like any chance for a logical explanation had just died. "Face to face. Like a real person. Like you and me talking right now?"

"Except He talks nicer to me," she said. "Not as uppity as you got to be." Maud gave Hazel an icy look.

"And He proved it was Him? How'd He do that?"

"He opened up His hand and there was your daddy and little Davie smiling up at me from His palm. They looked real happy to be sitting there, resting in the nail-scarred hand of Jesus."

That's when Floyd told Maud she was coming to live with him for a while. Hazel let out an audible moan. Maud shot her a look and then said she had to talk it over with Jesus first. And she did, right then and there. "Well, what do you think, Lord?"

As Maud waited for an answer, Hazel prayed to Jesus for the first time since Davie died. Under her breath she pleaded, "Tell her no. Please, oh, please, tell her no."

Maud nodded at the rocker and looked back at Floyd. "Jesus said it was fine by Him, but He was coming too. And to bring the rocking chair."

Hazel could have shat fire, as her daddy used to say. What was her husband thinking? Maud wasn't his real mother. He didn't even like her that much. Calling her a compromise name like Momma Maud told the story. This was the woman who made him sleep in the barn after she moved in with her own children; packed him a tomato sandwich and handed him a quarter when he was sixteen and told him to leave home, lie about his age, and join the war. She had called his own son retarded. Why weren't her own hillbilly children taking care of the mean old witch? No, leave it to Floyd to fix what wasn't even his.

"Well, it's fine by me if He comes, Momma Maud," Floyd said. "Jesus is sure welcome in our house anytime."

Johnny turned and saw his mother rolling her eyes. Maud saw it, too. But Floyd, seemingly oblivious to the declaration of war happening right under his nose, told Maud he would return the next day with the truck.

Hazel no more believed Maud's little charade than she believed in the Easter rabbit. Maud never had a religious bone in her body and all of a sudden she was on speaking terms with Jesus? But it wouldn't do any good to tell Floyd any of that. Right now he was blinded by duty. It would be up to Hazel to smoke out the old possum.

As Johnny and Hazel sat commiserating over their drinks, waiting for the impending arrival, Hazel thought she would use the occasion to give her son some last-minute instructions in their campaign against Maud. "She's not your actual kin," Hazel told Johnny. "She's only your daddy's stepmother.

"What's step mean?" Johnny asked

"It means not real," she answered, smiling like she did when she was pleased with herself. "I've found it helps to tell yourself that when you've got to be around her for a time. I just close my eyes and say over and over, 'That woman ain't real. That woman ain't real.'" Hazel hooted and slapped her knee. Johnny laughed at seeing his mother so happy for a change.

Then she got serious again and reminded Johnny he only had one real grandmother, her own mother, Granny Baby Ishee. "So don't go calling Maud 'Granny' or 'Memaw' or 'Big Momma' or 'MoMo' or nothing cute like that, you hear? If you have to call her anything, just call her plain old Maud."

"Plain Old Maud." Johnny repeated.

"No, honey, not all them words. Maud. Just the one word. That's all she'll get from us." She winked at Johnny and took another drink. "At least till we can run her out of town and then she might get a 'good-bye' and a 'good riddance.'"

Hazel meant it. She had Maud's number this time. The miserable old woman was going to be in her house under false pretenses and Hazel was going to show her up for the lying cheat she was. Floyd would see the truth and thank her for it. She took another drink, and felt the anger course through her blood like a tonic.

Maybe this could set everything right with Floyd. It was clear he was losing patience with her, waiting for her to come around. His bringing Maud under the same roof, considering how it worked out the last time, just proved how far she had sunk down on the list for success. Not that there hadn't been plenty of clues before this. Floyd had been complaining a lot to Hazel about her drinking and driving. It was far from being a family secret anymore. According to Floyd, she was on her way to becoming a legend across the county.

On several occasions the sheriff had personally driven Hazel and Johnny home, leaving the Lincoln behind straddling ditches or sunk deep in muddy fields. A few weeks after Davie's funeral, she had run a school bus off the road. Luckily the bus had just dropped off the last child and the driver had been drinking himself, so there were no charges brought, but word got out around town just the same. Hayes Alcorn had even made a joke about Hazel in a city council meeting. He cracked that instead of spending money on a siren for when the Russians attacked, that Delphi should have an early-warning system for when Hazel pulled out of her driveway.

To make matters worse, Brother Dear had done a thinly disguised sermon about Hazel titled, "You Can't Drive Jesus Away," which used a lot of traffic violations like hit-and-run and passing-on-a-bridge and going-the-wrong-way-down-a-one-way-street as metaphors for the deadly sins. Hazel sat red-faced through the entire service and gripped Johnny's hand until his fingers drained white.

She tipped the glass, finishing off the last few drops, and said to Johnny, "That's the last one. I'm going to straighten up and fly right from here on out."

For the first time since she could remember, Hazel felt alive again. Her husband needed her help. Her profound hatred for Maud had given her a new sense of purpose.

When Floyd returned with his stepmother and the rocker, he moved them both into the sewing room off the parlor. Hazel had positioned herself next to the stairs and watched silently, sizing up her enemy. Standing in the doorway of her new room, Maud was leaning pitifully on her sticks, with a saintly look on her face. But she didn't fool Hazel.

"I'm a little tuckered from the ride," Maud said to Floyd, ignoring Hazel's icy presence. "I think I'll spend some time with our Savior thanking Him for my safe journey." She shut the door behind her.

"Ha! Spend some time with your snuff is what you doing," Hazel said, not very quietly.

Floyd exhaled heavily. Then he turned to Hazel. "The best solution solves more than one problem."

Hazel waited for the translation for this new saying, even though it sounded an awful lot like the one about killing two birds at the same time. Or was it two birds living in the same bush throwing stones at each other?

"Well, the way I see it," he explained, ushering her into the kitchen, "Momma Maud just wants some attention. Afraid of being forgotten out there on the farm. She'll drop this Jesus stuff soon enough."

"You mean you don't believe her?" she asked, crestfallen.

"Course not. My plan is just humor Maud and get her to feeling useful. Let her help take care of the house while we help take care of her. That way, it'll save us from looking for a maid who won't gossip our affairs all over town. And who won't sit around all day and steal us blind while you're..." Floyd hesitated and then said, "while you're out driving."

He cocked his head to the side and grinned, but something about it looked strained. "See?" he said, "Two problems solved at once. We take care of her. She takes care of us."

Hazel felt the old dread returning. Floyd wasn't telling it all. There was something else. "How's she going to take care of us? She's too old and crippled to get around."

"Weeelll," Floyd said gingerly, like he was about to get to the real truth of the matter. "Maybe she could show you what to do. Maybe even teach you to cook and keep house. Don't you think it's time you started to stay at home and do them things?"

It was like a slap in the face. The first thing that came into her mind was the sampler Miss Ellen had made for their wedding present. In seven short years, Hazel had run through Faith and Hope and had moved right on to Charity. The same sense of obligation that made Floyd take in that horrible old woman was now the only thing that prevented him from throwing Hazel out.

When Hazel tried to speak, no words would come. There was only the opening and closing of her mouth, like a perch tossed up on the creek bank. But Floyd wouldn't have noticed because he was looking right past her and out the back door where the mower still sat broken on the porch.

Chapter 22
A MANGER SCENE

As much as Hazel hated cooking, she hated Maud worse, so meals usually consisted of some skillet-fried meat accompanied by a vegetable that didn't require anything more chancy than boiling water and tossing in a piece of fatback for seasoning. Any bread but bought loaf bread was out of the question. Even though Hazel felt she was now cooking for her keep, she was determined not to ask that old woman for a thing.

At every meal, Maud insisted Hazel set an extra place at the table for Jesus, always on her left side. Maud said that was her good ear. Sometimes she just chatted casually with Jesus, like a neighbor who had happened by at suppertime. "You wont some of these overcooked collard greens, Lord?" she would ask, filling his plate. "How's yore momma doing?"

Other times she would ask him for advice. Once after Johnny had come home crying, she consulted Jesus about it at the supper table. "What you think Johnny oughta do about that bully that keeps pushing him down at Sunday school?"

Johnny waited breathlessly for his answer from the Lord.

"What's that you say, Lord? The bigger they are, the harder they fall? You saying Johnny ought to ball up his fist and give that rascal his due?" Maud watched for Johnny's face to cloud up with worry and then smiled a satisfied little grin.

"What about turning the other cheek?" Hazel snapped. "Seems like I read Him saying something about that. You sure it's Jesus you got on the line?"

But Hazel had to be careful. Maud was just as liable to take down a message for her. "Well there you are!" she said. "Jesus, do you see the unchristian way Hazel treats me? Did you mark that down in your holy record book?"

Hazel just sighed into a forkful of collards, but Maud continued. "I don't mean to tell you your business, but sending her to H-E-double-L sounds a little severe. After all, I suppose I am just a burden to her. Why not give her another chance to be decent?" Maud smiled at her stepson, like she was doing him a special favor by keeping his wife and the mother of his child out of Hell.

"Where's Jesus taking Momma?" Johnny asked, almost in tears.

"Eat your peas, Little Monkey," said Floyd, who mostly ignored Maud when these impromptu prayer meetings erupted. He had told Hazel to pay no mind either, because the more upset Hazel got, the more it seemed Jesus had to say.

Sometimes Hazel just couldn't resist. "I sure don't need you asking any favors for me," she said. "In fact I'd appreciate being left out of y'all's little chats completely."

Maud ignored her. "Have mercy on her, Lord. I'm sure she's got other things on her mind. The way she been dranking and all. But I don't have to tell you about that, Lord. You got your eye on ever sparrow, don't you?" she asked the Lord, but peeked over at Floyd, who just kept right on chewing.

At supper on Christmas Eve, things came to a head. Maud clop-clop-shuffle-shuffled into the kitchen to join the others and commented that Hazel hadn't set a place for Jesus.

"Well, I figured he would be too busy delivering presents to eat," Hazel said as she dipped the butter beans from the cast-iron pot on the stove.

Maud got all huffy. "Jesus don't deliver presents. You know good and well you're talking about Santy Clause."

Even though Hazel swore it was an honest mistake, Maud wouldn't let it go. She insisted she was being persecuted for her beliefs just like the Pilgrims.

"Well, you might consider that other people have their beliefs, too," Hazel shot back. "You might notice that, if you weren't so busy hogging Jesus for your ownself." Two could play at this game, Hazel thought.

Without missing a beat, Maud said, "Jesus'll go anywheres He's called. And in yore case, Hazel Ishee, you ort best get yore hands on His emergency number." Maud leaned in on her canes. "And I'd give you the nickel to make the call if it would do you any good. But you ain't on speaking terms with the Savior, are you? He tole me all about it."

Floyd pinched the bridge of his nose and sighed. "Hazel, just set the Lord a place and don't argue."

But Hazel took the bait. "What He tell you?"

"He said you were blaming Him for yore own doing. Jesus said He didn't want to take away yore little boy. But you was too prideful. Yore like a horse that's got to be broke to saddle."

Hazel's face went slack. With the skill of a fisherman landing a ten-pound bass, Maud put a little play in the line. She smiled as close to a compassionate smile as she had probably ever come.

"Hazel, honey," she said sorrowfully, "that's why He took Davie. So you'll come back to Him on bended knees. Jesus said He's waiting for you with love in his heart."

Hazel just stood there frozen, a bowl of butter beans in her hands. Her eyes, dark and dangerous, were fixed on Maud.

"Hazel, are you OK?" Floyd's voice was full of trepidation. "Put the beans on the table, honey. Before they get cold. All right?"

Hazel didn't move. Floyd reached out for the bowl and carefully disarmed his wife. He set the beans on the table, but never took his eyes off Hazel.

Finally Hazel spoke. Her words were eerily calm and measured. "Floyd. If this woman is going to stay another night. Under this roof. She'll have to stop talking to Jesus. Do you understand what I'm saying to you? Floyd?"

Before Floyd could answer, Maud was back full-bore. "Well, God forgive you for that blasphemy!" she fired. "I know you don't mean to deny the Good Lord His say. I'll ask Him not to send you straight to H-E-dou-ble-," and then she barked, "HELL!" without bothering to spell it out.

The pronged vein leaped in Hazel's forehead and her voice got real thin and tight, like it would snap if she hit a word too hard. "That's exact-ly the thing that's got to stop. No matter how you try to wrap a smile around it, you just told me to go to Hell. You heard her, Floyd. Your step-mother tole me to go to Hell in my own house."

"No, I didn't," Maud protested, taking a step toward Hazel, her knuckles whitening on her canes. "I told you I would ask Him *not* to send you there. It's a Christian thing I'm doing." Her voice crackling like dead leaves, she said, "And what's more, I'll ask Him to forgive you for being such a vile little bitch!"

Hazel lunged for Maud's throat. Maud quickly aimed both her canes at Hazel. Before Hazel could fight her way through Maud's defenses, Floyd wedged himself between them, putting the flat of each hand against an opposing chest.

"You two got to stop this! My wife and stepmomma trying to kill each other on Christmas Eve. Right in front of the child here." Floyd looked around for Johnny to prove his point, but the boy was nowhere to be seen, having fled to watch the Christmas tree from his haven behind the couch.

Maud lowered her canes and then dropped her head and waggled it side to side. "Now look what I've done," she whimpered. "Just put me in the Jackson Home for Wore Out Women."

Regaining some of her composure, Hazel replied, "It ain't you being old that's the problem. It's your being mean and crazy. It's the Lunatic Asylum you ought to be packing your bags for."

"Hazel, don't rile her again!" Floyd snapped.

Crooking her neck to see around Floyd, Maud said, "You sayin I'm crazy cause I got Jesus on my side? You just jealous you can't get nobody to be on yores." She gave Floyd a tender, snuff-stained smile and sidled up next to him like an old yellow cat.

Hazel waited for Floyd to speak up. However, he stood there silent on the matter of whose side he was on.

"Like the Good Book says, Hazel," Maud proclaimed, "'If the Lord be for you, who can be agin you?' It's Jesus you ought to be asking to get on your side."

Maud's words, since they were obviously from the Bible, resonated with infallibility, and knocked the breath out of any possible comeback Hazel could have thought up. The old woman clop-clop-shuffle-shuffled victoriously into the parlor, plopped down onto the couch, and pulled the giant-sized family Bible off the banana table and onto her lap.

As a motorized wheel of tinted cellophane rotated before a bare bulb, turning the aluminum Christmas tree from red to blue to green and back to red again, Maud flipped through the Bible mumbling to herself. Behind her, scrunched between the couch and the wall, was Johnny. He hadn't meant to eavesdrop, but this was where he went every evening after supper to watch the tree magically change colors. He could make out bits and pieces of what she said.

"Pride and vanity...fancy automobiles...turning men's heads... whistling women and crowing hens never do come to any good ends." Her voice dropped to a low growl. "Why did you leave me, you sorry son of bitch?"

Johnny was quite surprised to hear her talk to Jesus that way. Now he was interested.

"Put up with your nasty temper. Your cheating and lying. Cooked and cleaned. Worked the fields. It was *me* what kept it all together ever time the price of cotton dropped and the bank threatened. It was *me* who got the crop in ever time you found you a woman to lay up with. We make it through flood and drought and boll weevils. We get through all that and then you die and leave it all to *him* and me to charity. To people who hate me. I ain't never gone get my home back. He gone kick us off for shore." Maud began sobbing, "It ain't fair! It just ain't fair." The words made pitiful gurgling noises in her throat.

Johnny jumped out from behind the couch and yelled, "Don't cry, Maud. I don't hate you!"

Maud's mouth flew open and, terrified, she threw her arms up in the air, which Johnny took as an invitation to clamber into her lap and give her neck a hug. But when she was able to speak, she said, "Where the hell'd you come from? You been spying on me?"

"You was crying," Johnny said, still clutching her around the neck.

"No, I wasn't!" she said pulling him off. "I was talking to Jesus. In private!"

"No, you wasn't," he insisted. "You was talking to Papaw Graham."

At that she jumped up to her feet, sending Johnny tumbling to the floor. "You callin me crazy?" she spat. "Papaw's dead. Jesus is who I'm talkin to."

Maud took off in a huff, abandoning her canes and tromping out of the room without the slightest limp.

Racing to the kitchen to tell his parents of Maud's miraculous recovery, he stopped short at the closed door. On the other side, he heard them hissing in whispers. His father was saying something about her trying harder and his mother said something about her having done everything but have the wise men over for coffee and his father saying something about her being too sensitive for her own good and then the back door slammed. When Johnny ventured into the kitchen he found his father sitting at the table studying his hands.

"Where's Momma?"

Floyd looked up with weary eyes. "Out driving."

Without Hazel, the house was graveyard quiet. Maud stayed in her room; Floyd sat at the table casting about for a plan to save his business from his wife; and Johnny fell asleep worrying about the whereabouts of both Santa Claus and his mother.

A little past one o'clock in the morning, Floyd grabbed the phone after the first ring. It was the sheriff. It seemed that Hazel had driven through his yard, smashed into Hertha's life-size nativity scene, and sent one of the sheep crashing through her parlor room window. Hazel had come to a stop in a clump of nandina bushes.

The sheriff sounded groggy. "I think she's OK. Just a little too much...well, driving. She must of really put on some miles tonight."

When Floyd said he would be right over to get Hazel, the sheriff told him not to bother himself. "Everthing's under control," he assured him. "I'm getting some black coffee down your wife and a sleeping pill down mine. Didn't even wake the girls. I'll carry Hazel over directly."

Hazel smiled at the sheriff as he came back into the kitchen. Then she wondered if she was smiling at all, her face being as numb as it was. So she tried harder.

The sheriff looked at her expectantly, like he was waiting for her to say what was so funny. Then he smiled back. Focusing the best she could, Hazel watched him as he poured her another cup of coffee. She felt sorry for him the way Hertha had gone on like she did. Probably embarrassed the poor man to death. Her shouting and carrying on over that silly old sheep. Nothing worse than a woman that can't control herself. Hazel pulled her shoulders up.

Leaning back with his hands propped against the counter, and his boots crossed at the ankles, the sheriff smoked his cigarette without removing it from his mouth, the cloud curling up into his face, his eyes squinting against it. Hazel figured he could finish an entire cigarette without out laying a hand on it. To her he looked like a cowboy star. But not the old kind that wore a white hat and drank milk. Not a goody two shoes. But the new sexy kind of cowboy. The outsider who had a dark secret in his past and looked like he could go either way and kept you guessing until the very end. Of course he would finally do right, but only reluctantly. Because down deep, his nature was basically good, in spite of what the small-minded townspeople thought.

"I'll take you home when you ready," he said. "I think we can get the car out this time no problem."

Sensing her head dropping forward, Hazel snapped it back with a jerk. She wiped her chin with the back of her hand where she had drooled just a bit. She hoped the sheriff hadn't noticed her nodding off like that. What was he saying? The car? Oh, yes, the Lincoln parked in the manger with the cows and the remaining sheep. And she was alone in the kitchen with the sheriff. That's right. He had sent Hertha upstairs. It was all clear to her again. She had a handle on things.

Hazel knew she needed to say something, even though her tongue felt as stiff as a sausage. Determined to sound sober, she weighed and measured each word as she said it. "You…make…'lishhuss…coffee. Shurff. I'd like anothern, don't mind."

"Well, I just poured you that one."

Hazel giggled and said he was right, she remembered him doing that now that he mentioned it. The sheriff just stood there smiling at her. Hazel wondered again what he saw in Hertha. He was such a nice-looking man. Almost pretty in a dangerous kind of way. Long black wavy hair. Sulking eyes with lashes a woman would envy. A face that looked hurt and angry and starved for love all at the same time.

She felt alive around the sheriff. Like something was about to happen that could change everything. Something that could knock the world off its dead center butt. Like the feeling she used to get riding with those route men in the hills. Like when Floyd first swaggered into the drugstore in tight-fitting bell-bottoms fresh from the Navy. Full of plans and hope and room for her.

"You just finish that one up and I'll pour you anothern. OK?"

Hazel thought she might have just winked at him. She hoped not. Sober, Hazel couldn't even look the sheriff in the eye. But after she had been drinking, she could feel the thrill that lay beneath the fear. It was worth getting stuck in the mud to have him come rescue her. Being with him was like riding danger piggyback. Like moving with the eye of a hurricane. Like driving eighty on the soft shoulder of a ridge road. Like singing a hymn at the top of your lungs while a storm raged outside, knowing you were safe and dry and it was only other people who were getting hurt. It was like having the devil on your side. Who needed Jesus anyway, when you had all that?

She wished she could tell him about the dream she had been having about Jesus. How He tells her to walk with Him across the Hopalachie River. She tells Him she didn't think she's up to walking on water but Jesus says all she needed was a little faith, hope, and charity. When they get to the middle of the river, she realizes that she is all bound up with barbed wire, and the engine to the Lincoln is tied around her neck. She begins to sink to the bottom.

But what she wanted to tell the sheriff was, it's not so bad. The water is dark and warm and the current caresses her like a lover. It's kind of peaceful down there where the only thing you can hear is the underwater rush in your ears. She wanted to ask him what he thought it meant. And what it means that in the dream he is standing on the shore watching, smiling knowingly, like he has seen it all before. But she couldn't tell him any of this. She knew her tongue was not up to all the words.

The sheriff reached up into the cabinet and pulled down a bottle of bonded whiskey and poured himself a shot. "Merry Christmas," he said, lifting the glass at Hazel.

"Happy Yew Near!" Hazel said, returning the toast by sloshing coffee over the side of her cup. It took a moment for her to realize that she had said the wrong thing. She laughed at her mistake to let him know she wasn't all that drunk. "I mean, Happy Near Yew." No, that didn't sound right either.

"Happy Near You, too." The sheriff winked at Hazel. Then he grinned and tossed back his drink. Hazel returned his wink and grin, not feeling at all like he was laughing at her. No, he liked her, she could tell. The sheriff was on her side.

Maud and Floyd were waiting in the door when the sheriff led Hazel up the walk, his arm around her waist pulling her tightly to him for balance. Lost in the aroma of cigarettes and Old Spice, she was disappointed when the porch steps came into focus. She could have strolled with him like this all the way down the bluffs and clear out into the Delta night.

"Hazel! Are you all right?" Floyd took over from the sheriff, but his handling wasn't as gentle. After he got her in the house, he grabbed Hazel by her shoulders and shook her once. "You could have killed somebody!" His eyes widened at the thought. "She didn't, did she, Sheriff?"

"Nope. Not that we know of. You didn't kill nobody, did you, Hazel?"

Hazel turned and saw her friend grinning by her side and she grinned back. "Only in self-defense." She winked at the sheriff like he understood what she meant, but he just shrugged it off with a grin and said his goodnight.

Maud didn't waste any time getting started. "Floyd, you've got to forgive Hazel. I'm sure she didn't mean to ruin your reputation by parking herself drunk in the sheriff's yard."

Hazel's face lit up. "That's how stupid you are, old woman. I *did* do it on purpose," she announced proudly.

"Hazel!" Floyd shook her again. "You're still drunk as Cooter Brown."

"Maybe, but I still did it on purpose. When I saw that tiny baby in that manger, I knew I had to kill it. Had to get it before it grew up and made my life hell. I aimed the car right for that little crib. I think I got Him."

"You tried to kill Jesus?" Maud said incredulously. "Girl, you as crazy as a betsy bug. You can't kill Jesus. He's going to live forever. Whether you like it or not!"

"Not in my house He ain't. If He can't talk nice then out He goes." Hazel flung her arm so hard showing Jesus the way out, she toppled over. Floyd caught her. She looked up into his face. It seemed frozen in disbelief. Didn't he understand? Everything was so clear now to her. Life could go ahead and roar past them like a freight train. She had everything under control. She had won.

Only Hazel wished Floyd would stop staring! What was he looking at? Then she turned and peered into the mirror that hung in the entryway. There she saw a madwoman, her hair in wild tangles and long black fingers of mascara reaching for her throat. Lipstick smeared almost to her ears, like a circus clown gone mad. A pair of dead eyes peered back at her from the farthest reaches of hell. This was what the sheriff had been grinning at.

Floyd spoke softly, carefully. "Hazel, it ain't Jesus' fault."

For a long time she stared blankly at Floyd. A cold rain began to fall. Through the window raindrops lit up like snowflakes as they passed through the halo of the yard lights.

When Hazel spoke, it was as a small girl. "Then whose fault is it, Floyd?"

His eyes offered her nothing.

"Tell me," she asked, "When is somebody going to be on my side?" Without expecting an answer, she dropped her head on her husband's chest and he led her off to bed.

1956

Chapter 23
BROKEN THINGS

"Git!" Johnny yelled from up on the porch. "And don't neither one of y'all stupid girls come back in my yard. I'll shoot you both." Nobody was going to get away with saying that about *his* mother.

He watched LaNelle and LouAnne Brister retreat and didn't take his eye off them until he saw the sisters disappear through their own back door. It was early February, his mother had been gone for a week and Johnny still didn't understand why, and the girls' answer had only infuriated him. It was true that his father had left his mother at a hospital called Whitfield down in Jackson, but he was sure the place wasn't a nuthouse like the girls had said.

Still indignant, he tramped inside to look for his father, whom he found sitting on the kitchen floor. "Daddy! What's a drunk?"

Floyd glanced up from the vacuum cleaner, the motor in pieces all about him. "Why? Who's been talking about drunk?"

"LaNelle said Momma was a drunk."

Floyd frowned. "That right?"

Billy Dean Brister's little girl had wasted no time in telling every person she saw about what had happened in her front yard Christmas Eve. The evening that, thanks to Brother Dear's ad-libbed quip to a packed house, became better known as "the night shepherds kept watch over their flocks in flight."

"LaNelle said Momma got sent to Whitfield with the crazy people for being a drunk and for running down baby Jesus."

"Um-hmm. Hand me that belt before you step on it."

Cautiously, Johnny picked up the greasy thing by his foot, catching it between his thumb and index finger and handing it to his father like a bait worm. Floyd inspected the belt and then looked up at Johnny again.

"Now, son, your momma might drink some, but she's not your average drunk. Your average drunk drinks to get drunk. For no better reason than that. Pure and simple. But your momma, now. She's different. She drinks when she gets mad."

"In fact," Floyd said thoughtfully, as if the conclusion was just congealing in his mind, "you might say your mother drinks *at* people." He smiled at Johnny. "So when she comes home, we got to make sure we don't get her riled up. You hear?"

"LaNelle said Momma was getting letter cooted."

"Electrocuted. Girl knows a lot for a six-year-old, don't she?" Floyd put the belt down and picked up the vacuum cleaner hose.

"It's like this," Floyd explained, "your momma's got all these thoughts backed up in her head that get her upset and make her want to drink. And when she's not drinking, they make her want to stay in her room and sleep. How come her to go to bed after Christmas and not get up."

"Momma was tired."

"That's right. They call it depression. And down at Whitfield they got this special kind of machine that will suck up all the sad thoughts that can't get out by theirselves."

He put the hose up to his head to demonstrate and made a sucking noise with his mouth. Johnny's eyes widened. "That way, she'll have room for some brand-new ones. You and me'll have to be extra nice so all her new thoughts will be happy ones."

Even though Floyd reassured him that his mother could be fixed, Johnny didn't feel any better. Once he had brought his daddy a cow that was supposed to moo when you turned him upside down, but the moo part was broken. Johnny had watched as the magical innards of his cow spilled out before him. With his father a simple tweak or twist would never do. Everything required a major overhaul. To give him credit, though, he did bring the moo back. But Johnny never wanted to play with the cow again. His daddy could put everything back but the magic.

"Understand?" his daddy asked, the hose still up to his head.

"Yes sir," Johnny answered dubiously.

When Floyd dropped the hose to the floor, one of Johnny's rubber balls came rolling out.

"Hmm," Floyd said. "I guess it waddent the motor after all."

When Hazel had retreated to her bedroom after Christmas, Maud took over the house with a vengeance, determined to make a permanent place for herself. Miraculously, Jesus told her to lay down her canes and dedicate herself to returning the household to the ways of the Lord. Refusing to let Floyd bring in a maid to help, she insisted on doing it all herself.

She rebuked what she called the vanity of household appliances, which she claimed had brought down many a family. So, instead of letting Johnny show her how to use the washer and dryer, she put all the clothes in a galvanized washtub on the back porch and scrubbed them on a rub board, in spite of it being the middle of winter. Every time Johnny tried to help her she would have none of it. Maud said that real boys didn't follow women around when they did their chores.

She was able to keep it up full steam for a few weeks, until Floyd took Hazel to Whitfield, and Maud began to slow. It was like without Hazel to push off against, she lost her ability to propel herself. Lately, Johnny was becoming worried about Maud. He thought she appeared to be shrinking and her color was fading to a chalky gray. More and more she would sit in the parlor with the big Bible in her lap, staring off into space, looking tired.

One afternoon he came into the darkened room to check on her, to see if any more of her had disappeared. When she saw him she snapped, "What you wont?"

"Nothing," he said, examining the reddened eyes that loomed large behind her glasses. "You tuckered out, Maud?"

"Don't you worry about me, Mr. Smarty Mouth. I got your number." She narrowed her gaze at the boy, and for a moment she seemed to be revived. "You just like her ain't you?" she said, almost hopefully. "Don't think for a minute I don't know what you doing sneakin in your momma's room when you think nobody's lookin. Jesus sees everything."

Maud tried to pin him down with her sharp-as-needles stare, but she didn't easily intimidate Johnny anymore. Since the night he had caught her crying to her dead husband, she wasn't nearly as scary. Anyway, he knew it was Maud, not Jesus, who had been skulking cane-less around the house spying on him. So Johnny just crossed his arms over his chest and pooched out his bottom lip defiantly.

Seeing she couldn't browbeat him, she said darkly, "You know, Jesus don't abide sissies. He's gone get you."

That made Johnny mad at Maud, even if she was old and pitiful. "You're mean and Jesus is mean, too. I wish He would grab you by your stanky old feet and pull you to Hell. And you were too talking to Papaw Graham!"

"There you are," Maud said, almost gloating. "Enough pride to choke a shoat. At least you come by it natural." Maud waggled her head pitifully and said she only hoped she wasn't too late. "That mother of yours teach you how to count?"

"Yeah."

"Yes, ma'am."

"Yes, ma'am," Johnny grudgingly obliged. "I can count to a hunnurd."

"There's more of that Ishee pride for you." She got out of the chair and grabbed his hand and jerked him out of the parlor, down the stairhall and into the kitchen, where she stood him in the corner.

"Since you're so smart, I wont you to recite a special verse I use on willful little boys like you." Maud assumed the shrill, monotone voice of a teacher in front of the class.

> *One-two-three. The Devil's in Me.*
> *Four-five-six. I will get several licks.*
> *Seven-eight-nine. I must get myself in line.*
> *Ten-eleven-twelve. I must conquer myself.*

The old woman dared him to say it. Johnny repeated the verse fast and without a mistake, which seemed to make Maud all the madder. "All right, Mr. Smarty Mouth, now get me the fly flap."

Johnny stomped over to the door and lifted up on his tiptoes to reach the swatter that hung on a nail in the frame. With his jaw locked in defiance, he thrust it out to her.

"Every time you make a mistake, you going to get a reminding switch on the back of your legs."

Holding on to his arm with one hand and gripping the swatter in the other, she said with a thin overlay of sympathy, "If somebody had only loved your momma enough to break her pride when she was a girl. It's up to me to make sure you don't get bit by the same dog." She tightened her grip. "Now begin, boy!"

Johnny said the verse ten times without dropping a stitch. On the eleventh verse, she loosened her handhold. Somewhere around fifteen she let go completely. But she said not a word and Johnny kept on reciting, flaunting his success. From behind him, he heard her draw a long breath, which rattled her lungs. When he turned to look up at her, her face had drained white. She wasn't even looking at him.

"I just don't know," she said to no one in particular. She slowly turned away and trudged over to the table, where she dropped herself down onto a kitchen chair.

She sat there quietly, her shoulders slumped forward, and her arms limp at her sides, the fly swatter dangling from a finger. Her glasses had slipped down the bridge of her nose, and her eyes stared over the rims, looking at nothing. "I wanna go home," she said to no one, like a little girl lost.

For a long while, Johnny studied the old woman. She had forgotten her teeth again and her mouth had collapsed into a series of snuff-stained furrows. Unmagnified by her glasses, Maud's eyes were like painful little sores in her head. Her breathing came in quick pitiful gasps. It was clear to him that she was suffering.

"Maud?" he said gently, and she looked at him blankly. "Don't be sad. You gonna see Papaw again." Thinking of Brother Dear's advice, he added, "Papaw ain't gonna stay dead if you remember him."

He couldn't tell if she had heard him or not. She just continued to stare at him through the little sores, unblinking. He carefully walked up to her, lifted himself up on his toes, and kissed her lightly on her cold, clammy cheek. She looked at him, pleading, and said softly, like he was the one to be asking, "I wont to go home now."

Not knowing what else to do or to say, he left her sitting alone in the kitchen. There were other things that needed tending to before his father came home.

Once in his mother's room, he locked the door and went into her closet. There he found the big straw purse his mother carried for their rides in the country.

Maud shouldn't have been surprised at his capacity to remember her little verses. Remembering and Forgetting had become all-consuming concepts for Johnny. Like Leaving and Staying and Returning. At the funeral, Brother Dear had leaned down and put his hand on his shoulder and said that Davie would live as long as Johnny remembered him.

Now his mother had gone away to forget. Too many things were getting lost.

Johnny walked over to his mother's dressing table. To get into the chair, he used a hatbox for a step. One at a time, he examined each item his mother had left behind on the tabletop—the tube of blood-red lipstick, the little mascara brush, the shiny pair of earbobs she had put on and then decided against the very morning she left. The silver hairbrush she used every night before she went to bed. Counting the strokes into numbers beyond Johnny's comprehension. What were those numbers called? he wondered.

Trying hard to remember, he began brushing his own hair. As he watched himself in the mirror, Johnny imagined his mother spread out in a million pieces on somebody's kitchen floor at the State Hospital in Whitfield, with men who were good with their hands like his father hovering over her, fitting her back together again.

What bothered him most was the possibility that those men who were so good with their hands might have a part left over, like his father did sometimes, and throw it away. What if the part they left out was the part that remembered him? Already, his mother seemed to have lost the part that remembered Davie. The last few times he had asked about his brother, she would just stare at him curiously, like she didn't know who it was he was talking about.

Not able to remember any more numbers, Johnny set down the brush and began to carefully pack up his mother's perfumes and lotions and powders and scented creams into the straw purse. When he had finished, he toted the purse into the closet with him. He quietly pulled the door closed. There, alone in the dark, he took out the containers, one by one, and uncapped them all.

Sitting cross-legged on the closet floor with his eyes shut tight, he summoned his mother's face into his mind's eye, and finally, enveloped by all of her smells, breathed his mother's memory into the deepest parts of him.

Chapter 24
LEAVING THE PLANTATION

It was bone-racking cold as Vida and Willie hurried down the road leading away from One Wing Hannah's. Since running into Sweet Pea there months earlier, Vida had taken to going quite regularly with her brother. Folks gossiped when they drank. It was a place to hear things. It was the first step in the plan she was brewing to close in on the sheriff.

Tonight the moon shone full across the desolate fields and illuminated thousands of dead stalks, a legion of skeletons waiting patiently for burial under the spring plow. The old army jacket Vida wore was missing all its buttons, so she walked hunched, hugging herself, keeping the front of the jacket shut against the icy wind.

Vida had been frightened all week. For the first time ever, when she closed her eyes, she could barely recall Nate's face. Even when she pulled his picture out of the crate underneath her bed, he seemed more like a dream she had one night long ago than a flesh-and-blood boy who had once tugged at her plaits, the fussy little child who couldn't get to sleep unless he was holding on tight to her father's gold chain.

"Hands, Momma. Hands," he would cry. She remembered his words but couldn't hear his voice. As the wind whistled past her ears, she repeated softly to herself, "Drivin a big black car for a big white man."

Willie was walking ahead of her, his gait determined tonight. As he stepped, Vida heard the sound of whiskey bottles clanking together. She could read his thoughts as clear as the glass that chimed from his coat. Her brother hadn't said it yet, but he had found a way out. He was ready to strike out on his own, leaving her behind with their father. She would never get away if that happened. Now was as good a time as any to start in on him.

"I been thinkin, Willie," she called ahead. The night was bright enough for Vida to see her words as she spoke. "I might take me a little work in Delphi."

That made Willie giggle and he slowed to let her catch up. "So that what you been doin sneakin off to Delphi ever chance you get. You been job lookin." He laughed again. "What you gone to do, sister? Find you a white lady to clean up after?" Willie bent over nearly double and acted like he was stirring with a washing stick. "Maybe get you a big ol' black pot and boil white folks' dirty clothes?"

Waving his hand at Vida, he said with a laugh, "Get on from here! You wouldn't last a week. Not with yo nasty temper. They find you grinnin over some dead white woman with an ice pick in yo hand, her wrong last word still warm on her lips."

"You funny like ringworm, Willie."

Again Vida noticed the clanking of glass. "I know what you up to, Willie. You got yore own ticket out. And me and Daddy can't make no crop. Not just the both of us. Not the way he is."

There followed a spell of silence. Just as she thought. Willie didn't say a word to deny her prediction.

"Besides," Vida continued, "the way the Senator keeps workin them cotton machines, won't be a cropper left on the plantation in a year. We all gone get tractored off the land, and still owin him money. Then he own us for sho. I guess we all need to be makin our plans."

"Yeah, but workin for a white woman? That ain't gone to suit you. Them neither. The only thing nastier than yo temper is yo cookin. And them white houses got all them washin and cleanin machines. And lectric cookers. You end up fryin yoself stead of the chicken."

"Well, that might be. But how somebody tole it to me, they is only two ways for a colored girl to get on. Find a white lady or git a white man. And if it's all right by you, I'm thinkin I'll commence with a white lady. I'll learn what I got to learn. Always have. Maybe I can find me a white woman that don't know no better."

Vida didn't mention she already had one in her sights. The time she spent in Delphi was devoted to learning as much as she could about the goings-on of the town's white inhabitants. She knew where the sheriff lived and had studied his house hours at a time from behind a holly bush. She had seen the crazy goings-on at the next-door neighbors, where the pitiful white woman lived. Nobody the man hired as a maid ever lasted, because he would accuse them of stealing from him before they finished out the day.

A sudden gust of stinging cold air hit them head on, making them haul their shoulders up to their ears. On the wind was the smell of wood smoke from the little cluster of shacks on up ahead. Not a mile beyond was their own cabin. They picked up their pace and the bottles hidden in the lining of the special coat Hannah had given Willie rang out louder.

Vida was panting now, trying to keep up with the pace Willie was setting. "You bein careful sellin that stuff?" she called up to him. "Hannah ain't gone git you shot, is she? That's the sheriff's money y'all messin with."

"One day I take more than his money," was all he said. He just kept moving forward, his chin tucked down against the wind.

Vida knew Willie hated the sheriff as bad as she did. They had both watched their father as he lost everything. The house, his churches, his respect, and according to Willie, his mind. As for Vida, she had found a way to stop the useless flow of tears. Even though it was the sheriff she wanted dead, she soothed herself with visions of murdering white people. She thought of smothering them in their beds with feather pillows. Tying up their children in croaker sacks and dropping them off the bridge over the Hopalachie River. Burning whole families alive in their houses. Cooking them in wash pots. Boiling them alive with the lye soap. Vida had come up with more than a hundred ways to kill a white person.

The one she liked best of all was getting every cook from all the white kitchens together and settling on a day to put rat poison in the soup. She figured she could wipe out the county's entire white population over supper. The fantasy helped the disagreeable idea of being a maid go down easier.

"Well," Vida said, moving in to close the deal, "since you ain't said nothin sensible against it, me lookin for some work and all, I reckon we both done with sharecroppin. It's gone mean lettin go of the place. Gettin a house in Delphi. How that sound to you?"

"How you gone settle up the Senator?" Willie asked. "We still owe him from what we came up short again last fall. He ain't gone let you go nowheres."

"I thought bout that. I say we let the plot go back to the Senator while we can, and hire on as day workers. Pay it off that way."

"That gone take a year. Maybe two."

"You right," Vida said carefully, "But I reckon if you set on runnin shine for Hannah—and you sure you ain't gone get shot—we might can settle by spring even. Might be you could ask Hannah for a little advance. If you willin, that is."

She waited, praying he would say yes.

After a short pause, he did.

When they approached their cabin, all the lights were out, but in the moonlight Vida could see a figure of a lone man slumped over in a chair on their porch. She hated seeing him like this, hated it because it tempted her pity, and pity was a thing she could not afford to feel.

"What you doin settin in the cold, Daddy?" Vida called out. "It's shiverin out."

Levi sat up, startled. He was wearing his full dress suit with the gold watch chain across his belly, leading now to an empty pocket. Still half asleep, Levi looked around to get his bearings. "Who that there? Who talkin to me?"

Reaching up under his father's arm and helping him to his feet, Willie said, "You been down to the bayou ain't you? You been preachin to the frogs tonight."

Levi jerked loose from his son. "I can walk. I ain't feeble. I ain't crazy neither."

"Willie didn't call you crazy," Vida said, even though she knew he thought it.

She didn't agree with Willie. Not really. Levi Snow had to preach, that's all there was to it. If the only congregation that would let him shout the words he loved were swamp animals and unseen spirits, then he would take that. It wasn't craziness. It was weakness.

She probably shouldn't begrudge him for that. At least he had found a way to be with what had been taken from him. As for Vida, there wasn't a night that passed she didn't worry about where Nate was laying his head. Nor a dawn that broke without her wondering was anybody feeding him breakfast. Nor did a storm approach without her fearing for Nate's being in its path. He was nine years old tonight and still her baby. But now his face was fading from her mind.

Vida closed the cabin door to the cold and pressed the flat of her back against the planks. The wind seemed to saw through the wood itself. He catches cold so easily, she thought. Was there somebody with him tonight to throw a warm quilt over him? Was Rezel there with her boy?

Driving a big black car
For a big white man.

As the wind seeped through the door and into her bones, Vida imagined she could soak up all the cold winds in the world until there was not a breeze left to do harm to her baby. She banged a fist against the door. How silly! she thought. The world was too big a place. Too cold a place. And she was too stupid a person. The time for wishing and waiting and piecing rhymes onto a shred of a song was over. For too long she had waited for news of Nate. She had made too many promises that she would get to him as soon as he sent word.

Vida listened to the wind. Maybe tonight he was trying to speak. She remembered late one evening, years ago, when she was still a little girl, she had been sitting out on Lillie Dee's porch, and the old woman told her of spirits that walked the land at night with secrets to whisper into the ears of the sleeping. Those who would not listen, they tormented with fevered dreams and madness. Vida couldn't help thinking again that it might be Nate whispering something to his father tonight. It was as if his voice was calling out on the howling wind that whipped around the corners of the cabin.

If his voice was coming to her through the fitful dreams of the devil himself, so be it. She would find a way to get near enough to listen and in listening, remember.

Chapter 25
HIDDEN IN CLEAR VIEW

At the county line, State Highway 51 abruptly darkened from the color of caramel to slate gray, as if to let people know things were done differently in Hopalachie County. Driving over, Floyd said as fast as he could, "Half in and half out!" and for a brief moment the car and its three passengers were caught in between counties, belonging entirely to neither. For an instant Floyd Graham had beat geography.

But Hazel didn't pay him any mind. What did it matter to her where they were going? Let him take the highway all the way up to Memphis if he wanted to. Or all the way down to hell for what she cared. It was all the same to her now. She just stared out her window, not at anything directly, mostly just away from her husband. It wasn't the silence of somebody who didn't have anything to say.

Doing his best to sound upbeat, Floyd chirped, "I know a little Mississippi town where the county line runs right down the middle of Main Street."

Hazel pressed herself against the door, away from Floyd. If she could she would have moved on through the wall of steel and let the summer-thick air bear her off in its swampy arms.

"They got a sheriff for each side of the road. Different laws and everything."

Johnny shifted a little on the seat. He still wasn't accustomed to having the entire back to himself. When the family used to go driving together, Davie would sit behind their father and Johnny directly behind their mother. Johnny scooted a few inches to the left and then to the right, trying to find the exact middle point between his parents.

"What I want to know is what happens if somebody shoots a person from across the street?" But nobody offered a solution to Floyd's dilemma.

When Floyd reached up to adjust his rearview mirror, Johnny saw his father's iron black eyes looking back at him. What did he want? Was he asking a question? Or was he sending a warning? His father's eyes were never easy to read, unlike his mother's, whose eyes couldn't hold a secret. You always knew what she needed of you. Johnny wondered if she would be in his room tonight, asking him, "Who do you love the most? Whose side are you on?" Checking for true center again, Johnny shifted a little to the right.

Floyd's eyes left the boy and scanned the horizon before him. Since they had left Jackson, the road had agreeably followed the contour of the gently rolling prairie. Now the terrain was lifting gradually, one rise at a time. "It's a straight shot to Delphi now," he announced. "We gaining sea level every second."

The wind gushed loudly through the windows. Since they had left Whitfield that morning, it had grown considerably warmer and more humid. Even though the car had air conditioning, Floyd never turned it on because he said it seemed standoffish to ride around with your windows rolled up. He liked to keep one arm on the ledge, ready to raise a friendly hand to everybody they passed. Johnny figured his daddy must be on waving terms with just about everybody in the world.

The breeze from Hazel's window carried the sweet smell of gardenias into the backseat. Even though Johnny had visited his mother in the hospital several times, she had never worn any of her familiar scents. She only smelled of things that stung his nose.

Johnny inhaled deeply once more, just to make certain, and then he smiled. Sure enough, his mother smelled right again. That had to be a good sign. For the most part his mother looked right. Back at Whitfield, when his father had walked her out of the stately, vine-covered building, Johnny immediately noticed her hair still drew a reddish glint from the sun. Her skin, too, was just as it was supposed to be, white as milk and sprinkled with the cinnamon freckles she hated so. The ugly bruises on her arms had disappeared, and when she got into the car, she still sat straight as a plumb line. His mother never could tolerate slouching.

But it was his mother's eyes that had disturbed him. They had dimmed from the crystal blue of a spring sky to the washed-out gray of winter. He could see no farther into her than into a pond on an overcast day. For the first time he did not know what she wanted of him.

Floyd slowed the car. "We're passing over the Big Black. Look out for gators!"

The tires of the Lincoln lowered their pitch, sounding out the hollow of the bridge. Beneath, the current was deep and the water dark like iron, and cypress trees and tupelo gums shrouded in moss rose from unseen depths. A sparkling white sandbar was strewn with dead pieces of wood petrifying in the Mississippi sun. The river gave off a coolness that, even on a summer-hot day in late May, gave Hazel a shiver. Hugging herself, she rocked to and fro ever so slightly in her seat, so slightly only the boy noticed. If she would only scoot over some, the boy thought, his father would surely put his arm around her.

The landscape began to break up into a series of cotton fields, bean fields, and cow pastures. Now and then they would pass through a little speck of a settlement. On both sides of the road, people were out on their porches fanning themselves against the midday heat. They waved and nodded at the Lincoln in a kind of heartfelt way, like they were greeting friends who they expected to stop by for iced tea. Then came the fields again.

"Hazel, honey, ain't you got nothing to say to us?"

Hazel wouldn't turn her attention from a pasture of strange-looking cattle, trying to remember what they were called. They had grotesque humps up high on their backs and seemed to be watching her with baleful looks, stirring a memory of warning from long ago.

"Momma Maud's gone," Floyd said. "Don't that make you happy?" Floyd waited for a response and then went on. "You know what it was? How come her to be so ornery and all? Her boys tole her I was selling the house out from under her. Said I was trying to get even for having to grow up in the barn. That's why she was acting so crazy and all. Trying her best to make me feel sorry and get on my good side. Bless her heart. I told her she could stay on the home-place as long as she wanted. I was never planning on kicking her off to start with. She'll be there till the day she dies, Hazel. I promise."

Johnny noticed that he didn't tell her the rest. How he told Maud she would be safer in the hills with Jesus than in the same house with Hazel.

"Everthing's going to be just fine now," Floyd assured her. "Just you wait and see. Everthing's gonna get back to normal."

Floyd beamed a reassuring smile over to his wife, who just kept a tight hold on herself, staring out the window. It was anybody's bet what normal was for her anymore. For all Floyd and Johnny knew, maybe this was exactly the way a body was supposed to act after weeks and weeks in the ivy-covered hospital getting fixed.

The boy had imagined worse. He dreamed of finding his mother with her hair standing on end and eyes bugged out like that cartoon cat on TV who got his tail stuck in the toaster. Once he woke up screaming in the middle of the night swearing he had seen his mother, her clothes afire and her eyebrows singed, dodging lightning bolts hurled from heaven.

On the left-hand side of the road, from a field of soybeans, rose a large billboard with a giant blue bottle painted on it. Almost on cue, Floyd dead-panned, "Y'all know that Milk of Magnesia plant down on the coast?" Next came the punch line. "It works more people than any place in the State of Mississippi."

Johnny knew this was supposed to be funny, but he never once, in the countless times he had heard it told, got the joke. On first sight of the billboard, grownups would push each other out of the way to be the one to tell it first. Still, he hoped it would make his mother laugh or cry or tell his father to "shut up and quit acting such a fool." Which she didn't, even though he was.

Johnny leaned over the front seat. "I know a joke."

"Let's hear it!" Floyd said like a man in bad need of reinforcements. "You want to hear it, honey? Go on and tell it, Johnny."

"I got to see your hand to do it."

Obliging, Floyd stretched out his arm along the back of the seat, and Johnny pointed to the back of his daddy's wrist with his finger. "You got a little white speck on your skin. I'll wipe it off." Johnny pretended to brush the make-believe spot away. "Now you're all black like a nigger!"

Laughing too hard, Floyd looked over at Hazel. "Get it, honey? He was pretending I only had a speck of white skin on me and then he knocked that off. He made a nigger out of me!" Floyd shook his head at such a thing. "That's a good 'un. Where'd you hear it at?"

"LaNelle tole it to me," Johnny answered, watching his mother, waiting for her to fuss at him for saying "nigger." But she didn't.

"The sheriff's girl? I shoulda known Billy Dean was behind it." Floyd shook his head again. "He's a sight."

His daddy's arm remained outstretched along the back of the seat. What was his mother waiting for? If she would just scoot over a foot, everything could get back to the way it had been. Johnny remembered one cool night in particular with his momma snuggled up to his daddy in the front seat, while he and Davie made smooching sounds from the back.

Hazel paid no attention. She was busy pretending to read the Bible verse somebody had painted on a barn roof. To hell with his nods and grins, she thought. Even though she had forgotten a lot, she could still remember well enough the way he got her committed into that nightmare of a hospital.

Floyd had told her he was taking her to Biloxi for a vacation. He was all nods and grins then, too. She even got herself out of bed and went to Gooseberry's to buy sundresses and Roman sandals and a pair of sunglasses that looked like a jeweled butterfly. She told everybody she was staying at the fancy Edgewater Beach Hotel. Then they packed up and headed south to the coast. Only she got dropped off at the state mental hospital on the way. It was going to take a lot more than a few jokes, a salesman's grin, and ninety volts to the temples to make her forget that.

Floyd switched on the radio. Somebody who sounded like a jittery colored man was singing about his hound dog. "Y'all listening to this?" He turned the music up loud. "That ol' boy's from Tupelo. Would you believe he's white to boot?"

Floyd tilted his head over at his wife and sang a verse. Then he smiled hopefully. "Hazel, honey, just think. You might of scooped him up some ice cream when he was little."

Even though his mother said nothing, Johnny wanted to sing along with his father. He felt the urge to giggle, tempted by the prospect that the world could be so wondrous a place, where giant blue bottles made grownups tell bad jokes and a white boy from Tupelo, Mississippi, could sing about hound dogs on the radio, and daddies were pure and honest in their desire to make you happy. But he thought better of it and decided to ignore his father like his mother was doing.

Floyd slowed as he came up on a farm wagon driven by an old man sitting slump-shouldered behind two brown mules. His daddy nosed the car so close to the wagon, Johnny could see the sacks of flour and cornmeal jigging on the wagon floor. Suddenly a mangy yellow dog leapt up from the bed of the wagon and planted his front paws against the endgate. He barked furiously at the Lincoln.

While Floyd waited for the southbound lane to clear, he lit a cigarette and eased back in his seat. Gripping the wheel with one hand, he placed his cigarette arm on the window ledge. "Yeah, boy, howdy," he said proudly to Hazel. "You and me come a long way since digging taters and chopping cotton and driving mules to town. Ain't we, honey?" Floyd nodded his head confidently, answering the question for both of them.

He never seemed happier than when he talked about how far he had left the past behind. Sometimes at home, when he was feeling especially proud, he would kick off his shoes, put his feet up, clasp his hands behind his head, and say, "I wonder what the po' folks are doing tonight." The way he did it always made Johnny laugh.

At the crest of a hill, Floyd tooted his horn and passed the wagon. After waving, he accelerated on the downslope. But in a few seconds the Lincoln was climbing yet another hill, and then another. The landscape had become like corrugated tin. As if to defy these hurdles placed in its way, the road stubbornly refused to bend an inch to the left or to the right. Instead it ran straight as a roller coaster bed and the risings and fallings were enough to tighten the boy's stomach. This rapid succession of hills and valleys meant they were now in the bluffs and approaching Delphi.

"'Home again, home again, jiggity jog. Home again, home again...' How's the rest go, honey? Something about a fat hog, waddent it?"

Hazel couldn't care less which words came next. She sighed heavily, her thoughts far away, trying to remember something important. What was it? It had to do with the bluffs. No, beyond the bluffs. Gradually, as the road entered familiar territory, it came back to her. Just on the other side of this narrow band of hills was that sudden descent into an endless flat flood plain. It was out there she had put mile after mile on her Lincoln, looking for god knows what. Or was it God she was looking for?

She remembered the day Floyd had taken her up into these bluffs for the first time. From where, with the wave of his hand, like the devil tempting Jesus, he had shown her the frightening secret of what lay on the other side of these soft, eroding hills. That sharp decline into the largest collection of flatness on earth.

It was strange what stayed put in her head and what went missing. Of course she knew she had been the mother of two children, and now she was the mother of one. Johnny had stayed. Davie had gone. But she felt nothing about his leaving. There was only a dead spot, like ground that had been scorched by lightening. It was as if, in her feelings, he was still falling.

Yet she remembered, like yesterday, that late afternoon she had stood by her husband on top of the bluff, and how her head had spun at the wonder of it all and how she had trembled at the thought of so much unbounded space. She remembered how she became terrified of falling into nothingness, until she had put her arm around Floyd for balance and how anchored he had made her feel. How she loved him so. She still had that memory. Now a memory was all it was. So, despite her husband's mindless jabber pulling at her, Hazel was unmoved, and stubbornly kept her gaze as unswerving as the roadbed.

Outside Delphi, Johnny's father nodded in the direction of a grim building made of bricks the same brown as potato peelings. "Hey, Little Monkey. That's where you gonna be starting school in September. Won't be long now. Bet you can't wait."

Johnny's stomach tightened up another notch. The school sat atop a bare dirt hill, worn bald by the wild animals the boy had seen spilling from its insides. Johnny winced. How he would survive among such savages, he didn't know. Looking back at his momma, who sat erect and distant, Johnny wondered if she would be well enough to get him through the ordeal.

The Lincoln crossed the bridge and began the direct ascent up Gallatin

Street, but instead of turning off on one of the residential lanes to bypass the Saturday crowds, Floyd decided to go right through the middle of town. He even turned at the courthouse, going out of his way to round the busy square.

For the first time during the trip, Hazel gave Floyd a look, and it was by no means a nice one. But she didn't say a word. She just put on her sunglasses and pulled down the visor. Her back was as straight as a fence post. Johnny could feel his mother's discomfort.

Like any Saturday in Delphi, the streets were awash with people. They were talking in friendly huddles on the sidewalks, calling to each other from across the road, and some sat in their cars with the doors open so they could sight neighbors as they walked by and holler them over to sit for a while and maybe share some fried chicken. On the square the old men who occupied benches under the pecan trees were busy keeping silent track of everybody who passed and everybody who didn't.

The Lincoln Premiere was a rolling advertisement of Hazel's last debacle. The car looked brand-new except for the prominent dent in the hood, exactly between the peaked headlights, from where Hazel had tried to run down the baby Jesus and sent the sheep flying the previous Christmas.

People stopped what they were doing to watch the Lincoln make its way through town. White and colored, everybody waved and nodded as Floyd drove past. But Hazel ignored them, staring straight ahead through her butterfly sunglasses, holding her chin up high, like she had a big insect balanced on her nose and was disinclined to disturb it. That way she didn't have to see people shaking their heads and blessing her heart as she passed.

It would have seemed natural for Floyd, the owner of Delphi Motors, to have had Hollis in his shop remove the dent long before now. But that's not how Floyd dealt with his family's embarrassments. He once told Johnny that in a town as little and high-hat as Delphi, everybody knew everything about everybody else, whether it was true or not.

"Except in your momma's case," he admitted with a pained sigh, "it probably is." He said a man looks plumb sorry covering up what folks already know. "Now just take the kildee," he explained. "She lays her eggs in the gravel, right under your nose. But you'd never see em cause they blend in so good. Yep, honesty is the best policy," his father had concluded. "Sometimes dragging the truth out in the open, every jot and tittle, is the best way to hide things."

So Johnny's daddy decided to display his wife for all Delphi to see the very day she got out of the mental hospital. He was hiding her out in public view like a bird egg.

Despite Hazel's obvious feelings on the matter, Floyd slowed down in front of Gooseberry's Department Store. The Gooseberry twins were standing out front in their usual Saturday spot, calling people by name—first and last—as they walked by. They knew everyone. If you wanted to get word out countywide, people knew to tell it to the Gooseberrys.

Sid and Lou were hard to tell apart. Each was the size of a small barn. They smoked fat cigars and hadn't a full hank of hair between them. Matching tape measures, draped around their necks, hung down their stomachs like limp yellow suspenders that had given up the effort.

The brothers lived by themselves in a house two down from the Grahams and belonged to that group of Delphinian families who passed down history as well as money. Floyd had once told Hazel the Gooseberry brothers were descended from Jews. "In fact their great-granddaddy was the South's only Jew Civil War hero."

"How come they to go to the Episcopal Church if they're Jews?" Hazel had asked.

"What I heard was that the family had to turn Episcopal when Jesus picked up such strong support among the Klan."

Hazel hadn't been impressed. She thought they were too pushy. She said anybody who supposedly sold high-class clothes for a living ought to have a little class themselves and not stand on the sidewalk trying to round up customers like barkers at a circus sideshow. Whether they were Jews or normal people, there wasn't any excuse for that.

Angling the car in front of the brothers' store, Floyd yelled too loudly, "Hey, Sid! How's business, Lou?"

Johnny noticed the tomato-size splotches rise up on the back of his mother's neck. There was something she needed of him now, but he couldn't figure out what.

Sid worked his cigar to the corner of his mouth and called out, "Why, it's ol' Floyd Graham." He loped over and placed his hands on the car roof and leaned down into Floyd's face, his cigar still burning. "How in the world are you doin today, Floyd?"

Lou came around to the other side. Hazel pushed the button for her window. Before the boy thought about doing the same, Lou had already placed his pudgy fingers over the ledge and thrust his jowly cigar-smoking face through the opening. He looked briefly at the boy and said, "Johnny Graham," like he was reading it out of a phonebook, and then peered up at Hazel. "Why, is that Hazel Graham up there in the front seat?"

"Welcome home, darlin!" Sid shouted through Floyd's window as if Hazel had lost both her mind and her hearing.

"You're a sight for sore eyes," Lou yelled at the back of Hazel's head, which was rapidly disappearing in a cloud of smoke.

Nodding in Hazel's direction, Floyd said, "Don't she look good, Sid?"

"I'as about to say it. She sho do look good."

"Bless your heart," the brothers said in unison.

Hazel's shoulders notched upwards. Johnny noticed that the blotches had joined up and now his mother's neck was a solid swatch of red.

"Why don't you come on in next week and buy yourself a pretty new hat?" Sid was saying. "We got just the one."

"A little yeller thing," Lou added. "It's right stunning."

The brothers traded embarrassed looks over the front seat.

"I thought it might come up a storm," Floyd offered, "but now I think it's fairing off. Maybe it's going to miss us after all."

Even though there wasn't a cloud in sight, Johnny was sure his daddy was right about it. The weather was one thing his father knew how to read.

"We'll have you over to the house real soon," Floyd said and then backed the car into the street, heading up Gallatin. The brothers waved them away.

Hazel finally spoke. "They all know, don't they, Floyd? The whole damn town knows."

Floyd smiled the same smile Johnny had seen his father use when an angry farmer had brought back his Mercury Coupe. "Sweetnin," he purred, "you know everbody would of found out soon enough. Now it's all in the open. Ain't that the way?" He smiled again sweetly and tilted his head to the side, not bothering to explain to her about the bird egg.

When Hazel didn't answer, he answered for her, "Well, it is, honey. You got to trust me on this."

Then Hazel uttered one syllable. "Ha." It was hardly discernible from a cough.

She pulled a scarf out of her purse, covered her head, and knotted it under her chin. Then she put a hand up to the side of her face like a blinder. Along with the sunglasses, Johnny thought she looked like one of those camera-weary movie stars she studied in *Photoplay*. "Floyd," she said coolly, "I don't feel like being on parade today. Would you please take me home?"

Floyd looked hurt. "I thought it might be good for folks to see that you're all right. That you're not—"

"Dangerous?" Hazel offered, looking straight down the middle of the road. "I feel like a solid-gold fool."

"I thought it was the best thing, Hazel. I'm sorry for it." He looked like he really meant it. "But everbody's so glad to see you. They all missed you." His face softened and almost in a whisper he said, "I missed you, Hazel. Forgive me, OK, sweetnin?"

She was cold and silent. Floyd decided to leave it at that and continued on up the hill toward the Baptist Church, which sat at the top of Gallatin Street.

As Hazel's luck would have it, Brother Dear was out front arranging the letters on the church announcement board. Even on his day off he was dressed in his dazzling white suit. Catching sight of the Lincoln, he set down his box of metal letters and waited for the Grahams to pull up and say hi.

Hazel caught sight of the sign, tensed her shoulders and looked away. She remembered a wedding. Or was it a funeral? But she was sure she recalled an old lady smelling sickeningly sweet of Cashmere Bouquet face powder. She had whispered something in Hazel's ear. At the time it had made Hazel happy. Now she wanted to cry.

Floyd slowed as he pulled in front of the church, but when he noticed the title of Sunday's sermon, "A Man Should Be Master in His Own House," he decided it might be best to keep on driving, leaving Brother Dear with a "bless your heart" on his lips.

Chapter 26

THE PREACHER CALLS

Johnny could tell his father was pleased with how things were turning out. For a while there, he said he was afraid his wife would cost him his business. People didn't seem to want to buy a car from somebody who couldn't keep his own out of a ditch. But as he told Johnny, they wouldn't have to worry about his mother's drinking any more. One of the pills she took would make her sick if she tried. A little blue pill would keep her from getting all knotted up inside.

Each morning before he went to work, Floyd stood by Hazel's bed and watched as she took her medicine. From the satisfied look on his father's face, it was obvious that the pills were a great comfort to him. Floyd was feeling so confident about things, he dared to leave Hazel at home with only Johnny to look after her, at least until he could find a full-time maid. One he could trust to keep her mouth shut.

The morning of her third day back, there was yet another knock on the front door. The Gooseberry brothers and Brother Dear had wasted no time spreading the word about Hazel's return, and casseroles had begun to arrive almost hourly from the time she walked in the door.

Hazel had refused to see anybody, as she was convinced that the whole town was dead-set on humiliating her. Since no suitable maid had been located, it was still the boy's job to take the visitors' offerings, tell them his momma was asleep, and turn them away firmly, but always with a "thank you kindly."

Johnny climbed up on the lounger and pulled back the chintz curtain to see Miss Pearl and Miss Hertha whispering closely on the front porch.

In her good hand, Miss Pearl held a basket of fresh-cut roses. His mother had complained repeatedly about how two-faced Miss Pearl was, but Johnny liked her just the same. He thought she was one of the sweetest-acting people he knew of and figured it might do his mother some good to get a visit from a person who was so good natured. She had been so grouchy since returning from the hospital. He ran up the stairs to announce she had company.

Hazel lay propped up on a bank of yellow satin pillows, flipping through her *Photoplay*. Just above her head, portraits of Pinkie and Blue Boy struggled to stay afloat on a sea of red and gold flocked wallpaper. When Johnny informed his mother who it was waiting on the porch, she repeated, "Pearl and Hertha," like she was trying to place their faces.

All of a sudden she puffed up. "Of all the nerve! Now that they convinced I'm crazy as a coot they obligated to do their Christian duty and pay their respects. Well, I ain't lettin em lay up treasures in Heaven by playing Good Samaritan at my expense."

"But it's Miss Pearl, Momma. She brung flowers."

Hazel shrugged and went back to her magazine. "You know what to tell em, honey. You been doing real good. Just say I'm asleep."

"That's a lie, Momma."

Hazel looked up at him and blinked once. "I reckon it is a lie."

Johnny really didn't mind lying. He had been lying for his mother on a regular basis lately, as well as keeping her own lies a secret. Like not telling his father how she spit the pills out from under her tongue after he left her room in the morning. So it wasn't the lying that bothered him. He just didn't want his mother to send Miss Pearl away.

"Now what can we say that ain't a lie?" she ruminated.

Johnny stood by her bed watching as she licked her thumb, and flicked through the pages of her magazine. Something caught her eye. She had stopped at a photo of some tormented film star, plaintively touching a wrist to her forehead, only wanting to be left alone. "Tell em I'm in-dis-posed." She grinned, pleased at the sound of it.

"Yes, ma'am," he said and rushed down the stairs rehearsing his line as he went, hoping it meant something nice. When he got to the door, he blurted it out before he forgot it. "Momma's in decomposed!" At first he was afraid he had gotten it wrong, but Miss Pearl's pleasant expression told him different.

"I can certainly understand that, in this heat and all." She smiled sweetly at Johnny.

Miss Hertha was grinning, too, but her smile twisted up in the corner. She raised a hand to her mouth and whispered, "Especially after you've been pickled for so long."

Miss Pearl pursed her lips together and lifted her eyebrows at the sheriff's wife. "Hertha, really!"

Not sure what they were disagreeing about, Johnny just watched Miss Pearl's poor hand as it brought the lacey handkerchief to her lips, to her neck, and then to her lips again. For a crippled hand it sure got around. Johnny couldn't understand what his mother had against her. She had blue cotton candy hair and carried herself like the fairy godmother in his Golden Goose Classics and was all the time as sweet as she smelled.

But Johnny was learning you couldn't trust your own assumptions about people. It paid to first get the real story from his momma. Where his daddy might see somebody as a good ol' boy or a sport or maybe even a might curious, generally he was tame in his appraisals. His mother, on the other hand, picked up on the fatal flaws that others missed.

"Will you tell your momma we hope to see her up and around soon?" Miss Hertha asked in a harsh nasal snort.

Johnny tried not to look directly at her face. At least he and his mother were agreed on Miss Hertha. The woman also reminded Johnny of characters from his book of fairy tales, mainly the ones who lived under bridges and put children into ovens. Her buckteeth gave Miss Hertha a mule-like appearance, an impression reinforced by a long sloping nose and protruding brows. His mother said that even though she herself had been born ugly and poor, she had managed to do something about both. But Miss Hertha, born ugly and *rich,* didn't have the least excuse to go around looking like a field animal. His mother had even made up a little joke about the woman.

"You know why they named her Hertha?" she would ask.

"Why?" was Johnny's part to say.

"Cause it 'hertha' look at her," and then she would giggle.

Miss Pearl now held her handkerchief up to her cameo choker. "Johnny, you tell her the least little thing she needs, to send you running. You hear, child? We'll be praying for her." Miss Pearl touched her heart with her crippled hand. "Well, I guess we'll be going." She handed Johnny the little basket of flowers.

"Thank you kindly," Johnny said. "And y'all come back."

"My, what a little gentleman," Miss Pearl said. "See, Hertha. Doesn't he have the nicest manners?"

Hertha reluctantly agreed and said it was probably credit to his father. Miss Pearl shook her head at Hertha and then they both turned and headed down the oak-shaded walk, trailing sweet perfumes and soft whispers. But no sooner had the ladies disappeared down the hill than Johnny caught sight of Brother Dear ascending.

"Tell him I died," Hazel told Johnny when he reported that the preacher was standing at the door. The boy waited while she reconsidered.

"No, that won't stop him," she sighed. "He'd just be back in three days with a crowd to watch him raise me up again. You better let him in."

Brother Dear was one person who had unlimited access to Hazel. Not because she wanted to see him; she didn't. It was because nobody could tell him no. He was the Baptist preacher, after all, the most powerful minister in town. Nothing happened of importance in Delphi without Brother Dear's blessing. Hazel had seen him make grown men cry, women faint, and teenagers turn crimson, their adolescent yearnings laid bare from the pulpit. There was a narrow path that led to Heaven and it was certain that Brother Dear knew the way.

Hazel pulled the covers up tight and folded her hands over her chest. "Before you let him in," she called out after Johnny, "go hide all the Bibles from sight. He might make me read verses with him."

Hazel never could find anything in the Bible on command. She wouldn't go to Sunday School because of how flustered she got when everyone else had their finger on the verse and they had to wait on her as she flipped around in the wrong direction.

Coming down the stairs, Johnny saw Brother Dear shining through the screen. The preacher wore his trademark white suit and red tie with the cross-of-diamonds stick pin and stood firmly planted only inches away from the screen door, his white teeth sparkling and his jet-black hair glistening. It was like looking directly into the sun. The only thing shabby about Brother Dear was the well-worn Bible he toted.

Johnny pushed open the screen door, and Brother Dear spread wide his arms like he was welcoming a church full of people. "Do you know how much Jesus loves the little children?" he cried out enthusiastically.

Brother Dear always greeted children this way, and Johnny answered like he knew how to. "With all His heart?"

"That's right! With all His heart, Johnny. What a smart boy!" Brother Dear fished a peppermint out of his suit pocket and handed it to Johnny.

"Do you love Jesus back with all your heart, son?"

"Yes, sir," Johnny fibbed. After his experience with Maud, he didn't know what to make of Jesus anymore.

Brother Dear was still beaming down on Johnny. "Are you saying your prayers? You know, Jesus smiles when He hears the prayers of children."

"Yes, sir," he fibbed again.

"That's good," he said tenderly, handing Johnny another peppermint. Brother Dear rested his Bible-less palm on the back of the boy's head.

Maybe Jesus wasn't all that bad. After all, Johnny did feel safe and loved under Brother Dear's touch. Like Brother Dear, Jesus was famous for liking children. Johnny had seen the pictures.

Brother Dear's smile was swept away on a heavy sigh. "Well, son," he said, now solemn. "I'm here to see your momma. Will you take me to her?"

"Yes, sir." Johnny led the way up the stairs.

The room was sweating hot when they entered. Except for the beads of sweat popping out on her brow, Hazel appeared to be a body lying in state, eyes closed and hands folded neatly on her chest. Johnny flipped the switch to the attic fan in the hallway, and as it began pulling a steady breeze through the house, the frilly lace curtains hanging on either side of Hazel's bed billowed out toward the middle of the room, reminding Johnny of the sails on a fairy queen's funeral barge.

Brother Dear walked to the foot of her bed, his face gravely composed. "Hello, Hazel," he said in a voice like thunder rumbling in the distance. "How are you today?"

Hazel opened her eyes slowly. She looked about the room bewildered, like someone regaining consciousness after a coma. Finally she focused in on the preacher as if just discovering him in her room. "Oh, Brother Dear," she said weakly. "How good of you to come see me. I'm sorry to be so tired. It's the medicine they give me. When you're up under the doctor, you got to do what they say." Her eyes closed heavily and then fluttered open.

"You certainly do, Hazel," he said, his voice full of sympathy. "We all want the best for you. God does, too."

Hazel smiled valiantly. "The Lord has certainly put a burden on my back. I must do my best to bear it."

"That's why I came," Brother Dear said, with a weighty nod. "To pray with you about that burden. To take it to Jesus in prayer."

Hazel shifted uncomfortably in her bed. "I been praying pretty good on my own I reckon."

"Well, that's just fine, Hazel," he said with a smile. "I imagine you been asking Jesus for His guidance?"

"Yes, sir," Hazel answered sadly, "I been asking Him why He done this to me."

Even from where he stood watching by the door, Johnny could see the preacher's face darken. His head swayed gravely from side to side. His mother had got a wrong answer already.

"Hazel!" Brother Dear was horrified. "Never, *ever* ask Jesus 'why.' Do you know what the first words out of the Devil's mouth were, Hazel?"

Hazel's face was still and sullen. Clearly she was done with being preached at in her own home. She hunkered up her shoulders and shook her head no.

Brother Dear was quick to answer for her. "The very first thing out of the Devil's mouth was a question. Look it up for yourself in Genesis."

Patting around on the bed like she was looking for something, Hazel

said with a dry grin, "I must of left my Bible by the sink when I was praying over the breakfast dishes."

Johnny's eyes grew big. Now his momma was going after the preacher!

"The point is, Hazel," Brother Dear said sternly, "God doesn't like
questions. If we question, it shows we doubt His will."

"Puts me in mind of some of them doctors I just met," Hazel said.

Acting like he hadn't heard, Brother Dear lifted his Bible, showing
Hazel the front cover with the engraved gold cross. "We got to have faith
in God's will. Without knowing the whys and the wherefores and the hith-
ertos. Jesus is no lawyer. And you," he said, aiming his pointer finger at
Hazel, "got to stop looking for loopholes."

Hazel wasn't responding to his threats. She simply lay there, glaring
back at him. Just when it looked like Brother Dear was ready to cast Hazel
from his sight, he changed his tactics. His entire countenance instantly
softened. The transformation was remarkable. He looked down on Hazel
as tenderly as he would on a lame child, and in a voice already filled with
tears, he pleaded, "Hazel, what you got to ask for is forgiveness. You got to
recommit yourself to Jesus."

Hazel stiffened again under the covers. "If you don't mind me saying,
it was Jesus who got me committed in the first place."

Johnny saw Brother Dear's jaw muscles pop and backed into the closet. It was like somebody had said "shit" in church. But the preacher's voice
was still patient. "Hazel," he said, "you got to let God know how sorry you
are for bringing all this down on your family."

Under the covers Hazel was pulling back on her shoulders, like the old
mule harness had tightened a notch. She was making it as clear as she
could that it was time for Brother Dear to leave. "I don't reckon I feel up
to repenting today," she said.

Brother Dear nodded at Hazel, like he was going to give her this
round, but he was not one to quit easily. He knew of many ways to skin an
unrepentant cat. He carefully dropped down to the floor, and knelt by her
bedside. His voice was now a soothing whisper. "I know you're weary,
Hazel. And Jesus knows it, too."

Hazel turned her head his way, but eyed him dubiously. Whatever he was up to, she was determined not to fall for it.

"Hazel," Brother Dear said in the gentlest of inflections, "Jesus wants you to set your burden down. He loves you, Hazel."

Johnny thought he saw his mother's expression thaw a little. Her shoulders seemed to relax.

Brother Dear reached out and lovingly patted her hand. "Hazel," he said softly, "you can set your burden down this minute. You can find true peace. True love. You can learn to have hope again. I know that's what you long for with all your heart."

Hazel's eyes began to mist up. It was clear that Brother Dear had touched her deepest desire.

"Close your eyes, Hazel and open your heart," he said. "The regret will haunt you for the rest of your life. It's only your pride that keeps you from being free. Release Davie to Jesus."

She snatched back her hand, like she had touched a hot stove. Her face went wooden again, but in her eyes, the terror was there for the preacher to see, letting him know he had hit paydirt. And he went for it. His voice began to break as tears rose up in his throat. He repeated, "Release Davie. Let him go. It ought to be Jesus you're holding on to, not the boy. Reach out to Jesus now."

A teardrop, as big and white as a pearl, rolled down Brother Dear's face. He leaned in closer, and said in a choked whisper, as if he were using the last of the air left in the room, "No amount of pills. Or electricity. Or whiskey is going to take your burden away, Hazel. Only Jesus can. Do you believe that?"

Hazel didn't move to respond. By lying there rigid, she hoped to shield herself from what was coming.

"Your husband loves you, Hazel. He worries and prays for you. He asked me to help you, Hazel. He told me about a bad dream. A bad dream you been having, Hazel. I think I can help you with it. Jesus might be trying to tell you something."

There was no hint of surprise on her face. Of course Floyd would tell. But the dream was hers. Not Jesus'. Not Floyd's. Not those doctors' at the hospital. He was wrong. It wasn't a bad dream. It ended with her feeling safe and warm under a dark, soothing current. The comforting sound of water rushing in her ears. No one was going to take it away from her.

Still on his knees Brother Dear laid his Bible on the bed and opened it. From the closet Johnny heard the whispering sound of the tissue-thin pages as the preacher's fingers skittered through the chapters.

"I want us to read the Good Book together, Hazel," he said and then he firmly pressed his finger against the page. "Here it is. Mark 9:42. *And whosoever shall offend one of these little ones that believe in me, it is better for him that a millstone were hanged about his neck, and he were cast into the sea.*"

He had read the verse as innocently as one would a bedtime story. He waited a moment to let the meaning sink in. Then he asked, "You know who that was talking, Hazel?"

"No," she said.

"It was Jesus, Himself. See, the words are in red." He showed Hazel the proof.

"You know what a millstone is, Hazel?" Brother Dear asked without a hint of guile.

Hazel shook her head. She wouldn't even look at him now.

"It's what they used to grind their wheat with in the olden days. It was mighty heavy. You see, Jesus was getting serious in this verse. He was talking about drowning. Did you hear that part, Hazel? You been dreaming about drowning, haven't you?"

Brother Dear leaned even closer to Hazel. His Aqua Velva was burning her eyes. "Our loving Savior didn't say, 'drop them in the shallow end.' He said 'cast them into the sea.' And with a five-hundred-pound rock around their neck." Brother Dear carefully touched his own neck. "Our gentle Savior was definitely upset here. You know what He was so upset about?"

"I don't want to hear no more," Hazel said. Her voice was hoarse.

Brother Dear nodded compassionately and said, "I understand, Hazel," but went on. "Leading children astray," he said sadly. "Neglecting their souls. Not bringing them to Jesus through a righteous example. Hazel," he murmured, as if it tore him up to tell her this, "that's the sin you're guilty of. Maybe the worst one of all."

He let the true sorrow of his words hang in the air for a moment, then held up a pair of fingers before Hazel. "You had two children entrusted to you. And now you've lost one." He buried one finger inside his palm. Davie's finger.

Hazel stared at Brother Dear's hand. There was horror on her face. She was remembering and the remembering was no longer split off from the feeling.

"Maybe little Davie was a warning. It's not too late to repent and save what's left. If not, well, you heard what Jesus said. He said you'd be better off dead." Now both sweat and tears trickled down Brother Dear's face in converging tributaries. He dripped onto the bedclothes. "Please, child, do you hear me? Do you hear the Word speaking to you?"

Hazel let out a deep sigh. Almost to herself she whispered, "Better off dead."

"That's right, Hazel." Raising his voice, Brother Dear called out to Johnny, "Come over here to your momma, son."

With Johnny now at the bedside, Brother Dear commanded, "Hazel, look on this child."

Hazel's eyes met her son's, but they seemed as blank as the marble angels in the graveyard. For all she felt now, he could have been made of stone. More than anything now she wanted to be in her dream. She wanted to be drawn beneath the dark waters, far below the surface, blanketed by watery layers of forgetfulness. The only sound she wanted to hear was that of the current sighing around her.

"Get on your knees with me, son," said Brother Dear.

Johnny did as he was told. His head sank below the mattress.

Then the preacher placed his elbows on Hazel's bed and pressed his folded hands against his forehead. Little beads of sweat popped out on his knuckles.

"Pray with me, Hazel." Brother Dear closed his eyes but Hazel was lost in a gaze somewhere out the window. "Jesus, you said that you were the Way, the Truth and the Life. Please have mercy on your daughter, Hazel Graham. Let her know that you have love enough to heal the deepest wounds. Light enough to brighten the darkest night. Truth enough to break Satan's stubbornest lie. Show her the way back to your loving arms.

We humbly ask it in thy name. Amen."

Brother Dear rose up and gently laid the flat of his hand on Hazel's brow. "I'll keep praying for you, Hazel. Night and day. As long as it takes." Reaching down, he placed his other hand on Johnny's head. "We'll all pray for you, won't we, son?"

"Yes, sir," Johnny sobbed.

Brother Dear took the boy's hand and they left the room with Hazel staring out the window. On the way down Brother Dear told Johnny that he was to do whatever his parents asked of him and to pray for his mother every night before he went to bed. He said it might be a good idea to pray where she could hear him. He reminded Johnny that Jesus loved the little children and He listened to them because they were still innocent and for him to stay that way as long as he could.

Johnny said he would. But he was beginning to get the feeling that even though Jesus and Brother Dear were partial to children, they didn't care much for grownups.

After Johnny saw him out, he ran back to his mother's room. Her eyes were closed and her head turned toward the window. The water glass his father had brought up that morning was lying close to her hand on the bed, drained. Then he noticed that the bottles of medicine sitting on the nightstand were all open and were empty. Under her breath he could hear her saying something over and over.

Chapter 27
THE KEEPER

Johnny kept his eyes on his mother as she stared straight ahead, seemingly into space. Except for two old farmers sitting across the opposite wall from them, the waiting room was empty. A nurse pushed through the big double doors and walked crisply up to the admissions desk. On her way she glanced over at Hazel with a detached look of professional curiosity and then shifted her gaze to Johnny. He got a sympathetic smile.

Floyd had told Johnny to keep an eye on Hazel while he went to pull the car up. As she sat there in her wheelchair, small and colorless and beaten down, a picture of ruined despair, Johnny held tight to her hand, afraid the reason she looked so miserable was because he had told on her, that she was mad at him for taking a side against her. But he had not known what else to do. His father had been counting on him.

On the very first day Floyd had left Johnny alone with his mother, he showed him how to use the phone. "In case," he said, "your mother does something funny."

Johnny didn't know what he meant. He and his mother didn't have *fun* anymore.

"You know what whiskey smells like, don't you?"

Johnny nodded. He instinctively knew all the smells that attended his mother, and what mood each signified.

"Well, then, when you think you smell it on her or if she gets to walking crooked or starts to talking funny, you call me right then." He led Johnny into the stairhall, to the little cubbyhole built into the wall. That's where the telephone sat, squatting there in the hollow like a giant black toad. Floyd put a chair against the wall so Johnny could reach the phone.

"Just pick up this part shaped like a door handle and put this end up to your ear and this one to your mouth. When the lady says, 'number please', you say real loud and clear, '4-0-3.' I'll get here before you know it."

He had told the truth. Within an hour of Johnny phoning to say that his mother was talking like her tongue had bloated up, Floyd had Hazel in the county hospital getting her stomach pumped. That was two days ago.

"Momma, are you mad?" Johnny asked. She didn't look at him, but stared straight ahead, her face bloodless and her lips dry and cracked. Strangers had handled her head roughly and her hair was in pitiful disarray. But his daddy said she was going to be OK. Johnny had been there in the hallway outside Hazel's room when the doctor talked to Floyd.

Dr. Barnes was a tall, sandy blond, movie-star-looking man, with shoulders like a sawhorse. "No permanent harm done," he had said. "We got to her in time. But an hour later...." at that point he reached down and tousled Johnny's hair. Then he looked back at Floyd. "Well, let's just say we'd be telling a different tale if it weren't for the boy."

Floyd looked down at Johnny and winked. But it was a wink without a smile. He could tell his father had been crying. It was the same look he wore on the nights he came to Johnny's room after Davie had left for the graveyard.

The doctor pulled a pad from the pocket of his stiff white coat. He talked as he scribbled. "Now, Mr. Graham, these are a good bit stronger than the prescription they gave her in Jackson. But I think under the circumstances...." He tore off the sheet and handed it to Floyd.

Nodding his head earnestly, Floyd took the prescription and, without reading it, folded the paper with trembling fingers and placed it in his shirt pocket—all the time continuing to nod, even though it had been a while since anybody had said anything to nod at.

Seeing his father act this way, so dutiful and anxious to please, was new for Johnny, and he didn't know what to make of it, but he had the sense his father had somehow shrunk standing there beside the doctor.

Dr. Barnes placed a hand as wide as a dinner plate on Floyd's shoulder. "Be patient with your wife, Mr. Graham. In cases like hers, time is the best healer. She's dealing with the greatest loss a woman can experience."

Floyd continued to nod. "Yep, you're right," he said. "Of course you are.

I know it." Placing his hand on Johnny's head, he said, "We all been put through the ringer. Everthing's going to be all right now though, ain't it, son?"

Johnny nodded weakly, not sure he was really being asked.

Poking Floyd's shirt pocket lightly with the tip of his finger, Doctor Barnes said, "And don't leave her in the house alone with this medicine. I'd strongly recommend that you get somebody to watch over your wife. Full-time."

Floyd winced and nodded even faster. But Johnny wasn't nodding. He didn't like the sound of that at all. His mother was never alone. He was the one supposed to be watching over her.

"Yeah, I know it," Floyd said contritely. "I shoulda done it before now. I just couldn't find the right one and all."

"I'm not saying you need a medical professional. Just someone reliable."

Floyd looked up at the doctor with immense gratitude, like he had found a man whose down-to-earth professionalism matched his own. "Now that you mention it, they's been a girl coming by for weeks now, pestering me for work. Persistent as the devil. Kinda made me mad. But after talking to you, that's probly just what it's going to take. A real no-nonsense colored to keep Hazel straight for a while. Till she gets back on her feet." Johnny could see that his daddy was standing straighter now, his voice stronger.

"That's real good, Mr. Graham."

"Yep. You right. I'm sure of it now," Floyd said. He stopped nodding for a moment. "I got to say, Doctor Barnes, I like the way you run your operation. You got class all right, but you tell it straight. Not like those fellows at the State Hospital. Poking around in the past. Sorting through garbage. Seemed like a mighty negative way to go about things. They never could tell me anything solid. Nothing I could bank on. Mostly full of excuses. But you seem to understand what we're up against here."

"Well," Dr. Barnes said, "I'm sure those psychiatrists do a fine job at Whitfield. I'm just a lowly GP."

"Now that's a gracious thing for you to say. Goes right to my point. Real class." Nodding excitedly, he said, "Doctor Barnes, I think we going to shift all our business your way."

The doctor donned a bemused look and left through a set of double doors, leaving Floyd there nodding to himself.

"Momma, are you mad?" Johnny asked again.

Hazel still didn't answer. Her eyes were focused on the two old farmers who sat side by side in the row of stiff wooden chairs. They were talking quietly together.

"How was you suppose to know it?" asked the stouter of the two, picking at his callused hand. He wore a broken felt hat banged down on his head like a helmet. His rheumy eyes peaked out below the brim. "You know how they'll do. Don't let on nothin's wrong. Till of coursin hit's too late."

The other man remained silent and straight-backed. His hair was plastered against his head and the fingers of both hands were splayed out on the legs of his faded overalls. His face was chafed and his eyes red, like they had been rubbed raw, and he appeared to be staring straight at Hazel. Or rather his eyes seemed to be resting on her, using her for support, like somebody tired out might lean against a tree or a fence post. She found herself using him likewise. Each gazed on the other, unblinking, unasking, with not the slightest sign of embarrassment, or even recognition that the other might be looking back.

The man with the hat continued talking in a low rumble. "When mine passed, didn't act sick till the end. Didn't want to put nobody out, I reckon. You know how they are." He brushed his nose with a finger. "Then one day she bolted straight up in her chair. Said calm as anything, 'Valgene, better get me to the doctor. I reckon I'm a-dying here.' Before I could lace my boots she was gone. I never knew a thing was wrong with her."

He took off his hat and leaned forward, resting his arms on the tops of his legs, fingering a hole in the brim. "Curious thing, though. I was only just looking at a pichure took of her six months afore she died."

The man's voice was even quieter now, so quiet Hazel could just make out his words. He might have been talking to himself. He said, "There was somethin about her eyes in that pichure. Somethin not right." He shook his head. "Peculiar I didn't see it then."

Johnny gently jostled Hazel's arm. "Momma, are you mad at me?"

He could tell she heard him this time. By the way she closed her eyes, took in a deep breath, and heaved it out like she regretted having drawn it in the first place.

With her eyes still shut, she said evenly, "No. I ain't mad. I ain't nothin."

When Floyd walked into the waiting room to pick up Hazel, he was sweeter than Johnny had ever seen him. "Things are going to be different, honey. From now own I swear it. Gonna git you a full-time girl. You wont something, you just say it. She'll get it for you. She can't, I will. Whatever yore heart's desire. We'll get it all sorted out. You just wait and see."

Not knowing her heart's desire, Hazel did not bother looking at Floyd. Her eyes went back to the farmers. As the attendant wheeled her out to the car, she watched them still, longingly, as if sad to be leaving their company.

A few days later, after Floyd had already left for work and Johnny was sitting at the kitchen table eating his Cheerios, there came such a loud knock at the back door it made him nearly jump out of his pajamas. Looking up at the kitchen door, he spied a set of dark, frightful eyes under a monstrous straw hat, peering hard at him through the top pane.

"Anybody to home in there?" came a shout.

The boy knew a new maid was coming today, but he had not anticipated this woman. He recognized her right away and was so shocked to see her up close, he ran to the bathroom off the kitchen and locked the door. Then he jumped up on the commode tank and peeked out the window onto the porch. It was the same woman, all right, but now she was dressed in a white maid's uniform, and at the present moment had the screen pulled back and was standing on her tiptoes, trying to peek through the flimsy curtains that hung on the kitchen door.

"My name Vida Snow!" the woman boomed in a voice too big for the little body.

"I told to be here this mornin," she continued to shout. "Y'all aimin to let me in or no?"

Johnny decided not to face the thundering invader alone and remained steadfast at his post, waiting for the noise to rouse his mother. Maybe this would make her mad enough to get out of bed.

"I ain't walkin all the way back to Tarbottom. Somebody better come on!" She beat on the door with the handle of a dirty umbrella.

She stepped back from the door and in a voice raised loud enough for the neighbors to hear, she bellowed, "I supposed to clean house for a po' sickly white woman!"

That did it. Johnny heard his mother's feet hit the floor with a blam! "Goodnight in the morning!" she cried out, banging the door behind her and clumping down the stairs. "Who's out there calling me names and it ain't even noon yet?"

Johnny's hopes rose. This was the most animate his mother had been in months. Excitedly, he ran to join her in the kitchen.

Hazel was already at the door, clutching her pink chenille robe at the throat and peering through the crack. She asked sharply, "What are you carrying on about?"

The visitor didn't back off one bit. "All I temptin to say is my name Vida Snow and I get paid two dollars a day. Done been tole so by Mr. Floyd Graham."

Hazel sighed and opened the door the rest of the way. "Yeah, I been told, too. Come on in, I reckon."

The woman walked straight over to the sink, leaned against the counter, and crossed her arms like she was setting claim to that very spot. As Johnny hoisted himself back into his kitchen chair, Vida studied him closely. "How many chilren you got?" she asked in a tone that said one was already too many.

Hazel didn't answer immediately. She poured herself a cup of coffee Floyd had made and eased herself into a kitchen chair. "Just the one," she finally said. "But I imagine Mr. Graham already told you that, too," she added coldly. "What else did he tell you."

Vida reached into the pocket of her maid's uniform and pulled out two bottles of pills. "Said I supposed to give you a blue one and a yaller one every mornin. No mo'. No less. And watch you close cause you be real bad to spit em out."

"He hire you to be my maid or my keeper?"

Vida took a clean glass from the drain board, filled it with tap water and then uncapped the pills. "Don't care what you name it. But I gets two dollars a day for doin it. Done been tole by Mr. Graham."

"So you said."

Moving no closer than an arm's reach from where Hazel sat, Vida bent over and cautiously slid the water and the two pills across the table, like she was setting out a plate of food for a dog of questionable temperament. She stepped back to watch.

Hazel reached for the pills. "Don't worry. I ain't going to jump you. No matter what you been tole by Mr. Floyd Graham." She swallowed the pills and then held her mouth open for Vida to see. "There. Ain't I a good girl?"

"Yessum," Vida said indifferently. She removed her hat and hung it on the rack behind the door. The strange little woman began bouncing on the balls of her feet, her eyes darting around the kitchen, appearing for the first time a little less than confident. "Where you wont me to start? Washin, ironin, scrubbin?"

"How would I know? Floyd hired you. He can tell you where to start. I'm sure he gave you his number." Lifting herself up from the table, Hazel added, "Just stay out of my bedroom, if you don't mind." At that she turned and trudged out of the kitchen.

Vida didn't seem to take offense. Johnny watched as she went about taking inventory of the kitchen, squinting her eyes, and shaking her head. She clucked her tongue at the sink. She bent over and whistled at the knobs on the stove. She scuffed her shoe against the linoleum, nodding curiously to herself. Only when she walked into the pantry did she lose her squint, for a long moment staring wide-eyed at all the cans and jars and boxes of food.

Her attention lit on Johnny again. The maid's eyes were now hard and alert. It was obvious this was a woman of very few words and very many opinions. "What you call yo name?"

He dropped his eyes to the linoleum. She had no right coming in here and asking his name and making his mother sad.

"Cat got yo tongue? Don't matter none. I done been tole. Johnny, ain't it?" She squinted at him and shook her head, rendering a silent opinion, which he did not feel was at all favorable.

"I'm Vida."

Still looking down, he said, "I know who you are. You the one been hidin in the bushes. I seen you there. Spyin."

"Hmm," she said. "Reckon you got somebody else in mind."

Johnny looked up at her. "Nope. It was you, all right."

"Could be I been in the neighborhood. That ain't no crime, is it?"

They glared at each other for a moment, and then she leaned against the sink once more, crossing her arms. "What's wrong with yo momma?" she asked.

He crossed his arms like she was doing. "Tired," was all he said.

"Tired," Vida echoed and then shook her head. "Nossuh! It ain't tired."

She poured herself a cup of coffee and sat down at the table with Johnny, crossing her legs at the ankles, all of her energy seemingly spent. "Nossuh!" she said again, mostly to herself. "I know tired. And that ain't tired."

Chapter 28

SWITCHING PLACES

Hazel lay in her bed waiting for the clattering of dishes, the fall of footsteps on the stair, the two hard knuckle-knocks on the door, and finally the scowling face of that horrible little woman who doled out oblivion, two pills at a time.

Each morning the maid followed on Floyd's heels after he dispensed his morning kiss as efficiently as Vida did her medicine. With that pitying look drooping from his face like a rag on a bush, he assured her, "You just get some rest and let me take care of everything for a while. Time is the best healer, you know."

She thought a moment about time. Since Vida began overseeing Hazel's medication, time ran like a clock somebody had thrown down a well. She could hear it ticking, loud and unceasing, and knew seconds and minutes and hours and days must be piling up somewhere, but she couldn't get a handhold on what it had to do with her. The arising and the passing of events constantly perplexed her. Wasn't Johnny supposed to be starting school soon? Or had he already begun? It wouldn't surprise her if he walked in with a high school diploma in his hand.

No, she could only deal with time in small doses. For instance now, just like every morning after she awoke, time was raw, and throbbed like a fresh wound. Each day she opened her eyes to see the world in a kind of stark, harsh glare. It was in the morning she knew she had a husband who barely tolerated her, and one child that was living and needy and the other dead and gone.

Vida took care of that. Clutched in that tight, dark fist she brought the next kind of time, a fluid, river kind of time. At first she tried to resist, knowing it would take her away from her remaining child, but eventually the medicine would catch her like a current and gently draw her below the surface, and soon she would only be aware of a beautiful refracted light, and hear nothing but the gentle hum of the water rushing in her ears.

Then there was the time of surfacing, when she would open her eyes and see her son, the remaining one, the determined one, waiting by her bedside, staring at her. His worried eyes trying to catch her like a net, beckoning her upwards. But she didn't want to go. She wanted to stay warm and caressed by the river. But his stare was relentless and finally the river gave her up.

Lastly, there was the night, when sleep would not come. During these hours it was as if she stood at the mouth of a secret cavern; and memories, indistinguishable one from the other, thick as bats at feeding time, swarmed at her in a great black cloud. They whirred past her ears and she could hear their screaming cries, their voices too familiar, but she could not make out what they said. In those late-night hours the voices forced her out of bed and she roamed the darkened house like a ghost, randomly picking up objects—a shoe, a toy, a photograph—studying them, trying to coax from them their secrets until, exhausted, she returned to bed. It was during this time she most wanted to drink, just to make the voices stop. Once she had sneaked a glass of Floyd's bourbon to bed with her, desperate enough to test the pill that was supposed to make her violently ill if she mixed it with alcohol. It did, and after another emergency visit to Dr. Barnes, Floyd had mentioned going back to Whitfield—for good.

From the bottom of the stairs she heard a rattling of the breakfast dishes. Here she comes, Hazel thought, right on schedule. Hazel eased herself up in bed to make a lap for the tray.

Sounding her two warning knocks, Vida entered the room and without speaking set the breakfast tray down in front of Hazel, then reached into her apron pocket and pulled out the medicine.

"Good morning, Miss Hazel," she said without feeling. "Take yo pills, and I'll sit here and keep you comp'ny while you eat yo breakfast."

Hazel glared at Vida. She knew the real story. The only reason Vida would stay was to make sure Hazel didn't stick a finger down her throat after swallowing the medicine.

When Hazel didn't respond at once, Vida waggled her hand in her face. "Come on now, Miss Hazel. I got ironin to do."

"Suppose you came in here one morning and I told you I waddent going to take your medicine. Supposing I locked the door on you. Then what?"

"First thang, it ain't *my* medicine. It's yores. And two, if you was to act ugly, I suppose I have to call Mr. Floyd at his work." She reached into her apron pocket again and produced a skeleton key. "Or maybe use this thang he give me just in case you was to try something funny like that."

"Y'all think you know me pretty good, don't you?"

"Nome. I ain't met nobody like you a'tall. Now take this medicine and swaller it down."

Hazel took the pills with a swallow of orange juice. There was never any doubt she was going to do as she was told. She just didn't like Vida bossing her like she did. Why make it easy on her? She didn't want to push her too far, either. Something about this colored woman scared Hazel. It was the determined set of her face. It signaled that this was a woman who would do whatever it took to get her way.

After eating a few bites of the scrambled eggs and toast, Hazel lay back in her pillows and waited for the warm current to rise up around her, gradually lifting her and then drawing her out into forgetful depths.

She cast an eye toward the maid, who sat in the chair across the room, staring stonily out of the window. With her anger and despair muted, Hazel found herself a little fascinated by this woman. She was so young. Maybe even younger than Hazel. But her bossiness made her seem so much older. How did a woman that young get to be so sure of herself? What does it take?

Hazel wondered if Vida had ever known loss. Maybe if things were different, they could be friends. Secret friends—the kind you tell secrets to. Hazel could tell her many things. About voices that spoke to her at night. About death and fading love. About faith, hope, and charity...and the greatest of these is charity...tied up and dropped in the river...cast away like trash...how it feels.

As the edges of her mind began to blunt, Hazel tried to stay focused on the woman's face. Really a pretty face.

But, no, Hazel thought, closing her eyes. It was a face that could have been set in concrete. Or carved from oak. Or painted on a screen door somewhere. But there was no heart behind that pretty screen. This woman probably didn't feel at all.

That evil little boy was at the dinette table when Vida got downstairs. He sat with his crayons and paper, looking like he had swallowed the cat-bird. What had he done now? She went to check the cabinets. Sure enough, he had switched everything around again.

Vida crashed about the kitchen, pulling out pots and pans, fussing out loud to herself. Johnny silently sat there, drawing the big letter "D."

"Now I know good and well I didn't put my pots here," she grumbled loud enough for him to hear. When she looked up at him he just rolled his eyes.

This was the third time this week she had to rearrange her kitchen. She couldn't turn her back ten minutes on that child without having him return everything to the way his mother had it.

"Pots don't belong by the sink," she complained at him. "They belong by the cookstove where they is used."

"It's called an oven. Never heard nobody call it a cookstove. That's stupid." He rolled his eyes again.

"What be stupid is for some little boy to go round switchin my kitchen on me. When he knows I just gone switch it right back. That's sho nuf stupid."

"Ain't your kitchen," Johnny mumbled.

Vida walked over to where Johnny sat and planted her fists on her hips. "I heared that. How you get so contrary? If you ask me, six years ain't enough time to work up that much orneriness. You as nasty-tempered as an old woman."

"Ain't your pots, neither. Them's my momma's pots."

"What's yo problem, boy?" she asked. "How come you gettin crossways with me?"

Rolling his eyes again at Vida, Johnny turned back to the table where he drew a big letter "H."

"You put me in mind of a boy I once knowed called Tangle Eye. Never would look straight at you. Always peekin out the corner of his eyeholes. Sneakin around and lookin cock-eyed at folkses. Real bad to wall his eyes at a person. Know how they come to call that boy Tangle Eye?"

Johnny exhaled loudly like his daddy, to show how exasperated he was getting. Bearing down hard on the lead, he put a cross on his little letter "t."

Vida was silent, still waiting for his answer.

"No, I don't," he said, trying to sound not the least bit interested.

"Well, since you so nice to be askin, I tell you. One day that boy roll his eyes a time too many and they got all twixed up. They cross so bad, he cried, and you know when he cried, his tears rolled right down his back."

Keeping his eyes down, Johnny acted like he didn't hear her. She'd get hers soon.

"Humph. Why don't you go outside? Ain't you got no little boy friends?"

"Ain't no boys around here. Just girls and I hate em." He looked up at Vida, as if to underscore his point.

"Well, then, play by yoself," she said. "Go fishin for a doodle bug."

"I can't. *He's* out there."

It only took Vida only a second to figure out who "he" was. Today she had brought her father, Levi, to the Grahams' with her. Knowing how much he missed his trips to the bayou, she let him bring his Bible so he could sit and read and preach at the bottom of the large backyard. She had hoped the yard was large enough for him not to attract attention.

Vida dismissed Johnny's concern with a wave of her hand. "I ain't got time for yo foolishness. He ain't studyin you."

"He's sitting in *my* back yard. Sitting on *my* bench. On top of *my* grass."

"He been eatin yo porich, too? Who you? Goldy Locks? They room for you and him both in that big ol' yard."

"He talks to himself. And he looks at me funny."

"Well, maybe you funny to look at."

"He called me 'Nate.'"

Vida was silent for a moment. Lord, she thought to herself, what was her daddy thinking of? "You ever playlike?" she asked.

"Sometimes," Johnny said hesitantly, sensing a trap.

"Well, that man out there is my daddy. And some days he playlike, too."

"But he's old."

"Old people can playlike. So when he call you 'Nate,' now you know he's playlikin."

"Does he playlike everday?"

"No. Some days he don't playlike at all. And then some days he talks to hisself. Like I heared you talkin to yoself behind my back." Then Vida shrugged her shoulders like the whole matter of people talking to themselves was no big deal. "So you see, there ain't no need tellin on him. He ain't gone bother you."

Johnny wasn't so sure. "Does he go round seeing Jesus? We've had plenty enough of that round here."

Vida gave Johnny a curious look. "No, he don't see Jesus I don't reckon."

"Well," he said doubtfully, "I better go make sure."

Johnny took off in a run and Vida watched as he scurried out into the yard, ducking behind trees as he went, like a movie Indian sneaking up on cowboys, until he was in spying distance of her father.

Vida shook her head. "Hope his mouth ain't as big as his eyes," she said to herself before going back to arranging her kitchen.

The rest of the day, like every other day, Vida found herself locked in a battle of wills with the fractious little boy. She tried her best to coax him into watching TV, but he would have none of it. He was like a buzzing horsefly—you were always aware of his worrisome presence, but never sure where he was going to light next. He just wore her out. The only peace she got was when he disappeared to play under the house, until she began fretting that he was starting fires beneath her feet.

The long day came to an end at last. As she was heaping food on a plate to carry home with her, she told Johnny, "Now yo daddy called to say he got a meetin way out in the Delta and he gone to be late."

Johnny wouldn't even look at Vida. He stood with his back to her, staring out the back door.

"Now listen here to me," she said louder. "I done took a plate to yo momma and I'm leavin you and yo daddy's supper on the stove. When y'all get hongry, jest warm it up. You unnerstand?"

Turning around, Johnny sniffed the air noisily. "Smells burnt to me. Don't you know how to cook?"

"Plain contrary," she said to herself, putting on her funny-looking hat. She reached for her flour sack purse, but her arm froze. "I didn't leave my sack on this peg." She looked down at Johnny. "*Somebody* been goin through my tote sack."

Johnny turned an accusing eye her way. "I was just looking for my momma's stuff."

Vida gave him a surprised look. "You thank I'm aimin to steal somethin from y'all? Boy, you callin me a thief?"

Johnny glared back. "You taking my momma's food, ain't you?" He dropped his eyes to the floor and said with a world-weary sigh, "You got to watch colored people in your house. They bad to steal things. That's what my daddy says."

"Contrary as the day is long," she said, shaking her head. Vida took Johnny by the shoulders and steered him out of the way of the back door. "Beatin'est mess of people I ever seed," she grumbled as she took the steps down into the yard.

When she got to the bench, she touched her father on the shoulder, waking him from his nap. "Less go home, Daddy. I done had my fill with white folks today."

Vida and her father made their way out of the Grahams' neighborhood and as they did, other maids also finishing for the day exited from the rear of their employers' fine homes, many also pan-toting leftovers. They formed a loose little procession of starched uniforms, some blue and some white, that gradually made its way down past the point where the expansive sprinkler-fed lawns gave over to a tangle of dusty trees and vines, and then still farther, on past where the pavement ended and the road changed to gravel, took a steep downward slope and wrenched itself around to the backside of the hill, as if turning its back on Delphi proper on its descent to Tarbottom.

Vida heard a familiar squeal. "Whoo-ee! Girl, don't I know you from somewheres?"

She turned. The woman wasn't hard to recognize, even without a man's arms wrapped around her butt. Although she was wearing a maid's outfit, her bright red earbobs and matching lipstick made her look ready for jooking.

The woman beamed her gold teeth at Vida and hollered, "I sees you took my advice. You went and got Miss Hazel for yo white lady."

Sweet Pea fell in beside them uninvited and Vida said coolly, "This my daddy, *Reverend* Snow," hoping that might water down the woman's enthusiasm a bit.

Sweet Pea batted her eyes at Levi. "Proud to know you," she cooed.

Don't this woman have no off switch? Vida thought to herself.

Levi touched his old felt hat and nodded politely at Sweet Pea. "It's good to know you likewise," he said, like he meant it. Vida could have sworn she saw him blush.

"I took my own advice," Sweet Pea told Vida. "I workin for Miss Cilly Satterfield on down from yo white lady. I'm done with the mens." Sweet Pea smiled again at Levi and then pulled a sassy red scarf out of her bag and tied it around her neck. "These ol' uniforms just ain't flatterin to a girl, is they?"

Levi grinned shyly and opened his mouth to speak. But when he saw Vida glaring at him, he put his eyes back on the road.

As the group continued on to the river bottom, the road lost all its gravel and became nothing more than two deep ruts. Sweet Pea prattled endlessly about the domestic goings-on in the neighborhood in which they worked. Which families lived in which houses and how they were connected to each other. Who was good to the colored and who wasn't. She talked without stopping until the road exhausted itself at a large flattened-out place, around which sat a community of wooden shacks.

Sweet Pea was saying something about how the sheriff's wife Hertha was Miss Pearl's niece as well as the Senator's daughter. That's when Vida took a sudden interest in the brash woman's babbling.

"And they all got maids, too?" she asked. "Them Pearl and Hertha women?"

"Sho. What you think? They do for theyselves?"

Vida's mind was working a mile a minute. "No, I jest...who...?"

"Speakin of the devil," Sweet Pea said, pointing, "see that big red woman down yonder sittin on her porch? That Creola. Miss Pearl be her white lady." A large freckled woman, her frame completely hiding the chair that was propping her up, waved a meaty arm in their direction.

"Miss Pearl," Vida repeated, carefully considering the prospects. "The Senator's very own sister." Then she asked anxiously, "Where the sheriff's maid live at?"

Sweet Pea gave Vida a sideways glance. "I recollect you askin bout the sheriff first time I seed you. Still got him on yo brain, huh?" She pointed farther down the lane. "See that painted house up on river stilts, lookin down on everbody else?" Sweet Pea paused a minute while her red lips curled up in a look of obvious disgust. "That Missouri's house. But we all call her Misery for short. She never let you forget who her white boss be."

"Missouri," Vida said slowly and deliberately, like she meant to remember it.

"Yeah, ol' Misery bout as whitewashed as the house she stay in. She so color-struck she think she poots Franch perfume." Smiling contritely at Levi, she said, "Pardon my langwich, Rev'run."

A plan began to formulate in Vida's mind. "Come to speak of it," she said, "I might could use yo help. I'm havin the beatin'est time figuring out how to work them washin' and cookin' machines. Why don't you come by tomorrow? I'll make some coffee and you can sit a spell."

"I know yo white lady ain't gone like that one bit."

"Don't give it a passin thought," Vida assured her. "I guarantee, we gone have the place to our own-dear-selves."

"Well, then, I be by after dinnertime," Sweet Pea said. Turning to Levi and batting her lashes, she cooed, "Maybe I see you tomorrow, too."

Vida's mind was buzzing, so she hardy noticed when Sweet Pea stopped at a tarpaper shack with a vine-strangled yardgate. As she lifted the wire noose from the post, she cut her eyes up at Levi. "Well, this be where I stays. All by my lonesome."

That got Vida's attention. Her father's, too.

"It was sho nice meetin you, Miss Sweet Pea," Levi said. This time it was Sweet Pea who seemed to be blushing.

It struck Vida that even though her father was almost sixty, he was still a very good-looking man. He was tall, lean, his face was creased with age, but his features still sharp. When he looked at Sweet Pea his eyes even seemed to twinkle. She had never thought of her father as a regular man with regular-man needs, and the thought made her very uncomfortable. She had not considered the effect of taking Levi away from his self-enforced isolation. Life was a lot closer here. People would be watching. Things could easily get out of hand.

As she continued down the lane with her father, Vida returned nods to neighbors who were sitting out on their porches, escaping from the heat of cookstoves and enjoying the cooling of the early evening. For the first time, she felt like she belonged. There was purpose for her here. She noticed how pleasant it was down in Tarbottom. How every porch was like a poor man's Hanging Garden of Babylon. Ferns and mother-in-law tongues and impatiens and verbena rose up from old enamel washpans, while petunias and moss roses and wandering jews, planted in rusted syrup buckets and coffee cans, spilled down from the eaves and railings. The yards, kept clean and grassless by the regular sweep of dogwood brooms, were filled with chickens pecking and dogs trotting and boys and girls racing around in games of chase. For the first time in a long time, she noticed the music that lives in the laughter of children.

Vida opened the front and back doors of the shotgun house to get a breeze channeling through the two rooms, and then pulled a couple of straight-back chairs up to the wood table that sat on a ragged patch of linoleum. She called to Levi, "Supper's ready, Daddy. Come on and eat."

Levi stood over the table and prayed, "Lord, bless this food to the nourishment of our bodies and—"

In the middle of the blessing, Vida plopped herself down and forked up a bite of squash. It didn't go without her father's noticing.

Levi finished his prayer and seated himself. "It wouldn't hurt to give Him His due, Vida."

"Hurt Him a lot less to give us ours," she said with her mouth full, not feeling angry tonight, just practical. "He the one got everthang. I reckon it gone be up to us to get our own."

"We got food to eat."

"Ain't even our food," she said, thinking of Johnny's meanness today. "If you got to bless it, put Mr. Floyd Graham's name on it. It's his holdovers we eatin."

A long silence followed while Levi stared at his plate. Vida knew she had shamed him again, but she couldn't help it. Looking at him was like staring defeat right in the face. Sometimes she just had to take a swat at it. Her father was lost without Jesus or the white man propping him up. She couldn't afford to think like that. Not now.

"All I'm sayin is we on our own, Daddy," she explained. "We got to be strong. Ain't nobody gone save us but us. You understand that? Time for wishin and prayin is long gone. We got to start bein' smart with what we got. And careful. If we make a mistake, ain't no sweet by and by for us."

"You wont me to leave, I'll go. You don't have to feed me. Anyways, I'd just as soon starve than hear you blaspheme the Lord."

"Where you gone go, Daddy? Tell me that. Down to the bayou to do some preachin? We too far away for that now."

Levi stiffened. "What I mean is I can find me a revival somewheres. Things ain't always gone be this way. Things gone be set right again."

"We been all over this," she said, knowing it would do no good to say it again, but she did anyway. "It's like the sheriff done put the evil eye on you. Ain't no board of deacons in this county gone stand against him. You can leave the county if you wont. But I ain't goin. I still got business here."

Vida studied her father as he sat there, his eyes cut down at his plate.

What would he do without her? It was too late for him to start all over. He was no longer a young man, and whatever ambition he had once seemed to have given way to wishful thinking. She had to be the strong one now for both their sakes. No, for all three of their sakes.

"Now, Daddy," she said, trying to soften her tone with him, "if you leave you ain't liable to make it on yore own. You need to be with yo family. I gone look out for you."

"But I need to be doin somethin. I can't just sit around on that bench all day. With that boy starin at me."

At that Vida tensed up in her chair. "Which boy?" she asked, her voice hard again. "Nate or Johnny?"

Levi blinked at Vida, not understanding. She didn't explain, but waited for his answer, testing him, until he had to ask, "What you meanin?"

"That white boy say you call him Nate. What you think those fine white people gone do if they catch you talkin crazy to one of their precious little lambs? Be back to the fields for both of us pickin scrap cotton. Or worser if it be the sheriff hearin you."

"I just took the boy for Nate's all," Levi explained. "He came up on me sudden like."

"I hope that's all it is. You better save that kind of talk for down at the bayou. We got to be careful now."

"He sho put me in mind of Nate is all."

Vida angrily crumbled a wedge of cornbread over her peas, wondering if her father even remembered what Nate looked like. Seemed like he tried his dead-level best to ignore his grandson. "That boy don't look nothin like Nate," she said flatly.

"Same colorin. Them thin lips—"

"Ain't nobody in they right mind gone mix Nate with that boy," she snapped. "Ain't nobody looks like Nate." Vida stopped herself, biting her lip. They both knew that wasn't true. If it were, Nate would be sitting at the table with them tonight. Vida ate for a while in silence, avoiding her father's look.

In a calmer voice, she said, "I'll talk to Mr. Floyd. Maybe he can fine you a little something to keep you busy in the yard."

Levi squared his shoulders. "I ain't no yard boy," he said. "I'm still a preacher of the Word."

Vida's temper flared again. "And I ain't got no business bein no maid. And Willie ain't supposed to be no two-bit bootlegger." Damn! she thought to herself. Why couldn't she ever stop short? Why did she always have to come out fighting? Seemed sometimes meanness was the only thing she had plenty of. She silently cursed herself again. Then she cursed her father for taking it from her, wondering when it was exactly that she had become the adult and he the child.

"It's been a fall for the both of us, I reckon," she said, now trying to be philosophical about it. "And neither of us caint pick ourselves up from no place but from where we fell. We ain't got a bushel basket of choices."

"One day it'll be different, Vida," Levi said, now sounding as confident as ever. "When the Senator finds out the truth of it all, things will get put back the way they was. The bottom rail will be on the top."

"I know, Daddy," she said, scraping a few more peas into her plate, "you lay more faith on the Senator than Jesus. And the both of em ain't listenin. Now my ownself," she continued, shaking her fork in front of her, marking her words in the air, "I find it best to keep my head down, my eye clear, and carry a ice pick in my tote sack. That way I kin get a quick handle on my faith when I needs to. We gots to be careful around them white people. And smart."

"They ain't all bad, Vida."

"Humph. They raised to be bad. Leastways to the colored." She chortled to herself, thinking of the fierce look on Johnny's face that afternoon. "You know, I figger that white boy would kill me if I kept my back turned long enough. He's some nasty."

Johnny eased open the door to the darkened room. A shaft of light from the hallway caught his mother's face and her eye opened to the light. He tiptoed over to the edge of her bed and carefully removed the tray with her uneaten supper from beside her. Then he stood staring into her face until she managed both eyes open. At last she recognized him with a half-smile.

Johnny pulled himself up into the bed with her, and burrowed into the space under her outstretched arm, putting his back against her ribs. Tucked up close to his mother, he dutifully reported to her the day's events, including the part about the strange old man on the bench, and the jumble Vida was making of their kitchen.

With outrage he told her of all the time Vida wasted. About how she would walk out to the front porch and stand there staring off in the distance at the sheriff's house, like she was waiting for him. And how sometimes, after the sheriff got in or out of his cruiser, she would head back to the kitchen, walking very slowly, like all that looking had worn her out, and stand over the sink, saying and doing nothing. Wasting his daddy's money.

"And Momma, one day she disappeared. She was out standin on the porch, looking at the sheriff's house, and then she was gone."

When his mother didn't ask where to, he offered his guess. "I bet she been over sneakin around the sheriff's house. She's sneaky mean, Momma. She's the one been behind the bush."

Johnny went on to list Vida's offenses and then waited for something to happen, as if his recollections would make her whole. Or mad. Anything. But she did not seem to care.

He had only one item left, one even he knew was minor. "She took some food home."

She just gazed at him with clouded eyes. Then from out of that dimness, he thought he saw a faint, familiar glimmer.

She whispered to him, "Nothing else?"

Johnny's heart began to beat faster, "No ma'am. I even checked her bag."

"You know your daddy won't tolerate stealing, don't you?"

Johnny nodded again, excitedly. They both knew that was one thing Floyd could not abide. He had fired other maids when he discovered they had taken something from the house. One time he even told the sheriff.

"But it needs to be something bigger than food," she said. "Something valuable."

"Yes, ma'am!" he said happily, interpreting this as a full-out declaration of war on the maid.

His mother's breathing became even again. When she closed her eyes. Johnny kissed her on the cheek and climbed down off the bed. Checking to make sure his mother's eyes were still shut, he carefully reached onto her nightstand, picked up a little garnet brooch, slipped it into his pocket, and tiptoed out of the room.

Chapter 29
VIDA'S DREAM

Vida is perched in her swing, the one that hung from the porch of her childhood home. Pushing off higher and higher, she kicks up her baby-doll shoes and ruffles her petticoats for the world to see, for Vida delights in the envious faces of the plantation girls as they walk by on their way to chop cotton, dressed in raggedy field clothes, and nappy-headed.

Her father in his best preacher's suit, with the golden hands hanging from his chain, tells her, "You are truly blessed to be the daughter of the Reach Out Man." He smiles upon her proudly as she reaches for heaven with the tips of her shoes.

From somewhere come the shrieks of a baby and the smile vanishes from her father's face.

"Is that baby yours?" he asks. She is too frightened to speak.

By now the plantation girls have come up into the yard, giggling wickedly. In the dream they play their ring games, holding hands in a circle and dancing and kicking. They chant those mean rhymes made up about Vida:

Vida was sewing a hole in her dress
From popping her tail so high
White man thread her needle,
Right through the eye.

Vida looks up at her father, hoping he will not hear, wanting to deny their accusations, but they begin to sing louder, almost shouting now:

Vida got her a baby boy,

Bright as a lectric light.
That's why she be grinnin'
Cause all she totes is white!

The crying starts up again. She sees Nate. He is at her father's feet, grasping for the golden hands. The hands seem to be alive, reaching down toward Nate. They almost touch.

"Tell me the truth, girl," her father says angrily. "Is this baby yores?"

Vida's throat is so dry she can't speak. She desperately wants to put the smile back on her father's face. Finally she blurts out, "No, Daddy. He ain't my baby." The crying and chanting grows so loud she reaches up to cover her ears.

When she awoke from the dream, it was Vida who was sobbing. "I'm sorry, Nate. I'm sorry," she heard herself moan. Through her tears, she saw the darkened form of her father standing in the doorway.

"Vida? You all right?" he asked, sounding worried. "You been callin out in yo sleep again."

Vida quickly wiped the tears away. "No. Ain't nothin wrong with me," she said sharply, suddenly angry with her father. But he just stood there, watching.

She saw that the man with hunched shoulders who stood before her was no longer the proud man in the dream. Vida said less harshly, "Get on back to bed, Daddy. I be fine. We both need our sleep."

Her father turned back to his bed. Vida bit hard on her lip. What was the reason Nate had been coming to her night after night? Was it just to remind her of what a bad mother she was? She knew that all too well. Caught between the love of her father and her son, she had chosen her father.

Or could it be that in the dream, Nate was asking her to undo the past? To put things right. Either way, as sad as it made her feel, she would not wish the dreaming to stop. It was proof Nate was still working in her life, doing his best to reach out to her, to show her the way.

⚜

A hundred miles north, the man's headlights washed across the road sign: WELCOME TO MISSISSIPPI, THE HOSPITALITY STATE. When he read it, he got the distinct feeling it didn't mean him, so he slowed the old Caddy to five miles below the speed limit. He'd heard too many stories about the kind of welcoming committees Mississippi convened for colored folks visiting from the North. Last year the papers couldn't say enough about that boy from Chicago they found at the bottom of one of those unpronounceable rivers of theirs. Sent that god-awful-looking corpse back up to his poor momma. They put him out on display like some kind of war hero. Thousands of people snaked by that casket to get a look at what Mississippi white people could do when they got it in their minds to welcome you properly.

And Jesus, the stories those Mississippi boys in Joliet told about home-sweet-home. No wonder they ended up robbing and stealing. Life spent bent over double in a cotton field, yassuhing and nawsuhing every white man that could knot a noose—such a life was bound to short-change a fella when it comes to making sound business decisions. Of course himself, his crime was the result of an understandable miscalculation. Cutting a man for drawing five of a kind out of a deck he himself had stacked. He figured if the brother could magically come up with an extra ace, he shouldn't have trouble producing a new ear. The law thought different.

Daylight shifted ever so slowly across the Mississippi landscape, carried on the back of a thick, ghostly mist. This was creepier even than the inky darkness that it replaced. As the shapes of trees emerged from the mist, he peered through the vaporous air to see if there were really ropes hanging from every limb.

Nope, he thought, if it wasn't for Rezel, you sure wouldn't catch my ass in this backwoods hell of a hole. But a deal was a deal. Anyway, Mississippi was on the way to the Big Easy, a town made for an expert gamesman like himself. In New Orleans, they never stopped dealing and the dice never stopped rolling. The best thing, nobody knew his face or his con. Be like taking candy from babies.

On top of anteing up a C-note, Rezel told him he could keep the car and the only thing he asked was to drop off a message to some girl he used to know. Must still be sweet on her after all these years. Acted like it was the most important letter he ever wrote. Didn't even have an address. Drew out a map to some hick town called Delphi and said to begin asking about her there. "But stay away from that sheriff," he told him. "Don't let him catch you."

The man had laughed. "What you think I am? Stupid? Might as well tell me to not slam my dick in the door."

Whether or not Rezel thought he was stupid, he didn't say, but he had made him repeat that girl's name about a hundred times and went on to say she always used to dress in white. It was like her trademark. Shoes, socks, dresses, and even little white bows in her hair and on her shoes. Sure sounded crazy, but Rezel was kind of crazy anyway. Everybody in the pen was sure Rezel was going to end up singing the blues for drinks and chump change. But the very day after he got out of prison, Rezel fell into working for some bigshot white lawyer who even put him up in a spare room. Let Rezel have his old Cadillacs like hand-me-down suits. A new one every five years. Rezel had said, "Go on and take the car. The boss and me is due to be refitted."

Crazy. Crazy like a goddamned fox. Again he wondered what con Rezel had pulled to make that white man do for him like that. Be nice to run that scam a few times in New Orleans.

As he was having his thoughts. the big Cadillac glided past a green metal road sign that read, "Delphi 58 mi."

While her father slept, Vida watched the flame gradually take hold of the kindling. Impatiently, she poked at the fire and then set the flat iron on the eye of the stove. If only Nate could know she was doing everything she could think to do. Every day for weeks she had studied the sheriff and his family, like a farmer studies the sky. Trying to decipher the comings and goings of the household. One day, when she was sure no one was home, Vida even ventured over to the house to check to see if the doors and windows were locked, before hurrying back terrified to death. But soon she would make her move. That house had to hold some clue about her son.

If there was one other person who could possibly care as much about Nate's whereabouts as she, it would be his father.

Then there were the maids. Vida had lost Nate to a world too big for her to grasp. But what she did understand, all too well, was that if anything was important to know in this oversized world, white people knew it first.

If anybody knew what was said in the white people's homes, it was their maids. Maybe it would only be a snatch of conversation overheard while putting peas on their white woman's table or ironing their white man's shirt. A piece of news from that Chi-car-go town. Or a mention about a boy somebody thought was the breathing image of a certain person they all knew. Or maybe there would be talk about a colored blues singer who traveled the countryside with a light-complected child.

It might not mean anything to them, but to Vida it could mean everything. Vida was working on a way to put her ear to every important keyhole in Delphi.

Vida spread her maid's uniform out flat on the eating table, getting it ready for the iron. She held her white tennis shoes up to the light of the fire to see if they were in need of wiping.

Even though she was new to being a maid, the other women had been helpful. It had also been a way to cultivate their friendships. Vida had made good friends with Creola, Miss Pearl's maid. Miss Pearl, after all, was the Senator's sister and Miss Hertha's aunt.

Vida had even gone out of her way to be nice to that awful Misery, the sheriff's maid. But there she would have to be careful. That woman was dangerous and loved the white man more than her own people.

Sweet Pea was doubly useful. Not only did she have a past "relationship" with the sheriff, as far as Vida knew she still slept with half the white men in Delphi.

There was the Gooseberry brothers' maid, Maggie. As addled as she seemed to be, surely she could pick up something from her bosses, who everybody knew were the biggest gossips in town. Now she had a plan to bring them all together. It might not be much, but it was something.

Vida touched a wet finger to the iron and heard a satisfying sizzle. She smiled, remembering how she once dreamed of bringing all the maids in

Hopalachie County together and conspiring to put poison in their bosses' soup. Well, as long as Miss Hazel cooperated and kept out of her way, and Mr. Floyd stayed gone working himself to death, this might be just as good.

It was almost dawn and the sign said simply, "HOPALACHIE COUNTY," no welcome to it. The name squirmed around in the man's head before it finally leaped to his tongue. "Hopalachie!" he hissed. "Good goddamned."

Now he remembered why it sounded so familiar. That was the name of the river they dragged the boy out of. And me driving in here like a fool with Illinois plates. He noticed that the air now hung heavy with the sour-sweet smell of swampland. Without thinking, he rolled up his window and knocked another five miles off his speed, all the while nervously checking his rearview mirror.

If he turned around and took the long way to New Orleans through Arkansas, Rezel would never know a thing. Why should he risk his neck going through some place named after a river like that? All he needed was some redneck sheriff asking him what a Yankee troublemaker was doing driving through his personal county.

The man turned off onto an overgrown path that led into a thick jungle of trees and vines and pulled to a stop, cutting his lights. Hidden from view he sat until the sun was well up, considering his options.

He had started this trip with a comfortable contempt for Mississippi Negroes. Mealy mouthed, slow-witted, foot-shuffling, spiritual-singing, haint-haunted, white-man-worshipping, rubber-spined cowards. Now, less than two hours in Mississippi himself, he was gaining a brand-new appreciation for what a person might do to stay alive.

He got out and, watchful for any tree snakes or jungle cats or alligators, or anything else that might be lying in wait, he tiptoed to the rear of the car. As the riot of strange insects closed in around him, he took out his pocketknife and hurriedly began to remove his license plate, thinking, If I'm gonna do this, I sho rather get a ticket driving without no tags than dropped in that Hopalachie River for being a meddlesome Yankee nigger.

Nearing the outskirts of Delphi, he told himself he would ask the first colored person he saw, and if they never heard of no Snow White, as far he was concerned, he had done his duty. He'd drive straight out of Mississippi and never look back.

Staying away from the fine homes, he took a gravel road that looked like it headed down toward the river. "I bet that's where they keep their colored folk," he told himself. Sure enough, as he descended the hill, trudging up the road toward him came one of the biggest colored women he had ever seen, puffing like she was late for a mess of ham-hocks.

"Hey, you! Big Momma!" he shouted out his window. "Come over here a second."

Creola planted her fists on her hips and scowled at the man, her red freckles aglow. The first thing she thought was that when this man was a baby somebody must have caught his head between a couple of two-by-fours. "Who you talkin to like that? I don't know you from jump, and if I did I'd sho nuf lie bout it. You one of the ugliest-lookin mens I ever seen. Somebody could use that face of yores to split wood. And why you talk so funny? I *know* you ain't from around here. People round here got some manners when they speakin to a lady."

The man held up a hand trying to stop the woman from making a scene. "Hold on, Momma! I didn't mean to get you riled. I'm just turnin a favor for a friend used to be from down here and I'm in bad need of a little southern hospitality is all. Sorry if I got off on a bad foot."

"What you want? Who you know from around here?"

"Never mind that part. The person I'm lookin for is called Vida. Vida Snow. You heard the name?"

Creola eyed the man carefully. "I ain't got time to talk with the likes of you. I'm already late for work, and Miss Pearl gone have my hide."

"You ain't answered my question. You know her or no?"

"Maybe I do and maybe I don't. How I know you ain't up to no good? Why you keep lookin over yo shoulder like that? The law after you?"

The man was becoming exasperated. "Look, Momma. It's a simple question," he said angrily. "Do you know somebody go by the name of Vida or not. Dresses like a fuckin' snowball. I got a message for her. It's important and she gone want it."

Creola snapped her fingers. "I bet you a fat man you a friend of her brother. Or Hannah one. You look like the kind they sociate with. You carryin a load of shine in that car?"

"Yeah, that's it, Momma. I'm her brother's best buddy. Now show me the way, will you?"

"Well," Creola said, eyeing the big, plush seats in the car. "I sho could use me a ride. You carry me in yo big fancy car and I show you where she be at. She don't work but two houses down from my white lady."

The man reached over and flung open the passenger door.

When they got to the Grahams' neighborhood, Creola told the man where to turn so he could drive up behind the house.

"Just climb up on that big porch and she probably be in the kitchen right this minute." With that Creola took off in a lope to Miss Pearl's.

Johnny was under the porch digging in the dirt when he heard the sound of footsteps above his head and then a knock on the door. "Anybody in there?" a strange voice called out.

He scrambled out from under the porch, brushed himself off, and clambered up the steps. "Who you lookin for?"

The man studied the boy for a moment. "You got a maid in there called Vida Snow?" he asked.

Johnny considered the man for a moment without answering.

"I'm askin if she works here. You followin what I'm tryin to say? You got a tongue?"

Thinking the man may have come to take Vida away, he decided to answer. "We got a mean ol' colored woman says her name is Vida."

"Well, where is she? I got to speak to her."

"She's on the front porch. Waiting."

"Waitin? Waitin for what?"

"Waiting for the sheriff."

The man swallowed hard. "The sheriff," he repeated, hardly believing his bad luck. "You say she on the front porch waitin for the sheriff. The sheriff of Hopa...Hipo...Hap...whatever the hell this county is. That what you sayin?"

Johnny pointed. "He lives next door. She waits for him every morning."

"Merciful Jesus!" the man spat. "I done landed smack in the middle of the snake pit." Looking around frantically, he pulled an envelope from his jacket pocket and held it out to Johnny. "Take it," he ordered.

Johnny took a step back.

The man jabbed the boy in the chest with the envelope, "You make sure she gets it, you hear? I ain't got time to hang around and chat with no baby crackers."

Johnny reached for it with dirty fingers. Relieved of his burden, the man flew down the steps, taking two at a time and headed straight for his car, idling at the bottom of the hill. He took off, spewing gravel behind him.

Johnny studied the sealed envelope. There was nothing written on the outside, except where somebody had typed the single letter "V." He glanced back toward the kitchen and then took the envelope with him under the porch. He knew he was doing a thing so bad, he could never tell anyone. Not even his mother. He would have to lie the very best he could.

And he did. When Creola came over later in the day to find out from Vida what it was Willie had sent the man for, Johnny pleaded ignorance, and in the face of all the hard looks Vida aimed at him, he stuck to his story.

Chapter 30
A GATHERING OF MAIDS

It was early afternoon and Hazel was fighting against the current. Johnny was standing there at her bedside, beckoning her upward. "Momma. They coming. Wake up."

That's right. Today was special. She remembered that much. Now what was it? Something good was supposed to happen. Something she and Johnny had been waiting for. But what?

Trying to draw herself up on her elbows, Hazel only succeeded in getting knotted in the bedcovers. She gave up and fell back on the pillows. Johnny came to her rescue and busied himself with untangling her covers.

"They coming today, Momma," he whispered excitedly. "We're going to catch em red-handed, ain't we?"

That was it! They finally had something good on Vida. Today they were going to give her hell. Today, after weeks of taking double doses of that woman's medicine and meanness, Hazel Ishee Graham was going to fight back. Now was the time. Anyway, what did she have to lose?

Over that summer of river rhythms, as the current took and then released her, from up in her bedroom Hazel studied the rhythms of her own household. Floyd floated in and out, but he no longer lived in this house. His heart had drifted elsewhere. His smiles and nods merely marked his coming and going, and meant nothing else, like Vida's two warning knocks when delivering food and medicine.

The afternoons brought Johnny, dirty from digging under the porch and breathless with fresh reports, mostly about Vida. Once in a while, he would tell on Vida's father, who had taken to working odd jobs in the neighborhood.

Sometimes Hazel could hear the sound of his mower in an adjacent yard. It had a strange comforting drone, like an old woman humming church songs on some faraway porch. So even though Johnny seemed indignant when he told stories about how the man would sit himself down on the bench under the live oaks, where he commenced to reading a raggedy Bible and talking out loud to himself ("*Real* loud," Johnny had said), she couldn't get mad at the old colored man. Even for breeding a monster like he had.

No. What little spite she could muster she saved for Vida herself, who over the summer had remained sullen, sparing no more words than necessary to get the job done. Sometimes Hazel would resist taking the pills just to hear the voice of another woman. But she always regretted it. Vida's words were as comforting as barbed wire. Hazel nurtured her dislike each passing day. That maid had become the living symbol of everything she had lost.

Once after dinner, Hazel thought she had heard the sound of strange voices, muffled laughter and the clatter of coffee cups. She put it down to dreaming.

That is, until Johnny told her about what Vida was up to—having her maid friends over for coffee, using the house as a break room for the neighborhood domestic help. The more Hazel heard about that, the more riled she got. Vida knew Hazel was helpless to stop her and she was just rubbing it in Hazel's face. Well, today she would show her different. Johnny had learned that after dinnertime, the whole raft of them were coming over to steal coffee.

"When they do," she had promised Johnny, "We'll go storming into the kitchen like Jesus into the temple and drive out that coffee-stealing gang of thieves." With right on her side, Hazel was going to show that heartless girl who the real boss in this house was.

"Johnny, you go on downstairs and watch," she whispered. "When they all get here, and Vida starts passing out my groceries, you come and get me."

Johnny innocently situated himself at the yellow dinette table, practicing his alphabet on the back of the electric bill. He could feel Vida looking over at him from where she stood at the sink, finishing up the dinner dishes.

"What you writin on?" she asked over her shoulder. "The light comp'ny ain't gone preshate you markin up they bill. You might be writin somethin that makes them people cut off the lectricity."

Johnny didn't bother to answer as he drew the big letter "V."

"You gone have them ABC's writ on ever some thing in this house before school even starts. Anyways, why you frettin so about it? You not spected to know nothin yet."

Ignoring her babbling, Johnny cut his eyes toward the porch. He hoped he had heard right about today being the day. Behind him he heard the clinking of china as Vida gathered the coffee cups and lined them up on the counter. Still looking down at his printing, he asked, as innocently as he could, "Are them ol' women comin over here today?"

"That's right. You got somethin' to say bout that?"

Johnny looked up at the kitchen clock in the shape of a chicken. "How many minutes are they goin to stay in my kitchen?"

"Til they gets up and walks out the do' be my guess." Vida turned around toward Johnny. "What you starin at? You caint tell time."

"Can't tell it what?" Johnny asked.

"Huh?"

"You can't tell Time what?"

"You can't read no clock, is what I tryin to tell you."

Johnny rolled his eyes at her. He knew that.

After disappearing into the pantry, Vida returned with a can of Luzianne, the brand that had a picture of a smiling colored woman pouring a cup of coffee on the front. Johnny wondered why his father couldn't have found a nice maid like that.

Vida broke off the little metal key, fit the tab into the slot, and coiled it around the top of the can, cutting away the lid. A thick smoky smell escaped into the kitchen.

"That's a new can of coffee, ain't it?" Johnny asked, grinding the dot on the little letter "i."

"Yessuh, I believe it is. Seein as how I jest opened it."

"I guess coffee costs my daddy a lot of money, don't it?" He used to see his daddy quiz his mother like this, asking her questions he already knew the answers to. "Have you been drinking again?" "Are you bound and determined to turn us into a laughingstock?" Sometimes his mother would cry. But Vida didn't seem anywhere close to crying. Johnny could feel her squinting down on him at that moment. He relented and looked at her. "I was just asking."

But she was still squinting. "What's yo problem now?"

He tried to hold her stare but finally exhaled loudly like his daddy, to show how exasperating she was, and then turned back to his work. She knew what his problem was—her and that squinty ol' face. He couldn't wait. She was going to get hers real soon.

A few minutes later, the screen opened with a screech and there stood Creola filling up the doorway and flinging a shadow over the whole kitchen. She was wearing a starched white maid's uniform just like Vida's, only a hundred times as large. Under one meaty arm, she toted an enamel dishpan.

"Come on!" Vida called out to Creola as she stood by the counter, waiting for the coffee to finish perking. "Set yoself down and rest easy."

Noticing that Johnny was busy with his pencil, Creola set the dishpan on the table and pulled out a chair next to him. She squatted down partway, and then, after waggling both hands behind her to locate the chair and center it, dropped into the seat with a groan. Johnny grimaced when he saw those poor chromed steel legs flare outward. These women would surely wreck his mother's kitchen. He sneaked a look down the hallway and smiled. Not too much longer.

Creola glanced over at Johnny's work and beamed. "Look at all them purty letters! Whachoo doin there, Mister John? You writin the guv'ner? Tell him Creola say 'How do.'" She winked at Vida. "And while you at it, ask him to let my ol' man out of jail for Saddity night. He can have him back first light Monday mornin when I'm done with him." Slapping her huge thigh, Creola burst out laughing at herself.

Johnny held up his printing for her to see. "I'm practicing my ABC's. I'm goin to school in Septober." He cut his eyes over at Vida, to see if she noticed how nice he could be to somebody who was nice to him first.

"I tole you, ain't no September," Vida corrected. "They be a September. They be a October. But ain't no Septober."

"Well, ain't you a big boy!" Creola exclaimed brightly. She grabbed the corners of her apron and fanned her face with it, but she made sure to include Johnny in the breeze, too. "Hardly bigger than a porch baby and kin already cipher. You sho nuf gone be teacher's pet."

While Creola bragged on him, Johnny wished again that his father had hired somebody else besides Vida. Even Creola would be an improvement.

The screen door sounded again as Vida was unplugging the percolator. "Just in time for coffee," she called out.

"Lawdamercy it's so hot I'm bleedin to death!" exclaimed Sweet Pea. Beads of perspiration glistened on her smooth black face. In her arms, she carried a paper sack from the Jitney Jungle. Sweet Pea let out a high laugh. "Y'all I saw Misery comin up the lane from the sheriff's house, and I swear that woman don't sweat. She as cool as a cuke."

She placed a hand beside her mouth like she was going to whisper but didn't. "I guess them albino niggers ain't got no sweat holes." Glancing out in the yard with a contrite look, she said, "I better mind myself. She tell her boss on me, he haul my butt off to jail."

"Won't be the first time he haul yo butt somewheres," Vida said under her breath. When Sweet Pea shot her a look, Vida asked innocently, "You wont some of this here coffee, Sweet Pea?"

She gave Vida a forgiving smile. "It might be better if you had some thang cold to drank. It be uphill from the store and I run the whole way." Checking the bright yellow chicken, she said, "I can't stay too long today. Miss Cilly be spectin me back with her grocies." She set the bag on the counter.

Looking into the refrigerator, Vida called out behind her, "We got some sweet tea left from dinnertime. Got some orange juice."

"Ice tea hit the spot."

"Well, stand there in front of the fan and I'll po' you some."

Johnny watched as Vida cracked open a tray of ice and fixed a glass for Sweet Pea. Now she was giving away his mother's tea, too. It was a good thing his momma was going to put a stop to it today. If Vida's club got any bigger, pretty soon they wouldn't have anything left in the house.

Sweet Pea drained half the glass in one gulp. Smacking her lips she exclaimed, "Y'all, it's hotter than a billygoat in a pepper patch!"

"Now I reckon that be hot!" Creola giggled, as she wedged the dishpan into the valley between her massive thighs.

Pushing back a strand of her shiny black hair, Sweet Pea said, "Yessuh! It be as hot as a one-legged ho' in—"

"Mind the boy, Sweet Pea," Vida interrupted. "Ain't nothin he don't remember."

"Oops," she said, "I clean forgot he was here."

Sweet Pea leaned over the fan that sat whirring on the counter. Johnny peeked through the corner of his eyes as she stretched open the top of her uniform, aiming the breeze down her bosom. Noticing him staring, Sweet Pea winked at Johnny. "How you doin, precious?"

Johnny snapped his eyes back down toward the table and pretended to be writing. Whenever Sweet Pea spoke to Johnny, he would blush, finding it impossible to speak back. He had never seen anybody like her. Brassy and big-hipped. She always wore shiny red earbobs as big as moon pies and her dress hugged tight every curving and rising of her body. He preferred to watch her when she wasn't looking.

"Cat got yo tongue, baby?" She fluttered her eyes at him.

"Dat boy be cipherin up a fog," Creola said with a chuckle. "Ain't got time for no women's fussin over him."

While Sweet Pea continued to flirt with Johnny, the door silently opened and closed, and before anyone knew it, a bony, light-skinned woman was standing among them, looking around the kitchen with her nose up. When her eyes lit on Sweet Pea, she sniffed once and then sat down at the table without speaking.

"How you, Missouri?" Vida asked, cutting her eyes at Sweet Pea, warning her to behave.

Missouri ironed out the lap of her crisp uniform with the flat of her hand. "I swear I ain't had a minute to sit till now. We been workin night and day gettin things ready out at the Columns." Then she fell silent, as if waiting for someone to ask her what exactly she had been doing out there at the Senator's, and while she waited, she ran her hand over the top of her head to smooth out her fine white hair, even though it was pulled back as tight as a snare drum.

After a long moment of quiet while the other maids traded amused looks, Missouri said, "Me and Miss Hertha been helping the Senator get ready for Miss Delia's birthday party."

"Miss Delia, that's the Senator's younger daughter, ain't it?" Vida asked, knowing good and well it was. "The flirty one."

"Yeah," Sweet Pea giggled. "She be the daughter that *don't* belong in a zoo. Missouri, yo white lady so ugly, she has to sneak up on a mirror...."

"The *Senator*," Missouri said, not letting Sweet Pea finish her meanness about Miss Hertha, "the Senator is invitin ever important person in the State. I spec the guv'nor hisself be there."

Behind Missouri's back, Sweet Pea prissily placed her hands on her hips and made a sarcastic "la-dee-da" face. Vida had to put her hand over her mouth to keep from laughing out loud.

"So Miss Delia done been resurrected, huh? Praise the Lord," Sweet Pea said rudely. "And everbody thinkin she was murdered."

"She got back home last week," Creola offered. "Tole y'all she took off to Memphis. And I heard she paid money to get a tattoo put on her patootie."

"Where Miss Delia tell her daddy she been gone to?" asked Sweet Pea. "After the Senator done searched half the county for his poor little lamb."

"Nowheres," Creola answered. "And he don't ask. Fraid she might tell him the truf. And that girl would, too. Don't give a hoot bout what folks thinks. Always been wild like that since she was a baby." Creola lowered her voice. "I heared the last one she took up with was a colored boy from Tchula."

The crowd got real quite for a few moments, and a feeling of danger hung in the air.

Vida broke the tension. "What you wont, Missouri, sweet tea or coffee?"

Missouri pressed her lips together into a thin taut line and smoothed her hair again. "You ain't got nothin else? Feel like a sof' drink, my own self."

Looking back into the refrigerator, Vida said, "I just mixed up some purple coo'lade for the boy. Reckon he wont mind sharin."

Johnny shot Vida a murderous look.

Seeing the reaction on Johnny's face, Missouri smiled a tight little grin and patted her head again. "Po' me a big glass of that coo'lade." Obviously pleased with herself, Missouri raised an eyebrow at Johnny, daring him to say something. But Johnny just held his peace. Her time was coming. There was only one maid left to go. The craziest one of all.

No sooner than he had the thought, there came a long slow creak as the screen door pulled back once more. Everyone looked up. It was the Gooseberry brothers' maid, Maggie. Her hair was its usual state—a jumble of black and white bristles, as tangled as a squirrel's nest. Maggie walked with great difficulty, by rocking side to side, like her legs had rusted long ago and had lost their bend. Her cotton stockings had completely given up their grip and bunched loosely around her ankles.

"How you doin, Maggie?"

"Ain't it good to see you!"

"You a little down in the hind today, Maggie?"

Seemingly deaf to the chorus of hellos and inquiries about her health, Maggie pulled out the last empty chair and eased herself into it.

Johnny shifted his focus to Maggie and studied her for a while. She was a gruesome sight to behold. Where her left eye should have been, there was only a shallow crater, permanently sealed shut with a ragged flap of skin. When she looked right at a person, which was rarely, it appeared like she was giving a sustained wink. Mostly she kept her good eye looking down at her leathery hands in her lap.

"Maggie, you wont a cup of coffee?" Vida called out.

Maggie continued kneading her hands. Vida brought the coffee pot over to Maggie and then lightly touched her shoulder. Maggie jumped. Her one eye shot open as wide as a silver dollar. "That be the Lawd's truf. Sho is!" she said emphatically, but to no one in particular.

Vida poured Maggie a cup and eased it in front of her. Eyeing Maggie closely, Johnny tried to figure her out. Whatever she said never seemed to match what was actually going on at the time, like she was a hoofbeat off from the rest of the herd. Anyway, his daddy would call them all a crazy bunch of niggers.

"Johnny," Vida said, interrupting his thoughts, "You get up and gimme yo seat. Go on outside and play."

Defiantly rolling his eyes at Vida, flouting the fate of Tangle Eye, Johnny dropped down from the chair. He didn't need to be told twice. This was his cue to go tell his mother it was time.

As Creola began a story about Miss Pearl, Johnny left through the back door, made a dash around the house and tiptoed in through the front. He was startled to find his mother already out of her room, wearing a robe, hunched on a step halfway up the stairs, her ear cocked toward the kitchen.

"Momma, they all here!" he whispered. "Let's go!"

But to his surprise she shushed him.

"But…"

"I'm trying to hear," she said. "Now they low-rating Miss Pearl."

"But…"

Hazel shushed him again. "Maybe they'll do Hertha next." She was enjoying this better than radio.

Disappointed that their plans had obviously changed, Johnny slipped down to the foot of the stairs, and quietly crept up to the kitchen door so he could keep one eye on the maids and the other on his mother.

Creola sat there hunched over Miss Pearl's dishpan, shelling Miss Pearl's butter beans, and was still badmouthing the woman she worked for. "Well, you all know how Christian my white lady believes she be." Creola dropped a handful of hulls in a paper sack Vida had set by her feet.

"Whachoo say!" Sweet Pea said with a laugh. "Miss Pearl think she so sweet, she stay out the rain less she melts."

Out of the blue Maggie exclaimed, "Praise Jesus!" like she was in church.

Smiling affectionately at her, Creola went ahead with her story. "Last week Miss Pearl come traping in the house and took a perfect good chair and busted it with a hammer. I ask her, 'What you doin, Miss Pearl?' She say, 'If you has to know, Creola, I'm buskin up this here chair so Mr. Ramphree from the hardware sto' can fix it.' That what she tole me. My word is my bond."

"That woman is crazy!"

"Sho nuf is!"

Missouri, who was always up for defending the white folks, seemed doubtful. "Now why she be bustin up her own chair? That don't make no sense."

"I tole you it was curioussome," Creola said. "Know what she say when I ask her how come?"

"Tell it sister!" Sweet Pea whooped. "You done started somethin now."

"Well, seems while Miss Pearl was downtown on her way to the beauty parlor she pass the hardware sto'. Some gennelman think she was goin inside so he hole open the door for her. Miss Pearl too nice to tell the man he be wrong and she didn't have no notion of going in that sto', that she was on her way to get her hair fluffed out. No, ma'am, she don't tell him that. So she say 'thankie very much' and walks on in the hardware sto'."

Vida and Sweet Pea both told Creola to "hush up," which Johnny knew meant just the opposite to colored people.

"You ain't heared it yet!" Creola dropped another handful of hulls into the sack. "When Mr. Ramphree sees Miss Pearl in his sto' he ask her if he kin help her find somethin. She don't wont to be ugly and tell the man she come traping into his sto' by mistake, so she lies and say she got a broke chair and was lookin for some nails and glue."

"Bless her own dear self," Maggie intoned sweetly, rocking her head back and forth, probably lost in a story all of her own. Missouri frowned at her.

"Well, that Mr. Ramphree thinks she so sweet he say he be glad to come by and fix up her chair."

Vida slapped her leg. "No, ma'am, she didn't!"

"Yes ma'am she did," Creola laughed. "Stead of saying 'no thankie' like anysomebody with the sense God gave a billygoat, she go straight home and busts up a chair so the po' man would find somethin to fix when he got there." Throwing her head back, Creola raised both arms to the ceiling and shouted, "Law, Law! I tole you that woman was a pure-dee mess."

Maggie looked up with her good eye and saw Vida and Sweet Pea bent over in laughter. Judging the story to be over, she nodded her head vigorously. "Uh-huh. That's right. Sho is."

Johnny thought he heard something behind him and was amazed to see his mother with her hand over her mouth. Had she really laughed?

Suddenly, Missouri shushed everybody. Her ear was cocked toward the stairhall. "I thought I heared somethin stirrin." Both Johnny and his mother froze.

Vida, who was wiping her eyes from laughing so hard, reassured them. "All you probly heared was Miss Hazel's radio. She ain't comin out that room before suppertime. We got the kitchen to our own selves. I tole y'all who was boss in this house."

Again Johnny looked at his mother. The muscle in her jaw was jumping, but otherwise she was still.

"Now?" he mouthed. But she shook her head no.

Sweet Pea fished a couple of ice cubes from her glass and twisted them tightly in her handkerchief. "You right bout that Miss Pearl. She tries to act so nice it be scary." She daubed her throat with her ice pack. "Every time that Miss Pearl comes visitin my white lady, she bound to sneak back to the kitchen and gimme some trashy love story she done read."

"Uh-huh," Creola said. "She got herself into a love book club. When one of them books comes in the mail she runs and hides it so Mr. Hayes don't see what she be messin wit. She gives em to you just to get em out the house. And who you gone tell?"

"Whachoo sayin! She say she gimme them books cause I went to the eighth grade and don't hardly never say 'ain't.' And she say she like how I straightening myself out by givin up the mens and gettin respectable work." Sweet Pea shook her head at the compliments and then continued. "I read em ever one but they all the same. Bout some weak-kneed white woman waitin for a big strong man to come along and pull her butt out of trouble. Miss Pearl say, 'Sweet Pea. It's so nice to know some of *our* colored can turn themselves around and 'spire to life's lofty pursuits.'"

"You soundin just like her now!" exclaimed Creola.

"What I wont to say is, 'Why thank you kindly, Miss Pearl, but if what you callin the lofty pursuits is countin on a man to rescue pasty white ass, you can keep yo books. I'll carry myself down to One Wing Hannah's and punch in some Bessie Smith records on the Seeburg. That's one lady who know what a man is good for. If Bessie's man ain't home by suppertime, she be moved on to the next pair of britches.'"

"Uh-huh!" Creola agreed. "When the men go huntin, the womens can go fishin." She hooted at herself.

Vida laughed at Creola. "Whachoo know bout that. You been with the same man for forty years."

Sweet Pea whistled. "Never met a man worth forty years. Whoo-ee!"

Missouri patted the bun on the back of her head and sniffed at Sweet Pea's common talk. "If you so down on men, how come you always seem to be knee-deep in a fresh supply?"

"Don't gets me wrong. I like a man's comp'ny. But if'n his comp'ny turns bad, then out the do' he goes. You can't do that if you countin on love to pay the rent. I pays the way for my own dear self." Shaking her head, Sweet Pea crunched a piece of ice. "Nothin worse than havin to bide bad comp'ny."

"Praise the Lawd," Maggie said in a low whisper. She appeared to be nodding off.

Vida tried to steer the conversation back onto the Senator and his family. "What was y'all sayin bout Miss Delia a while back? Bout her bein crazy and runnin off to Memphis."

"*All* them womens in that family is crazy," Sweet Pea said. "Startin with Miss Pearl and ending with Miss Delia. Ever time that girl go missin, which is bout once a month, it's katy-bar-the-door and hide yo purties, cause the Sheriff ain't long behind."

"What you mean, hide my purties?"

Creola, who had begun to sweat in the hot kitchen, nodded her soggy head at Vida, "That's right. You ain't been here long nuf. You don't know bout the little show the white folks put on ever time Miss Delia gets a wild hair to take off and mess around." Creola, having seen all this many times before, told Vida that the Senator would right away get in a terrible state, convinced some ungrateful nigger had done his daughter harm. Next he would ride his son-in-law the sheriff until he did something official.

"That's like sending the fox after the hen," Sweet Pea said under her breath.

"But the fact of business is," Creola continued with a chuckle, "everbody in Delphi know that Miss Delia gone come home by her own self. Probly after sneakin off up to Memphis and alley cattin' with some man. They say she like the colored boys and white trash the best."

Like a wet dog, Creola shook her head furiously to throw off the sweat from her mop of red hair. Everybody ducked. "How be ever, you caint tell the Senator that," she said, pushing back the limp strands of her hair with both hands. "No lawd! Both them girls—Hertha and that Delia—is the apples in his eyes. Caint do no evil. So he tell the sheriff, 'Boy, you better git yo ass in high gear and do somethin bout my little precious *now.*'" Creola whooped and stamped her foot. "And you should see that man move that skinny butt of his. Lawd!"

But Vida wasn't laughing. "I still ain't seein what it got to do with hidin' my purties."

"That's the part I'm up to now." Creola took a loud sip of coffee. "To *keep* his job, the sheriff got to prove to the Senator he *doin* his job, so he put on these house-by-house searches. Cept they ever one start and end in Tarbottom. He go down there and poke through a few of us's houses. Just to stall the Senator till Miss Delia drags her own dear self home."

"So the sheriff just gone walk right in my house one day?" Vida asked.

"That's right. Prob'ly already has," Sweet Pea said. "He likes to go when nobody's home. And he bad to pick up thangs from folkses houses that don't be his. Triflin thangs. Caint be worth nothin to him. How be ever, to some po' colored person it is."

Creola frowned. "Last year he stole the locket my little niece gimme for my birthday."

"Why he do that?" Vida asked.

Creola shrugged her shoulders and picked up a swatter lying on the table and waved it at her face. "Why white people do any thang they do? Cause they can, I reckon."

Again Johnny looked up at his mother. What was she waiting for?

A heavy silence fell over the group, until Missouri spoke up with a sputter. "You all ain't nothin but a bunch of gossipin ol' hens. Sheriff Brister ain't no man to be disrespectin. The sheriff chosen by a wise God who knows when the peoples need a firm hand."

"Don't blame God for that man," Creola shot back. "He married Miss Hertha how come he be the high sheriff. The Senator's money what keep him runnin for office. And Miss Hertha's uglies keep him runnin after anysomebody with a tail to switch." Creola winked at Sweet Pea, who looked away too quickly, none too anxious for Missouri to know about her times in the woods with the sheriff. Creola continued anyway. "Why, I bet you a fat man he got fifty chillun both white and colored runnin all round this county."

Now it was Vida's expression that had darkened. She dropped her coffee spoon on the floor with a clatter and then went down after it. By the time she was up again, she was smiling pleasantly. She looked over at Missouri admiringly, and cooed, "I bet you like part of that family, ain't you, Missouri? I seen how they always makin 'mirations over you."

Missouri glanced at Vida suspiciously. "They do good by me. If you pay respect, you gets respect."

"Ain't that the truth," Vida said. "I bet you know just about everthang that goes on in they house."

"I reckon. What you rootin around for?"

"Nothin mostly," Vida said, trying to affect only mild interest. "Just somethin I been meanin to ask you."

"Like what?"

"Like what become of that ol' uncle used to be his deputy?"

"Humph!" Missouri sniffed. "That ol' fool? Sheriff run him off years ago."

"Did?" Vida refilled Missouri's glass. "Now ain't that somethin? How come he went and done that to kin? Sounds cold."

"Sheriff got good reasons, I'm sho. Anyways, ain't none of your business. Best kept in the family." Missouri said, letting everyone know that included her.

Vida sighed and let it go.

Glancing up at the clock, Creola said, "Look at the time in that bird's gizzard." She caught a hold of the table, and hoisted her massive bulk vertical. "I reckon I best be gettin back to Miss Pearl. She wake up from her beauty nap and find me gone missin she be some mad. She liable to turn out the hounds."

The rest of the group followed suit and rose from their chairs.

Sweet Pea lifted her grocery bag from the counter and then stamped her foot. "Mercy! I plum forgot Miss Cilly her dish soap and I been gone all this time. She gone raise sand at me."

Vida disappeared into the pantry and returned with a new bottle of Lux. "Here, take this," she said, handing out Hazel's soap. "We got us plenty of ever thang in this house."

Johnny shot a glance at his mother. *Surely* that would set her off. They were stealing right from under her nose. But she just sat there. If he didn't know any better, he would even say she seemed a little glad they had said all those mean things about white people.

The boy watched as the little club headed for the door. After almost an hour of gossiping and grunting and waggling their heads at each other, and the one with the scary eye mumbling and humming to herself, they exited the kitchen, one by one.

His mother had let them go. Scot-free. She had them dead to rights and now they had escaped. He looked back up the stairs and watched disappointedly as she carefully drew herself up and turned back toward her room. Suddenly he became frightened. Why was she letting Vida win?

Chapter 31
MISSING THINGS

No matter how many times she had been here, she was never prepared for the gloom the house exuded. Inside, it was darker than the Grahams', and cooler, almost tomblike. The furniture was ponderous and grave. Latched shutters behind silk damask drapes, their golden rope tiebacks loosened, both kept out the afternoon sunlight and kept in that morning's run of the air conditioner. The ceilings were higher, probably fourteen feet, and although the rooms were densely furnished, the house eerily echoed the slightest sound. It seemed to repeat even the galloping of Vida's heart.

The floor in the hallway was constructed of long, wide planks of heart pine, waxed to a deep honey glow. Over the century the soft wood had been dimpled countless times by the sharp, pointed heels of white people now long dead.

The creaking beneath her feet sounded out like thunder as she cautiously made her way into the library. She came to a stop before the fireplace. On the marble mantelshelf, the tick-ticking of the gold clock was loud enough to wake the dead. For a moment she stood stock-still on the ancient French wool rug of muted colors and stared up at the oil painting that hung above the clock. It was of a white man with curls cascading onto his shoulders, dressed in a frilly blouse; short, tight pants, with white stockings that rose almost to his knees. He wore slippers with bows on them, like she used to wear. She remembered back in school, she had seen men wearing clothes like this in her history books. It was said that the Senator's grandfather and great-grandfather had lived in this house, and Missouri said that before this there were plantations in Virginia and castles across the ocean.

Vida slowly looked around the room, taking in its contents. She wondered if her own ancestors could have dusted and shined these very heir-looms. A great-great-grandfather could have planed and laid down the very floorboards beneath her feet and maybe even felled the trees from the extinct Delta forests she had heard about, before cotton took over the world.

Vida's interest turned toward more recent times. She had stolen inside the house to watch and to listen, to touch and to gather up smells. She came to glean from the house any trace of a living, breathing inhabitant. Yet, in the midst of all this splendor, she could detect no sign of the sheriff. She closed her eyes and tried to imagine him in the house. Where did he sit? Where did he eat? Surely not at the grand mahogany table, in a chair with a hand-embroidered seat. Where did he sleep? In the giant four-poster bed upstairs with the canopy as big as the night sky?

No, this was not where he lived. Even though she kept up with his comings and goings, watching him swagger to his patrol car in the morning and disappear into the house in the evening, she couldn't imagine him existing once he passed through those doors with the polished brass handles and the beveled glass, distorting like prisms. There was nothing of him here. This was old, and elegant and civilized. Where did a low-rate man like him disappear to in a house like this? Where did they hem up the sheriff so he wouldn't upset the ways of fine, civilized white people?

One careful step at a time, Vida softly padded up the stairs. She wanted to see the bedroom again. Maybe there was something she had missed before.

Vida knew her way around the house very well by now. When Hertha took the girls out to the Columns to see her daddy, sometimes she would bring Missouri along, leaving the house empty and unlocked. If she could get Johnny to take a nap, or sneak away while he was busy under the house, Vida was free to roam through the rooms, touching their contents, hoping in some way to brush up against an understanding of Nate's daddy, and perhaps bring her one step closer to her boy, all the while remaining alert for sounds of an approaching car. But so far in all her visits, she had not run into the sheriff here. Not even the stink of stale cigarette smoke lingered. The only scents were those of Hertha and her blood relations.

In the bedroom, she opened the giant doors of the mahogany armoire, where his clothes were kept. Taking her time, she went through the inside drawers and fingered each item, lifting it up to her face, smelling the fabric of undergarments and socks and handkerchiefs. Vida had never forgotten the sharp, piercing odors of the sheriff when he had fallen upon her.

But it was not here. Everything had been so finely laundered as to be absent his presence. Missouri was more of a fact in this house than he.

She closed the last drawer and turned to look at where he slept, a massive four-poster bed with a flowered canopy. Did he ever dream of his son there? she wondered. Did he ever call out Nate's name in the middle of the night as she herself had done countless times? Lord, she thought, did he even know his own son's name?

She knelt and looked under the bed. There was room enough for her. If she found out that the sheriff had harmed her son, in the middle of some night, the man would awaken with an ice pick in his heart.

Vida crossed the room and climbed the bed steps. Carefully she sat herself down on the elaborately embroidered coverlet and ran her hand over the duck-down pillows. Did he ever feel any emotion for his son besides hate? she wondered. If not, she would settle for even that. For if he still hated Nate, if in his heart he still raged at the boy, then that was a strong testimony to Nate's being alive. Knowing even that would be a great comfort. Yet where in this house was the proof he had not tracked Nate down and killed him?

She descended from the bed, and smoothed away with the flat of her hand any evidence she had been there. Her visit today was almost done. There was only one more place she wanted to look.

Downstairs, Vida stood for a moment in the stairhall, listening and watching. The house had darkened even more. It was getting late and the sheriff would be arriving soon. But she heard no engine sounds or tires against gravel, only the clock in the library marking the seconds.

Vida made her way stealthily to a little room off the parlor. She wanted to check the drawer again. In all the house, that one drawer in an old rolltop desk was the only thing kept locked, while silver, gold, and crystal lay out in the open for the taking. Whatever was in that drawer must be important indeed. She was determined to find the key.

She tried the drawer as she always did and it resisted as usual. But then it lurched open. A fold of paper had wedged itself between the drawer and the desk and had kept the lock from catching. Someone must have been in too much of a hurry to notice when they turned the key.

She removed the paper and there in the bottom of the drawer was strewn a trove of treasure, glinting even in the darkening room. Astonished, Vida reached down and stirred the contents about. On closer look, she saw breast pins with colored stones, bracelets going green, broken pocket knives, a tarnished Sunday school attendance pin from her father's old church. Junk.

She picked up a dime-store locket, realizing what she had found. These were the trifles Creola had complained about, the ones the sheriff had pocketed on his raids down into Tarbottom.

Holding the locket in her hand, she debated whether to steal it back for Creola. Deciding against the risk, she dropped the locket back in the drawer and pushed it shut. As she did, she shook her head in wonderment. This had to be the queerest place in the world! A house where a man can walk in through the door and then completely vanish, without leaving a trace. Where treasures are laid out for the taking, but trash is kept under lock and key.

As she turned to leave, she noticed she was still holding the paper that had jammed the lock. She flipped the purple and white paper in her hands and saw that it was an envelope. It smelled strongly of perfume. On the front somebody had written simply, Billy Dean.

All at once the house seemed to shake with the chiming of the clock in the library. Vida stuffed the envelope in her pocket and fled.

The very moment he saw Vida leaving through the sheriff's side door, Johnny thought, "That's where she's been sneaking off to. Now she's gonna get hers." From his bedroom window, he continued to watch as she scurried back across the yard with her hands in her pockets. He knew he finally had the goods on Vida Snow.

For reasons he could not understand, his mother seemed to have softened her views on Vida. Each time the maids came by, taking over the house, she sat on the stairs and listened, but never sprang their trap. He was beginning to fear that Vida was taking over his mother as well. That his mother was going to be on Vida's side.

But *this* she couldn't ignore.

Johnny was on his way to his mother's room before Vida had even got back to the kitchen. He found her sitting up in bed with the curtains pulled and the radio on, half-hidden in the shadows. Tingling with excitement, Johnny ran and jumped up beside her, and breathlessly told her all he had seen.

When he was done, she said very softy, "I swan. Tell me again." After he had finished his second rendition, she asked, "Did you see her tote anything out?"

"No ma'am. Her hands was poked down in her pockets."

"I swan," she said again. "Ain't that something."

Johnny thought he could see a ghost of a smile flicker across her face. He had done well.

He thought she might have winked at him when she said, "Let's have us a secret. OK?"

The news seemed to be making her feel better already. She even asked him to pull back the curtains, to let a little light and air into the room.

Turning toward the window, Hazel indeed felt her spirits begin to lift. Johnny's news confirmed what she had already suspected. Lately, she had lost a silk scarf and a hairbrush and a garnet pin. But she had put it down to the pills and her volt-damaged memory. That is, until Floyd started complaining that he couldn't find his new gold-plated tie clip or his favorite hammer. The pieces were falling into place.

For the longest while Hazel was silent, gazing off into the distance, like a gambler considering how to play a very good hand.

The next morning Hazel heard Vida stomping up the stairs, rattling the breakfast tray. Normally this was the part of the day Hazel hated the worst. Vida coming in sullen, as gracious as a prison guard, plopping the tray down on the bed and jutting her fist out. "Medicine time, Miss Hazel,"

being the only words she spoke now. But this morning, Hazel was certain there would be more words passing between them than just those.

Vida rapped twice with a free knuckle, then pushed open the door with her foot. She took one step into the room and spied the empty bed. That stopped her cold. But she almost fell over when she spotted Hazel in the armchair over by the closet door, wooden-backed and defiant.

Hazel had dressed herself in her favorite riding clothes, a navy blue poplin with a box-pleated skirt and a little round hat bobby-pinned to her head. She had even managed some makeup.

"What you staring at?" Hazel asked, not able to hide a satisfied smirk.

"Nothin. I don't reckon," Vida stammered, like she wasn't trusting what she saw. "Maybe I just ain't never seen you in nothin but bedclothes." She set the tray on the foot of the bed and considered Hazel again. Finally, she asked, "What you all made up for, Miss Hazel? You goin' out today?"

Sizing Vida up, Hazel said, "Thought I might. If that's all right by you."

"What I got to do with anything?" Vida reached for the glass of orange juice on the tray. "I'm just yo maid."

"More like my overseer," Hazel muttered.

"Yessum. Well, here yo medicine." Vida stuck out her hand. In her palm were the two round pills, one blue and one yellow. In her other hand was the glass of juice.

Hazel set her jaw. It was now or never. "I don't reckon I'll be taking no pills today." Her voice was a bit shaky.

"I reckon you will, Miss Hazel."

"Not if I don't want to."

"Miss Hazel, 'wont to' got nothin to do with it. Mister Floyd say you got to. You don't take yo pills, I don't get my little bonus."

Hazel's mouth dropped. "He pays you a bonus?"

"Yessum. Two bits a pill," Vida said matter-of-factly, as if this were common practice in households across Mississippi.

Her hand was almost in Hazel's face. "Here you go. Swaller em on down."

Hazel took a breath to steel herself. She knew she didn't have a lot of energy to waste. "Vida," she said, deciding to get to the point, "things have been going missing around the house."

Squinting hard at Hazel, Vida asked in a measured voice, "And what that got to do with me?"

"Well…" Hazel hesitated. This was going to be harder than she had imagined. "Well, who else could have took them? I mean, after all…" Then she blurted, "Vida, please don't make me take no more pills!"

Vida, still squinting, thought it out and said, "You tryin to blackmail me, Miss Hazel? You callin me a thief?"

"You don't understand. I don't care about the things you took. You see, nobody has to know," Hazel explained in a rush of words. "I just don't want to take them pills no more. They make me tired. I can't think. I can't feel nothing. Vida, I don't care what you took. Keep it all. Take some more. I won't tell. I promise. Please. It'll be our secret."

"Miss Hazel, since the day I got here the onliest thing I took from this house is nasty looks."

"But things are missing," Hazel said, desperate now. "Floyd's going to be upset when I tell him it's been you. Don't make me have to tell him."

"You go on ahead and tell it on me if you wont. Come on down to Tarbottom and search my house. Everbody else is. But you ain't gone find nothin cause I ain't took nothin." Vida waggled her open palm at Hazel. Her voice was firm. "Now you swaller these pills, Miss Hazel, before you get me and you the both in a fix."

The little gumption Hazel had been able to muster for the confrontation was ebbing fast. She was beginning to panic. Her one opportunity was slipping away. "But Johnny said he saw you sneaking around in the sheriff's house."

"You think I ain't got the sense of a June bug? If I gone take up thievin the neighborhood, you reckon I'm gone commence with the high sheriff's house? If you think that, then let's me and you call Mr. Floyd and see who he believes." Then she waited, patting her foot to the passing seconds.

Hazel sank back in her chair, defeated. What Vida said was true. Floyd would certainly side with his maid over his wife. Her explanation would be best because it was the simplest, the easiest to live with. Poor ol' Hazel was just acting crazy again. It explained everything. It was the shortest distance between two points. Hazel dropped her head.

"Wont me to help you in bed, Miss Hazel? Or you wont to sit up for a while? Same difference to me." Again Vida held out her hand. "Long as you done took yo medicine."

Hazel remained slumped in the chair. Couldn't even get a colored maid to be on her side. She had handled it all wrong from the start. She shouldn't have tried to blackmail Vida. Now she had made her mad. She would never listen. And there was so much she needed to tell somebody, even if it was a colored somebody.

She needed to tell about dreams and drowning, and about how it feels to be beat up, bound up and thrown away, like that poor colored boy in the river. She needed to tell how he still haunted her.

She needed to tell about losing a child she never really knew to begin with, and about how it feels to see the remaining one fretting his childhood away, constantly staring at her like she was already a dead body on the bottom of the river, waiting to be dragged up, his worried eyes scanning the surface above her, calling out for her; and about how she wanted to reach up through the currents for him, but was pulled back by the weight of knowing nothing she could do would make a damn bit of difference. She needed another woman to tell it to. That and more.

About how she believed her husband had other reasons for wanting to keep her down. How Gardenia Paradise was last year's fragrance and now when he leaned over to kiss her goodnight, he smelled of something French and sophisticated. She wanted to tell how her own reflection had vanished completely from her husband's eyes and been replaced by another's.

She lifted her head to see Vida still standing there, unmoved, her hand outstretched. Hazel was a fool to think that just because she and Vida hated the same people, they themselves could be friends and share secrets. So instead of telling Vida all these things, Hazel took the pills like she was told and let herself be put to bed like a child.

Closing her eyes, she drifted back to that day she had stumbled across her father's jug in the woods, and how its wondrous contents had lifted her spirits higher than the chinquapins along the creek below her. Higher than the hills that had hemmed her in. She had been nothing but a silly, full-of-feelings girl. She should have listened to her parents and kept her eyes shielded against hope. Now she understood. It was important for her kind to steer clear of hope. Not because they weren't capable of it. But because they were unable to sustain it.

Chapter 32
IT'S ONLY MAKE BELIEVE

It was Wednesday, and regular as clockwork, Delia had arrived just before twelve, ready for her weekly test drive. Floyd, like all the other business owners in Delphi, took each Wednesday as a half-day, closing shop at noon; and, rain or shine, she would be there, just before he locked the doors. That way they could drive off together and no one would notice how long they were gone.

"Well, look who's here!" Floyd said, acting surprised. "Think I might could interest you in trading up today?" He grinned and cocked his head.

"Depends, Floyd," Delia purred.

"On what?"

"On how well you service after the sale."

Floyd blushed. She could always made him blush, which to her thinking was like winning. No matter how hard he tried to play along, attempting to match her insinuation for insinuation, she would up the ante to the point he became so embarrassed he had to retreat.

So instead of thinking of something clever to say, he just admired her proudly for a moment. Today she had on a misty sea-green dress, made of some delicate fabric as wispy as smoke, causing her to shimmer there before him like a mirage. He looked up into her eyes. Even with all her joking, something was different about her today. It was something he did not know she was capable of. Delia was noticeably sad. Even though Floyd wasn't one to encourage negative feelings, he asked her about it.

Laughing unconvincingly, she said, "Nothing's wrong with me that a test drive with you won't cure, Floyd."

But still her mood bothered him, somehow making what they were up to more real, harder to deny. "We got to be more careful," he said. "I think we better find another way to meet. You been test-driving that Mercury Montclair for three months now. If word gets back to the Senator—"

"Daddy?" She rolled the bluest pair of eyes Floyd had ever seen, even bluer than Hazel's that day in Tupelo Drugs. He struggled to push Hazel out of his thoughts.

"It's coming up on ginning time," she said. "He'll be too busy to care about anything or anybody except getting his cotton picked."

Floyd knew that wasn't true. The Senator doted on both his daughters, Delia as well as the ugly one. "The Beauty and the Duty," as the sheriff himself had once let slip about his wife and her sister. The Senator would first ruin and then kill any man who harmed either one.

He got up from his desk and walked across to where she stood. His office had windows on three sides and jutted like a peninsula into the showroom, and he came as close to her as he dared, close enough to catch the smell of her perfume and see the flecks of gold in her eyes. How could someone like Delia really want to be with him? he thought. Real high class. Somebody who had come out at the Delta Debutantes Ball. A woman who wore cashmere like a second skin.

"You sure there's nothing wrong?" he asked again. "You ain't tired of me, are you?"

"Tell me again, Floyd," she asked, sounding very much like a little girl.

"Tell you what, Delia?"

"Stop teasing. You know." She reached out and moved her finger slowly up and down his tie, tracing the vertical lines in the pattern. "The reasons you like me." She looked up at him like the fate of the world rested on his opinion.

His face fired up again and he quickly scanned the showroom to make sure no one was getting an eyeful. He cleared his throat. "I like you because you're the most beautiful woman I ever seen. I like you because you know what you want and go after it." Floyd smiled bashfully. "Me included."

"Serious, Floyd."

"OK, serious. I like you because you understand the way the world works. And you keep me positive. That's important to a man like me. I like you because you make me feel like I can do anything. Like a winner. You—"

Delia interrupted Floyd's earnestness with a burst of laughter. "Do I really, Floyd?" she teased. "Do I make you feel like a winner? Well, I guess I wasn't head cheerleader at Ole Miss for nothing. Go Floyd Go!"

Her laugh was hard-edged now, derisive, and Floyd felt his face coloring again. "Now *you* be serious," he said firmly. "You're good for me, Delia. That's all there is to it." Floyd moved closer than he should.

Delia's mood shifted again. No longer laughing, she said sadly, "I merely distract, I'm afraid. I help you forget all you've lost."

Maybe, thought Floyd. It was true Delia kept him positive and sure, like he was before family, death, and craziness ganged up together and conspired to bring him down. Being with her was like spending an afternoon with Norman Vincent Peale. Well, almost.

When Delia looked back up at him, he saw the tears in her eyes. She said, "But I use you, too, Floyd. It's like we cover each other's losses."

He waited for her to say more, only to see her smile at him sadly.

But later that afternoon he found out what she meant by her comment. They were two counties away and across the river in Arkansas, at their little honky-tonk hideaway on the levee. Instead of her usual beer, Delia was drinking bourbon, and lots of it. She began making jokes about the live entertainment, some local tractor driver with an impossible name, tuning his guitar not five feet from where they sat. Delia tried to think of all the funny words that rhymed with Twitty, some of them not very nice, and laughed out loud in the boy's face.

The boy looked right at Delia and said he was going to sing something he had just written about illusionary love. When that plowboy began growling out his song, Floyd could tell from the tragic expression on Delia's face she wasn't going to make it through the whole tune.

And he was right. When the boy got to,

My only prayer will be
Someday you will care for me
But it's o-o-o-o-o-nly make believe,

Delia burst out into loud ugly sobs. Everyone was staring.

Panicking, Floyd rushed her out of the honky-tonk and back to the car, where she cried uncontrollably into Floyd's shoulder. Eventually, sitting there in that hard dirt yard, the poor white boy still grinding out his music from inside the shack and Floyd nervously scanning the darkening grounds, she confessed her secret.

"Oh, Floyd," she cried. "I'm pregnant."

"But we never... How could...?" As yet, Floyd hadn't done much more than hold her close and stroke her hair. She had not even allowed him to kiss her on the mouth.

She pulled back and looked up at him through her tears like he was an imbecile. "Not *you*, Floyd."

"Oh," he said, at first relieved.

"Oh," he said again, hurt.

"Yes, exactly," she cried. "Oh."

"You been seeing somebody besides—"

"That's right," she said. "And I'm in love with him, Floyd."

As it slowly sank in that he had lost Delia, or rather never had her to lose in the first place, he was overcome by that old crippling sensation. The same one he had had when Davie died, a trapdoor feeling where it was like he was doing a free fall through space, all his insides floating up, and bunching high in his chest. Gripping the wheel tightly, as if to keep from being pulled through the car by an ancient gravity, he stammered, "Who... Who..." even though he was certain he didn't want to know.

She wouldn't tell him anyway. But she did go on to tell him other things he would rather not hear. She said she was frightened. Her lover had been outraged when she had asked him to marry her. He had even made threats. With tears glistening in those cobalt-blue eyes of hers, she looked up at Floyd and said, "It just hurts all the more knowing the man you cherish would even bring up the topic of killing you."

Through his own sorrow, Floyd could see her point. "Maybe we should tell the sheriff, Delia," he suggested.

That had stopped her tears. "No. No. No," she said, as if that were the stupidest idea in the world. But all at once her face unclouded and she became thoughtful. Looking at Floyd with an expression of pure earnestness, she said, "But Floyd, if anything does happen to me, even though in my heart I don't believe he would hurt me, you tell the sheriff then. Only afterwards. OK?"

Floyd thought it a strange request. "After?"

"Promise me," she insisted. "Not before. Only after."

He promised. But she still wouldn't reveal the name of her lover.

The incident with Delia had sent Floyd for a loop, and his lapse in emotional control caused him to do one of the silliest things he had ever done. Something worthy of Hazel. On that last test drive Delia had left a bottle of her perfume in the car pocket, and one day Floyd rode around in the red-and-white Mercury for hours, all the way to the river and back, the windows up and the Chanel open, crying his eyes out.

That was like hitting bottom for Floyd. It forced him to get a grip on himself. Using his best logic, he began to reason himself out of his grief. He told himself it was to be expected. Everybody knew Delia was a bit on the wild side, with two ex-husbands up north. Take it as a lesson, he told himself.

After all, he counseled, there ain't a thing you can do about it. There's no future in looking back, he reminded himself. Look at it this way, he reasoned, Delia's love for you never really existed. Why should you mourn what never was? If you want to be happy, act happy. Get glad, not sad.

Floyd mostly put it all behind him after only a few days. It was a sterling testimony to the Science of Controlled Thinking. If anybody asked Floyd what his secret to success was, as he often imagined them doing, he would have to say it was his ability to take feelings that would sink a less mentally trained person and discharge them like so much ballast.

He only regretted he couldn't tell Hazel how he had handled the thing with Delia. If he could just get that one thing through Hazel's head: when you can control your thoughts, you control your emotions. No need for hospitals and pills and such. But no, some people refused to put out the mental courage that it took.

Chapter 33

MANY MANSIONS

From where he sat in the shade of an oak in his own backyard, Johnny could see clearly the crazy old man over at Miss Pearl's, raking the ground beneath her stand of pines. Even though he had been studying him for quite a while in the mid-afternoon heat, Johnny couldn't figure out what he was up to, besides raking straw. After he filled his barrow, he would bow his head over the load of straw. Then he appeared to talk at it and make gestures over it. When the man was done with his little ritual, he would wheel the barrow over to the flowerbed and spread the straw among the gladiolas and azaleas and then talk at it some more.

Johnny decided to get up close and hear for himself what the man was telling the pine straw. It might be something his mother needed to know about.

"The harvest is great, but the laborers are few," the man said, in a voice unlike any Johnny had ever heard before. It was like thunder rumbling and rivers rushing and trees bending in the wind. Yet it wasn't loud on the outside. It only felt loud on the inside. The words still rang in Johnny's head.

The man wheeled his harvest over to the flowerbed, with Johnny tagging behind. It occurred to him that the man was wearing overalls, a hat, and a long-sleeve flannel shirt in the afternoon heat. The shirt was dark with sweat. Johnny thought he should be wearing khaki shorts and a thin nylon shirt like him if he was going to stay outside. "Ain't you burning up?" he yelled out to him.

Levi started at the voice coming from behind him. When he turned and saw the boy, all he said was, "No," and then went back to his straw.

Even though the man still sat out on the bench once in a while, Johnny had mostly avoided him. He was Vida's father, after all. But now he decided to get a closer look. As he ventured nearer to the man, he saw that his face was lined with deep wrinkles like the folds in his mother's black velvet dress. When the man completely uncoiled himself to give his back a stretch, only then did Johnny notice how tall he was.

Johnny threw his head back to see into the man's face and Levi returned the stare. Johnny decided those had to be the largest, roundest, deepest eyes in all the world. They were like oceans of chocolate and big enough to see him all at once. Most people's eyes took in little parts of him at a time, his dirty hands or his uncombed hair or his untied shoes. This man's eyes swallowed him whole.

"How come you wearing them long sleeves?" Johnny asked.

The man quickly looked around, as if to see if anybody was watching. "I ain't studyin you," he said very low. "Get on from here fore you get us both in trouble."

Even though the man wasn't being very nice to him, for some reason Johnny wasn't afraid. He just wanted to be looked at again with those big eyes of his. So he asked once more, "Ain't you hot dressed up like you are? Did Vida make you wear them clothes?" It would be just like her to do something that mean.

The man gave Johnny a bemused look. "Vida? You think Vida puts my clothes on me?"

"I don't know," he said, secretly pleased he had got the man to look at him again.

"Well, she don't. And if you has to know, young man, I dress like this because it makes you sweat more."

"Yeah, but why you wanna sweat more?"

Levi took off his hat, revealing hair so white and fleecy, it reminded the boy of a lamb he had petted once. Johnny would have petted the man's head if he had offered.

Taking a bandanna from his back pocket, Levi wiped the inside brim of the hat, but he still didn't answer the boy. So Johnny asked again. "So why you want to sweat more, huh?"

"You ask a lot of questions," Levi said. He replaced his hat and then looked down at Johnny.

"Yeah but why?"

"It be like this here. Sweatin makes you cool. Sometimes you got to get hotter before you can get cooler. Like sometimes things got to get worser before they get better. Can you understand that?"

Johnny thought it sounded like something his daddy might say. Maybe the man wasn't crazy after all. But just to make sure he asked, "You know what my name is?"

The man hesitated, not knowing what to make of this boy and his questions. He quickly looked up and again surveyed the yards around him, as if to see who had put this child up to testing him like this. Finally he said, "I reckon they call you Johnny."

"What's yours?"

"Levi Snow."

"Why was you saying them Sunday school words to that barrow?"

Levi shook his head at the boy's question and then leaned over the load of straw to resume his work.

"You playliking you a preacher today?"

Levi quickly drew himself up again. "I *am* a preacher," he said stoutly.

Johnny doubted it. If he were telling the truth, where was the man's preaching uniform, the snow-white suit with the cross-of-diamonds stickpin? "You ever bury anybody?" he asked, testing again.

"Course. I done tole you I'm a preacher. Now you best get on away from here and let me work."

"Davie got himself buried."

"Yeah, I heared bout that," Levi said, his face softening and his eyes swallowing Johnny whole again. "If you believe in Jesus, you gone to see him again."

"We been waitin on him," Johnny said.

Levi nodded. "In my father's house there are many mansions."

Yep, Johnny thought, that sure enough sounded like something a preacher would say.

Then Levi picked up an armload of straw and scattered it in the bed of red and white gladiolas, while speaking in his special voice. "I send you like sheep among wolves."

As Johnny contemplated how pine straw was like sheep and wondered where the wolves were, the scent of face powder drifted their way. Miss Pearl was strolling through the yard showing her niece, Miss Hertha, her prize roses. Always happy to see her, Johnny called out, "Hey, Miss Pearl."

She looked over and, upon seeing him, waved her handkerchief and began approaching, Miss Hertha by her side.

"What are you all doing out here?" Miss Pearl asked.

Fascinated now by the woman's hand, Johnny watched as she used her handkerchief to dab at the moistness which had gathered in dewy drops above her rose-tinted lips. Then he realized she was looking at him for the answer to her question. "Just talking to Mr. Snow," Johnny said, trying to be proper around Miss Pearl.

Miss Pearl smiled, but Hertha was quick to reply. "No, no, child!" she said, shaking her head at Johnny. "Levi here is not a Mister. Levi is a nigruh."

"Leave the boy alone, Hertha. He's just practicing his manners."

Hertha wouldn't be stopped. She motioned in Levi's general direction. "He's just plain Levi. Understand, child?" she asked. "Only white people get to be Misters. And one day Levi will call you Mister, but never the other way around. Isn't that right, Aunt Pearl?"

Pearl said nothing, but simply patted her throat with the lace handkerchief. Then she turned to study her gladiolas.

As for Johnny, he really couldn't discern any meanness in Miss Hertha's voice. Instead, it was like someone telling him firmly not to talk with his mouth full or to keep his elbows off the table. When he looked back at Levi, he saw that the old man stood there looking much smaller, his shoulders humped down. He was turning his hat round and round in his hands and his huge eyes studied the grass at his feet, but his face did not contradict anything Miss Hertha had said. If Levi didn't mind, Johnny figured that must be the way things were. Anyway, Miss Pearl would say so if it were wrong.

"Well, let Levi get back to his work, now, child," Miss Pearl said. She looked over at the man and said sweetly, "When you finish up with the beds, Levi, the verbena by the front gate needs shaping."

"Yessum," he said, studying the ground. With his head still bowed, he looked up out of the tops of his eyes and addressed the woman he had known since childhood. "Miss Pearl, ma'am. If you don't mind me askin, next time you see yo brother, would you tell the Senator, Levi Snow sends his regards?"

Miss Pearl smiled affectionately at Levi. "Now Levi, when you want some ice water, you just knock at the back door and Creola will fix you some, do you hear?"

"Yessum, I sho will do that," Levi answered, and then bent himself down again to the wheelbarrow.

As Miss Pearl pointed out her gladiolas to her niece, and Johnny stood there wondering if he had missed the woman's answer to Levi's question, the big reddish maid Creola came bounding out of the house and down the hill to where they were all standing. As usual, she was out of breath when she arrived.

"Miss Pearl!" she puffed, holding a hand to her heaving chest. "It's the Senator on the phone. It's bout Miss Delia."

"What now!" Miss Pearl said, sounding exasperated.

Miss Hertha exclaimed, "I just knew Delia would do something to scandalize Daddy right before her party. What's she done?"

"She gone missin," Creola said, puffing.

"Oh, is that all." Miss Pearl dismissed Creola's message with a wave of her handkerchief. "Tell my brother there's a difference between an emergency and a predicament."

Creola looked at Miss Pearl quizzically and then said, "All I know is the Senator say it's for real this time. He say Miss Delia went out hossback ridin and that hoss done come back empty."

"Oh, my," Miss Pearl exclaimed, her eyes shifting to her poor broken hand. "Her horse. That is different."

Hertha wasn't convinced. "She's up to something. I know it. Always trying to get attention."

"Po Senator," Levi said as he watched the women rush back up the hill. "It gone sho nuf kill him if some bad thang happen to Miss Delia."

"Miss Delia?" Johnny asked, at first not remembering. Then it hit. "She's the pretty one," he blurted proudly.

Miss Hertha, who was already halfway to the house, whipped around and gave him a look that made Johnny take a step behind Levi for safety.

"Um-hmm," Levi said, still raking. "Boy, you better hide. Least till you learn who you can practice yo manners on and who you can't."

Then Johnny heard him give out a soft chuckle.

Vida was in the parlor dusting the furniture when Johnny got back to the house. It was a task she saved for this time of the day, just before her programs began. Sure enough, when she finished wiping off the television, she clicked it on and settled back into a Strato-lounger. Even when the maids came over for coffee, they had to leave before the start of her first show, the one about the butler who gave his boss's money away, a million dollars at a time, tax free, to complete strangers. Vida always got a real kick out of that.

Johnny stood furtively in the stairhall, waiting for the set to warm up and the sound to blare out before he crept past the parlor doorway and slipped upstairs. This was one of those few times during the day he could spend with his mother without fear of Vida calling out for him, trying to meddle in his business.

When he came into her room, the lights were off, and the radio was on. She hardly ever went down to watch TV, and when she did, she seemed to tire quickly of all those happy families doing their best to make her laugh.

Today, the radio was playing a song without words. It was the kind of music he and his mother used to make up rhymes to as they drove fast in the Lincoln. But for now, Hazel lay there quietly, with her eyes closed. Without making a sound, Johnny pulled the dressing table chair to her bedside and seated himself. He stared through the filtered afternoon light at his mother.

Her hair was flattened against the sides of her head, and pitifully pooched out on top from lying on it all day. Later that evening he would ask her if he could brush it for her. He looked at the arm that lay crooked on her stomach. Her skin was the same pasty white color as the china poodle that sat next to her on her night stand, the one his father had given her for a surprise present, for no reason at all. Her fingernails were ragged and chipped, the last vestiges of polish from her aborted escape about to flake away. He noticed how the bedspread rose and fell at regular intervals and knew that to be a good sign, having watched his father lean over Davie, yelling at him to breathe.

She needed to get up soon. Time was coming unloose. Countless days and hours and minutes were passing undesignated and unaccounted for, flowing into one another like little streams coursing into an unnamed river. Although Time lived in the clock, his mother was the only one who could tell Time, who could tell it what to do. Time to rise and shine. Breakfast. Dinner. Supper. Time for a story. Time for bed.

Without her, all the ticks of the clock bled together and he couldn't be sure the day had been done right, that some things hadn't been left out. He sighed. So many things to be remembered. Nobody talked about Davie anymore. He needed to be remembered so he could come back home.

His mother took in an extra-deep breath and then, forcing it out, opened her eyes. Neither of them spoke, each watching the other. His mother's face was expressionless and he tried to make his likewise.

Once, while out driving, his mother had without warning pulled the car to a stop on a country road. She had reached over, touched him on the shoulder and pointed, all in a way that told him to be as still as he could. Looking along the line of her finger he saw the lone doe. For several minutes he and his mother gazed upon the deer, and the deer gazed back. The world stopped breathing. It was as if the slightest movement of the tiniest muscle would break the spell and frighten the deer back into the woods. So now, Johnny watched his mother quietly, asking nothing from her except that she keep her eyes on him, to notice that he was there.

A single tear trickled down her face. "Johnny, I wanted to be a good momma," she whispered. "I really wanted to."

A few moments passed, and her face went heavy with the weight of some realization. Johnny watched as she closed her lids and said sadly to herself, "Damn."

After tiptoeing downstairs and sneaking past Vida, who was at that moment fussing at a contestant on a quiz show, he went out through the back door, catching the screen so it didn't slam, and descended the porch steps.

The elevated porch was supported by brick pillars, and between the pillars on three sides were giant partitions of criss-crossed green lattice, framing in a dirt-floored, cool space underneath. Parting the confederate jasmine that climbed the latticework, Johnny removed a small inset wide enough for a worker who might need to get at the pipes underneath the house and crawled through, replacing the little latticed door snugly behind him.

Squatting down there in the dirt, waiting for his eyes to adjust to the dark, Johnny remembered what the old colored preacher had told him earlier in the afternoon about funerals and believing in Jesus and seeing Davie again. It certainly sounded like what Brother Dear had said.

Maybe Levi Snow was just another crazy nigger. After all, he *had* been talking to pine straw. Johnny was beginning to think that the world was chock-full of crazy grown people on the loose, seeing Jesus and preaching to pine straw and sneaking in and out of other people's houses. To think, his mother was the one that got picked on.

Johnny took the little china poodle out of his pocket and cradled it in his palm and hummed to it the lullaby his mother had taught him about sleepy sheep in pretty fields of daffodils. He kissed the dog on its nose. "Who do you love the best?" he asked the dog. "Whose side are you on?"

Setting it gently on the ground, Johnny took a silver spoon from the box and began digging among the dozens of little mounds arranged in neat rows in the dirt. After he had dug his hole, he placed the dog in a bread wrapper and then laid it carefully in the grave.

"Now, stop that crying. Close your eyes and go to sleep. Jesus is gonna come by soon and get you up. And then you can come home again. I ain't gonna forget."

He scooped dirt over the dog with the stolen tablespoon. There were so many graves now. Johnny was having trouble remembering what was buried where. He crawled along the ground, touching each grave with his finger and as he did, he said the name of the person who had forfeited some possession to his graveyard.

Over the hammer he said, "Daddy," and over the garnet pin he said, "Momma," over the toy tractor, "Davie," and "Vida," over the envelope he got from the man with the straight-edged face.

He went on like this until he had recalled them all. Little lost things that others would miss and consider gone forever, and only he knew how to stop their grieving. It was up to him to remember where everything was buried. This was, after all, his graveyard, and here, he was the one who measured out death, one tablespoon at a time.

"Johnny!" came Vida's voice. "I know you up under there. Get on out right now! Got to get you cleaned up befo yo daddy gets here."

The boy took another moment to finish his remembering. Then he told them all, "Good night. Sleep tight. Don't let the bedbugs bite."

Chapter 34
TRUE STORIES

The next afternoon found Vida hurrying upstairs to make sure Hazel was set for the next hour or so. She hated being disturbed when her friends were visiting. In the bedroom, the lights were off and the radio was on low. When she was convinced Hazel was sound asleep, Vida gently closed the door behind her and quietly descended the stairs.

Hazel flipped opened her eyes and turned off the radio. She rose up out of bed, groggy, put on her robe and dragged herself to the door. Carefully easing it open, she peeked out and, seeing that the coast was clear, took her listening post on the stair. By that time Johnny had tiptoed up to join her.

For Hazel, in this summer of drugs and depression, the time she spent listening to those maids carry on in her kitchen, loud talking and low rating everybody they knew, was the only thing that kept her going. She wouldn't miss a session for the world. Something about the way those colored women could tell it on people. It was one of the few things that did her heart good anymore.

When Vida returned to the kitchen, Creola was already telling the maids about how she had overheard her boss, Hayes Alcorn, Miss Pearl's husband and Delia's uncle, carrying on about a men's club he was forming.

"That man gettin crazier-actin ever day," Creola said. "Ever since that hoss came back by hisself, he keeps tellin Miss Pearl, 'This nigger problem done got outta hand.'"

Pulling out a chair for herself, Vida said, "How come he already knowed a colored man done it? How come he knowed anybody done it? Ain't even found her body yet."

Creola shook her head. "She dead all right. They found her pretty silk scarf dangling on a branch reaching out over that whirly pool near to Bryson's Bayou. She probly floated all way down to the Mis'sippi by now."

"Well, she might a fell off in that whirlpool by accident," Vida suggested. "It's slick on that bank." She knew the spot well. It was near her father's praying ground, where he used to cry out to Heaven, pleading with God to show His face once more, while Vida secretly looked on.

"Girl didn't slip," Missouri said, her eyes blaring at Vida. The sheriff's maid was acting like it was her own sister who got drowned instead of her white lady's. Missouri even wore a black armband on the sleeve of her maid's uniform. But Vida would bet good money she didn't go sporting it around Miss Hertha.

Enjoying how riled Missouri was getting, Vida said flippantly, "Maybe she flung herself in there on purpose. Don't always take a colored man to make a white woman do somethin crazy. Sounds like they's a dead cat on the line if you ask me."

The group was quiet for a moment, as if waiting for Vida to hang some meat on her suspicions. But she said nothing more. For now she wanted to keep the contents of the purple-and-white letter a secret. Especially with Missouri there.

"Mr. Hayes say it's got to be a colored man done it," Creola said. "Mr. Hayes say the colored done got above theyselves. He say we gettin some dangerous ideas from the outside."

"What kind of ideas we been gettin?" Vida asked.

"Oh, bout votin and integratin and sleepin with the white folks. He tole Miss Pearl his little club gone take care of the colored problem onced and for all. White supremer he calls hisself now."

"Praise Jesus," Maggie sang out. "He rule supreme."

"He sho do, Maggie. But we ain't talkin bout Jesus right now," Creola said, growing angry, which was not at all like her. "We talkin about a little no-assed varmint callin his own self supreme. Mr. Hayes is foamin at the mouth bout some colored preacher over in Alabama. Said he done outfoxed the bus company and the whole town of Montgomery. He say Mis'sippi gone be next."

"Colored man do that?" Vida asked. "How?"

"He got all the colored folks together and tole em to stay off them buses till they could ride up front like first-class citizens."

"Sho!" Sweet Pea squealed. "I read bout it in one of them Chicago race papers somebody was passin round at One Wing Hannah's. But it waddent no man who got it started. It was a colored woman done it."

"Goodness gracious!" Creola said. "If Mr. Hayes know that, he sho nuf have a hissy fit."

"Her name Rosie somebody," Sweet Pea continued. "She ridin back home from work on the bus and wouldn't let go her seat to a white man. Say she was too tired to move."

"That what she say? Too tired to move?" Creola started laughing like that was the funniest thing she had ever heard. She began singing the words like a gospel song. "Too tired. Too tired to move. Law! Law! Too tired to move." She laughed again even harder, setting her mighty breasts to wobbling.

Sweet Pea and Vida broke up, too. Maggie mouthed the words, but didn't seem to recognize the tune.

"Um-hmm!" Creola said, wiping her eyes. "I know just how she feels. Bone weary. Ain't that somethin? So that what started it all."

"They hauled her off to jail for it," Sweet Pea said.

"Thank you, Lord!" Maggie sang out, sounding like she thought the more colored folks in jail the better.

"She a maid?" Vida asked.

"No. Weren't no maid. I believe it said she sewed clothes."

"Law. Law," Creola chuckled to herself. "That's what we sho nuf need around here. Somebody too tired to move for the white man."

"We ain't got no buses here," Missouri said flatly.

"That ain't the point," Vida snapped. She wasn't in any mood to hear Missouri take up for the white man today. "Somebody need to teach the white folks in this town a lesson or two. Can't keep messin with us the way they do."

"Who been messin with you?" Missouri challenged.

Creola answered for Vida. "That boss of yores for one. He been tearin up ever colored house in Hopalachie County lookin for who drownded

Miss Delia. How many white doors you spec he busted down?"

"The sheriff just doin his job," Missouri said. "What he elected to do."

Creola stomped her foot, rattling the dishes and sloshing the coffee out of the cups. "*I* sho didn't elect him. *Us* caint even vote in this county."

Vida had never seen Creola this upset before. Her face freckles were glowing like lit cigarettes on the inhale.

"What you wont to vote for?" Missouri spat. "Why you care what white man get elected?"

Vida couldn't help but smile, seeing Missouri tempt her fate with Creola this way.

The large woman shifted her bulk in her chair and then leaned in toward Missouri, getting right in her face. "I tell you I care. My baby niece only just turned fo'teen and that man already messin with her. If I gets the vote, yo sneaky-eyed, bony-assed, fork-dicked boss sho be out of a job."

Missouri's face swelled up like a biscuit in a hot oven. "Votin is the white man's business," she said, clenching her teeth. "Ain't no colored preacher or any uppity girl from Alabama gone make it otherwise. All they gone do is make a mess everbody else gone have to live in." While they all shot her furious looks, Missouri continued to lecture them righteously, "We need to keep our minds on the Lord, not on the vote. Like the Good Book says, 'Pay honor to God.'"

"And everthang else to the white man," Vida snapped.

When Missouri smiled her tight little grin at Vida, she knew she was about to get it. "We could all take a lesson from Vida's daddy," Missouri said. "Sheriff say he used to be a biggety preacher out in the county till he got hisself mixed up in this votin mess. Course y'all see how he do more yard work than preachin nowadays." Looking quite satisfied, Missouri puckered her lips and took a noisy sip from her coffee cup.

There followed a charged silence. Vida knew they were looking for her to say something in defense, but she kept quiet. What could she say? "You wrong bout that! Daddy was a white man's nigger just like you, Missouri!" Vida could tell them how he had curried favor with white folks, thinking he would have him an angel when he needed it. Look where it got him.

Then Vida smiled. She had come up with a way to get even with

Missouri. Thinking again of the letter she found at the sheriff's house, she said, "I bet I know who Miss Delia was carryin on with."

Before Vida could tell her theory on the matter, Sweet Pea piped up. "You mean it be true? Here I was thinkin it was just crazy talk. "

Vida was confused. Had Sweet Pea heard about Delia and the sheriff? "You know?" she asked.

"Bout Mr. Floyd and Miss Delia? Sho! I heard some old drunk down at Hannah's talkin bout how they seed the two of em out by Friar's Point. Bein mighty close."

Up on the stair, Hazel's shoulders slumped. Johnny looked up at her. "Momma," Johnny whispered. "Are they talking about Daddy?"

Hazel didn't answer. She didn't even breathe. Slowly she rose up from the stair, went back into her room, and closed the door behind her, shutting Johnny out.

Johnny looked back down the stair. These women had hurt his mother. It was all Vida's fault. If his mother wasn't going to get rid of her, he would have to. And he knew just how to make it happen. Didn't the sheriff arrest bad people and haul them away? What would the sheriff do if he found out Vida had been sneaking inside his own house, stealing things? Later that afternoon, Johnny thought to himself, Vida wouldn't be the only person watching for the sheriff's patrol car.

Chapter 35

THE CITIZENS' COUNCIL

Back at the dealership, Floyd stubbed out his unsmoked cigarette and slowly got up from his desk, pulled the blinds and clicked off the light. Standing there alone in his darkened office, he took a handkerchief from his back pocket, wiped his eyes, then blew his nose. He needed to be alone for a few minutes and pull himself together.

Settling back behind his desk again, he took a deep breath and closed his eyes. He needed to get his attitude right. Get back on top of things. After all, attitude determines altitude. Floyd blew his nose again and dropped his head down on the desk, tapping his forehead against the laminated surface. "I'm a winner. I'm a winner. I'm a winner," he repeated weakly.

He had just got over losing Delia. But now it looked like he would have to start all over again. Two days ago, after he had got his attitude back on track, Brother Dear called, saying Delia had been drowned. It almost killed him this time, imagining her lithe body floating lovely face down, her blonde hair glistening in the sun, a silky net for leaves and twigs and river trash. He imagined her wearing her sea-foam-green blouse with the bouffant sleeves, fragile and shimmery, spread wide on the water surface like failed butterfly wings.

Only Wednesday, she had been standing right there in front of his desk, smiling at him, tossing back her hair in that free and easy way of hers, eyes bluer than they had a right to be. For a moment he even thought he could detect a whiff of her perfume and hear her silvery laughter once again. He wiped his eyes again. If he could just have one more taste of the way things used to be.

Used to be? Just listen to yourself, he silently scolded. Wallowing in the past like a loser, crying over the way things used to be? Now get over it.

This very minute, you hear? Focus on the future, he told himself. The past is deader than beef.

No matter how hard he tried to push Delia back to the past where she belonged, she refused to budge. He tried muttering his favorite motivational sayings, but his guilty mind would have none of it and countered by churning out dire prospects for his future. It occurred to him that he was probably one of the last people to have seen Delia alive. That would make him a suspect. She had made such a scene at the honky-tonk, somebody was bound to remember the two of them together, her drunk, crying her eyes out, and him shocked and embarrassed and guilty-looking, probably as red as an Indian peach.

Wasn't he a witness of sorts? Delia told him directly her boyfriend had threatened her life, surely crucial information the sheriff would want to know. He had promised her he would tell if anything happened. But how could Floyd explain to the sheriff where he got that little piece of news without revealing his own lusting heart?

She was the Senator's daughter, for God sakes! No matter what he did, he would never get out of this alive. He was as doomed as an upsided turtle.

He could see the newspapers now. "Local Businessman Keeps His Poor Wife Drugged as He Conducts Illicit Affair." That's the word they would use, all right. Illicit. Even if he had never kissed her. It didn't matter. He would look as guilty as sin.

Oh, my God! he thought as he began mixing and matching facts in his head. There was that phone call he had got from Hayes Alcorn earlier. About a meeting at the barbershop. He had said it was important and had to do with the future of Hopalachie County and he needed Floyd's help. And that the sheriff and some others were going to be there. Maybe it wasn't a meeting at all! They were setting him up for an arrest. That was it. It was a trap. They were going to surprise him so there wouldn't be a scene.

Floyd flipped his face over, and with the change in perspective a surge of sadness overtook the guilt. "Oh, poor, sweet Hazel," he sighed.

"Delia," he corrected himself.

"Floyd, you awake in there?"

Floyd snapped his head up. He hadn't even heard the door open, but there stood his shop mechanic peering at him, unblinking through blood-shot eyes, his face an ugly red. How long had Hollis been standing there watching him? Floyd cleared his throat a couple of times, afraid that if he spoke, his voice might break up.

The stalling didn't seem to bother Hollis any. He just leaned against the doorsill and began working the grime from around his fingernails with the grease rag he always kept hanging from the back pocket of his striped coveralls. Was that a smirk on Hollis's face? Maybe he thought he had something on Floyd. Maybe he knew about him and Delia.

"Everbody else done gone," Hollis mumbled. "I can lock up fer you if you wontin to get on to yore meetin." He cut his eyes up from his rag for the answer.

The meeting! Floyd checked his watch. The meeting wasn't for anoth-er hour. Hollis probably just wanted to get Floyd on his way so he could have a nip or two before he went home to his wife. That's probably what his shifty look was about. Most likely it wasn't about Delia at all. Floyd needed to get a grip.

Well, it might not be such a bad idea to leave a little early, drive around town and collect himself. Maybe arrive at the barbershop before Hayes started up the meeting. That way he could get a sense of the crowd. Get the lay of the land, so to speak. Not that he had anything to be worried about.

Floyd cleared his throat again and stood up. Avoiding Hollis's stare, he reached down for some papers to shuffle and then aligned them precisely with the edge of his desk. "Yeah. Sure thing, Hollis," he said, keeping his voice even and controlled. "Lock 'er up when you're done."

Pulling down the visor of his truck, Floyd re-read his saying for the day: *It's no good being a mental giant if you remain an emotional pygmy.* As he drove up and down Gallatin, committing the saying to memory, trad-ing nods with folks as they emptied the stores and headed on home for supper, Floyd's spirits gradually began to lift.

He gave himself a little pep talk. Attitude was everything and he need-ed to keep his on track. Couldn't let this Delia thing get him down again.

He had overcome worse. Just like yesterday's saying, *Whether you think you can or you think you can't, you're going to be right either way.* It was all a matter of not getting detoured into negativity.

By the time he got to the barbershop and stepped in through the door, tripping the little bell, there was already a crowd there. Hayes Alcorn, Brother Dear, and half a dozen others looked up and nodded at Floyd, and said their heys and howdys. The old shoeshine boy grinned his usual grin. Nobody looked at Floyd with the least bit of suspicion, not even the sheriff, who just sat slouched in his chair acting bored.

The others quickly returned to the amusement at hand, making fun of the new Yankee in town who was at that moment up in the chair getting his hair cut by Slats. As usual, Marvin was taking a ribbing about his accent.

Hayes Alcorn was the one talking now. "Say 'school' again, Marvin."

Marvin said it, making it sound like two words. Everybody howled.

"Y'all hear that?" Hayes said. "'Skew all.' Don't that beat all."

Marvin joined in the laughter. He even looked like a foreigner, with his swarthy complexion, severely pocked, probably from some northern affliction. Marvin had married a local girl and got the job managing the Nehi bottling plant in Granada. But he was a real sport, never taking himself too serious.

Floyd sat down in the chair next to Hayes and felt so relieved he decided to join in. "What's that thing on top of your house, Marvin?" Floyd asked.

"Roof," Marvin said good-naturedly. There was another round of laughter.

"Sounds like a dog barking. Don't it?" Floyd said with a chuckle. "Ruff. Ruff." Then he asked, "How y'all say it when you run water over your hands?"

"Rinse?" Marvin guessed.

"Nope," Floyd said. "It's rench." He looked around, wondering why nobody else was laughing.

Hayes nudged Floyd and grinned. "Naw, Floyd. That's how they say it in the hills. You still ain't got it right."

This time there were a few snickers at Floyd's expense. Not very pleased that the laughter had turned against him, Floyd smiled contritely and decided just to listen for a while.

Marvin cocked his head so Slats could get the stiff little hairs on the side of his neck. "Now that you mention it," Marvin said, "a Negro family who lived in our town pronounced it that way. Rench. I think they were from down south."

An ugly silence gripped the barbershop. It was Hayes who finally spoke up. "A *neee*-gro?" he said derisively. "What's that?"

Marvin's face reddened. "Negro. The colored. You know."

"How many *neee*-gros lived in that town of yours in New York?" Hayes asked, dead serious.

"Illinois."

"Same thing."

Slats whisked the back of Marvin's neck. It was almost quiet enough to hear his falling hair touch the floor.

"There were two families, I believe," Marvin answered carefully. Everybody shook their heads in amazement.

"Well, you ain't no expert then, are you?" Hayes said. "What we got down here is *nigruhs*."

Then Hayes glanced over to the shoeshine stand. "That right, Ben?"

The balding colored man who had been sitting there quietly smiled bashfully and said, "That's right, Mr. Hayes."

"See," Hayes said. "We expert at nigralogy."

Trying again, Marvin said carefully, "Nig-gruhs. Is that how you say it?"

Hayes slapped his leg and guffawed. "We gone make a Mississippi boy outta you yet, Marvin. You know you just can't marry into it."

There was an immediate burst of laughter from the crowd that sounded a lot like relief. Slats carefully loosened the barber's apron from around Marvin's neck and then whipped the cloth in the air with a loud crack. Snippets of coarse black hair rained on the floor.

Marvin paid Slats for the haircut, and bid the group good-bye, chuckling to himself and repeating, "Nig-gruh. Nig-gruh," as he walked out the door.

Turning his attention to Floyd, Slats asked, "When you gonna let us in on the big secret, Floyd? Or you gonna stay hush-mouthed about it?"

Something the size of a catfish wobbled in Floyd's stomach. "Wha...? Wha...?" was about all he could manage.

"Them '57s are due in a couple of months, ain't they? You gonna keep em under a tarp this year?" Then he winked at Floyd. "Or will you give your friends a little peek ahead of time?"

The blood that had drained from his face now rushed back up with a vengeance. He figured he was probably candy apple red by now. "Oh, yeah!" he said, feeling like he might get sick. But he stammered on. "That'd spoil the surprise, now wouldn't it, now. I spect it would." Floyd remembered to breathe. "But I got it on good word they real beauts. Something to behold." Floyd wiped his clammy hands on his pants. "Yessiree. That's what I'm told, all right."

Thankfully, at that moment Shep Howard, the insurance agent, walked in with Gaylon King, the publisher of the *Hopalachie Courier*. After another couple of rounds of greetings, they took chairs along the wall with the others.

Hayes Alcorn rose to his feet, which everybody always joked was a quick trip for Hayes considering how short he was. "I think that's everybody. Slats, would you mind pulling the blinds? It's time we started up."

Hayes stepped up into the barber's chair, and looked down with great satisfaction upon the gathering of county leaders. Not a hair over five-foot-four, Hayes Alcorn was a man who liked being looked up to. Even though he was Princeton-educated, he made every effort in word and deed to prove to people that he was still one of them, only more so. Neither a fancy education nor that Communist cell of liberal college professors could intimidate him from saying "ain't" or soften his Mississippi attitudes about the natural order of things. More than one in the room thought he might be announcing for governor come next election.

While Slats pulled the blinds, and the rest kept their eyes on Hayes, waiting for him to speak, Ben hurriedly packed away the tins of polish, trying his best not to make a sound. He carefully folded his blue apron, lay it up on the shoeshine chair, and then moved like a phantom across the shop floor, opening the door in a manner that kept the bell from ringing. Even though the day was fair, Ben stuffed his fists in his pockets and hunched up his shoulders like he was stepping out into a storm. Slats locked the door behind him.

Hayes cleared his throat. "Before we get started, I just want to thank y'all for the prayers and all the kindness you've shown to my wife Pearl and me. And I'm sure I can speak for Billy Dean and Miss Hertha, too. You all made the unbearable a bit more bearable."

A quiet murmur rose up from the group of men as they crossed and uncrossed their arms and shifted in their chairs. Again Floyd imagined all the eyes were now on him, fearing that Hayes was about to dramatically point a finger at Floyd and accuse him of illicit test drives with his niece. Illicit. He was growing to hate that word. Maybe he should just get it over with and confess, he thought. He made a bargain with himself. If he got through this meeting without being arrested, he swore that he would let the sheriff know about that death threat. Floyd began thinking of ways to tell it without mentioning his and Delia's drives to the levee.

To Floyd's relief, Hayes turned his attention to Billy Dean. "And I think we should continue to keep the sheriff in our prayers as he pursues whoever it is responsible."

The sheriff, who was sitting cross-legged, slouching down in his chair, did no more than nod in Hayes's direction, seemingly more interested in flicking the lid of his cigarette lighter.

After Hayes let a little memorial silence pass, he announced, "Well, that brings us around to why I asked y'all to come today." He reached down and gave the lever on the chair a little pump, sending him up a couple of inches, and then continued. "All this integration mess coming out of Washington, D.C., is giving the nigruhs ideas that they can get away with other things. Y'all know as good as me this talk about equality is nothing but a Jewish-Communist conspiracy. A way to mongrelize America by letting the nigruhs have their way with our women." Hayes let the obvious sink in.

Floyd wondered if Hayes was implying that Delia had been molested by a colored man. A surge of feeling for Delia welled up in Floyd. He gripped the arm of the metal chair and tried to think of something positive to stem the sadness. Well, at least they were looking for a colored man, he told himself. That got him off the hook. Then he hated himself for thinking it.

Hayes continued, "Seems every other county in Mississippi has already formed them a Citizens' Council to resist it at a local level. Now, Delphi, being the progressive town we are, needs to get on the bandwagon before we get left behind. I think it's up to us as forward-thinking county leaders to get the ball rolling."

Denton Satterfield, who had planting interests in the Delta alongside the Columns, asked, "How's the Senator going to feel about this council thing? I can say for a fact, he don't abide the Klan in this county."

Hayes nodded. "You right about that. Why many a time I myself have heard the Senator say, 'Hayes, the only thing worse than the Klan in their white sheets is the Supreme Court in their black ones. Neither one,' he'd say, 'got no business telling me what to do with my niggers.'"

There was a round of appreciative laughter for the Senator's sentiments and Hayes's fine impersonation—laughter from everybody except the sheriff, that is. Floyd was keeping a close eye on him and right now Billy Dean seemed bored to tears. As Floyd watched, the sheriff lit a cigarette and inhaled, blowing a jet of smoke up at Hayes in his barber chair throne. It might have been judged to be an aggressive gesture if Billy Dean's expression revealed anything other than pure indifference.

Hayes cranked himself above the cloud and continued. "But I know for a fact, if the Senator wasn't grieving, he'd be here with us this evening lending his support. You see," he said, "the Citizens' Council is not the Klan. We're not a bunch of yahoos out to lynch nigruhs. We are a legitimate association of civic leaders who will work with the Sovereign State of Mississippi to protect its constitutional right to be led by white people." He paused to survey the group, face by face, and then concluded, "We'll have the full support of the State and its governing bodies, as well as the complete backing of my brother-in-law, the Senator. We're talking respectable."

"Like the Rotary?" Floyd asked hopefully. He sure didn't want to be involved in anything mean-spirited.

"Yes," Hayes heartily agreed. "Exactly. Upright, patriotic men operat-

ing by the full light of day in the community's best interest. Why, just
between the eleven of us here and the Senator, we can evict, cancel credit,
cut off commodities, or fire any nigruh who wants to make trouble. No
need for lynching anymore. This is a new day for Mississippi." Hayes
paused while a murmur of agreement rippled among the men.

Then he continued. "Why, over in Indianola, they got it locked up so
tight that if a nigruh even starts thinking about voting he has to leave the
county to earn penny one. And it's all on the upright. No violence. Ain't
that right, Sheriff?"

Not bothering to look up, Billy Dean stubbed his cigarette on the sole
of his boot and yawned. "Yep," he said. "That's the way to do it, awright.
Lawful."

Floyd noticed Brother Dear nodding vigorously, throwing his vote
firmly on the side of nonviolence. He didn't know what it was about some
of these people in Hopalachie County. Back in the hills there was a hanging now and then, but these people were damn near nigger-crazy. Even the
Baptist preacher there. Talking about how the colored wanted to take over
the schools and the churches and the bedrooms. To hear them tell it, every
white woman in the county was in danger of waking up one morning and
finding herself impregnated with a colored baby.

On the other side of the coin, it certainly was an honor to have been
asked to be a founding member of this thing. The way Hayes explained it,
maybe this Citizens' Council wouldn't be so bad after all. What harm could
it do? It sure wouldn't hurt business any.

"Well, if we all in agreement," Hayes said, "I think we should start by
electing officers and then plan a recruiting drive to get the rest of the county involved."

Floyd even took vice president.

Floyd stuck close to the sheriff after the meeting broke up, pretending
to be going in the same direction. As the sheriff reached for the door of his
cruiser, Floyd stopped in his tracks and snapped his fingers, like the
thought had just hit him.

"Sheriff!" he called out. "Something come to me this here second. Something that must of slipped my mind before." Floyd hurried over to where the sheriff stood waiting for his revelation.

Floyd began talking in a rush. "Delia was at the dealership one day last week looking to trade in, and she said she sure liked that Mercury Montclair we had on the side lot, but then she said she didn't know if the fella she was seeing would like it and I tole her why not surprise him and see if he don't, and she said he didn't like surprises and that he had threatened to kill her over the last one she give him."

Floyd waited for the thousand follow-up questions he had practiced the answers to, but the sheriff just looked at him unblinking. "Well, how come I didn't bring it up before," Floyd said, proceeding with the interrogation he had imagined, "was I didn't think she was serious about it. You know how you can get so mad at somebody you love, you liable to say things you don't really mean in a million years? I was thinking it was that kind of thing. How come I didn't mention it before now."

Floyd knew he was talking too much for an innocent man and his face began to burn hot, but he couldn't seem to get his mouth stopped. "You know what I mean," he rambled on. "I thought it was one of those things, like we all do. Like 'I'm gonna kill you, Hazel.' You know what I'm saying, don't you, Billy Dean?"

Floyd was finally able to get himself to shut up. The sheriff studied him coolly. After a long moment, he reached to open his door and turned back to Floyd. Without a hint of emotion, Billy Dean said, "I'm sure you're right about that. Done the exact same thing myself on occasion."

The sheriff drove off, leaving Floyd on the sidewalk, a free man.

Pulling up to the house, Floyd had convinced himself for the thousandth time everything was going to be fine. Things were going to work themselves out. Like his book said: "To rise above your petty problems, tackle even bigger problems. Successful men are known by the size of the problems they choose to focus on."

Today his fellow citizens had entrusted him with important and grave responsibilities. By anyone's standards, Floyd was becoming a successful man. An important man. A man of the community. A man who could be trusted with larger problems and purposes.

The house was dark when he stepped in the door. Vida had left hours ago and Hazel would be asleep in her room. It was the solid, reassuring quiet of things under control. Yes, he told himself again, things were going to be fine. "Johnny!" he called out in the dark. "You here?"

Johnny came bolting down the stairs at the sound of his father's voice. "Big Monkey!" he called out. The boy ran over to his father and bounced happily up and down at his feet.

"Hey, Little Monkey," Floyd said.

Floyd lifted Johnny up, not thinking. He only felt love for the boy, wanting to share with him the exhilaration of that moment. He swung the boy downward and then raised him fast on the upswing, like he was about to toss him into the air.

Even before Johnny's scream, Floyd felt it. That terror of standing on a precipice, the only real thing in the world being the inevitability of plummeting and never stopping. He was pierced by a panic so absolute it shut down his senses, and then losing his balance, he staggered forward, holding on to his son for dear life.

After reeling there in the dark for what seemed like an eternity, drenched from the heat of an unseen blaze, gripping his frightened son, Floyd felt his senses slowly return to him, until he was able to set Johnny down, carefully, both feet on the floor. Still trembling, Floyd knelt down before the boy and looked into his face, only to see his own terror repeated in his son's eyes. Floyd reached out and drew Johnny to him again. This time he began to sob uncontrollably, clutching his boy to his chest.

Chapter 36
ABDUCTED

The sheriff parked his cruiser behind a curtain of kudzu-strangled pines so that he couldn't be seen from the road. As he sat waiting, he flicked open and closed the lid of the nickel-plated lighter. He didn't know why he bothered taking it. Just couldn't seem to help himself when he saw stuff lying around. He had quite a collection now. Mostly dime-store flash. The kind of thing niggers hold dear. Junk his mother would get from his daddy after a bad drunk. Trinkets so cheap not a one held up during the fire.

A couple of maids walked by yammering. He cricked his neck out the window to get a look, but resumed flicking the lighter. Normally Billy Dean wouldn't mind driving down into Tarbottom in broad daylight to pick up a nigger. It was sport for him to see if he could get his cruiser to the bottom of the hill before he was detected. But usually by the time he cut his motor and coasted down the hill, emerging from around the curve into plain sight, he was too late and everything had already come to a dead halt.

On the porches, women had stopped fanning themselves in mid-stroke. The bucks had already got themselves hid in the woods. The pick-aninnies were at their stations, standing stock-still and wide-eyed at the windows, ready to relay messages like Western Union from the women to their men. Even the yard dogs appeared to be waiting for him, their ears flattened back and tails tucked. Everything might be graveyard quiet, but Billy Dean could feel the hidden busyness under the surface. It was like a bed of fire ants. Sometimes he just wanted to kick the top off.

But it wouldn't do any good. When he did grab one by the collar and question him, Billy Dean always got that "nossuh-sheriff-we-don't-know-nothin" hangdog look. In eight years as sheriff, he had learned that niggers were like animals, the way they stuck together and communicated danger to the rest of the pack. If you wanted to surprise one, you couldn't do it alone, and you had to come at them from more than one direction.

Today, however, he didn't want to be seen in Tarbottom, risking it getting back to the Senator. He had to be careful. When it came to Levi and his family, the Senator made it clear they were off-limits. He hadn't trusted Billy Dean from the very beginning on that count. He remembered how suspicious the Senator had been when Billy Dean told him somebody had burned down Levi's church for starting up all that voting business.

The Senator had been infuriated. "Levi's church hell!" the Senator shouted. "That was my goddamned church!"

How was Billy Dean to know the Senator had built it himself to keep his niggers contented? "I reckon the Klan burnt it down," he had said, thinking as fast as he could.

"What Klan?" the old man asked, eyeing Billy Dean doubtfully. "I don't tolerate Klan in my county."

"Must a been from somewhere's else. Lusiana Klan maybe."

"What about that little nigruh boy?" he asked. "Who shot Levi's grandbaby? That don't sound like no Klan to me."

"Boy's daddy done it," Billy Dean answered. "Found another mule kicking in his stall. Got crazy jealous and shot wild. He probly up to Memphis by now."

"All this happen in one night?"

"Big night," Billy Dean said lightly.

"Yeah, big load a somethin." The Senator had been blunt. "Here's the quick of it, Billy Dean. From here on out you let Levi and them alone. If anything happens to him or his, I'm going to hold you personally responsible. Got it? I done run the Klan out and it'll take a lot less to dropkick your sorry ass over the county line. The niggers in Hopalachie County are *my* business."

He blew a thick cloud of cigar smoke at Billy Dean. "I'll take your word this once about that voting business, but I swear, if I ever hear anything different, if anything ever happens to Levi, if you lay one hand on him or his girl or his boy...." The Senator stubbed out his cigar in his silver ashtray. The gesture wasn't lost on the sheriff.

"Yes, sir. I hear it. They your niggers. Not mine."

"Good. And now that we having this nice father-son chat," the Senator had continued, "let me tell you one more thing I got on my mind." Then the Senator tilted forward in his chair and slammed his elbow on the desk, pointing his trigger finger straight at Billy Dean. "I know your kind, Billy Dean. If I ever find out that you been fooling around on Hertha, I won't bother kicking you out of the county. I'll personally bury you ass-up, right under my back step, just so I can tromp on it every morning on my way out the door."

Thank god for the Senator's stubborn pride. If him and Levi ever had a heart-to-heart, Sheriff Billy Dean Brister would be history. Sometimes he wondered who got the best end of this deal. For two terms, he had done the Senator's bidding as his plantation sheriff—patrolling the train station to make sure no tenants skipped town owing the Senator money, keeping the local yahoos away from the nigger prisoners until the traveling electric chair could get to town, closing down the jooks and keeping the blues singers in jail during times of short labor, shooting up any stills not personally sanctioned by his majesty, not to mention trying to keep his ugly-as-sin daughter happy.

Now, to add to it, every day the Senator was hounding his ass to "find the nigger that killed my little girl!" He was going to have to come up with something pretty damned soon to satisfy the Senator on that count.

Billy Dean tossed the lighter and snatched it in midair. But on the other side of that same nickel, he had become accustomed to the jangle of the handcuffs and the tug of a pistol on his hip, deputies who had to do for him. For the first time in his life, Billy Dean knew what it was like to have something to lose and it wasn't that bad of a feeling. He sure wasn't going to let some nigger maid come between him and that.

Through the tangle of trees and vines, Billy Dean saw Vida and her father. That gold-toothed whore was with them. He pocketed the lighter. After letting them walk a little farther down the road and out of earshot, he cranked the engine. Then he slowly pulled out from the trees and rolled after them, coasting at a snail's pace with his foot on the brake. They never even glanced around.

Pulling up alongside the threesome, he leaned across the seat and glowered at them through the opposite window. None of them paid him any mind. They just kept walking with their eyes straight ahead, unfazed. How do they do that? the sheriff wondered. They had known it was him without ever turning around. He hollered out, "You! Girl! Get in the back."

All three stopped and cut their eyes at one another, probably sending some kind of animal SOS. These niggers were something else entirely.

Vida didn't respond at once. The sheriff slammed the car into park, sprang out, and marched around to the other side. He jerked open the back door and shoved Vida inside, striking her head against the roof ledge in the process. "I ain't got all day," he said, banging the door shut.

As Vida sat hunched in the backseat, holding her head, he looked at Levi and Sweet Pea, whose faces were stupid and blank. "Y'all just keep on ahead, minding your business, you hear?"

The sheriff got back in the car without another word. He just drove. A light rain began to fall, enough to muddy up the windshield before stopping again. Every once in a while he checked Vida's expression in the rear view. Cold as a stone. Just like she looked every morning and every evening when she stood outside the Grahams' house, staring him down. No sir, he thought to himself, no nigger girl was going to kill his gold-shitting goose.

They were miles out of town and speeding down a road that coiled through the bluffs as it ran north. The sun had already dropped below the tree line and the fields were mostly shadow. The road was empty except for the cruiser and scores of yellow sulfur butterflies. One butterfly had not made it clear of the sheriff's windshield and got hung up under the wiper, wings whipping and ripping in the wind, and its fine powder streaking yellow against the glass.

Eventually the sheriff turned off the blacktop and onto a gravel road, cut on a deep downward slope that would inevitably strike out into the open Delta. But before reaching the bottom of the descent, the sheriff turned again, this time onto an ungraded and much narrower road, cut between high earthen banks, and for a while it wound like a stream between the walls of a canyon. The farther they traveled, the narrower the road became and the more disused it looked, until it was nothing but two footpaths, with goldenrod and jimsonweed growing up between.

When there was no path left at all, the sheriff pulled to a stop. Sitting off in the growth of weeds and brushwood sat a half-burned, rotting shack, much of it overgrown with vines. It leaned crazily to one side, as if the green twisting tentacles were ever so slowly luring the house down into the underbrush.

The sheriff lit a cigarette and then sat motionless, looking off in the direction of the house. Vida also remained dead-still in the backseat, but she was damp with fear. Her hand was down in her bag, her fingers firmly gripping the wooden handle of the ice pick.

Opening the glove compartment, the sheriff pulled out a half-pint of whiskey and got out of the car. He opened her door and simply said, "Out." It was the first word spoken between them since they began their journey.

Still she didn't move. Looking down at his boots, considering her options, she tightened her grip on the pick. When she saw him reach for her arm, she jerked her hand out of the sack, empty. She struggled to exit the car on her own, detesting the thought of his touch. On her feet, Vida's legs buckled and she nearly fell, finding her balance just before the sheriff shoved her, sending her stumbling into a wild tangle of a yard.

Briars bit her legs, but she kept moving toward the house, clutching her sack. She stopped when she got to the fire-scorched porch, warped into great valleys. There were no steps.

"Keep on ahead," came the dry growl from behind her. He pushed her again and she caught herself against the plank edging.

She hoisted herself onto the porch and walked toward the door. Each step made a loud hollow sound that seemed to reverberate through the woods. The sheriff followed close behind.

Once inside the shack, Vida saw that the far wall was mostly burned out, nothing left but charred boards. But the vines had stitched over the breaks, keeping the house dark and cool, the smells thick and musty. All the windows were busted out, and dirt daubers busied themselves around the stone fireplace, filling in the gaps where the chinking had fallen out. It was past twilight and the house was alive with shadows, half-real shapes that seemed to loom in the room, vanishing when looked at straight on.

Vida's eyes adjusted to the dark. She noticed broken chairs and pieces of a table strewn across the floor; and against the wall was an empty pie safe, its screened door hanging askew like a broken arm. The place gave off a sense of death and despair.

Vida estimated the distance across the floor to the window. If she didn't get shot first, she figured she'd make it in three steps and then take off into the woods. But again, she felt his hand at her back. He shoved her forward.

The clump, clump of their steps echoed even louder now and seemed strangely out of place. Like cow hooves on a plank bridge. He shoved Vida so hard it sent her stumbling through a doorway into the back room. On the floor in the corner lay a ruined cotton mattress, its once-striped ticking darkened to a uniform dingy brown. Strewn about were dozens of empty whiskey bottles, a chair with the cane seat busted out. It was exactly as Sweet Pea had described it.

A flicker of hope rose up in her chest. Maybe Sweet Pea would find Willie and tell him what had happened! Willie had a gun. Could Sweet Pea remember where this shack was? But just as suddenly, the hope vanished. She remembered Willie had gone to Louisiana on a run for Hannah. Vida was alone in the world with this man.

The overpowering smell in the room was not of old smoke, but of rot and mildew. The stench, laced with her own terror, gripped Vida's stomach. More afraid of the mattress than the gun, she turned to face the sheriff. She did not dare look into his eyes, but she could feel them running over her body like cold hands.

The sheriff screwed open the whiskey and flung the cap across the room. "Go on, girl. This what you been wanting ain't it? To get a close-up view? Well, here I am. Take a look."

Vida began to shake. But she kept her eyes riveted to the floor.

Then he roared, "I said look, goddamm you!"

She tried, but was only able to raise her eyes to the level of his badge before dropping her head again. She felt a warm stream of urine run down her leg. Tensing her body, she tried to control her bladder, all the time praying he couldn't tell.

He said nothing. The only thing she heard was the pounding in her ears and the ugly grunts his throat made as he drank from the bottle. When he spoke at last, he no longer shouted. His voice was like the cold edge of a blade to her throat. "What kind of games you playing with me, girl?"

Still, she remained mute. She closed her eyes and saw Nate's face.

"What's the idea you working right next door to me?"

"Needs the money," she was able to mumble.

"The Senator know how you done run off his place?"

"Yessuh," she said. "He know it. We all paid up with the Senator."

"And what you doing with that whore?"

"Who that?"

"You know the hell who. The one you was walking with."

"She ain't a whore no more." Vida bit her lip, not meaning to contradict him.

He laughed. "Sure thing? She been re-virginated, I reckon."

"Yessuh. She Miss Cilly's maid, now."

There was another pause while the sheriff raised the bottle and took a long pull. She lifted her eyes for only a quick moment and saw him wiping his mouth with the back of his hand. He had seen her look. Again he laughed. "You still wearin white, I see."

"Yessuh," she mumbled.

"Like the first time I seen you. I bet you remember that night good, don't you, girl?"

"Yessuh," she said, thinking again of the ice pick the sack held.

He took a step closer to her. "What was his name?"

"Who name?" She knew, but she couldn't believe he had really meant it. In a hoarse whisper he said, "The boy's name."

"The boy..." Vida said, stopping short of what she had intended.

"*Your* boy," he said. "His name. What was it?" He moved closer again.

Her head still bowed, she could see the pointy toes of his boots. She began again, "The boy...the boy you kilt."

Once that was said, from somewhere she had to find the courage to study his face. His reaction meant the world. Would his expression deny or confirm? She lifted her eyes. The room went perfectly quiet. In that moment, nothing else existed but the man's face and the message it held.

She saw his thin, pinched lips, his jaw that jutted out sharply, the dip in the chin like a thumbprint. But nothing in his face moved, except a muscle under his ear that hardened and released and hardened again. Then she dared to glance quickly into his eyes. There was nothing. Nothing but cold and darkness. She shut her eyes to him.

"Wha'd you call him?" he asked, terrifyingly patient with her.

"Nate," she said, thinking how peculiar to be telling a father the name of his own son. What would he do with it? What *could* he do with a name?

"Nate Snow," he said almost to himself. "How many years would he a been now?"

"Nine."

She waited for more, but he just stood there holding his bottle at the level of his star, still nothing telling on his face. She glanced quickly at his eyes again. They were like burnt-out coals.

No longer able to bear not knowing another second, Vida blurted, "How come you askin me that?"

He smiled, as if amused at her boldness. He said coyly, like he was playing with her, "No reason particular. Just making conversation." He took another drink, wiped his mouth, and then continued talking in that odd, loose way. "Just puts me in mind of that nigger boy from Chicago a while back. Down visiting his old auntie. Know the one?"

Vida didn't answer. Everybody knew. Why was he asking?

"Smart-mouthed a white woman. They pulled him out of the Hopalachie if my memory serves me." He shook his head in mock sadness. "Shame. Real shame. Mississippi can be a dangerous place for a nigger ain't been brung up here. Don't know the ways."

Vida's heart leaped to her throat, and her fear was pushed aside by a sudden upswell of hope. There was only one reason he could be telling her this. It was a warning. And a warning meant he hadn't tracked her boy down and killed him! It meant Nate was as lost to the sheriff as he was to her.

But her excitement chilled again. He knew he had been tricked by the empty coffin. This was no man to be made a fool of. "What you gone to do with me?" she asked, even though now she was certain he meant to hurt her bad. "Why you carry me out here? What you wont?"

The sheriff drained the bottle and tossed it out the open window. She heard it land with a clink somewhere out in the bramble. Sensing that his eyes were no longer on her, she looked up and watched him as he slowly surveyed the room, as if he were able to see what she couldn't. Vida half expected something to melt out of the shadows.

That's when she knew it. What this place was. If thinking about someone made it so, she knew this man better than any man in her life. Fearing him. Studying him. Turning him over and over in her mind, until she believed she could prophesy his movements. This is where Billy Dean Brister belonged. This was his home.

It was as if Billy Dean had snared her thoughts and didn't like them one bit. He struck like a rattler. Sudden and swift, in the blink of time between two thoughts, he had her by the throat.

Vida fumbled at her bag. Before she could touch her pick, he had snatched the sack away and lifted her by the neck to her toes. He flung her bag across the room and tightened his grip on her throat, choking off her breath. "You listen to me. I know that nigger boy ain't dead. I know bout you sending him away. Think you smart, don't you?"

The sheriff's face was in hers. His breathing was hard and she could smell the sourness of whiskey. His eyes had caught fire. "You know what I'm going to do to you now, don't you?" His spittle flew into her face. "Answer me," he said. "Don't you?"

He had cut off her breath. "Nossuh," she gasped.

"Nossuh, Sheriff! Nossuh!" he raged. "That it? That's all you niggers know how to say?"

But Vida couldn't say anything else if she had to. The sheriff's face was now a glowing ember at the center of a darkening sky.

He pulled the gun from his holster and carefully placed the bore against Vida's temple. He eased back the hammer and like thunder she heard it lock into place. "Girl, shooting you ain't gone mean jackshit to me.

Take a look around you. Let this broke-down shack be the last thing you see. This is how far I come from. And I ain't never going back. No ashes to ashes…"

The red ember that was his face burned out.

When Vida came to she was lying with her face flat against the stinking mattress. She had no idea how much time had passed. She only knew she was still alive. The second thing she knew was that she hadn't been raped, not yet.

The house was darker and cooler now. A breeze stirred in the room. She reached to touch the searing pain in her throat. When she turned herself over, the sheriff was standing several feet away. He seemed to be studying her through the dark.

"Girl," he said, his voice low and even. "I'll say it once. Stay out of my house. Away from my wife. Away from my girls. Do you understand that?"

"Yessuh," Vida whispered hoarsely, her voice clawing the inside of her throat.

"And next time your daddy tries to get a message to the Senator, through Pearl or anybody else, he'll be one dead nigger. Tell him."

"Yessuh."

"Now, you be a good girl and let sleeping dogs lie." The whites of his eyes shone in the dark. "Remember, I'm watching you just like you watching me."

He reached down and picked up her sack. After he removed the ice pick, he tossed the sack on the mattress. "I'm glad we have reached this understanding," he said, eerily formal. "Now, let's you and me get on back to the car."

As the sheriff headed toward Delphi, Vida rubbed her throat, thinking hard about the man driving. She had more questions now than ever. Why hadn't he killed her? He could have easily. Nobody would have been the wiser. Killing now must be so easy for him. The letter she had taken from his house proved that.

Yet he had let her live. Why? she asked again. To carry back a warning to her father? Why hadn't he killed them all long ago? She could think of no reasonable answer. Any more than she could figure out how a little colored boy could draw so much hate from a grown man.

As the headlights split the darkness before them, Vida thought of what Lillie Dee had said so long ago, about the spirits who walked the land at night, calling out the names of the sleeping. When a sleeper answers, the old woman had said, the spirits come to him with his own special truth and whisper it into his ear. Then they leave him in peace.

But Lillie Dee said that most white folks don't know their names anymore. They had lost themselves along the way in all their grabbing and taking of what belongs to others. So they can't answer when they're called. It is these people that the spirits taunt with bad dreams and fitful sleep, leaving their brains fevered with madness.

Maybe that was it, Vida thought. This was a man who didn't know his name or even where he belonged. Who ran to the shadows of a rotting-down house where maybe once he knew who he was. Maybe the sheriff had him a praying ground, too, like her father, where he went to remember the face of God, before the world went dark.

Vida had no idea of the time when the sheriff pulled the car over, almost to the spot where he had picked her up a lifetime ago. He simply told her to get out. In the dark of a starless night, Vida stumbled down the hill and through the mud to Tarbottom.

When she neared her house, she could see Willie's car parked in front and his silhouette on the porch.

"Vida!" he shouted, jumping to his feet and scrambling down the steps to meet her. As he approached she noticed the pistol he was toting.

"Vida, you all right?" He strained to see her face in the dark.

"I'm fine, Willie, but please, put up that gun."

He shoved it in his belt. "I been drivin round the country for hours lookin for you. Sweet Pea was waitin at Hannah's when I got back from Lou'siana. She was cryin so hard I couldn't hardly make it out. Then she tole me bout the sheriff. I tried my best to find you, but…" He paused, narrowing his eyes at his sister. "What he do to you, Vida?"

She looked up at the darkened cabin. "Where's Daddy at?"

"Inside, sleepin. We ain't tole him nothing. Said you was out visitin."

Vida was relieved. "Don't wake him up. Come on. Let's go around the back to the kitchen."

Once inside, Willie got the lamp lit, then turned to Vida. Seeing her holding her neck, he grabbed Vida's wrist. She resisted, but Willie was stronger.

Her skin was already bruising. Willie spat, "That son of a bitch! I'll kill him." His hand automatically touched the gun.

Gripping Willie by the arm, she drew him down into a chair, then sat next to him. "Willie, I'm all right," she said in her calmest voice, trying to soothe him. "It don't hurt. Just let it alone." She managed a smile, "Willie, I got good news."

Willie stared angrily at her throat, his jaw clenched. Vida could tell he was ashamed, probably because he had not been there to stop it. "Willie, listen," she said, "Nate's alive! I know it. The sheriff ain't never found him. Don't know where he is."

"That's real good," he said evenly.

Vida reached over and shook him by the shoulder, trying to break him out of his mood. "Don't it make you happy, Willie?"

He looked into her eyes, and as if hearing for the first time what she said, smiled tenderly. "Yes, it do, Sister. It really do."

Willie got up, went to where his special coat hung on the back of the door, and retrieved a Milk of Magnesia bottle from a pocket. Setting it on the table beside Vida, he said playfully, "How bout a drink? Might do you good."

"What you meanin by this?" Vida asked, having to smile.

"Open it and take a swaller."

"You crazy? I ain't backed up."

"Go ahead on and open it. It ain't what you think."

She unscrewed the top and lifted it to her nose. "This is hootch!"

Willie laughed. He was suddenly his smooth, charming self again. "It was my idea," he said proudly. "I make deliveries to white women all over the county. They rather get it from a colored man who ain't gone tell it on them, like a white bootlegger might do. Smart huh?" He laughed again. "I pretend I'm from the drugstore dropping off medicine to constipated white ladies."

"You crazy," Vida said, not able to keep from laughing with him. She gave his hand a pretend slap. Vida screwed the top back on and handed the bottle to her brother. "But leave me out of you and Hannah's schemes." She reached up and touched her neck.

Willie's face went serious again. "Sister," he said gravely, "I thought you might could use you a drink."

"No," she said, "It don't hurt that bad."

"No. Not that." Willie was speaking very carefully now. "I got some news, too, Vida."

"What's happened?" she looked toward the front room. "Is it Daddy? He done somethin, ain't he?"

"No, it ain't Daddy." Willie reached for her hand. "Now listen to me. While I was in New Orleans pickin up a shipment, I stopped off to shoot a little craps."

"Willie, I tole you no good gone come out of that kind of livin. What trouble you fell in now?"

"Just listen, Vida. There was this fella in the game and when I tole him where I was from, he said he had been through here once. Back in June he said it was. Vida, he said he came to Delphi lookin for you."

"For me? Why…" Then it dawned on Vida. "Creola said there was some man come lookin for me at the Grahams'. I tole you bout him. The one Creola said was a friend of yores."

"Never laid eye on him before, Vida. He told me he brung a letter for you. From Rezel."

"Rezel!" She gripped his hand tight enough to stop the flow of blood. "Oh, my Lord amighty in Heaven! You got the letter, Willie? Give it to me!"

"I ain't got it, Sister. He said he left it with the boy."

Then her eyes flared. "That damned white boy! He got my letter!"

It was everything Willie could do to keep Vida from taking off that minute to grab Johnny out of his bed and shake him senseless. But she agreed to wait until morning.

She didn't sleep the whole night through and by first light she had figured out where the letter had to be. She didn't bother with breakfast or even with waking her father. Instead, she threw on her wrinkled uniform and raced up the hill toward the Grahams'. She was the only one on the road.

Halfway there, the sun had already disappeared behind a weak gray sky. A misting rain had started to fall. She had forgotten both her parasol and her hat, and the fine mist gathered on her skin into droplets that trickled down her face and neck. She didn't notice to mop it away.

When she arrived at the Grahams' house, she didn't bother going inside. She headed straight for Johnny's digging ground under the porch. After she crawled through the little door, she stopped.

At first, she couldn't see a thing. She waited there, on her hands and knees in the dirt, for her eyes to adjust, and when they did, she saw a piece of white paper that seemed to be growing out of the ground. Her heart began to race. Was that it? She crawled in that direction. There was another one. And then another. Rows and rows of scrap paper—used envelopes, grocery lists, bills, paper plates—each piece run through with a popsicle stick and stuck in a dirt mound like a sign. Dozens of them.

She plucked one out of the ground. In crayon was written the single word, "Daddy." Scooping up the dirt with her hand, she found buried one of Mr. Floyd's tie clips. Other signs read "Momma" and "Davie." Frantically, she began tearing the sticks out of the ground, one after the other, reading the names, until finally, Vida found the one she had been looking for. A marker with her name drawn in black crayon. She frantically dug down into the ground with her fingers, pulling out fistfuls of dirt. Until at last she saw, lying in a bread wrapper coffin, an envelope with a neatly typed "V" on its face.

Vida's first reaction was disappointment. "This can't be from Rezel," she told herself. "This writ with a typin machine."

With her heart pounding in her ears and her hands shaking like leaves, she carefully tore off the end, blew into the envelope, and fished out a single page of white stationery.

Sitting there under the house, the light of the dim morning strained through lattice, she moved her lips to the words.

Dear V,

I'm sorry I haven't tried to reach you before this. There are too many reasons, none of which make any difference now. Besides, I know how the white folks down there like to read the colored's mail. I was especially afraid to send something with your name on it. After Momma passed, there was no one I could trust to send a letter to.

For years, I told myself it would be best if you knew nothing. I'm still not sure I made the right decision, but when my friend said that he was going down that way, I took the chance of him finding you or your family.

First off, your son is fine. I don't know if you heard, but soon after I left Memphis I was sent to prison for a couple of years. It was impossible for me to keep the boy. There was a man who was real good to me through it all and he said he would take him. He and his wife are raising him like one of their own. They are white people. V, they love him and he has nothing to want for. The white life is the only life he knows.

I can't tell you where he is. It may break your heart to hear this, but you must realize that he doesn't remember Mississippi or his short time there.

Please try to see that it is best this way. Mississippi is not a place for a colored man or boy. Pray for your son and wish him the best, but let him have his chance now.

I won't be back either. I hope you and your family are well and weathered the storm all right. I'm sorry I let you down.

Sincerely,

R.

She stared at the paper for a long time, unblinking. Then she hardened her face and said out loud, "Nossuh. Rezel didn't writ this letter. This was writ by somebody with book learnin. Reads like a teacher done it." She shook her head at the letter, denying what it said. "Ain't none of it the truth."

She forced herself to read it again. Upon finishing the second time, disbelief had bled away, along with any hope, leaving her emptied and desolate, leveled by the truth.

She wasn't aware of how long she sat there under the porch, amid Johnny's graves. She didn't even notice when Floyd walked out the kitchen door and descended the steps to his car parked between the house and the dry-docked Lincoln.

At some point, she told herself she should be grateful. "Least he's alive," she said without conviction. "That's somethin."

But she also knew that he was alive to some white woman. A white woman he was now calling Momma. He didn't know Vida at all.

"And if he ever do see me," she thought, "who he goin to see? A nigger is who." She breathed in and forced out the breath, her shoulders caving in on the exhale, as if all at once feeling the cumulative strain of eight years of waiting without word.

"I'm dead to my boy," she said bitterly, staring at the letter. "Worse than dead. He one of them now. Nate, you ain't never gone wont me for yo momma."

Later inside the Grahams' kitchen, Vida sat trancelike, staring at the letter spread out on the table before her. She only moved to touch her throat. This morning she had even forgotten about Hazel's pills.

The kitchen had grown steadily darker with the weather, but she hadn't bothered to turn on the lights. As the thunder began to rumble outside, her only response was to clasp her hands and lay them on top of the letter. The unlit kitchen rapidly filled with shadows.

She looked up. There was the boy, wearing his pajamas and sleep still in his eyes. He stood there, a grave look on his face, considering her carefully. Knotting his brows, he asked, "What's the matter? Why's your dress so dirty?"

She gave him a searing look. In a bloodless tone, she said, "I been up under the house. You wont to guess what I found?"

Johnny's eyes cut down to the letter and then back up at Vida. He took off in a frantic dash for the bathroom. But before he could get the door closed, Vida was on him. She pushed back so hard, the door flung Johnny to the floor.

Not thinking at all now, merely acting out of a blind rage, she yanked him up by the waist and hauled him under her arm like a sack of cornmeal, his legs flailing in the air. She plopped him standing up in the tub. Then she grabbed him by the wrist.

"Ow! You're hurting me!" he shouted.

"Stand still or I'll shake you like a 'simmon tree." He tried to pull away from her, but she yanked him viciously.

"Momma! Momma!" he yelled.

Vida turned on the faucet and a loud rush of water splattered into the tub, drowning out his screams.

"Go ahead and holler yo head off," Vida shouted. "She ain't gone hear you. She ain't gone do nothin to save her little white boy. You and me both knows that. Now who you gone tell it to?" She scalded him with her eyes. "You gone tell it to the sheriff agin?"

She gripped his wrist even tighter and reached for the bar of soap. "You know what they do to bad little boys with dirty, lying mouths, don't you?"

"Leave me alone. Nigger!" he shouted.

That did it. Vida flung the bar of soap against the tile wall and it hit with a *twhack* and then splashed into the tub. "Damn it, Nate!" she screamed, "shut your god-damned mouth!"

"I ain't Nate!" Johnny screamed back. "I'm Johnny Earl Graham. Big letter J! Little letters o! h! n! n! y! That's who I am. Don't you people call me Nate no more!"

It was like somebody had slapped Vida across the face. Her mouth still agape, she looked at Johnny long and hard. His breathing was furious, his bottom lip quivered, and his little fists were clenched.

In a voice strangled with a murderous rage, he seethed, "And you better leave my momma alone or I'm gonna kill you."

For certain, Vida thought, this boy would kill her if he had half a chance.

She let go of his wrist, and, like that had been the last thing holding her up, she slumped to the floor. She sat there in a heap with her eyes closed and her hands limp in her lap.

Johnny remained tensed, ready for whatever this crazy woman might do next.

Vida looked up at Johnny. Here was a boy prepared to kill for his mother, and for the first time she knew why she hated the white woman so.

She shook her head slowly. "Johnny Earl Graham," she said wearily, just over the sound of the running water. "You got a wagonload of fight in you."

Now with tears streaming down her face, she carefully reached up toward the boy. He raised his fists at her, as his own tears fell.

"And chile," she said as she gently wiped a single teardrop from his cheek, "in this bad ol' world, I spec you gone need ever last ounce of it."

Chapter 37
MORNING PICNIC

Vida's steps were leaden as she slogged down the muddy road to Tarbottom. She couldn't work today, that was all there was to it. Anyway, Miss Hazel didn't need her. She had her son to tend to her, to love her, to worry over her. As for Vida, her thoughts were of her own bed, in her own room, her own dreamless sleep.

When she got to her cabin, her father was sitting out on the porch. She felt his eyes on her as she climbed the steps, and she knew he was waiting for some explanation, but she said nothing. She passed through the open door and didn't stop until she fell hard upon her bed, as if collapsing under the weight of losing her son for the second time. It seemed to have crushed the very breath out of her.

Levi followed her into her room. "Vida, are you sick?"

How could she answer him? How could she put into words her sickness. Years of plotting and scheming. Childish plans that had put them in Delphi, within striking distance of the man who wanted her whole family dead. Thinking she could weave a web around an entire town, and snatch up every word spoken about her son. Only to be undone by a six-year-old. She had been so foolish.

"Daddy," she said, her eyes closed, "I ain't never going to see Nate again. I know it now." She wasn't sure why she told him. Maybe she just needed to say it out loud to someone. To make it real. To let go of the folly. She looked up at Levi.

He was watching her with blank eyes. Did he even understand? She had lived so long with her silly connivance, never telling him what she was feeling or thinking or hoping. Her plans had been all she had needed. But now she was alone again with her father. How could he ever understand her loss?

A faint smile appeared on Levi's face. He looked down on her dirt-streaked uniform and her muddy tennis shoes. "Snowflake Baby," he said, finally. "You still my Snowflake Baby, ain't you?"

She could feel the emotion rising in her throat. "Yes, Daddy," she said, her eyes filling with tears, "I reckon I am."

Her father sat down on the edge of the bed and held open his arms to her. Reaching up around his neck, Vida lay her head against his shoulder.

"That's real good," he said softly. "I been so sad about losing her."

Hazel had waited and waited for Vida's approach, but it never came. When Floyd had dropped in earlier to deliver his morning kiss, at first she could hardly look at him. She had long stopped asking if he loved her. He couldn't say it without that "anyway" sound to it. She wondered how much patience he had left with her. How much time did she have before he moved her out, and moved in the one with the French perfume?

The maids had given her fears a name. Delia. The same woman who came into her house and laughed at her. Humiliated her. Made fun of her furniture and her food. All the time scouting Hazel's home for her third husband. Not for one second did Hazel believe she was really dead. Mainly because her own jealousy was so alive.

When she did manage a look at him, even with his salesman's grin and head-tilt, he seemed nervous.

"What's wrong?" she had asked.

"Nothing," he said too quickly, glancing at his watch. "I really got to go." He made a beeline for the door.

"Floyd," she called after him, desperate, "maybe we could get away from here. Take a trip together. Maybe drive down to the coast? Maybe stay at that Edgewater Beach Hotel for real this time."

With his hand on the door handle, he turned over his shoulder and for a moment she thought he was going to cry. Or confess, maybe. Her heart stopped.

Then he seemed to recover and said, "It's ginning time. Everybody's flush. I'm going to be plenty busy, what with the new models arriving soon and all the trade-ins. Now's just not a good time."

It had to be Delia. Maybe she was hiding out somewhere, waiting for Floyd to run away and join her. Why else would he be acting so jittery?

"What about Johnny?" she almost blurted after he had shut the door, wanting to remind him there was more to consider in this world than just him and Frenchie. But she said nothing, knowing that in a few moments, the river would be there to fetch her and, for a few hours, wash away any regrets.

However it was Johnny, not Vida, who came to her room. For some reason, Hazel thought he looked as guilty as Floyd.

"What's going on here?" she asked the boy. "Where's Vida?"

Johnny looked down at his feet. "She's gone home."

"Why?"

But he only shrugged.

A cold shiver ran her through. If Floyd had fired Vida, did that mean he had new plans for her, too? Had he decided to send her to Whitfield again? That sounded about right, she figured. "New models and trade-ins," he had said. Hazel guessed that was as nice a way as any to be told. Floyd could be all alone with his new model while his trade-in was getting rewired.

"We don't need her no more," Johnny said, breaking into her thoughts.

"Huh?'

"Momma. I can take care of you. We don't need Vida coming in our kitchen. I can feed you."

"Johnny, what are you talking about?"

"I made you a picnic. It's ready. Come and get it."

"A picnic? You mean outside?"

He nodded excitedly. "A breakfast picnic. Orange juice and toast and Cheerios and grape jelly and chocolate cake. Vida never did that, did she?" He reached for her hand and tugged. "Come on. It's on the ground. We got to go before the dogs get it."

"But…"

"Please," he begged. "I got it all ready. Come see."

Hazel didn't have the energy to argue. Anyway, with Vida gone and no anti-drinking pill this morning, she was having her own picnic ideas.

Johnny found her pink quilted housedress in the closet and selected a scarf for her hair. Hazel slowed briefly before the makeup mirror, but talked herself out of looking. But she did make a stop at Floyd's collection of Jim Beam decanters in the kitchen. Finally, with Johnny leading the way, Hazel walked out of the house with her yellow tumbler and into the dreary morning light.

Deep in the yard under an oak, on his cowboy bedspread, Johnny had laid out plates and napkins and knives and forks and most of the food from the house. He had even set out a large bouquet of fresh-cut roses in a Mason jar of water—roses that looked suspiciously like the ones from Miss Pearl's garden. Somehow he had managed two kitchen chairs out of the house and down the porch steps.

"Johnny, it's so nice," she said, really touched by his efforts.

"Better than Vida. I told you so."

Carefully, Hazel sat herself down in a chair. She balanced her bourbon on her lap, trying to remember how long that doctor at Whitfield said the Antabuse stayed in her system. Was it fourteen hours? Or fourteen days?

As she contemplated her drink, sitting before the spread laden with the odd assortment of foods, Hazel began to get a strange, haunted feeling. As if she were acting out some memory from long ago. Where had it been?

She raised the glass to her nose and took a whiff of the liquor. Yes, that smell was part of it. But there was more. What was missing?

Johnny climbed into the dinette chair beside her. "It's wet today. So we got chairs to sit down on."

"I see," she said, still trying to remember.

"But on a real picnic," he explained, "you supposed to sit on the ground."

"That's right," Hazel said.

"Like we did by the river. Remember? We had Moon Pies and grape Nehis. And remember how Davie took off and I caught him? Do you remember, Momma?"

"Davie," was all Hazel said and she began to cry, only a little bit at first.

"What's the matter, Momma?" Johnny asked, panicking. "What did I do wrong?"

"Nothing, honey. Nothing." But the more she tried to reassure him, the harder she cried. "It's...not...you," she sobbed.

Johnny didn't believe her. He started to dance frantically around the bedspread, picking up servings of food and bringing them to her. And when she shook her head, trying to tell him it wasn't the food, she would break out into a new round of sobbing, which only sent him back to the spread in search of the dish that would make her stop.

Not able to bear his repeated efforts to make her happy, she hid her face in her hands and wailed and would have probably continued for hours if it had not been for the sudden intrusion of a voice.

"What a lovely idea," said the univited caller, her crippled hand flourishing a handkerchief over the feast. "A morning picnic. Now whose idea was this?"

Shocked tearless, Hazel peeked up over her fingers into the perfectly composed face of Miss Pearl Alcorn.

"I suspected something special was up when I saw Johnny in my rose garden."

Johnny looked up guiltily at Miss Pearl.

She said nothing about the roses. Instead she turned to his mother. "Hello, Hazel."

Hazel didn't speak at first. All the ugly things she had rehearsed over the summer to level at Miss Pearl had vanished from her head. Still holding her hands up to her dripping face, a soggy "Hello" was the best she could do.

Miss Pearl smiled sweetly and then scanned the sky. "Who ever said picnics are best saved for sunny times? I think we have more need of them on gray, gloomy days, myself."

Then looking down at Johnny, she said, "Child, would you hand your mother and me a paper napkin from your elegant setting there? The ragweed is dreadful this time of year."

Pleased on learning how to be of specific help, Johnny quickly did as he was told.

With her good hand, Miss Pearl took the napkin and touched it to her perfectly powdered face, giving Hazel a chance to blow her nose and dry her eyes.

"It's been a fretful season, hasn't it, Hazel? So many offensive things in the air. Pollens and such. Smells of cotton poison wafting up from the Delta."

Hazel nodded, not sure what the woman was talking about.

"I want to apologize for not visiting more this summer. But to tell you the truth, I was a little intimidated by that unpleasant little maid of yours. Levi's girl. How did a sweet man like Levi manage to raise a…. Oh, never mind. I'm sure it's a shoddy excuse on my part." Miss Pearl looked down on Hazel and smiled sadly. "I know it's all been a trial for you."

Hazel studied the woman curiously. Something offensive in the air? That dreadful little maid? Was Miss Pearl attempting to sum up Hazel's entire hellish summer? This woman was sillier than even the maids had imagined.

"Anyway, even though I haven't called, doesn't mean you haven't been on my mind." With what Hazel discerned as a definite look of pity, Miss Pearl asked, "Hazel, dear, how are you?"

Hazel dropped her eyes to the glass in her lap. How in the world was she supposed to answer that question? My husband is cheating on me with your niece? I'm one sip away from the nuthouse? I'm the sorriest excuse for a mother since Ma Barker?"

She wished Miss Pearl would just leave so she could down the tumbler and several more like it, not caring now if it made her sick or not. But Miss Pearl's regal presence kept her from moving at all. She tried to remember what the maids had said about Miss Pearl. She seemed so laughable then. But today she was as scary as ever. Hazel was able to smile weakly and make a feeble attempt at straightening her dress and smoothing her hair.

"And how's that hard-working husband of yours? A regular Horatio Alger, isn't he? I haven't seen him around much."

Hazel opened her mouth to answer but found herself having to choke down a sob. She put the napkin up to her mouth and dropped her head.

"I see," was all Miss Pearl said. And for a moment they were all very quiet. Miss Pearl handed her napkin back to Johnny and said, "Child, would you be a dear and get me a glass of ice water? And some fresh napkins."

"We got tea," Johnny offered, eager to do anything for Miss Pearl.

She smiled and nodded. Johnny took off at a dead run for the house.

Miss Pearl looked into the distance again and waved the handkerchief entwined in her fingers in an arc over the neighborhood. "You know, my ancestors used to own all this land. Most of the county as a matter of fact. In the days when this part of the world was considered frontier. The backwoods."

Miss Pearl seemed to be speaking more to the landscape than to Hazel. "We go way back. Man after man in our family put their names to the deeds and handed them down to their sons. It's always been that way. We bred some great men, they say. Big part of this state's history. And you know what I'm struck with, Hazel?"

Hazel was getting irritated. She was not in the mood for another history lesson that ended up exposing her own poor-as-dirt roots. "No," she said at last, "What strikes you?"

"That most of the men I have known personally, especially the ones they call great, are dull to the point of genius. Don't you find it so?"

"Huh?"

"No imagination. They really don't seem to know what they want." Miss Pearl solemnly touched the handkerchief to her bosom. "Not deep down."

She turned to Hazel, "You see, I have a theory. I think men are able to see only one thing at a time. And that is the thing that happens to be in front of them at any given moment. The more shine and glitter the better. As you might imagine, this gives them the tendency to lurch a lot. This way and that. To and fro." She waved her handkerchief in time to her words. Her whole body was undulating absurdly, like she was acting out her theory to some audience larger than just Hazel. The maids were right. This was one of the silliest women she had ever met. The thought brought a little smirk to Hazel's face. All the woman needed was a Maypole.

Miss Pearl continued her little dance. "Always unbalanced," she said, leaning farther to one side to demonstrate. "They break the surface like pond minnows striking at shadows." Miss Pearl giggled at the thought. "And the little ripples they make convince them they are oh so very dangerous and bold. But in the end it merely makes them predictable."

Hazel had no idea what Miss Pearl was trying to say, much less why she felt so strongly about it, acting it out the way she was. Hazel was beginning to feel a little embarrassed for the woman.

Unabashed, Miss Pearl went on with her theory. "Women, on the other hand, aren't as prone to lurching. You know why?"

Hazel shook her head.

"Because we *do* know what we want and we hold on for the duration. We know what will fill us up. We are more attuned to life's vital essences."

Without warning, Miss Pearl thrust her crippled hand into Hazel's face. "*We* grab and hold onto what is important." Hazel snapped her head back, frightened by twisted fingers.

"Hazel, *we* don't let ourselves become distracted by the fancy of the moment. *We* are the steady ones. Never, ever," she said fiercely, shaking her hand in Hazel's face, "lean on a man for balance. You know why?"

Staring at the hand, Hazel took a wild guess. "Because they lurch a lot?"

"Exactly!" Miss Pearl exclaimed, throwing her hand over her head.

Not knowing what to say now, but pleased to have gotten the right answer, Hazel just shook her head knowingly, as if she had grasped this vital difference between the sexes. It did sound familiar. Hazel wondered what Miss Pearl would say if she knew how much she sounded like Sweet Pea.

Miss Pearl sat down heavily in the chair next to Hazel and took a few moments to catch her breath. Then, in a much more somber tone, she said, "Hazel, let me tell you the story of someone who will never be in the history books. Or have a statue in the Capitol rotunda at Jackson."

She drew her handkerchief to her heart, as if swearing to the truth of the story, and began. "Many years ago, my great-grandmother on my mother's side was abandoned by her husband. For an octoroon in New Orleans, no less. He left her with forty acres of undrained swampland, six children, and a blind mule. But the woman knew what she had to do. Somehow, she was able to raise her a plot of corn, and with that produced her first batch of whiskey. Once a month she loaded up that whiskey on the back of that blind mule and led it and six children twenty miles to an old beech tree that grew on the Natchez Trace. She camped out under that tree until she had sold ever last drop. To travelers, drifters, and highwaymen. To whoever had a dollar. Later she built her a little house on that very spot and hired two girls to work the back room, if you know what I mean. She may have even pitched in herself."

Hazel thought she saw the woman's pale blue eyes mist over.

"No," Miss Pearl said sadly, "you won't see her picture in the history books. But I once saw a photograph of her when I was a little girl. It was hidden away at the bottom of an old steamer trunk. I still remember. It was taken when she was eighty-two years old and she was still a beautiful woman, if you can imagine that. She sat erect, her head unbowed, unapologetic. When my father saw me looking at that photograph, he took it from me and tore it to pieces. I was told I would risk scandalizing the family if I ever spoke of her in polite company. Hazel, that woman raised a governor and a Secretary of War, but nobody today even knows her name."

Hazel nodded. She liked the story very much, but had no idea why Miss Pearl was telling it to her. "Sounds like she was a fine woman," Hazel offered.

Miss Pearl smiled. "I thought you would like her, Hazel." As if she had read Hazel's thoughts she went on to say, "Now, I know they say the women in my family are silly. Maybe even crazy. Well, perhaps we are. But, you see, we come by it honestly. We don't make it a habit of leaning on men. Now Hertha, bless her heart, wanted Billy Dean, God knows why, but hell and high water, she got him and she's kept him. But I know good and well, once he's outlived his usefulness, she is not above pitching him out in the street. And poor Delia…."

"Delia," Hazel repeated, wincing. For a moment Hazel had forgotten. But now she had to ask. "Is she really…I mean…?"

"Dead? Yes, probably. But I don't mourn her. I'm quite certain she died going after her heart's desire. And in Delia's case, that would probably be an insatiable taste for variety. But she was true to it up until the very end."

Suddenly Hazel wondered about Floyd having been in love with the dead woman. Would he mourn Delia? Would he come back to her now? Was the point of Miss Pearl's story that she shouldn't even care?

"And you, Hazel…." Miss Pearl said.

Hazel looked up into Miss Pearl's penetrating gaze. "Me?"

"The first day I saw you, at the little gathering at your house, when you answered the door…do you remember that day?"

Hazel grimaced and nodded.

"Well, the minute I laid eyes on you, I said to myself, this woman has something special. She has a deep, unquenchable thirst."

Hazel looked down at her glass, embarrassed.

"A deep thirst for life, Hazel," Miss Pearl clarified. "I saw it in your eyes, the way you dressed. Oh, my! That elegant blue dress you wore. And the manner in which you wore it. The way you stood there. Like a queen. I was so impressed, Hazel. I never in my life saw anything like it." Miss Pearl smiled fondly. "Except maybe once."

The world had gone dead quiet around Hazel. All she wanted to hear was Miss Pearl's voice. Nobody had strung that many nice words together about Hazel in years. Since she and Floyd first dated. It was like somebody finally had really seen her. She was so enrapt, she wasn't even aware that Johnny had arrived with Miss Pearl's tea and a handful of napkins.

"Now, correct me if I'm wrong, Hazel, but the way you were dressed that day. The way you held yourself. You weren't born to that, were you?"

Hazel shook her head, now mesmerized.

"No, I thought not. That's what makes me so sure that at some time, you must have wanted that more than life itself. Didn't you?"

Hazel nodded. It was true, she had.

"You grabbed ahold of something deep inside yourself. Some private hope or dream. And you started pulling. Regardless of what other people said."

"You're right," Hazel said, amazed. "They all laughed at me cause I wanted to look nice."

"But Hazel, don't get me wrong. I'm not merely talking about assembling a fine wardrobe. What I saw that day was not about pretense or presentation. Or even style. It was something else."

"What was it?" Hazel asked breathlessly.

"It was a heartfelt yearning for something more. And I wager, if you are absolutely, rigorously honest, it didn't have to do with any man, did it?"

How did she know this? Hazel wondered. Her hoping had begun long before Floyd Graham ever showed up.

"That thing you grabbed hold of. You know what I believe it was?"

"What?" Hazel breathed, ready to be convinced of anything that came out of the woman's mouth.

"Dignity," Miss Pearl said. "That's what I saw that day." Miss Pearl extended her arm out before her, her handkerchief fluttering in the breeze. "A woman reaching out with all her might for her share of dignity."

"Dignity," Hazel said reverently, thinking she never heard such a beautiful word in her entire life.

"Diggity," Johnny whispered, deciding that the word must be like abrakadabra, and that somehow things would never be the same. Even the little breeze that ruffled the handkerchief in Miss Pearl's still-outstretched hand seemed to confirm it.

They both watched silently as Miss Pearl receded into the distance like a lovely illusion. For a very long time Hazel sat without moving, with Johnny resting just as motionless in her lap. She knew she needed time to think. Not just about the future, but about the past. It was like that decoder ring they offered on the radio when she was a girl. Miss Pearl had given her something that turned the whole alphabet on its head. A was really D and E turned out to be Z. Hazel started paging through every memory, decoding them, reordering all the letters. So many lies she had believed.

It was Dignity! Not silliness. Not stupidity. Not worthless and ugly and helpless and hopeless and crazy and bad, bad, bad. Dignity, that was it all the time.

Chapter 38

FIREFLIES

Wearing a slightly dazed expression, Hazel got up from her chair and returned to the house, softly repeating to herself the new word Miss Pearl had given her. She emptied her tumbler back into the decanter and went to her room. She spent the rest of the day there, alternately sobbing, calling out Floyd's name, and then becoming very quiet once more, staring out the window, seeming very far away. Johnny found her sitting before her makeup mirror, looking blankly into the glass. When he asked about her, she looked at him oddly, as if she were surprised to see him, but assured him she was fine. But he didn't know anymore. Miss Pearl's visit had upset his mother in some way he didn't understand.

The good thing was Johnny had a whole day without Vida and he certainly needed it. There was a lot to do. Part of the day he spent in his graveyard, digging up the mounds. His father was going to be furious at him, not only for taking things from the house, but for stealing from Vida as well. When Vida came back, she was sure to tell on him.

Later he sat at the table practicing his name for school, which he understood would be starting Any Time Now, whatever that meant. "Almost Time for school," people would say. "Are you getting excited?"

Sitting there in the empty kitchen, he studied Time—right where it lived—in the wall clock shaped like a chicken. There Time stretched its arms and pointed to the numbers that told everybody where to go and what to do and when to stop doing it. Always circling. Widening its reach only to bring its arms together again, squeezing out the space between, and slowly opening its embrace once more.

Johnny had yet to figure out the secret language of Time, but as soon as he did, he believed Time would tell him important things. Like when it was going to heal his mother and send Davie back home. He copied down the numbers from its face. "Time is the great healer," his father was always saying. Time, he thought, must be almost as powerful as Jesus.

His father arrived home later that afternoon looking tired and worried. He headed straight for the TV. As Johnny sat on the couch, Floyd aimed the rabbit ears toward Jackson and then leaned back in his lounger, letting the gray and white men who pointed fingers and shook hands and signed papers on the evening news cast light and shadows across his face and send him directly to sleep.

He thought about crawling up into his father's lap, waking him. There were questions he needed answers to but did not know how to ask—the questions of Time and the secrets it held, but he had put these questions to his father before, and his father had only become frustrated, not understanding what he was asking. "Time is the currency of life," was the best he could get from his father.

There was someone else who might know about Time and Death and Jesus. He had heard the sound of his mower coming from Gooseberry's yard earlier in the day, and because he had watched him all summer, he knew the man often liked to work into the cool of the evening.

It was already first dark when Johnny stepped outside and the shadows had finished their lengthening and let go completely, flooding the entire yard in deep, cooling shade. Mourning doves welcomed the evening by cooing softly from somewhere nearby. As if in rebuttal, a brown thrasher protested with a harsh cry from a cherry laurel.

Amid the sounds of the evening creatures, Johnny heard a lone voice deep in the yard. It was exactly the person he was looking for, sitting down the hill on the cast-iron bench.

Johnny slowly approached the man until he was right up behind the bench. Vida's father wasn't exactly talking to himself. It was more like he was talking to someone who wasn't answering back.

Levi spun around on the bench, surprised. For a moment he searched the boy's face with those dark, bottomless eyes, and Johnny could almost feel the earth come up to meet his feet. Levi said, "How long you been standing there spying on me?"

Johnny didn't answer, still watching the man's eyes. He only shrugged.

"What is it you wont?"

The boy was still silent, not sure of that answer either.

"You go inside now," Levi said, "It's getting dark and time for supper. They gone come looking for you and put the blame on me."

Johnny took one step back, but stopped, still staring up at the man. "Ain't nobody home," he lied.

A few more moments passed while Levi considered this. Finally, he said, "Well, you best come over here, so I can see what you is up to. No good, be my guess."

Doing as he was told, Johnny walked right up to the man.

The man asked simply, "You lose somethin?"

Johnny considered the question for a moment. It was a good question. The right question. Before Johnny could answer it, he somehow knew the answer. Death was not a hide-and-seek game you played with Jesus. You can pray. You can be good. You can try hard not to forget. You can do everything right, but some things will stay lost forever.

But he decided to ask anyway. "Is Davie coming back?"

Levi's gaze softened. "Yo little brother?"

Johnny nodded.

Shaking his head gravely, he said, "No. I don't think he's coming back."

Johnny considered this for a moment. "I don't think so neither. I used to believe it when I was little. But I don't believe it no more."

"I can tell that," Levi said. This time they both sighed.

Then looking up at Levi, Johnny asked. "Why you always sitting back here in my backyard?"

Levi eyed the boy tentatively. "You got a problem with it?"

"No. I just wondered who you been talking to back here."

Levi considered the question. "Ever man need him a place to talk to God."

Johnny nodded to himself. "God," he echoed softly, and climbed up on the bench next to Levi.

Minutes passed as they both looked down the hill, into the darkening distance. As they sat there silently, little breezes began to play high up in the trees. Levi had his arms stretched out over the back of the bench and he gave off smells of earth and sweat and to Johnny they were substantial and comforting. He leaned into Levi and felt the dampness of his shirt. Levi squirmed a bit, as if trying to push the boy away with his movements, but the boy held fast. Levi looked around and then carefully lowered an arm around the boy.

"You seen Him?" Johnny asked.

Levi quickly looked about. "Seen who?"

"God. You seen God?"

"Oh. Yes, I have."

"How'd He look?"

"Well, it's hard to say. The first time He showed Hisself to me He was in a mighty whirlpool of churning water. But I knowed it was Him all right."

"Maud said she saw Jesus. But I don't believe that no more neither. I think she made the whole thing up." He asked Levi, "You seen God around here lately?"

"No. Not for a while. He got His own timetable, I reckon. But you can be sure He always seeing us. His eyes don't miss a thing. Not even the smallest sparrow."

"He looking at us right now?" he asked, wondering if God's eyes were as big as Levi's.

"No doubt in my mind. Ain't that a comfort?"

Johnny shrugged. "I want to see His face."

Levi laughed. "Me, too, I reckon."

For a moment they scanned the yard together, as if trying to pick out the face that was supposed to be turned their way, invisible and unblinking. A firefly flickered in the twilight.

"Lightnin bug winking at us," Levi said.

"Uh-huh. I seen it. He's gone now."

"He's out there," Levi said. "Why you say it's gone?"

"Cause I can't see it no more. He's gone dark."

But the firefly blinked again. "There he is over there!" Johnny whispered, not wanting the firefly to know they were on to him, figuring they might be as skittish as fish. He pointed in the direction of the porch.

"But he's gone dark again, ain't he?" Levi asked, making his voice sound as though the disappearance was a worrisome thing.

"We got to be quiet and wait till he blinks," Johnny explained, not wanting him to give up too soon.

Levi laughed like he had known it all the time. "That's the way it is with God, don't you reckon? He always around somewheres, if you can see His face or not. He's out there watching through the dark. Sometimes that's got to be enough, I suppose. Knowing He sees us even if we can't see Him back."

Johnny didn't know what to say to that. He thought they had been talking about fireflies.

Levi surveyed the yard again. "You know, I'm starting to think it's more God's nature to move unseen through the darkness like them bugs out there. He ain't gone stay put in no church or on no riverbank or even in no Bible. I know. I done found Him and lost Him again in all them places."

"Me and Davie used to catch lightnin bugs in a mayonnaise jar," Johnny said, thinking it much easier to talk about fireflies. "Daddy poked holes in the top with an ice pick. But they died, anyway."

Levi nodded. "Can't keep God in no jar neither, I reckon."

Levi continued talking about God for a while, in a voice that seemed at home with the croaking and whirring and cooing and the rustling of leaves, all the night music that was rising up around them. Like those sounds, his words didn't insist upon answers nor require understanding. Johnny found himself wishing his mother could hear him talk. He asked him, "You know my momma?"

"No. I can't say I do. Vida tells me some."

"She don't feel good no more. Stays in bed all the time."

"That's what I heared," Levi said taking off his hat and setting it on the bench. "You know, I reckon what we been talking about is the same with people. They can sho nuf go dark, too, can't they?"

Johnny nodded, not really knowing. But he was willing to believe.

"Myself, I got so used to seeing the faces shining their love at me, I thought it would stay that way forever. My wife. Vida. Nate. My flocks.

They was so much love in them days. All them faces shining just for me."
Levi brushed his nose. "But pride goeth before the fall. The Lord giveth
and the Lord taketh. And God done took it all from me. Put out them shining lights."

Then Levi squeezed Johnny's arm gently. "I reckon that's got to be the
hardest thing about loving, ain't it, child? Calling out in the dark. Pleading
with love to show its face again." He laughed sadly. "Maybe we all just living from one blink of love to the next."

The firefly winked over by the elephant ears. It seemed to be working
a wide net around the yard. Levi lifted his finger in the direction of the bug
as if he were about to say something, but instead he formed a fist and
brought it down hard on his leg. "Old fool!" he said with so much intensity Johnny jumped. "The dark *was* His sign! Right in front of my face!"

Levi's gaze was firmly fixed on a spot somewhere beyond. Afraid,
Johnny peered out into the deep dusk, wondering if somebody had come
up on them. But he saw no one. There was only the firefly.

But Levi kept talking in a slightly raised voice, leaning into the gathering dark. "All this time I thought it was *you* abandoned *me*! Cursed me
with your darkness!" Levi shook his head with strong feeling. "Old fool! I
been cursing the darkness. Thinking it was hiding you away from me."

Levi sprang to his feet. He held his arms extended and shouted, "I see
it now. My own church, going up in flames. It was a burning bush. A sign.
All things working together for the glory of God!"

Surely his voice was loud enough for his father to hear. Then Johnny
noticed that the insects and frogs and evening birds had gone into riot, rising up like a night choir, as if to cloak his words. The wind picked up and
the trees shuddered and swayed.

"I see it, Lord. With the eyes of a child. I see it clear. I will build You
an everlasting church. A church of rock with a pulpit of iron."

He fell back on the bench, as if now under a heavy load. "I know what
must be done. I hear Your voice calling to me, 'Step with Me into the darkness. Step with Me into the darkness.'"

As if in reverence to Levi's now-heavy heart, the wind died to a whisper, and the creatures around them hushed to a deep, soft murmur, almost

like a lament. Levi dropped his head to his chest, which was heaving mightily. Just before he covered his face, Johnny thought he had seen tears glistening in the man's eyes.

No longer afraid, he reached out to touch Levi's other hand, which lay open by his side. Now it was Levi who was hurting. So many people were hurting, he couldn't keep track of them all.

Johnny stroked Levi's hand, trying to soothe away his sorrow about the darkness. He thought of Davie in the dark. About his mother, lying in the dark, fading a little more every day. Everything seemed to be going to darkness.

Almost imperceptibly, his body began to tremble. His breathing became shallow because it hurt his chest to bring the air deeper. He moved his eyes around the yard. Now there was a second firefly, circling and flashing. It was impossible to tell which firefly was his. He had lost it.

The little breaths hurt and the tightening continued upward to his throat. He squeezed Levi's hand, trying to hold it back.

"What is it, child?" came the voice from above him.

He looked up. Levi was not crying at all! His eyes were burning bright, his face shining. Before Johnny himself knew what the words were going to be, he blurted, "My momma's gonna die forever, ain't she?"

Levi gripped Johnny's shoulder and pulled him close. He held on to the boy tightly and let him sob open-mouthed into his shirt. His tears ran fast and free, like pent-up rivers flowing finally to the ocean, as if all the fear and dread in the world was thawing to sorrow, and not until the tears had slowed did Levi move. He took Johnny by the shoulders and looked him solidly in the face.

"Listen to me, child, and remember what I'm saying." His voice was clear and strong now. It was the same voice that had once prayed over pine straw, the kind of voice that made Johnny quiver on the inside and caused his flesh to tingle. "Even though you can't see Him, and even though you can't feel Him, He's loving you, right now, through the darkness. He's lovin' yo momma, too."

Searching Levi's eyes, Johnny wanted to believe.

"I know it for a fact. Everthing gone be all right. He promised it to me."

Levi paused for a moment, smiling down on the boy. "I been wrong. As wrong as a man can be. The darkness ain't been hiding God at all. He revealed the truth to me and I'm gone tell it to you."

His eyes like pools of light, he whispered the secret to Johnny. "Child, the darkness is God too. And you and me and yo momma and Vida—we all been moving through the very heart of God." Levi motioned out into the night. "See? He ain't forgot about us."

Johnny looked to where he pointed. The yard was now studded with fireflies, their twinklings multiplied through the prism of his tears. It was like all the stars in heaven had settled in around them.

Chapter 39
THE MAMMY

Vida had never before spent the entire day in bed. But yesterday she did. A good thing too, because her father had kept her up most of the night. He had come home late, scaring her half to death with wild talk of visions and lightning bugs blinking in the night, going on about God giving him a new story to live. He was worse than she had ever seen him down at the bayou.

"God done set me out a path to walk," he had said, "a path out of the wilderness. It was Him who set my church afire. Like the burning bush. The Lord was trying to speak to me, like he spoke to Moses. But I didn't hear Him then. But now I know. It was a sign. A sign that God has a greater story in mind for me."

Vida wasn't sure she could take any more. It was through a story that he first told her to let go of her son. It was his stories that kept him wandering in the past, blind to the present. Now she feared his stories had set him adrift downstream in his mind for good.

Even though she tried her best to draw it out of him again this morning, what it was God was telling him to do this time, all he would say was that he was called to preach, and preach he would. And how at that very moment God was preparing him a church like none other—one that could never be set afire. "From there I will deliver a sermon that will touch the hearts of our people. Vida, God said, 'Don't fear the darkness.' He said to be ready to step into the darkness with Him."

She tried to dismiss his talk as nothing to worry about, the wishful thinking of a man on the short end of his life. But so far she had not yet convinced herself. All she knew was that she would need to watch him closer than ever.

The first thing Vida noticed as she climbed the hill up to the Grahams' house was the boy sitting hunched on the back porch steps, his shoulders drawn close, shadows veiling his face. Then the boy's father stepped outside, and watched her approach intently. Oh, Lord, she thought, something bout this don't look right already. Levi probably scared the boy so bad last night that Mr. Floyd was going to have her daddy run out of Delphi on a rail.

The closer she got, the more her mind kept churning out dire possibilities. The boy most likely told Mr. Floyd about her being so rough on him yesterday. That was it! She was about to get fired. Or maybe even arrested for attacking a white boy. No telling what the boy had piled on top of that story, bad as he hated her. Vida quickly looked over toward the sheriff's house, to make sure he wasn't at that moment storming across the lawn with his pistol drawn.

As she came up to the porch, Vida avoided the boy's face.

"Morning, Vida," Floyd called, his voice pleasant enough. "The boy said you were feeling poorly. Left early." He took a sip of coffee and then, peering at her over the rim of the cup, asked, "Let's see, what did he say was the matter?"

Vida opened her mouth to answer, but before she could utter a sound, Johnny said, "She had a headache."

"That's right," Floyd said, remembering. "Well, I'm glad you made it back today." Still watching Vida, he asked, "You gave Hazel her pills yesterday before you left, didn't you?"

Again before she had a chance to answer, Johnny said confidently, "Yes, sir. I saw her do it."

Seeming satisfied, Floyd set his cup on the railing and headed across the porch. As he took the steps, he reached down and playfully tousled Johnny's hair. "Bye, Little Monkey."

"Bye, Big Monkey," he said, overly cheerful.

First thing Vida thought was, that little devil can lie like a convict. But why?

Floyd turned back to Vida. "By the way, where'd you find my cufflinks and tie clip and all the other stuff that's been gone missing? I've looked high and low for them things."

She looked down at Johnny again, who was looking back at her with pie-pan eyes. That was it! The rascal was striking a bargain with her.

"Just round, Mr. Floyd," she said casually. "You know how thangs likes to wedge up in and betwixt."

"I'm sure glad, " he said with an awkward laugh. "I was ready to think you been takin them. If I didn't know any better."

Johnny beamed at Vida.

After Floyd left, Vida went into the kitchen with Johnny following close behind. When she got to her spot at the sink, she turned to watch him as he pulled himself up into his regular chair. They looked at each other awkwardly for a few moments, both remembering their fight.

"You know," Vida said finally, staring uncomfortably at her feet, "I'm sho sorry about yelling at you. And for treating you so rough like. I just wont you to know I don't hold no madness against you."

He studied her for a moment and then said, "I'm sorry I called you a nigger." Then he dropped his eyes and added softly, "And for hiding your letter."

"Well," she said with a long exhale. "I guess we both just done a big thang, ain't we? Ought to proud of our selfs."

"Yes, ma'am," he said.

"Ma'am?" Vida laughed to herself. "Well, I be."

Vida had turned back toward the counter to pour her coffee, when Johnny asked straight out, "Who is Nate?"

It caught Vida off guard. "What?" she blurted.

"The one y'all always calling me. I was just wondering. Levi said Nate don't smile at him no more. Is Nate dead, too?"

"Daddy said that?" she said, surprised.

"Levi said Nate don't smile at him and his light went out and that makes him sad, and I figured he might be dead like everbody else."

"No," she said thoughtfully, touched that her father would say he missed Nate. "Nate ain't dead."

"I know a lot of dead people," he said with a heavy sigh. "Papa Graham is dead. Davie is dead. Old Miss Floy down the street is dead. You know, Vida," he said gravely, "the dead stay gone forever and ever."

"Nate ain't dead," Vida said again, firmly.

The boy was now looking at her with wanting eyes. Her father had tried to get her to feel sorry for the boy last night. Said that boy's mind was too much on death. Well, this white boy was looking to the wrong person. Her own loss was too fresh. Anyway, Vida Snow was not one of those old-time mammies the white folks were so fond of—treated like slaves when they were alive and buried like family when they died. No, ma'am, she told herself, I ain't no Lillie Dee.

She turned back to the sink again. There was work to get done. No telling what that white woman was going to be like this morning, after being without her medicine for a day.

Sensing something at her back, Vida turned and saw the boy still star- ing. "You want something?"

"Un-uh," he said.

"Then why you drillin holes in me?" she asked. Whatever he was up to, she told herself, it wasn't going to work. Not like it had on her father. Finagling. That's what he was doing. Trying to boll weevil his way into her feelings. He wanted something from her that wasn't his to have.

"If all you got to do is stare at me, you might as well give me a hand with breakfast. Get me fo' eggs out of the ice box. And the orange juice. Then count out three pieces of bread for toast."

Johnny hopped down and did exactly as he was told.

He'd be off to school in a couple of days, she thought to herself, out of the house *and* her kitchen. She cracked an egg into the skillet, shaking her head and thinking, that white momma of his been so busy feeling sorry for herself, she probably don't even know school is about to commence. Mr. Floyd is sure too busy to worry about such things.

Looking down at the boy whose gaze was locked onto the toaster, she asked, "You ready for school?"

His eyes shot up at her. "What do I have to do to get ready?" The bread blasted out of the toaster, making them both jump.

Just as she thought. Nobody even talked to him about it.

"Not much," she said, buttering a piece of toast and trying to sound as casual as she could. "I magine you need you a letterin pencil and a doodlin pad."

"I ain't got none. What they gonna do to me?"

"Don't fret, so. I'm sho yo daddy gone find you some. Plenty of time befo school commences."

"But what they gonna make me do with a pencil and a doodlin pad?" he asked, his eyes beginning to jump about again.

"Nothing you can't already do," Vida said. "I spect they gone show you thangs to copy down. Like them ABCs you been practicing all summer. And yo name. I seen you writin that down on everthang in the house."

The boy was hanging on every word. "What else they gonna make me do?"

"I spect they gone show you thangs and tell you to count them up on yo fingers. You can do that. And probly draw thangs out of a book. Know you got that licked." Why did she even bring this up? They had been doing so good. "Now settle down," she said in her most even voice. "You gone get the fidgets. I spec the teacher will be real sweet and think you mighty smart. I know you will do very well."

It didn't work. He let loose with a torrent of questions. "Can I come home if I don't like it? What do I do if somebody pushes me down? What if I get sick? What will my momma do without me?"

Vida became more annoyed by the second. I ain't gone be this boy's mother, she told herself. Anyway, he has a perfectly good one. Well, maybe not, but no reason for him to go round actin like an orphan. Vida had lost her own boy, but it had been out there in a big, wide world. How, she wondered, could a boy get lost in his own house?

But there he was. With his own momma in a bedroom not ten feet from his. And him as lost as a babe in the woods. What kind of mother would let that happen? A white one, she answered to herself. With nothing better to do but feel sorry for herself, that's what. Vida took a spatula and flung the eggs at the plate.

The tears surprised Vida. She quickly wiped her eyes with the back of her hand and thought angrily, why couldn't nobody see it but her? Cause everbody around here had their damned heads up their butts, that's how come! Mr. Floyd seein whatever he wants to see. And not seeing what needs to be seen. Right under his own nose. And that white woman? She done lost one boy to death and afraid to touch the other. Lest she kills him, too. Don't need no doctor to tell Vida that.

The whole thing landed squarely in Vida's lap. Just like a white woman to cause this much trouble and get off Scot-free. Laying up in bed. Acting so helpless and piteous. Not so helpless she couldn't blackmail her maid so she can go out and get drunk. Vida might have bought the whiskey herself if Hazel would put in a little time being a mother. It just made Vida's blood boil. That white woman was aiming to turn Vida into a mammy, sure as rain.

Well, she thought, dropping the plate on the tray, that Hazel woman was not going to get away with it. She had another think coming if she thought she was going to win this easy. Staring hard up at the ceiling like she could see right into Hazel's room, Vida said under her breath, "Lord give me the strength to help this child without killin his momma first."

Chapter 40
HELP ARRIVES

One day off those pills and Hazel felt like a new woman. She was in no mood for that foul-tempered maid with her hard looks. The idea of treating a white woman in such a way. It was...it was...undignified! That's what it was. Why, Miss Pearl would never stand for such a thing. Neither would the new Hazel.

This morning, Hazel Ishee Graham was itching for a fight.

From downstairs she heard the sound of Vida clattering the china worse than usual and taking the steps upward in heavy tromps. Suddenly the bedroom door flung open and in fumed Vida jostling the breakfast tray. She practically dropped the tray on the bedside table, rattling dishes and sloshing coffee, and then stood over Hazel's bed with her fists planted on her hips. She narrowed her eyes at Hazel.

But Hazel narrowed hers back. "What!" she said. "I ain't done nothin to you." This morning Hazel believed she could take this woman if she had to. Wrestle her to the ground if there was need.

"*No, ma'am!*" Vida said expansively. "You ain't done *nothin.*" Bending over the breakfast tray, Vida mumbled under her breath, "That be the nub of it, awright. Ain't done one damned thang." Vida turned toward Hazel with the most unreal smile plastered to her face. Handing her a cup of coffee, she oozed venom, "I spect you wont cream in that, don't you, *Miss Hazel?*"

"What was it you said?" Hazel asked, doubting her own ears.

"I spect you wont cream with that coffee," she cooed ever so sweetly. "I membered the little cow jug this time."

"No. Before the cream part. About the nub of it. What did you say to me?"

"Oh, that," Vida said, with the coat-hanger smile still on her face. "I was just meanin this house sho is gone to hell in a bucket. If you don't mind me sayin it, *Miss Hazel*."

Hazel eyed Vida warily. At the moment she was holding out the little cream pitcher shaped like a heifer with a painted-on grin, much like the maid's. Hazel took the cream and poured a cloud of it in her cup. "Well," she said, stirring her coffee, "I wouldn't count on seeing me up anytime soon if *that's* what you getting at."

"You seem feisty enough this mornin. If you don't mind me sayin that too."

"What? You think I been putting on? You think I like being kept up here like a two-headed uncle?"

"Who been keepin you up here?"

"Who?" Hazel looked incredulously at Vida. "You the biggest one. And Floyd. And them doctors. And them pills. And—"

Vida cut in on her list. "Like I say, you seem mighty fit this mornin. Fit enough to get outside and walk. Take that boy with you, maybe."

"Not after you give me them pills, I won't. In less than an hour, I'm going to be fog-bound and you know it."

Looking up at Vida out of the corner of her eye, she said, "Reckon you got them pills right there in your pocket, just itching to put me out so you can go back to having the house to yourself." She strained at a smile and then took a sip of coffee, but Vida didn't bite.

"Of course," Hazel continued, almost wistfully, "they tole me one day I'd get used to feeling like I've got a sack of seed on my back and cotton lint between my ears. They say I'll come round to it."

Hazel looked up, sad-eyed, but Vida didn't appear very sympathetic, standing there like a wooden Indian. There was just no getting to that woman.

Hazel fussed with the napkin on her chest. "Anyway," she said lightly, "I don't know why you need to fret about it. You still get your little bounty for every pill you can cram down my throat." She looked up and grinned, "Ain't that right?"

There was a moment of frozen silence as the two women stared at one another, each smiling mightily and neither meaning an inch of it.

Vida threw her hands in the air. "Calf rope!" she cried out. "I give up. It ain't worth puttin up with yo mess no more. What's yo price, white woman?"

Hazel pulled back at the maid's outburst so suddenly she sloshed coffee on her bed jacket. "What the hell are you babbling about? My price for what?"

"To make you do right!" Vida said, clearly exasperated. "What it is you wont out of me?"

"What I'm wontin' is a little dignity!"

"Dignity? Dignity! What you talkin bout dignity?"

"I didn't think you'd understand. What would somebody like you know about dignity?"

"Enough to know you ain't done nothin to rate none of it."

"Well, then, if you can't give me none, then what I want is for you to leave me alone."

"Lord, that be what I wont too. I just love to leave you alone. That be my fondest dream. But it ain't just you and me. They's that boy downstairs. What we gone do bout him?"

"We? Ain't no we to it. He's my boy. Do you hear?"

"I hear it, but I don't see it."

"Listen to me," Hazel said, her teeth clenched. "What I don't need is you coming in here and making me feel guilty about what a bad momma I am. The whole county knows that already. Why, I been sermonized in the Baptist Church and writ up in the Hopalachie Courier. Ain't you read it yet?"

"Lord, girl! You got enough pity in you to float a boat upriver."

Hazel gave Vida a look of pure viciousness. "I don't think you ought to be talking to a white person like that. I hear it ain't healthy."

Vida's eyes blared out. "All I'm askin is what's it gone take to make you wont up!"

"That's between you and Floyd, ain't it? He the one paying you to keep me down."

"Well, it ain't nowheres near enough," Vida shot back. "I got me a boy downstairs worrying me like a bone. Askin me questions his momma ought to be answerin." Hazel opened her mouth to protest, but Vida kept it up. "All summer he been letterin his name on everthing in the house. Like he leavin a trail for somebody to follow. Like he lost. Why he doin that?"

"I…"

"Well, I don't know neither. And that ain't all. Did you know he got him a graveyard up under the porch? Spends all day in his hidy-hole buryin Lord know what all. Makin funerals and sayin prayers over graves. It ain't natural. What's all that supposed to mean?"

"I don't know. Why you asking me?"

"Well, you his momma, ain't you? Who else I got to ask? That bed-post?"

Hazel tried to answer, but again she wasn't quick enough.

"And he frets like an old woman. Talks like a undertaker. I swear! I ain't seed the boy in him yet." Vida gave Hazel a scalding look. "That boy is in a plumb mess and I ain't the one who gone clean it up. You his momma."

"I know it!" Hazel shot back and glowered out the window.

"Well, don't that mean *nothin* to you?"

When Hazel wouldn't even look at her, Vida said, "Miss Hazel, that baby is plumb lost and a momma is the one that tells a child where he belongs. Every child need to know that. He got to know where home is. That's the biggest thing what a mother does."

For a moment, Hazel thought the woman sounded half-human, but when she checked, her expression was hard as ever. "I done told you," Hazel said. "It's them pills you got in your pocket. They keeping me down. That's all's wrong with me."

Vida reached into her apron pocket and pulled out Hazel's daily dose of medicine. Rolling the pills around in her palm, she studied them seriously. Finally she said, "But these here pills is supposed to keep you from drankin, ain't they?"

Hazel didn't need to answer. The way her face colored up told Vida she was right.

"Now I ain't dumb," Vida said. "I heard bout you gettin all looped up and galavantin across the countryside in yo car." Vida cocked her head to the side, looking at Hazel with disdain. "Tryin to act like you somebody."

That right there was enough to set Hazel off. "That ain't it!" she shouted. "That ain't it at all. And why should I tell you about it?" Without waiting for Vida to answer, Hazel let loose on the maid. It was her turn now. "I drive because then I'm free. All my whole life it's felt like I got a fence around me, bull high and hog tight. No way out. Being moved from one pasture to the next. But when I'm in my car it's *me* who's deciding which road to take. Or *not* to take. Or even if I want to take any road at all. Sometimes I just head off through a field. I can go as fast as I want to. I can laugh, I can cry. I can stick my fool head out the window like a gold-plated idiot and hoot to high heaven. I can cuss God and my momma and my daddy and Floyd and Jesus, too. Then step on the pedal and make them all disappear in a cloud of dust. And yeah, I can get as drunk as I damn well please."

Vida stood there open-mouthed, gazing at a red-faced Hazel. It was like the woman had come uncorked.

"So maybe you right," Hazel said after finally taking a breath. "Maybe you hit it on the head. When I drive, I do feel like I'm somebody. Not *somebody's* somebody. Not somebody's pitiful wife. Not somebody's sorry excuse for a mother. Just plain somebody. Me. Hazelene Brenda Ishee. A woman in a car with a full tank of ethyl, reaching for a little dignity. Is that selfish?"

Vida almost answered, but Hazel beat her to the punch. "OK. It is selfish, I'll give you that one. But if I can have that two or three days a week, maybe four, the rest of the time is tolerable. Who's it hurting, I'm asking? You don't know what it's been like." Hazel clenched her teeth. "And you know as good as me, Floyd's been cheating with another woman. And then he pays you to prize my mouth open and poke pills down my throat. How would you feel? Well, I'll tell you exactly how I feel." She looked at Vida fiercely and then crossed her arms over her chest, her whole body shaking. "I'm just sick and tired of feeling beat down. Can you understand that? I'm sick and tired of plowing other people's fields. When am I going to get some acreage of my own? My own little piece of dignity?"

As Hazel lay there, breathing heavily after her outburst, Vida looked back and forth between the white woman and the pills in her hand. Then she asked carefully, "This here dope you takin. It supposed to make you forget about all that?"

Hazel sighed. "That's the big end of it, I reckon."

Looking back at the pills, Vida said, "I reckon forgettin can be a blessing."

Hazel shut her eyes and sank back into her pillows. There was no way she could ever win with this woman.

After a long pause, Vida continued. "I heard tell of this colored woman called herself Rosie."

"Yeah, seems I heard tell of her too," Hazel said, her eyes still shut, not saying she had heard about Rosie the same time Vida did, from downstairs in her own kitchen. Hazel seemed to remember her husband's affair had also been on the program that day.

"Well, anyways," Vida continued, "Rosie stirred up a lot of trouble for the white folks. They say she forgot who she was. Forgot her place." Vida shook her head. "But I figger, it was the other way around. I figger she remembered who she was. Remembered she was as good as anybody else. That's what folks didn't like."

Hazel flipped one eye open. "What's a colored girl got to do with me?"

"Well, I spect if Rosie was takin these here pills, she might of give up her seat and dragged herself on to the back of the bus. Just like ever other day. Forgot all about how tired she was."

The other eyelid went up. "I ain't asking to ride in no bus. It's the Lincoln I want."

"Don't matter," she said, still looking into her palm, "All I'm gettin to is this. I ain't no doctor, but I say you done forgot too much already. I spect it's time you start rememberin, like Rosie done."

"Remembering what?"

"Rememberin you a momma for one," she said. "I don't know about all that other craziness. About the drankin and the drivin and the yellin out the window and such. Don't sound like no dignity to me." Vida shrugged. "But maybe that just goes along with the rememberin."

Hazel thought about that for a moment. "You know," she said softly, "I never was a very good momma, no way."

"I don't doubt that for a minute," Vida said, like she figured they were both telling the truth now. "But that boy don't know it. Good. Bad. You be the one he wont. That there is a blessin. More than you know, Miss Hazel. What could be better in this whole world than having a little boy who don't wont nobody but you for his momma?" Vida smiled sadly. "A little boy who would kill to keep you safe."

"That ain't all," Hazel said, touching a freckle on the back of her hand. "I lost my Davie. You just don't know what it's like to lose a child."

"Well," Vida said. "I reckon—"

"Vida," Hazel whispered, tears filling her eyes. "I could see it coming. I knew. I might could have stopped it and I didn't. There's just no makin up for that."

Vida dropped her eyes. "No ma'am, there ain't no makin up for that," she said, rolling the pills around in her hand. After a few moments she looked back at Hazel and said knowingly, "And Lord knows, they sure ain't no forgettin it." There was a tremble in her voice.

Vida dropped the medicine back in her pocket. "Now you listen," she said, suddenly tough again, "I ain't gone be no mammy. How be ever, if it means gettin that boy out from under my feet, maybe I can figger something out."

"Why should you?" Hazel asked.

Vida shrugged and exhaled heavily. "Beats me." But when she spied what could have been a misty look of gratitude well up in Hazel's eyes, she said sharply. "Just remember one thang. I ain't doin it for you."

"Then why?" Hazel asked again.

"Maybe there ain't no reason," Vida said, poking both fists into her apron pockets. She looked past Hazel and out the window, as if she had spied somebody strolling through the yard. "And then again, maybe if I did have a little boy walkin round lost, I'd sure wont somebody to get him back to his momma." Nodding to herself, still staring out into the distance, she said, "Maybe it's as simple as that there."

But Hazel wasn't fooled. "No, it ain't that simple, is it, Vida?"

"Ma'am?"

Hazel smiled sadly at Vida. "You been a momma, ain't you?"

Vida caught her breath and stared incredulously at Hazel. "What you meanin?"

For a long time the two women looked at one another, each searching the other's face, wondering who this other person had become before their very eyes.

At last Hazel patted the side of her bed. "Sit down here next to me, Vida," she said. "Tell me about your boy. I wont to know."

On Johnny's first day of school, Vida broke an egg into the skillet and then hollered at the top of her lungs, "Scrambled or fried?"

"Scrambled!" came the answer from upstairs.

Stabbing at the yolks with the spatula, she yelled again, "Well, get on down here. Breakfast almost ready."

A moment later, Johnny came tearing down the stairs. "Vida! Vida! Momma ain't in her room! Where's my momma at?" He was on the verge of tears by the time he burst into the kitchen. Then he stopped dead in his tracks.

Hazel was already at the breakfast table, sitting plumb-line straight, in her red sateen dress. Her hair was brushed and her makeup was on neat. The scent of Gardenia Paradise mixed gloriously with the smell of frying bacon. "Momma!" he gasped.

"I been wanting me some sugar from a real live school boy this morning. You know any?"

Johnny reached his arms around her neck. She kissed him and then rubbed the lipstick off his cheek with her thumb. "Momma," he said, "you look beautiful."

"Why, thank you!" she said, like she really believed it. "And don't you look nice and growed up! Your hair all smoothed down. I swan! You even dressed yourself!" She reached over and finished tucking in a shirttail. "When did you learn how to do that?"

"Vida showed me."

"Well, she did real good, didn't she?" Hazel smiled at the maid, who continued setting the table.

"Now sit down and eat," Vida said. "You gone to be late yo first day."

But Johnny couldn't stop staring at his mother. "You ain't tired no more?"

"I feel just fine. Ready to dance a jig."

Vida set the biscuits on the table and then leaned against the sink, her arms crossed. "All right now," she said, her tone businesslike. "What all this young man need to know about his first day at school, Miss Hazel?"

Hazel looked up at Vida blankly.

"You know. Like you was tellin me about." She gave Hazel a piercing look. "Remember? Like when he need to go peepee. The part you was saying bout holin up his hand."

There was a flicker of recognition in Hazel's face. "Oh, yeah! If you have to go to the bathroom, raise your hand."

"That's right!" Vida said, reaching behind her for the coffeepot. As she filled Hazel's cup, she prompted again, "And how about not sassin the teacher?"

"Yep. Don't break your manners," Hazel said. "Be real sweet and say 'yes ma'am' and 'no ma'am.'"

"Anything else?" Vida asked. "Like maybe, don't cut up in yo seat and don't leave the school yard and be sure to get on the bus right after school lets out?"

Hazel nodded. "Yep, all them things is important, too, Johnny."

Taking her spot against the sink again, Vida asked, "You wont to give him the stuff *you* bought him?"

"Oh, yeah!" Hazel reached under the table and pulled out a little plastic satchel with a picture of a cowboy painted on the front.

"This is for you."

"It's the Cisco Kid!" Johnny yelled. "It's so pretty!"

"It really is!" Hazel said, looking up at Vida.

"Momma! You know what Vida calls him?"

"No, what?"

"The Crisco Kid!" he said, laughing hard, pointing at the maid.

"Now ain't that funny?" Hazel said, smiling up at Vida. "The Crisco Kid. I swan if that ain't funny."

"Ain't y'all gone look inside?"

"Good idea!" Hazel said excitedly. "Let's open it up and see what's in it."

Inside they found a blue plastic ruler, a box of crayons, a pencil nearly as big around as Johnny's wrist, and a lined tablet with the ABCs on the cover—big and little letters—and a banana Moon Pie. "My," Hazel said thoughtfully, her eyes on the Moon Pie. "They think of everything, don't they?"

Vida just shook her head at Hazel.

Johnny climbed up into his mother's lap and held her close, not caring in the least that he was smearing her makeup and mussing her hair and that he would spend the day smelling of Gardenia Paradise.

"We're going to be fine now, baby," Hazel whispered to him. She smiled warmly at Vida, then kissed her son again on his cheek. "I'm your mother and I don't know a lot of things, but I know exactly where you belong, honey. You never have to worry about that. We ain't going to be lost no more."

Vida slapped her hands together. "Time for the bus! We need to get movin.'"

"My boy ain't gonna take no bus his first day!" Hazel proclaimed. "Nosiree! I'm gonna drive him." She turned sheepishly to Vida. "You know where Floyd hid them?"

Vida hesitated for a moment. Still reluctant, she opened the icebox and reached into the freezer. She handed Hazel the keys to the Lincoln.

As she held them there in her hand, Hazel looked at the keys with an expression of real affection. She grinned big and clenched her fist tightly, warming the cold metal. "Vida," she announced, "don't expect me home no time soon. I'll be out driving some." Hazel winked at her maid. This time it was Vida who needed prompting. "You know, what we talked about. What you promised?"

"Oh yeah," Vida grumbled. "So much for that dignity." She walked across the kitchen and reached into her bag in which she toted her apron and her walking shoes and a plastic rain hat and her ice pick. Pulling out a cobalt blue bottle, she muttered, "If you ask me, which you ain't, you just swappin the devil for the witch."

Not really understanding her little saying, Hazel just grinned at Vida, and then, as if the maid might suddenly have a change of heart, Hazel snatched the bottle from her outstretched hand. Clutching the bottle in one hand and the ignition key warmed and ready in the other, Hazel made a dash for the Lincoln with Johnny scrambling close behind.

Chapter 41
HAZEL GETS A FRIEND

Hazel Graham swung the Lincoln in front of her house and pulled to an easy stop, the front passenger-side door lined up flush with the sidewalk steps. It was a crisp fall afternoon, the air golden with sunlight and thick with the smell of burning leaves. She honked the horn twice, bringing Johnny tearing out the front door down the walk, with Vida following a moment later, her bag swinging from her shoulder.

Clambering up into the front next to his mother, Johnny breathed deep and hollered, "We got a new car!"

"Ain't it nice?"

Hazel waited for him to close his door and then eased the car up a few feet for Vida. The back door now in position, Hazel leaned down to receive her peck on the cheek. "How was school today? You do good?"

"I got to tell another story," he said.

"In front of the whole class?"

"Yes, ma'am. And the teacher told them to clap."

"I swan."

Vida opened the back door and ducked inside. She gave the back seat a couple of bounces, checking out the springs under her regular spot.

"How you like my new car, Vida?"

Vida rolled her eyes. "Same as the old one, ain't it?" Like Johnny, she took a sniff. "Cept it don't smell like medicine," she said tersely, "and it ain't got no caved-in hood. Musta just now got it."

"I did! I just picked it up at the dealership. It's a '57."

"Make it squeal, Momma!"

"Hold on to your taters!" Hazel yelled, and then, leaving the smell of rubber in her wake, and neighbors scurrying to their windows, they headed off to Tarbottom, with Vida in the back gripping the door handle.

Hazel was simultaneously touching up her lipstick and turning down the hill toward the river when Johnny shot up in his seat with alarm. "Stop, Momma!" he screamed. "You gonna hit him! Stop!"

Hazel stomped on the break pedal, throwing gravel and fishtailing the car within inches of the ditch. Vida went hard up against the front seat. The car skidded to a stop and Johnny hopped out, scampering back up the road through the dust. Watching him from the rearview, Hazel saw him pick up a very lucky box turtle she must have straddled with her tires. Johnny took the turtle back to the side of the road, aimed him the other direction and patted him on the shell. When he got in the car Hazel asked him, "Why'd you point him thataway?"

"So he could get on home before he hurt hisself."

Vida gathered herself up in the backseat, growling. "Just gone turn hisself around again." She pulled the apron out of her sack and mopped the nervous sweat from her brow. "He gone cross that road no matter what you do. You see if he don't." Vida cut her eyes at Hazel in the mirror. "You see, Johnny, some of God's creatures you can't tell *nothin* to. Hardheaded as that turtle's hull. They ain't gone change their ways even if it kills them and a load of other folks."

Nodding thoughtfully, Hazel said, "Johnny, Vida's right. You get out and put that turtle on the other side of the road. If you want to help a thing, you got to help it in the direction it's headed." Hazel beamed, delighted with herself. Floyd wasn't the only one who could come up with snappy little sayings and she told Vida so. Vida rolled her eyes again.

In Tarbottom, Hazel pulled the car close alongside Vida's front porch. Johnny and Vida got out, but Hazel made herself comfortable where she was. Sucking on a peppermint, with her legs dangling out the car door, she was feeling especially good. She always did on her driving days. "Vida," she said, "today I drove clear past Parchman Penitentiary and went to a little town I ain't never been to before."

"Don't say," Vida replied from where she sat up on the porch. Her eyes were on Johnny, who was playing pretend with a family of cornshuck dolls she had made for him.

Hazel worked the peppermint to the opposite cheek, and then continued. "I knew right off there was something different about that town."

"Do tell?" Vida said, crossing and re-crossing her legs at the ankles.

"Know what it was?"

"No, ma'am," she sighed, "I sholy don't."

"Neither did I at first. Just couldn't put my finger on it. Then I parked on the main street and walked around a bit. I went into the dry goods store and the drug store. A real nice restaurant that had a green parrot that hollers 'howdy partner' at you when you walk in the door. And then it hit me. Everbody was colored! The storeowners, the clerks, the waitresses, the customers. Folks sitting out on their porches. Everbody! They said even the doctors in the hospital was colored. Ain't that something?"

"Sho is peculiar," Vida said evenly, shooting Hazel an annoyed look.

"It was a colored town!" Hazel said, not sure Vida was suitably impressed.

"Yes, ma'am, sounds like that's just what it was. Might be you should be gettin on home now." Vida cut her eyes anxiously up and down the row of cabins.

"Well, I never heard of such a thing," Hazel said. "I spied this colored man wearing a suit and I asked him if he was a preacher and he kind of looked at me funny and said he was the *mayor*! And a Harvard-trained lawyer to boot. Real fancy talker. I thought he was deviling me. He tole me the town was started by the slaves of Jefferson Davis hisself! Them coloreds was running the whole shebang. Been running it by theyselves for a hundred years, I reckon."

Hazel shook her head and laughed at such a thing. "Not one white person around to tell em what to do."

"Must be glory," Vida said as she glanced nervously down the road at the distant sound of laughter.

Hazel loved these chats with Vida. It was a perfect ending to her driving days. A driving day would start with Vida showing up early in the morning with a little blue bottle in her flour sack purse. After they got

Floyd off to work and Johnny off to school, Hazel would pack a couple of sandwiches or some cold fried chicken and head out by herself, staying gone until late afternoon. When she was done, she would pick up Johnny and Vida at the house and then head back to Tarbottom. Hazel was getting good at angling the Lincoln within a hair's breadth of the front steps. That way Vida and Hazel could hear each other talk without Hazel having to get out of the car. It went hard against tradition for a white man or woman to put both feet on a colored person's porch. A man might could put one foot up, as long as the other stayed on the ground. Hazel didn't mind pushing a few conventions but she wasn't taking any chances on getting sent away for being crazy again. Besides, this way was just fine. Vida seemed to be able to hear Hazel perfectly as she related from her car all the strange and wonderful things she had seen during her drive. At least, Vida had never asked Hazel to repeat anything.

"And that's not all, Vida." Hazel said.

"There's more? It's gettin kinda late—"

"I saw some real live gypsies today!"

"Gypsies?" hollered Johnny, jumping to his feet.

"Yep. I was saving the best for last. I was coming down off some old ridge road and there they were, camped out by a branch. A whole herd of gypsies."

"A *band* of gypsies, Momma." At six Johnny knew the name of every family group under the sun. That was his specialty.

"Mighta been," Hazel said grudgingly, not too pleased at being corrected. This was her story, after all. She gathered up her excitement and continued. "They had these wagons with roofs. You should have seen them. Painted red and blue and green and yellow. Pictures of flowers and animals and such. And there were snow-white horses grazing on the hill. Their bridles had these little gold bells."

"And real live gypsies?" Johnny asked.

"Shore! A mess of em. I mean a band of em. With gold hoops in their ears and the men wore bright-colored head rags. They had real dark skin and these mysterious black eyes. They was something! And real friendly folk."

"You talked to em, Momma?"

"I did. I said, 'Nice day to be outdoors, ain't it?' Invited me to sit around their fire. Gimme a drink of something called tequila with a worm left right there in the bottle. Brought it up all the way from Mexico. They tole me they was on their way to where the Queen of all the Gypsies is buried. Right here in Mississippi. Going there for some kind of a gypsy powwow." Fishing another peppermint from her bag, Hazel sighed contentedly. "The things you learn in this ol' world. I swan."

Hazel looked on contentedly as her son pretended the dolls were gypsies and made them do a little gypsy dance. At first Hazel had been leery about Johnny playing with those dolls instead of his cowboy toys. But that boy had his own way about him. After living under the house in the dirt for most of the summer, he now insisted on dressing in his Sunday clothes for school. Refused to put on a pair of jeans. He looked like a little businessman with his white starched shirt and dark blue pants, toting his Cisco satchel. Even his teacher said he was special. She told Hazel that Johnny knew his numbers and ABCs better than anybody in three counties. She said Johnny was always turning every lesson into a yarn about families. Like with numbers. 10 was the grandfather of the family who walked with a cane and the grandmother was 9 with a humped back. They had grown twin boys, the 5's who have big stomachs, he said, like the Gooseberry brothers. Each of them had five skinny boys, the 1's who wore baseball caps. There was an aunt, the big fat 8 who had four lovely swan-necked daughters, the 2's.

It was the same with his ABC's. Each letter had its own personality and a story to go with it. The teacher said that some days she even let Johnny tell his stories in front of the whole class.

Hazel smiled proudly as Johnny sang a peppy dance tune. She figured she would take her own advice about helping a thing in the direction it was headed. Vida said a mother is the person who shows a child where home is. But Hazel figured there was more to it than that. A child's not going to stay at home forever. Like her, Johnny was reaching out for something. It took Miss Pearl to recognize and name what Hazel herself had been reaching for all these years, and now Hazel wanted to do the same for her son.

She figured that even though a mother might not be able to change the direction her child was heading, at least she could make sure he got there with a fistful of hope. If acting out stories with cornshuck dolls was what it took to make Johnny happy, then more power to him.

Maybe I'm not such a bad mother after all, she dared thinking.

With her friend close by on the porch and her boy lost in play, the sun setting on a world with plenty left to explore, for the first time in a long time, Hazel was actually at peace. It was as if her own far-flung hopes were coming home to light.

Then, after glancing at the car clock, Hazel breathed into the palm of her hand and popped a last peppermint into her mouth. "Pack up them gypsies, Johnny," she called up to the porch. "Your daddy's going to be to the house any minute. And remember—"

"—it's our secret," Johnny finished for Hazel..

Her boy climbed in beside her and she cranked up the car, gave Vida a snappy little wave, and headed home.

Chapter 42

ANSWERED PRAYERS

Levi reached on top of the chiffarobe and retrieved the brown paper sack. Very carefully he drew out his felt hat with the oval crown and the brim that was stiff as new. After removing the newspaper stuffing from the hollow of the crown, he held the hat out before him and lightly touched the small satin bow on the shiny band. This was the hat he had worn only to deacon meetings and to conferences with the Senator, on occasions when he needed to use his sway. The hat hadn't seen the light of day for years. He hadn't needed it. There wasn't anybody who would listen to him. But today they would listen. The Lord had deemed it so. He set the hat on the bed.

Next Levi pulled out his gray preaching suit that hung flat against the back wall of the wardrobe. He remembered those early dawns after he had lost his churches, when Vida would lay this suit neat across the bed with a fresh starched shirt and dark tie. She would tiptoe soundlessly around the bedroom, trying not to disturb him as he prayed on his knees to the Lord to give him another chance. He would dress and spend the day traveling the county, begging every cotton-field church he came across to let him say a few words. All Levi had ever wanted was to preach and be heard.

Today his prayers were being answered, exactly forty years from the day he stood on the banks of the Hopalachie River and first saw the face of God looking up at him from that whirlpool of churning water. Forty years. The same amount of time Moses spent in the wilderness before leading his people to the edge of the Promised Land, telling them to go on without him.

He held the suit up before him. The moths had got to it, but it would do for today. He smiled sadly, thinking there might be bigger holes in it by sundown.

Levi put on the fresh white shirt he had paid a woman to boil and starch so Vida wouldn't know. Standing before the cracked mirror that hung on the chiffarobe door, he knotted his tie, then put on the vest and coat. The cracks in the mirror broke Levi's face into four distinct pieces. Levi smiled at that, too. "Thank You, Lord," he prayed simply, "for today is the day You make me whole again. I step into the darkness with You."

The only thing left to do was to loop his gold chain across his vest, the watch having been sold years ago to put gas in the old Buick. He rummaged through the fruitcake tin and the bottoms of all the drawers, in the pockets of his clothes. The chain was nowhere to be found. Vida would probably know where it was, but she had already left for work. He wouldn't have asked her anyway. She wouldn't understand. He gave up the search and took it as a sign from God against his vanity. Levi carefully positioned his hat on his head.

He looked up into the sky when he stepped out the door. He had never seen such a sight! Curiously shaped clouds in a multitude of unearthly colors, moiling and swirling, like heaven was still mulling over what kind of a day to turn out. When he understood, tears came to his eyes. It was the whirling, ever-changing face of God, looking down upon him, showering him with blessings, showing him the way out of the wilderness.

Billy Dean Brister sat in his office with his new air conditioner going full bore. It was coolish for November, but he liked to watch the lazy curl of smoke rising innocently from his cigarette, until the shaft of cold air from the vent blasted it. The unsuspecting smoke would rupture and be whisked away across the room in a thin cloud. It helped him think.

Delia had really put his ass in a crack this time. What had she been thinking of? Now the Senator was telling him not to bother putting his name up for sheriff again if he didn't find either her body or the nigger who killed her. Pompous old fool. All the time going on about how they were *his niggers* and nobody knew *his niggers* like him. But just wait. The minute somebody or something goes missing, he's the first one yelling, "Which one of them sorry ingrates did this to me!" Don't even have a body to examine and he knows for sure that Delia was drowned by some grudge-holding darkie specially out to get him. Served one term at the lousy state house a hundred years ago, and that supposed to make him some kind of know-everything god?

Billy Dean blew another jet of smoke into the stiff current of air. The question was, what the hell was he going to do to buy some time? Wasn't as easy as turning over a few shacks in niggertown. If the Senator found out about him and Delia, he would do more than ask him to resign. The Senator would have him take Delia's place at the bottom of the river.

He should have known Delia would bring him nothing but trouble. Trouble was her middle name. Always living on the wild side. Doing things to shock everybody. Like marrying those nose-talking Yankees. The woman even had the nerve to bring them down here and rub everybody's faces in it. And those love letters of hers. Leaving them under his windshield wiper. On the seat of his desk chair, right in his office. Any reckless place she could think of. That purple-and-white paper was like a personal calling card. He told her a million times to leave off with them purple letters.

"Don't say purple, Billy Dean," she purred at him. "That's too common. Like you. It's lavender and cream. With a touch of *Chanel*. Like me."

Once, when Hertha threw a dinner party, Delia had sneaked off upstairs and put a steamy one right under his pillow. Right there in her sister's own bed! It was like she reveled in the possibility of getting caught. But when she got pregnant, the game got serious. She taped one of those purple-and-white envelopes to his front door. It said that unless he left Hertha, whom she despised in a way only a sister could, and ran away with her, she would make sure her daddy knew everything. She would ruin him. If Hertha had come home thirty seconds earlier, he would have been ruined anyway. Plus castrated and shot. As it was, he was just able to get the desk drawer shut and locked when she walked in. Billy Dean had been furious. That's when he threatened to kill Delia. That had been a big mistake.

Goddammit! When was he going to learn to keep it in his pants! He couldn't put it in a woman without her spitting out a mimeographed copy of him.

Just then his deputy flung open the office door, barging in on his thoughts. "Dammit, Lampkin," he snarled. "Ain't I tole you to knock first.

I didn't hang no screen door there for a reason."

"Sorry, Sheriff," the baby-faced Lampkin said, not seeming to take the Sheriff's mood too personal, "but I thought you'd wont to know it first. They's trouble over at the courthouse. Nellie Grindle is pitchin a fit."

"What's wrong this time? She trying to take all the Senator's dead friends off the voting rolls again? She knows he ain't gonna stand for that."

"Nope. You better come on. They's a nigger over there says he wants to vote."

Billy Dean got to the circuit clerk's office to see the colored man still there, his hat in his hand smiling respectfully at a pinched-faced woman with pointy glasses who by now had gone purple in the face.

"Sheriff!" she cried out in an annoying squeak of a voice, "It's about time you got here. This nigger's tryin to register for the vote. And when I told him to leave the premises he flat-out refused."

It took a moment for the sheriff to recognize the man dressed in the suit as baggy as a rodeo clown's. Then it hit him. "Well, lookie who it is!" he said. "I always said you was a troublemaker, boy. You been biding your time, ain't you?"

Levi smiled shyly at the sheriff. "You sho were right bout me, Sheriff. I been bidin my time like you say. I been weighin the matter and now I wonts the vote."

The sheriff studied Levi's face and then frowned. This is all I need, Billy Dean thought to himself. The Senator watching me like a hawk and now his old pet nigger has gone crazy. Strolling right in here in front of God and everybody. No telling what he was liable to say. Billy Dean walked over to Levi and shoved him hard, slamming Levi in the doorjamb. "Get outta here!" he shouted.

When Levi opened his mouth to speak, the sheriff shouted even louder, "Now, goddammit! Not another word out of your sassy mouth."

Nellie dropped her chin. "Aren't you going to arrest him for disturbing the peace or something?"

"Nellie, don't you know, Levi?"

Nellie stared at him mystified.

"Well then, let me introduce you two. This here is one of the *Senator's* niggers," Billy Dean sneered. "You know we got special rules just for them." He looked back at Levi, who remained by the door with a pleasant grin on his face. "I don't see you moving, boy."

"That's right, suh," Levi said politely and bowed his head. His manner was almost courtly. "Like I was tellin Miss Nellie, I come to take that votin test."

That set Billy Dean back for a moment. "Are you deaf? Did you hear what I tole you to do?"

"Yessuh," Levi said. "But like you splained to the Senator, I'm a born troublemaker. Don't know no other way to be. Guess you gone have to do like Miss Nellie say and toss me in the jailhouse."

Nellie clutched her old woman's breast and gasped, "Of all the…I've never in my…"

The sheriff looked at Levi warily. "You actin like you want me to arrest you. That it? You want to go to my jail? You tryin to rain the Senator down on my ass?"

"I wonts to vote, suh," Levi said again, respectfully. "And I reckon if I can't vote, I might as well go on to where they puts all the colored that try."

Billy Dean grinned. "The years ain't been good to you, has they, old man? I believe you crazier than a coot." All the more reason to get him out of here fast before he starts to raving, thought the sheriff. Something sure wasn't right here. Smelled fishy. If he arrested him, people might take Levi serious. The Senator would get involved for sure. The sheriff had another idea.

He grabbed Levi by the arm and yanked him out the door and down the corridor. By the time they got outside to the courthouse gallery, a small crowd of whites had already gathered on the lawn, all the black faces having pulled back to the safety of the opposite side of the street.

What everybody saw, black and white, was the overworked sheriff of Hopalachie County clutching an old colored man dressed in a ridiculous suit, with a foolish grin on his face. People started smiling at the pitiful sight even before the sheriff pushed him down the steps.

As he lay there sprawled out on the sidewalk, his hat crushed beneath his backside, Levi nodded respectfully to Billy Dean, who stood with his hands on his hips at the top of the steps. "Sheriff, suh, I still wonts the vote. Now all these good people is my witness. So if you ain't gone let me take that votin test, you best take me on to jail."

People in the crowd looked at one another, bewildered. Now they didn't know what to think. They looked back up at their sheriff.

Billy Dean was at the top of the steps, shaking his head and grinning. "Crazy as a coot," he called out loudly.

Relieved, the crowd let out with a roar.

As the sheriff walked back through the door, he said to himself, "Now let him tell his story and see who listens."

But not everybody was laughing. Later that afternoon, Floyd got a frantic call at the dealership from Hayes Alcorn convening an emergency board meeting of the Citizens' Council. He said to be over at the bank in fifteen minutes.

Floyd was convinced that it was about him and Delia. The sheriff was still looking for the murderer, and Floyd, a nervous wreck for more than three months now, had decided somebody was bound to inform on him sooner or later. He would probably be called in for questioning and interrogated about all the time he stole from his poor, nervous wife to be with the Senator's twice-divorced daughter. All the sordid details of their pathetic little affair would be on the front page of *The Jackson Daily News.* The word "illicit" haunted him in his dreams. "I feel healthy! I feel happy! I feel terrific!" Floyd repeated over and over to himself as he crossed the street to the Merchants and Planters.

It was after banking hours, but Hayes was standing at the entrance, holding the door open to the members as they arrived, and then pointing them one by one to the conference room across the marble lobby in the far corner of the bank. "Glad you could make it," he told Floyd, looking truly appreciative. "These are troubling times."

Floyd breathed easier. From the grateful look on Hayes's face, Floyd could tell he was still considered to be on the right side of troubling times. Much relieved, he went on in to join the other members.

Floyd was met by a weary look from the sheriff, who sat back from the mahogany conference table, his legs crossed, the Stetson pushed back on his head, flicking that old nickel-plated lighter. Billy Dean looked like he had been run through the wringer all right and it showed—months of chasing leads and tracking down suspects, running the hounds till they dropped, tromping through woods and thickets and digging up fields, dragging miles of creeks and swamps and rivers by the light of day and by torch at night—and so far only coming up with a couple of bodies and neither of them white. Everybody knew his job was on the line. Floyd forced a smile at Billy Dean and then took a chair, angling it so his guilt-ridden face was out of the sheriff's line of sight.

Hayes walked to the head of the table and cleared his throat. He always ran the meetings standing up, all five-foot-four of him. "Like I told ever-body already, we got a crisis on our hands. A well-known nigruh agitator walked right in the circuit clerk's office as big as broad daylight, and demanded to be registered to vote. Nearly scared poor ol' Nellie Grindle to death. Twenty years and she ain't never had no nigruh to suggest such a thing."

"Who was it?" asked Gaylon King, the newspaper editor.

"Levi Snow," Hayes said as if the name itself would raise alarm. He plopped down dramatically in his personal chair with legs six inches high-er than all the rest. "You can see we got a problem."

The county attorney, Hartley Faircloth, looked at Hayes incredulous-ly. "You mean that old colored man who tends yards? What he do, threat-en Miss Nellie with his rake?"

Everybody laughed.

His face pinking up, Hayes shot out of his chair and leaned over the table. "The man is a known agitator. Ain't that right, Sheriff?"

The sheriff didn't bother looking up from his lighter. "Was once," he mumbled.

Hayes waited for the sheriff to tell the rest of the story, but it was obvi-ous Billy Dean was all talked out on the subject. Narrowing his eyes at the sheriff, Hayes said pointedly, "Nellie told me you didn't even arrest him. That right?"

"I took care of it," the sheriff said.

Hayes shook his head and pulled back to address the whole group. "The way I understand it, he use to be one of them NAACP preachers trying to stir up the colored. Y'all might remember that nigruh church getting burnt down out in the county a few years back."

Nobody seemed to. But Hayes said, as if they did, "Well, that was his!"

Hayes planted his little balled-up fists on the table and leaned in toward Billy Dean again. "Ain't that right, Sheriff?"

"Fore I was elected," Billy Dean said, clicking the lid of the lighter shut.

Johnelle Ramphree from the hardware store piped up. "That old man's harmless, Hayes. Maybe a little addled is all. I don't think we got nothing here to worry about. Not from a poor ol' afflicted colored man."

Hayes was not one to be dismissed so lightly. "That's just a front. He's been biding his time. He told the sheriff as much. Right in front of Nellie. Now with this stuff in Montgomery with that King nigruh and the Supreme Court going pinko, he knows the climate is right. No telling how many nigruhs he can get stirred up if we don't do something immediately. Gentlemen, it's up to us. Hopalachie County is in the grips of a Jewish-Communist conspiracy. We might have another Martin Luther King right in our midst."

Floyd shifted uncomfortably in his chair. It was Floyd who had first talked his neighbors into using Levi in their yards, and he had the man's daughter working right under his own roof. He decided he better weigh in on this thing before it turned on him. "Now I agree with Johnelle," he said. "I been around Levi and he seems a pleasant enough colored…" he stopped and corrected himself. "I mean nigruh." He better talk in Hayes's language if he was going to head this thing off. Something he learned from that book about influencing people.

"Floyd!" Hayes said, "You ought to be more concerned than anybody. I've seen him out there talking with your boy. Johnelle said he was criminally insane."

"I believe I said 'addled,'" Johnelle corrected.

"No matter. Did you ever see how big that nigruh is? Six and a half feet if he's an inch." Hayes was reaching up over his head as far as he could, but Floyd figured he still came a few inches short. "And those hands could choke a cow," Hayes added.

The nickel-plated lighter shut with such a crack, everybody snapped their heads toward Billy Dean. That's it! he thought. Straightening up from his slouch. Billy Dean said, "He might well be dangerous, at that." It would give him the chance to get the Senator off his back and buy some time. Voting was one thing. Murder was another. He stuck the lighter in the pocket of his khakis and pulled up to the table like he had decided to join the meeting after all.

Thrilled to finally be getting support from the sheriff, Hayes went after Floyd. He looped his arms out in front of him dramatically. "Why, I've seen him tote a two-hundred-pound tree trunk the length of my yard. Ain't you the least bit worried, Floyd? At least for your boy's sake? For your wife?"

Of course, Levi had also been seen by the whole neighborhood talking to Hayes's wife, Pearl. That wasn't being mentioned. But Floyd decided not to be antagonistic. Try to see the other person's point, he remembered his book had said. Don't alienate by being too defensive. After fully listening to the other fellow, it advised, you are in a better position to tell him where he is wrong. "Maybe we should hear Hayes out," Floyd said, settling into a reasonable position. "Why don't you tell us what it is you're suggesting, Hayes." Floyd liked the sound of that. Almost statesman-like.

"Thank you," Hayes said, acknowledging Floyd's contribution. "It's not like I'm advocating violence. I told y'all from the beginning that's not what the Citizens' Council stands for. Like our charter says, we stand for a peaceful yet firm response to any attack on our way of life. I suggest we make an example of this nigruh by guaranteeing he never works again in this county. We boycott him. Nobody hire his time. And what's more, he doesn't get credit from any Delphi merchant nor service from any professional."

"Seems like a little overkill for a poor ol' broke-down colored man, don't you think, Hayes?" Gaylon King from the paper asked. "By the way," he added with a sly grin, "this wouldn't have anything to do with the rumors about you announcing for governor, would it? How about a quote for the paper?"

There were a few sniggers. Gaylon went on. "I can run it as my lead story. HAYES ALCORN SINGLE-HANDEDLY STARVES OUT POOR OLD NIGGER MAN."

That drew an even bigger laugh. But Hayes ignored it and continued outlining his all-out campaign to save the county from the conspiracy at hand. "And I suggest we extend this boycott to all members of his family." Hayes looked down at Floyd. "That means you need to get rid of his girl, of course."

Floyd sat up in his chair. "I don't see why that's necessary, Hayes," he protested, the idea not sitting well with him at all.

"Well, exactly what do you see as *necessary*, Floyd? What does our vice president suggest?"

"Well," Floyd said, taking a breath and diagramming the situation in his head. He could already see the sparks flying if he had to tell Hazel he was going to fire Vida. She was sure to throw a duck fit. Things around his house had changed dramatically over the past month. Hazel was all fired up and full of git, dressing nice and out driving the Lincoln like the old days. Maybe even drinking, but not enough to tell it. She seemed happy. Though he would like to believe his positive mental attitude had rubbed off on her, he was more convinced Vida was somehow behind it.

"Well?" Hayes said impatiently.

Floyd cut his eyes to the ceiling and exhaled deeply, letting Hayes know he was still in a mulling mode. Maybe it would be better if Vida were gone, he thought, taking the other side of the issue. He had probably trusted her too much. Truth was, Floyd had no idea what was going on in his home. This thing with Delia had sapped all his extra energy. Floyd got the feeling that as a result of his lack of attention on the home front, he was now surrounded by a conspiracy between his maid, his wife and maybe even his own son. But still he didn't want to rock the boat. Floyd also had the vague feeling that Hazel knew about Delia and he wasn't anxious to find out how much. Let sleeping dogs lie.

The room was still waiting for Floyd's best thinking on the subject. He cleared his throat. "Well, maybe we can just give Levi a good talking-to and tell him to get back to his yard work," he said hopefully. "I bet that's all it would take."

Hayes's response was immediate. "No! No! No! That's not the way it works at all," he cried, sounding like his chances for governor were slipping away before his eyes. Hayes's reaction was so violent, Floyd began to worry about the extension on his business loan.

Then Hayes started strutting around the room like a banty rooster. "We the Citizens' Council! We supposed to strike fear in the hearts of agitators. We don't give them a good *talking-to*. Now, y'all got to get behind me on this. And Floyd, you of all people. The vice president for Christ's sake." He glanced quickly at the other end of the table. "Sorry, Brother Dear."

Brother Dear, sheathed in his white linen suit, had been listening intently to the debate and used the opportunity of Hayes's blasphemy to insert himself on the Lord's behalf. He smiled at Hayes forgivingly and then leaned forward to address the group. "I've been listening carefully to what's been said here today. Now I know that each of you comes here with the well-being of your community foremost in your thoughts and prayers. So I think it's safe to put aside any doubts you might be having about the motivations of others at this table."

Hayes nodded aggressively.

Brother Dear's beatific smile and melodious voice had already given a new gravity to the proceedings. The men around the table now wore the sober expressions of civic responsibility. "I believe what Hayes says bears listening to," he continued. "Our community institutions are under attack from Washington. Our local government. Our schools. Our businesses. Next in logical sequence, like the falling of dominoes, will be the church. And finally it's the family that will topple."

He let that sit a minute before he went on. "Our local traditions make up a complex weave." Brother Dear made a dramatic sweep of his hand over the sleeve of his white suit to demonstrate. He was well known for using visual aids in his sermons. "That weave, our community fabric if you will, is a living, breathing testimony to our shared Christian faith." To emphasize that point, Brother Dear reached up and lightly touched his cross-of-diamonds stickpin.

Then he shook his finger at the group. "And this is not about prejudice and discrimination. Why, just look at us here. We have Baptists and Methodists and Presbyterians and Episcopalians all sitting around the same table together."

Everyone grinned sheepishly, acknowledging the private reservations they had had about just such a thing in the beginning. Everyone grinned, that is, except for Billy Dean, who, when Floyd glanced over at him, seemed to be deep in thought. From where he sat, Floyd could see the sheriff's hands under the table, and instead of the lighter, he was fiddling with a gold chain of some kind, fingering the links one at a time.

"Nor is this simply about a yard man and a maid," Brother Dear was saying. "It represents a kind of gnawing at those fibers that hold together our community. We need to take righteous action before more threads are broken and the fabric loosens. Before we disintegrate—desegregate if you will—into social chaos. You all know what that means."

Floyd rolled his eyes. Yeah, he figured he knew what it meant. All those colored men had been biding their time for three hundred years, working in the fields, getting out from under slavery, getting themselves lynched, burned and drowned, and finally going all the way to the Supreme Court—all that, just to get them a white woman. If that was true, Floyd thought, they ought to get some kind of blue ribbon for pure determination.

No, he just couldn't figure out the logic of some of these people. But what he could figure out by the silence around the table was that Brother Dear's sermon had pretty well clinched the deal for Levi and Vida. All that was missing was the amen and hallelujahs.

Her husband would hardly look at Hazel all through supper, and when he did, his expression was tinged with guilt. But it wasn't like she hadn't seen it coming for a long time now. Hazel prepared herself for the worst, the other-woman confession. Even though Delia might be dead and gone, it was obvious, so was Floyd's affection for Hazel. She was certain that he had already replaced Delia with another.

She watched apprehensively as he took the last bite of his minute steak and then carefully folded and unfolded his napkin several times. Then he glanced at Johnny. "Go up to your room and play. OK, Little Monkey?"

"All my doll people are at Vi—" Johnny caught himself before he broke his and his mother's secret. "Yes, sir," he said and took off upstairs like a guilty man set free.

"Hazel," Floyd said gravely, unfolding the napkin again and laying it over his plate like he was covering the face of a dead friend, "I got something I need to tell you."

She closed her eyes and bit her lip. Here it comes, she told herself.

"Bad as I hate to…" Floyd said.

"Oh, God," Hazel moaned, slumping down in her chair.

"Bad as I hate to…we going to have to let Vida go."

Hazel burst out crying, "What's she got that I don't…" then it registered what he had said. "Vida?" She sat up straight.

"It's for her own good, Hazel." He flashed her one of his grins.

Hazel knew she should be thankful he wasn't asking for a divorce, but it wasn't gratitude or even relief she was feeling now. Not even fear. Something else was taking hold.

"You're going to fire Vida? That's what you're trying to say?" There was a boiling down deep in her gut. The floor seemed to quake under her chair. In her mind she saw a tattered lace handkerchief tied to a flagpole and whipping valiantly in a gale-sized wind.

Shifting into his most logical voice, he said, "Now she's only a maid, Hazel. I can find you another one just as good by suppertime tomorrow." He cocked his head to the side and grinned again, like the deal was done.

When she saw him begin to rise up from the table, it was like another person took over inside. Her fist came banging down on the tabletop, hard enough to rattle the silverware in the drawers.

Floyd fell back in his chair, covering his head. Hazel heard herself telling her husband in a voice that was flat and final, "Ain't no way you getting rid of Vida." Her face burned hot, and she was not sure where the voice had come from, only that it had been too long in the coming.

It took a few moments for Floyd to regain his composure. His voice still a little shaky, he said, "Now don't upset yourself. You been doing so good and all. You're letting your emotions get the best of you. Calm down and listen."

She crossed her arms over her chest and shook her head vehemently, trying to block out his words. He reached for her hand, still clenched at her side. "Hazel, we got to be a team on this now."

"Team?" She erupted in a burst of angry laughter. She snatched her hand from his. "My whole life long I ain't never had a real friend before. Somebody in this world who would be on my side no matter what. Somebody I can tell everything to. Who listens without interrupting. Who don't list out everything I should have done different. Who don't want me to be nothing but what I already am. No way you're gonna make me give Vida up, Floyd Graham. No way in hell. Vida stays! She's the one on my team."

The words had tumbled out in such a rush that Hazel wasn't altogether sure what she had said. When she looked up at Floyd he seemed to have been struck dumb. He cleared his throat a couple of times and struggled to give her one of his trademark grins, but the rest of his face wasn't able to get behind it.

"Hazel, you're talking about a colored woman," he said. "She can't be your friend."

"Don't go telling me what Vida is or ain't. You got no right."

"Now, I got to insist, Hazel," Floyd said, his tone less confident than his words. "It might come down to staying in business or not. And I know you want what's best for the family. Please, Hazel." Floyd was pleading, and she almost felt sorry for him until he said, "It might seem like a problem now, but we got to look at it like an opportunity."

This time Hazel banged both fists on the table. "Stop spouting those things at me!" she screamed.

Floyd covered his head again. "What things?" he called out from his crouched position.

"Those sayings of yours. About how what is really ain't. And what ain't really is. About if you call something by a different name, all your troubles will disappear. Floyd, all you doing is tying my brain up in knots."

"All I'm saying," he ventured, "is if you take what looks like your very worst problem and think about it positively, what you might have before you is something you can use. I already told you all this. Remember? Lemons and lemonade?"

Floyd found his salesman's grin again. "Now all I ask is if you would take ten seconds and think about what I just said. See if you can make the problem work for you. Make some lemonade, so to speak."

Hazel eyed him dubiously, but did as he requested. She gave it seven seconds, then she said, "OK, let me see if I got it. If I take the most awfullest thing, and look at it different, try to hang some hope on it so to speak, then I might can figure a way to make it turn out good?"

"Exactly, honey. That's all I'm saying." Floyd was real excited now, like there might be hope for her after all. "It's the Science of Controlled Thinking."

"I see," Hazel said. "Like if I thought you ever cheated on me with another woman, for instance. There might be a way to make that work *for* me instead of *against* me?"

Floyd opened and closed his mouth several times like he was straining for air. He stammered, "Wha...wha...what are you asking again, honey? Would you repeat that question for me?" But his voice was ludicrous. All bluff.

She smiled innocently and said, "I'm asking, is that the way it works, Floyd? Am I a controlled thinker now?" There was a long moment of silence while Hazel's big blue eyes looked expectantly at Floyd, waiting for his answer.

Floyd blurted out, "Hazel, I ain't cheating on you! I swear it!"

Maybe he wasn't...not now. Maybe there was no new woman in his life. But even if Floyd was technically right, he was still cheating with his words. He was sacrificing his dignity for a lie. He didn't have the courage to tell her the truth. To give him another chance she asked, "What's the matter, Floyd? You look like you going to be sick at the stomach."

"What's got into you?" he shouted. "Stop it whatever it is, you hear?"

She knew she had won something and lost something at the same time. Sighing sadly, Hazel said, "Maybe I don't understand your little saying after all, Floyd. Maybe I'm not smart enough."

She pushed herself away from the table and rose to her feet. When she stood, she noticed how strong and solid her legs felt beneath her. Hazel said more sarcastically than she meant to, "But please don't fire Vida. Would you do that one thing for your poor, ignorant wife?"

Chapter 43
SET UP FOR A FALL

Vida had the fidgets so bad she had cracked two of Hazel's dishes, and it wasn't even noon yet.

Levi had dumbfounded her the evening before with the news about his day at the courthouse. His eyes had shone bright, the way they had the night he came home raving about the lightning bugs and his church that couldn't be burned. But that had been over a month ago. She thought he had got it out of his system.

"I wisht you could have seen it, Vida," he told her. "You would have been proud. It's what God been leading me to do. I'm walkin with the Lord again. Steppin out in faith."

Vida had been so stunned she collapsed on the bed in disbelief, hiding her face in her hands.

"You should have seen how they looked at me, Vida," he said. "Like I was dangerous or something. Like I was a man to be dealt with. It was like Moses calling on Pharaoh."

Vida looked up at him and shouted, "Don't you never say nothing about no Moses again! You hear? We ain't people in no book. You can't just go ploppin us down in some make-believe story cause it suits you. We is real!" She jumped to her feet, furious, and held her arms out to her father. "See. Flesh and blood. We got feelins. We can hurt. We can die. You got no right."

Levi acted bewildered by his daughter's reaction. "Vida, you don't know what you're saying. It was God's will. I had to do it."

"No, you didn't!" Vida spat. "You didn't have no right gettin up one day and out of the clear blue decidin you was gone be Moses. Cause tomorrow when you wake up, you gone go back to bein Levi the nigger yard boy. You gone still be livin in Mis'sippi. The white man still gone be on top. And then what you gone do? You think God gone get you out of this mess? Well, He ain't. Case you ain't noticed, He ain't parted no seas for us lately."

Levi had been undeterred. "It was what was set before me to do, Vida. I got to go where the Lord leads me. Don't you see it? It was God sent the sheriff to burn my church down. Made him spread the lie about me workin for the vote. But the sheriff's lie was God's truth. God wonts me to stand up for my people. Like that King preacher in Alabama. Like that Rosie girl you tole me about. I reckon she had to live the story the Lord set out for her."

"Don't lay it on Rosie," Vida said sharply. "That ain't our story neither. No more than Moses is." But when she saw his look of incomprehension, she gave up. All she could do was to shake her head sadly, bite her tongue and walk away.

They hardly spoke the rest of the evening. Levi sat out on the porch praying, and Vida stayed inside, terrified the sheriff might show up any minute to set fire to their house. After an hour passed with the cabin still standing, Vida had almost convinced herself that her father had imagined the whole thing. For the first time she found comfort in his delusions. But then Creola came chugging into the yard and crashing up the steps. After nodding uncertainly to Levi, who was still praying on the porch, she rushed past him and into the house to Vida's side. She breathlessly confirmed Levi's story, saying that it was all Hayes Alcorn had talked about over supper.

The next morning at breakfast, things had been strained between Vida and her father. Clearing away the dishes, she suggested the only workable idea she had been able to come up with. "Maybe we ought to go on up to Memphis," she said. "Borry some money from Willie and leave Delphi. I ain't got no reason to be here no more. Crazy just waitin around to get killed."

"No. I ain't runnin," Levi said firmly. "I got to wait right here. This is where my new church will be. The Lord promised it to me." His face softened and he smiled patiently at Vida, like she was a little girl who didn't understand her Sunday school lesson. "Don't be afraid, Snowflake Baby. He ain't deserted us. He been watchin us from the darkness. Directin our feet all the time."

He reached over and cupped her face in his giant hand. She knew then there was no way she could talk him out of this. Her father had finally set his world right again. He had found a story he could weave himself into. He was a self-proclaimed prophet of God, a leader of his people again, the kind they wrote up in newspapers and put on TV. It didn't matter that not a soul was following him. He was the Reach Out Man once more.

Vida looked out the Grahams' back door for the umpteenth time that morning, hoping to get a glimpse of her father working in the neighborhood, when Hazel came up behind her and said, "What's got you on edge?" Vida nearly jumped out of her skin.

"You expecting company?" Hazel asked. "Your friends coming over later?"

Vida yanked the screen door shut. "Ain't nothin the matter with me. Didn't sleep much, is all." She walked over to the oven to check on the cornbread.

"Well, if it's about what your daddy did, I don't want you to worry one bit," Hazel said, sounding proud as could be. "I done fixed it."

Vida gasped and slammed the oven door shut. "Fixed it?" she repeated. She spun around to face the white woman. Hazel had a satisfied look on her face. That's all I need, Vida thought, a woman the whole town knows to be a crazy drunk coming down hard on my side. She'll get us all killed. "What you mean you fixed it?" she asked.

"Floyd's little boys' club told him he had to fire you," Hazel said. "But I put my foot down. 'No way in hell,' I said. I said, 'Nobody's gonna fire my Vida.'" Hazel's eyes seem to mist up. "Oh, I wished you could have heard me, Vida. I really stood out for you."

Hazel looked like she expected a "praise the Lord" and a "thank you, Jesus" to come bubbling out of Vida's mouth. Instead, Vida's face went to steel and she angrily wrenched herself around to the sink. She began scrubbing a pan so hard, it looked like she was trying to take off the enamel.

But Hazel hadn't moved. She kept standing there in the middle of the kitchen like she was waiting for her due.

Rinsing off the pan, Vida said curtly, "Why don't you go on and do your drivin now. Your hootch is in my sack behind the door."

Hazel was unfazed. "How about I carry you on home later. We can chat for a spell at your house." Hazel stood there, as dense as molasses, waiting for her answer.

Vida began scrubbing the same pan again, cursing to herself. White women! God, she hated white women! Vida slung the pan into the sink with a splash and whipped herself around toward Hazel. "Tell me somethin, Miss Hazel," she snapped. "What you wont from me exactly?"

"What do you mean?" Hazel asked, caught short.

"Why you bother savin my job for me? It can't be the hootch. You can get that for your own self now."

"But Vida—"

"And I been meanin to ask, why you all the time comin down to Tarbottom and lettin peoples see you sittin in my yard talkin to a colored woman?"

Hazel opened her mouth to speak, but closed it again. Vida could tell she had hurt the woman, which only made her want to strike again. "Why you wont to talk with me at all? Why don't you talk to Mr. Floyd. Or some white womens?"

"You don't like our little chats, Vida?" asked Hazel, sounding small.

"You the onliest one chattin. I the one jerkin my fool head up and down like a chicken in a yard full of corn. It just ain't natural." Vida dropped her eyes to the floor. "Anyways, my peoples is startin to talk. And I reckon so is yours."

"Well, let em talk. What they gonna say anyway?"

"I can't speak for the white folks, but my peoples is askin if you tryin to be colored. And some wont to know if I tryin to be white."

"That's the silliest thing I ever heard!" Hazel said. "I talk to you because you understand me. I can tell you things I can't tell nobody else."

Vida shot Hazel a look sharp as a pick. "Why is that, Miss Hazel?"

"Because—"

"Cause why?" fired Vida. "Cause I won't tell nobody?"

Hazel gripped the back of a kitchen chair, like her legs were going wobbly.

"How do you know I don't tell nobody?" Vida pressed. "How you know I don't tell my friends everthing you say? And all about you drankin and drivin?"

Hazel looked as if she could cry. "But I don't care what you tell your friends."

"No, I reckon you don't. All my friends is colored. Don't matter what colored folks think."

"Vida, you're putting words in my mouth. I care about what you think."

"Then tell me," Vida demanded, "What do I think? What I thinkin right now? Tell me what it is I fret over everday? Tell me what it is keeps me up at night worryin. Tell me what you know about *my* sufferin. What it is *I* done lost."

"The both of us lost our boys, Vida. Ain't we got that together?" Hazel's eyes were tearing up. "I thought we was friends."

"I clean yo house," Vida said sullenly. "That makes me your maid, not yo friend. That's the difference between colored folks and white. You get to pick me as a friend and I ain't got no say about it."

Vida turned back to her dishwater, so she couldn't see the hurt on Hazel's face any longer. But her insides felt like they were crumbling, caving in like a house afire, one floor at time.

The sheriff was tilted back against the wall in his chair, boots up on the desk, waiting for his deputy to return with the evidence—evidence the grand old man would insist on before he would let Billy Dean act. It just might work, he told himself again. At least it would buy a little breathing room. Give him some time to figure his way out of this fix Delia had put him in.

If he worked it right, he could put a stall into things for a couple of months. Get the good citizens off his back. Give the newspapers somebody else to crucify besides him. And most of all, keep the Senator from replacing Billy Dean with Lampkin Butts as sheriff like he was threatening. Said he didn't even need an election to do it. Billy Dean was his personal sheriff. Like all them *personal* niggers he looked out for. Billy Dean reached into the drawer, pulled out Delia's note and read it one more time.

> *I'm holding you to your promise, Billy Dean. Leave her or I'll tell Daddy. It's me or nothing, sugar. And you know you could never stand nothing.*

He studied the handwriting. All those pretty swoops and curves and curlicues masked the cold hand of steel that wrote it. He brought the letter up to his face and sniffed it. "Oh, Delia. You sweet, conniving thing," he whispered. "Why didn't I do it your way from the start? It wouldn't have come to this."

It wasn't the first time he wished he had just gone ahead and given her what she wanted. Done it before the threats began. Gone ahead and told Hertha the truth. Hell, it would have been worth it to see the look on that godawful face of hers. Anyway, it wasn't like he was ever going to get his hands on the Senator's money. He used to be under the impression that when the old man died the plantation and the gins and the bank shares would pass on to him. He would be fixed for life. Could do things his own way. But Hertha said there was no way he was getting his hands on it. She said *she* would keep him on as sheriff, but the Columns was a separate thing. A family thing. *Her* family, not his. And the family lawyers would make sure of it.

To hell with her family. And their land and their money and their personal niggers nobody could lay a hand on. You touch one, you touch them all. That was the problem with the Senator and them. They couldn't tell where one thing ended and another began. They were all wrapped up in one ball and it was *theirs*. Billy Dean couldn't imagine such a thing. With him, the fewer strings the better. He'd cut them all loose if he could.

To hell with them all, he thought again. The only one of the whole bunch he ever gave a good goddamn about was Delia. And now....

In the middle of his thought, the door flung open and in rushed his deputy, panting like an overworked mule. The sheriff quickly shifted himself about and got his boots back on the floor. He shoved the letter into the drawer and slammed it.

"I tole you about knocking, Lampkin."

The deputy was trying to catch his breath. "Look-a-here what I found out yonder," he said, puffing. He handed Billy Dean the watch chain. "You was right. Funny how we missed it all them other times."

"How bout that? I just had a feeling."

It has to work, the sheriff told himself again. What was the worst thing? The old preacher might spend a few weeks in jail until this thing was settled. He sure seemed willing enough. Of course he might get lynched before things unknotted themselves, but that wouldn't be Billy Dean's fault. Not if he played his cards right with the Senator. The sheriff pocketed the chain. For the first time in months, he walked out of the redbrick jailhouse with a spring in his step. He got in his cruiser and headed straight to the Columns.

The ederly houseboy met Billy Dean at the door and showed him into the library. The Senator was standing over by the marble fireplace, staring into the coal grate. It had been more than three months and he seemed to be getting worse every day.

"We found something, Senator." The sheriff was talking to the back of the grieving man's head. "Thought I'd show it to you and get your thinking on it."

The old man turned. Taking that as permission to approach his majesty, Billy Dean sauntered over to him and dangled the chain. "I tole Lampkin to look over the alleged crime scene again with a finetooth comb, and there it was. Tromped down in the mud. Right near that whirlpool where Miss Delia's scarf was. Even though I ain't saying she went in."

The Senator held out his shaky palm, and Billy Dean let the chain coil like a rattler in the old man's hand. He cast a weary eye on it. Billy Dean noticed how much this thing had aged the man. His once meaty jowls had wasted to sagging flaps of skin.

Finally the Senator spoke. "Don't look like it's been laying out in the weather for no three months."

"No sir," the sheriff said quickly, "I cleaned it up first. See if I could identify it."

"And?"

"It sorta looks familiar to me. But I can't say for a hunnurd per cent. Take another look and see if it don't ring a bell with you. You probably know everbody in the county."

The Senator narrowed his shaggy brows at the chain. "Hell, I can't tell. Do you know or don't you? Stop playing games."

Billy Dean had hoped the Senator would have guessed it himself. "Don'cha see that little charm on it. Them's praying hands."

"So?"

"You know. Maybe like a preacher would wear? Don't you reckon?"

The Senator sighed wearily. "Billy Dean, just tell me what you got to tell me."

"Well, id'n it just like the chain that nigger preacher wore. You know the one. He used to come by here all the time. Remember?"

"Levi," the Senator said softly and went quiet for a moment. Looking up at Billy Dean, he asked, "But how you know this one's his?"

"Now I don't know for sure. That's a point we need to consider real careful."

The Senator tried to give the chain back to Billy Dean, but the sheriff quickly poked his hands down in his pockets and said, "Now what I do know for a fact is he showed up yesterday at the courthouse trying to vote." Billy Dean watched the Senator for a reaction and, when he saw the old man's face crease, went on. "When I seen him then he was all dressed up in his Sunday-go-to-meeting, minus what you holding there in your hand. To make sure, I checked my recollection with Nellie Grindle. Needed to get a second opinion on such an incriminatin detail. She said she would swear on a stack of Bibles he didn't have it neither."

"Nellie said that?"

"Yes, sir. And I guess you remember better than anybody how he used to flash that chain around. Anyway, hard to miss on a darkie. Like curtains on a outhouse."

"But why would he? He used to dote on Delia. Somebody could have stole it off him."

"Now you could be right. Yes, sir," the sheriff said, stroking his chin. "I'm thinking that, too. Somebody could have framed him. After all, he'd be the perfect one to frame, wouldn't you say? If I was going to frame somebody and make it stick it'd shore be him."

The Senator bit. "Why's that?"

"Think about it. He probly blames you for his churches. His pretty little house. Fine car. Making him work for a living. Refusing to talk to him. All them things."

"So?"

"Well, now," the sheriff said carefully, "a reasonable fella might could say he's trying to make you pay. First by drowning Delia, even though I ain't saying that she's drowned, mind you. Then by trying to vote. Going right up against you like that." Afraid he was sounding too eager, the sheriff backed off some. "I just wanted to come by and tell you before I checked him out's all. Might should let it drop. You right. Probly framed, like you say."

The Senator shook his head in disbelief. "Ol' Levi. Treated him like family. I never would've thought it."

No, you wouldn't, Billy Dean said to himself. You and your niggers. Well, he told himself, whatever happens to this nigger is on your head, old man, not mine. And he believed it.

Again the Senator held the chain out to the sheriff, who took it this time.

"I suppose you better go see about it, Billy Dean," the Senator said. Then, with an old man's groan, he eased down into his wingback chair and with a voice full of regret said, "It's the ones you've done the most for that you have to watch the closest."

"Ain't that the truth," Billy Dean said, shaking his head sadly.

That night, Vida sat up alone, waiting in the pitch-blackness of her shanty for her father to return, trying not to think the worst. The truth was she didn't know what to think anymore. The last twenty-four hours was proof her father was liable to do anything. Already several of the other maids had come by to tell Vida the pieces they knew of the last day's events. Even Missouri. She said that everybody laughed at Levi when he tried to register. That Vida had nothing to worry herself about except having a fool for a father. Vida had been so happy to hear that, she had wanted to kiss the woman. Next it was Sweet Pea who said she had overheard a call between her white lady and Nellie Grindle. Nellie was all upset because the sheriff had refused to arrest Levi. Said he just laughed it off.

So, for a few moments, Vida felt some welcome relief. Then Creola came panting up Vida's steps, sweat drops as big as bullets glistening among her freckles. Vida could tell Creola had something to say and was fighting hard against it. Finally she blurted, "Mr. Hayes is telephonin all over the state bout Levi. Callin him an agitator. A civil righter. An NAACP nigger. Going on bout how dangerous he is. Say somethin got to be done. And the sooner the better."

Creola reached out for Vida's hand. The woman was trembling. "Vida, I shore would feel a lot better if you come and stay with me and Rufus tonight."

"I can't go, Creola. Things gone work theyselves out. I be all right."

Creola bit her lip and then said what she had come to say all along. "Vida, when a colored person starts up with that votin business, his whole family liable to get hit. Nightriders drive by shootin off they guns. Even fling dynamite sticks through yo window." Creola's whole body shook. "Vida, I'm afeared for you."

Vida reached out and took the big woman in her arms and thanked her. But Vida still wouldn't go, determined to wait up for her father. "I owe him that," she told Creola. "It's cause of me we come to Delphi in the first place. I ought to got him out from this county a long time ago."

Reluctantly, Creola left the cabin. Vida closed the door behind her and dropped the crossbar. She would wait for her father in the darkness. As she sat in a corner of the room, Vida heard the coonhounds down by the river, their barks high-pitched and sharp, like they were on the scent of game.

"Please, God," she whispered. "I ain't spoke to You in too long a time. I been holding a lot of madness against You. And You got to admit, You ain't been the easiest thang to love. But I promise, if You let my daddy live through this, I see what I can do bout softening up some on You and him both."

Vida heard the hounds again. Their barking was different. Harsher now and lower, like their heads were slung back. The dogs had something treed.

Vida's heart almost stopped. It wasn't the sound of dogs this time, but the low whine of a car engine. Easing cautiously across the floor, as if a careless creak would give her away, she peeked out her window. Sure enough she saw the approach of a pair of headlights, painting the row of shacks in a gleam of white.

There was nowhere to turn. All the houses around her were darkened now. Word had spread fast about the trouble the Snows were in, and nobody wanted to be lit up when it came calling.

Vida went back to her chair and waited, listening to the sound of the engine coming closer, and closer and closer still, until she imagined she could hear the tires whispering against the dirt track. She said a last prayer for Nate and another for her father.

The shack exploded with light. The headlights were aimed right through her window. In that instant, Vida was hurled back in time, to the awful night the sheriff had come for Nate, when her room had lit up, distorted images thrown against the walls, the horrible glare in her eyes.

Vida pinched her lids shut and sat there holding her breath, as if she could make herself disappear under the lights. Her mind was a muddle. Maybe she could make it to the back door and run to the river. At least crawl up under the bed, she told herself. At least do that. But she couldn't move. It was Nate who had given her the legs to flee so many years ago. Now, alone, with no one to save but herself, she could only sit there, frozen.

The engine cut off, but the headlights remained on. Her heart pounded like a wild animal trying to bang its way out of its cage, but she still did not move. She sat there listening, waiting for it to happen: an explosion. Gunshots. A voice summoning her out into the lights.

But so far there was only silence behind the lights. Finally, the lights themselves cut out.

She waited in the darkness for what seemed like an eternity. Being able to stand it no longer, Vida rose up on wobbly legs and peeked out the window. She couldn't believe her eyes. There was the Lincoln sitting in her front yard. "Miss Hazel," Vida whispered. Then louder, "Miss Hazel!" Her voice raw with fear, "Is that you out there, Miss Hazel?"

"I got to talk to you, Vida."

Vida was never gladder to see anybody in her entire life. Tonight, at least, nobody would dare hurt Vida with a white woman in her yard. "Sho thing, Miss Hazel," she called out the window. "I'll cut on the porch light. You can talk as long as you wont this evenin. I even got coffee."

Vida quickly lifted the crossbar, but by the time she had opened the door, Hazel had both her feet on the porch. "Miss Hazel...?"

"Let's go inside, Vida," Hazel said, her voice small. "Can we please?"

"I reckon we can," Vida answered, but what she was thinking was, what has this white woman gone and done now that would make her ask to go inside a colored person's house? Once inside, Vida turned on the light and offered Hazel a chair. She's looped up and can't go home, Vida guessed. "You wont that coffee, Miss Hazel? Won't take but a minute or two."

Hazel shook her head. "Vida, sit down here beside me, will you?"

Vida eyed Hazel warily for a moment, and then retrieved a chair from the kitchen to join her guest. Seated across from Hazel, Vida could see there was something very wrong. A look of physical pain had settled on Hazel's face. "What is it?" she asked, her voice flat. "Tell it."

Speaking carefully, Hazel said, "I got some real bad news, Vida." She searched Vida's face for a clue as to how she might continue. But she saw nothing. Vida had already hardened herself against the news.

"Vida, it's about your daddy. He's been arrested." Again Hazel studied Vida's face, looking for any sign that what she said had registered. "Vida, I'm so sorry."

Vida closed her eyes and sighed heavily. But strangely, it sounded to Hazel like a sigh of relief. "Then Daddy ain't dead," Vida finally said.

"No, Vida, no!" Hazel exclaimed. "He ain't dead at all."

"All right now, Miss Hazel," Vida said, cool and in charge. "Tell me everthang what happened. Don't jump over nothin."

"I don't know it all, but I'll tell you what I heard. Floyd got a phone call a few minutes ago and I picked up the upstairs extension and listened in. Thinking it might be…" Hazel dropped her eyes just for a second, and then continued, "That part's not important. It was Miss Pearl's husband, Hayes, on the line. He tole Floyd that the problem was taken care of." Hazel stopped for a moment, making the connection. "Oh, Vida, if Floyd had anything to do with this…."

"Go on, Miss Hazel. What Mr. Hayes say?"

"Hayes said he guessed they wouldn't have to worry about Levi doing anymore agitating for the vote."

"So let me get it straight what you sayin, Miss Hazel. Daddy ain't been hurt. He's alive and they got him in county jail."

Hazel nodded, relieved Vida seemed to be taking it so well.

"I see," Vida said, "but they gone see he ain't no agitator. Just feeble-thinkin. They ain't gone hold him for that silliness at the Courthouse. They bound to see."

Hazel was confused. "What silliness at the courthouse?"

"For tryin to get his vote!" Vida said impatiently. The woman couldn't keep her own story straight! "You the one said it. The reason he got hisself in jail. Agitatin for the vote. Them's yo words."

Hazel shook her head sorrowfully. "No, Vida, no. That ain't why he's in jail." She was trying to get it out as gently she could. "Your daddy got arrested for killing Miss Delia."

Vida's eyes widened. She cupped her hand over her mouth and let out a muffled cry, one that Hazel thought could have come from the opposite side of some imaginary hill that separated them. So far away. So all alone.

Vida started shaking her head stubbornly. "No. No. No," she said. "That don't make no sense. They talkin about somebody else. Probly not my daddy at all. Probly you heard wrong. They got Daddy in jail for votin. But he was just confused in his head. He didn't mean nothin by it. They let him go in no time."

"No, Vida. I heard what Hayes said." Hazel took another deep breath. "Vida, there's more. I hate to tell you but you need to know it."

Vida's eyes seemed to have veiled over. Hazel reached out and gently shook her shoulder. "Vida? Are you still listening?"

"Go on," she answered, deadlike.

"Vida, Hayes told Floyd that they might could overlook a crazy colored trying to vote, but not a crazy colored murdering a white woman. That the Senator and his family ought to be spared the spectacle of a public trial. That Levi was going to be…" Hazel reached for Vida's hand. "That they were going to bust your father out of the jail and…" Hazel began to cry. "Oh, Vida, it's…Hayes said they were going to lynch your father."

At first Vida didn't catch what Hazel had said, because she was so shocked to suddenly find her hand in the white woman's. But those words, "lynch your father," kept beating against her brain like birds throwing themselves against a windowpane, until she at last had to let them in. As if the truth had weight to it, Vida's shoulders caved and she dropped her head, shaking it slowly from side to side. Still, Hazel held tightly to her hand.

Vida lifted her face to Hazel, who with her other hand reached out to gently stroke Vida's cheek. To avoid Hazel's touch, Vida quickly jerked her head away. Her hand still in Hazel's grip, Vida rose up to her feet and stood for a moment on wobbly legs, but then dropped to her knees. She tried to wrench her hand from Hazel's, but Hazel refused to loosen her hold. With no place to go, Vida laid her head on Hazel's lap and at last began to cry. As she gently stroked Vida's hair, Hazel wept also. Loss filled the room— fathers and mothers and husbands and sons, dead and forfeited and snatched away. Vida looked up to see the other woman's tears. She rubbed her cheek against Hazel's hand. In their private grieving, each tried to comfort the other.

Having seen the lights of Hazel's car, others showed up at the door. The big reddish woman, Creola. The smart sassy one, Sweet Pea. Half-blind Maggie, ancient and befuddled. Women whom Hazel had listened to from up a flight of stairs and through the worst of times. They all gathered around and made tender sounds above the two weeping women, their voices fluttering above them as softly as feathers on a dark, sheltering wing.

Chapter 44

THE FREEDOM RIDERS

School was letting out early because of the storms breaking out all across the Delta, not to mention the tornado sighting over toward Little Egypt. As children were inching their way in orderly lines from the school building, lightning lit up the dark skies and thunder shook the ground and rattled the windows. The children broke ranks and ran screaming for the buses. Just as the yellow-and-black lumbering giants began backing out one by one, the troubled sky opened up and the rain fell in sheets. By the time Johnny's bus had turned down his lane, roofs had become waterfalls and the streets gushing rivers.

From the bus, Johnny made a run for it up the sidewalk and through the front door. He was halfway down the stairhall, wiping the water from his eyes, before he noticed that the house was unlit. The rain, noisily beating down on the world outside, contrasted eerily with the dead silence inside the house. Suddenly he worried that his mother and Vida might be somewhere out in this storm. He scurried back toward the kitchen, calling out "Momma! Vida!" as he ran. But no reply came back to meet him.

He tore through the kitchen door, but then stopped in his tracks. He was taken aback by the sight of the maids sitting silently in the shadows. They looked up at him with weak smiles that quickly faded.

Vida got up without speaking and walked into the laundry room. She returned with a towel and began to dry Johnny's head. "You gone catch yo death," she said, but she sounded like she was thinking of somebody else.

"Where's Momma?"

"Out drivin."

"What y'all doing in the dark?" he asked, peeking out from beneath the towel.

"Lights is out," Sweet Pea answered.

"And we can't go home cause the river suppose to flood," Creola said. "Again."

The way everybody slowly nodded their heads up and down, Johnny could tell they were really sad. Since Levi's arrest yesterday, they had been low. Even Maggie's "Praise Jesus" sounded wobbly to him.

"Fourth time this year," Sweet Pea said glumly. "Get a little rain and the bottom gets flooded out ever time." She was slumped over in her chair, her arms propped against her legs. The cleft between her breasts was more prominent than ever. Vida jerked Johnny's eyes away as she continued to towel his hair.

"Nobody gone build no levee for colored folks, that's for sho," complained Creola. Her wet red hair was hanging stringy from her head, making her already huge round face appear more balloon-like than usual.

"Yeah," Sweet Pea grumbled, "Miss Hertha put Misery's house up on stilts. I bet she down there grinnin like a pink-eyed albino possum, sittin high and dry up in her tree."

A clap of thunder shook the house, but only Johnny jumped.

The sound of stamping feet came from the back porch, like somebody trying to shock the mud off their shoes. A moment later, Hazel entered smiling at everybody, but when she opened her mouth to speak, the dreary scene in her kitchen silenced her. She walked over to Vida, who was standing at her place by the sink, looking forlorn. "Oh, Vida, I'm so sorry. I heard em tell it on the radio."

"Tell what?" Johnny asked.

"Now I'm sure it's for the best. Your daddy will be better off in Jackson. The sheriff was right to ask for it."

"He ain't there yet, Miss Hazel. You don't know the sheriff. Lot can happen between here and Jackson," Vida said, close to tears. "And Miss Hazel, the sheriff won't let me see my daddy. Only way I gets to see him is if I stand in front of the jailhouse and stare up at him in his window. He always there, lookin down through his bars like a zoo animal. Everbody pointin they fingers at him. Callin him names. Laughin."

Hazel put her arm around Vida. The other maids glanced at each other, their eyes big.

"He didn't do it, Miss Hazel. They framin him."

"I'm sure they are, Vida," Hazel comforted her. "It's a shame on everybody claiming to be a white person."

"But I know for a fact he didn't. I got Miss Delia's letter. I knows who did it."

"Who?" Hazel asked. "If you know, you got to tell it to the sheriff and get your father set loose."

There was a disbelieving silence. Vida and the maids shook their heads and then laughed sadly at Hazel.

"What?" Hazel asked, hurt. "Why y'all laughing at me?"

"Nothin, Miss Hazel. Just what you said. You done marked off the difference between being white and being colored as clear as if you drawed a line in the dirt."

The maids laughed again.

Flustered, Hazel said, "I don't know what you talking about."

"Let me count it out to you plain. First off, we colored. We ain't got no sheriff. And second off, I seen the evidence. I know who kilt Miss Delia. But it comes back around again to me bein colored. How's a colored woman gone speak out and get believed? Well, she ain't."

There was a chorus of "that's right" from the maids.

Vida picked up steam. She started counting on her fingers for emphasis, which reminded Hazel uneasily of Floyd. "And third off, I'm *still* colored. How can I speak out the first word if that word is against the sheriff *hisself*."

"That's the truth," Creola hollered and Sweet Pea chimed in with an "amen."

"And fourth off," Vida said, "if I do say that first word, it will sure as hell be my last one. You know why?"

"Cause you colored?" Hazel ventured.

That brought a response of grievous howling from the maids.

"That's right, Miss Hazel. That's why we was laughin at you."

"You saying Billy Dean Brister did it?" Hazel sounded doubtful.

"Makes me so damned mad," Vida grumbled to herself and then surveyed the room. "We a piteous sight. Things keep comin down on top of us like that storm outside and all we can do is just sit around in the dark with our tails tucked."

Hazel pulled up a chair, let Johnny climb into her lap, and sat with the maids in silence, listening to the rain drumming on the tin roof over the porch. Finally, after the rain had slacked off to a sprinkle, Hazel spoke up. "You know what helps me when I don't think I can take it no more? A little drive. Never fails to get me cheered up."

Vida looked at her like she had cracked, but Hazel insisted, "Let's all go for a ride. Come on, now! Everybody in the car."

Johnny jumped down from her lap, excited to go with his mother, but the maids only stared at her. Hazel went around the room grabbing their arms and pulling them up off their chairs, one by one. By the time she had herded them onto the porch, the rain had completely stopped and the wind had died. It was deathly still. The skies were an eerie coke-bottle green. There was an unholy calm all around, like tragedy suspended in midair. Tornado weather.

Hazel wasn't deterred. On the way down to the car she told them all about a man she met last week on one of her drives who said when he was a boy he was picked up by a tornado and carried clear into another county, at a mile a minute, and set down unharmed into the Pearl River. Hazel said, "He tole me you got to cooperate and not fight it. Since I had heard that, I've felt real peaceful about the weather."

Hazel situated herself behind the wheel and Vida scooted over next to her. Sweet Pea took the front seat window. Creola and Maggie loaded in the back, wedging Johnny between them.

"Lawdy, Mercy!" Creola called out from behind. "We gone sho nuf bust out the sprangs in Miss Hazel's new car!"

"Don't you worry about nothing, Creola," Hazel reassured her. "Everything's paid for." She opened up her purse, retrieved a little blue bottle, and handed it to Vida.

"This is yo hootch." Vida said, taken aback.

"It just don't do nothin for me no more," Hazel explained. "Take it. Y'all just sit back and relax. Enjoy the ride." Hazel mashed the gas pedal and the big Lincoln roared, taking off like a rocket for where the sun was about to break through the clouds.

They drove along winding roads, through masses of trees and vines growing so dense that the inside of the Lincoln would grow dark and cool, until they burst out again into the dazzling light of open fields. Confident and in charge, Hazel worked the wheel like a Talledega pro. No terrain could discourage her. She took back roads—gravel, dirt, sand, washboard, rutted, overgrown, and completely washed out. She navigated abandoned logging trails and mere pig paths. When it looked too muddy to continue on and everybody swore she would have to back herself out, Hazel would swerve off onto a shift road appearing out of nowhere and skirt the bog completely.

Even Vida was impressed.

Hazel drove up along ridges and down into the hollows, splashing full speed across wet-weather branches where there seemed to be no path at all and picking up a trail again out of thin air. Hazel took them to places the Indians had never seen. Deer and wild turkey and foxes seemed as surprised as the maids when the Lincoln stole into some uncharted patch of wilderness. Now and then, when everybody was sure she had gotten them lost, Hazel would pull the car over, and heading off on foot, she would reach behind a log or into the hollow of a tree or under a gnarly root and return with another blue bottle and hand it to Vida, telling her to pass it around. But Hazel didn't touch a drop.

The passengers surrendered to Hazel's driving, as they might lose themselves in the lament of a soul-scarred blues veteran or in the words and cadence of a revivalist burning with the holy spirit or in the rhythm of an old woman piecing up a quilt with fingers skittering along patches at the speed of lightning. It was obvious that Hazel was inspired. Creola turned to Johnny and said with reverence in her voice, "Yo momma can drive like Peter can preach." That sounded about right to everybody.

As the sun began to set, they came upon a pasture blanketed with a smoky mist. "Look," Creola said pointing to the field. "The rabbits is cookin they supper!"

"Ain't it purty," Sweet Pea said wistfully. "Looks like a cloud bedding down for the night."

With the cool November wind blowing gently in her face, Hazel inhaled deeply. "Don't this make you feel free as a bird? Nobody in the world to bring you down."

Turning to Hazel, Vida said in a sad voice, her words a little slurred, "But that's just it, Miss Hazel. We ain't free. Don't seem like we ever gone get free."

Hazel nodded like she had heard it all before. However, she was careful not to say anything, lest she encourage this kind of talk. No telling where it could lead.

But Vida continued. "One day we gone take our freedom. Gone stop waitin for somebody to give it to us in the sweet by and by." Vida took a quick little nip. "Anyway, I figger freedom really ain't yores unless you take it. Nothing free if you owin somebody for it. Nobody give it to Rosie. No ma'am. She reached out and snatched it from the white man."

The maids erupted into a chorus of "uh-huhs" and "that's rights." Nobody could mention Rosie without soliciting some kind of heartfelt response from the maids.

"Now Vida," Hazel cautioned, "that's civil righter's talk. You got to mind where you say things like that. We all free in this car, but when we get out, we got our places. You have to be careful. People might take you for an agitator."

Feeling no pain, Sweet Pea stuck her head out the window and yelled "Agitator! Agitator!" She snatched the bottle from Vida and took a swig. Wiping her mouth she said, "I'm sick of y'all white folks blamin ever thang on agitators." She passed the bottle back to Maggie.

Maggie just held to it tightly, looking a little confused as to why somebody had handed her a bottle of laxative. "Take it to the Lord in prayer!" she sang softly.

Reaching across Johnny, Creola eased the bottle from Maggie's grip. "I'm sick of it, too," Creola added. "And I don't even know what a agitator is. Sounds like somethin go crawlin round in the swamps."

Hazel said she wasn't real sure herself what one was, but whatever it was, it was up to no good, and that they should make sure they didn't mess with any. It might get them shot or hung or drowned. "And I seen it done," she said, thinking of the boy in the river.

"We all gotta die sometime," Vida said, sounding resigned to it. "What's the difference how? Only matters why."

"Might as well be somethin you believe in," Sweet Pea said.

"That's right," Vida said. "My daddy sittin in jail thinkin he gone die for the vote. Instead everybody wonts to get at him for drownin a damned white woman. And he didn't even do it." Vida pounded her fist on the padded dash. "White man done took everthang he got. Only thing left was his story. And I'll be damned if they didn't go and snatch that too."

"Poor Rev'run Snow." Sweet Pea began to cry. "Now he was a righteous man. He was surely lookin on the face of God. And such a good-lookin man, too."

"Y'all stop talking like that," Hazel said firmly. "Levi ain't dead. And Vida, you wrong. I do care how you die."

Vida thought about that for a moment and turned to Hazel. "But do you care how I got to live?"

"I don't understand what you saying," Hazel said, not at all enjoying the turn in the conversation. They had been having such a nice time.

"I know you don't wont me to die, but that ain't enough," Vida said, and took a quick pull on the bottle before continuing. "Bein my friend and all like you say, you got to wont me to live my life free and equal."

"You talking to the wrong person. I ain't free neither. Just one mistake away from being sent back to the State Hospital myself. They got a bed with my name on it."

"Well, maybe you got some figurin to do, too, Miss, Hazel. But for me, I'm getting more like my daddy everday."

"Tell it now," Creola called out.

"You know I got a little boy out there I ain't never gone see. He ain't ever gone know me for a momma. I has to live with that I reckon. I can't raise him up to do right nor wrong. Can't help him with his homework. I missed teaching him everthang a momma needs to teach a chile. But my daddy say they is one thing I can leave him."

No one spoke. Except for Hazel, this was the first anyone had heard of a boy wandering the land without his momma.

"Daddy say I can leave Nate *my* story. And my story is how I live out my life. I can live it afraid or I can live it strong. I don't understand it all my own self. But Daddy say if we live our story, we get to pass it on. If I try to live strong and free, somehow that make Nate mo strong and free, where ever he be at."

Nodding to herself, she said, "That's what I done decided to leave my son. A free life."

Hazel was nodding now, too. "What you want me to do, Vida?"

Without hesitating, Vida answered, "Walk with me to the courthouse and say 'this here is a first-class citizen who wonts to vote.'"

"Amen!" Sweet Pea seconded, before Maggie could even open her mouth.

But Vida wasn't through. "Let's you and me go to Micky's Diner and tell the waitress you wont a table for the two of us."

"Uh-hunh!" Creola called out from the back. "I wonts to go in there with y'all. Where it's air-cooled and they set yo food down on a table in a china plate and not shove a greasy bag at you through a window in the alley."

"And," Vida said, "when we pass somebody you know on the street, I wont you to say, real proud like, 'This is my friend, *Miss* Vida Snow.'"

Everybody in the car was quiet now, imagining such a thing. Finally, Sweet Pea announced, "I gots to pish like a racehorse."

They decided it was a good time to drop into One Wing Hannah's and see her brand-new indoor toilet. They heard she had put a sign above the tank that said, "Flush God Dammit!"

As they sat about the table at the jook with a new bottle, Johnny in his mother's lap, the women told their secrets. For the first time Vida told about how she came to have a boy named Nate. And Hazel told about how she came to lose a boy named Davie. Creola cried about never having chick nor child to lose. Trembling like a virgin, Sweet Pea told about her first and only true love. Hannah came over scratching her wig to see what all the crying was about and plopped herself down and told right out about how she once loved a woman like a man, and damned if she had found anything since to beat it. Maggie sang a hymn so fractured nobody could recognize it to sing along, but everybody knew it was from her heart anyway.

It was going on ten o'clock by the time Hazel had dropped off the maids and returned to the house. She hoped she might be able to sneak Johnny up to his room before Floyd discovered them home, but he was waiting for them in the kitchen and fit to be tied. Word had already got back to him that his wife had been seen as far as fifty miles away riding around with a carload of colored maids. Somebody from the filling station called and said most of the bunch looked pie-eyed drunk. And with tornadoes touching down all over the county!

First thing, he threatened to take Hazel's car away. She drew herself up and said fiercely, "You do and I'll leave you for sure."

"Where would you go?" Floyd scoffed. "How would you live?"

Without missing a beat, Hazel shot back, "I'd move in with Vida. I'd help her clean houses. I'd wait tables at One Wing Hannah's. See what that does to your year-end closeout."

That stopped Floyd, but only for a moment. "Do you want me to send you back to Whitfield? You know I could have you committed again. There ain't a judge in four counties that ain't already heard about you riding those niggers around and having a high ol' time." Floyd looked down at Johnny, as if noticing him there beside his mother for the first time. "And with innocent children!"

"Don't say nigger no more. It ain't dignified and we don't like it."

"Don't tell me what dignified is, not after what you been up to. And who the hell is 'we'?" Floyd asked. "You're a white woman, for god's sakes. You got it all. Any other woman'd be proud to be the wife of a Lincoln dealer. Any other woman would take advantage of that situation and make a place for herself in the community. Get in the Trois Arts League. Join the Baptist Ladies Auxiliary. Raise money for the Lottie Moon Offering so the missionaries can save the niggers in deepest Africa."

Hazel opened her mouth to object.

"Excuse me," Floyd said bitterly. "*Colored* people. But not you. You want to throw it all away. And take me down with you. Well, no deal, Lucille! I won't let you do it."

"Send me away then, Floyd," Hazel yelled back. "Tell them to snip the wires in my head this time, why don't you? Matter a fact, why don't you cut out a magazine picture of the kind of woman who would make you happy, tack it on my forehead, and tell them doctors to have at it. Don't accept delivery till I meet your factory specifications."

Turning on her heels, Hazel stormed away, and Floyd, stunned, listened to her stomps recede up the stairs. Her bedroom door slammed shut.

Johnny and Floyd now stood alone in the kitchen. As Johnny watched his father, waiting for him to say something, he noticed a color in his face he had never seen before, a kind of cherry-red heading toward grape. His daddy's eyes were anxiously searching the kitchen, as if he were looking for something to turn off or on. Up or down. Anything he could make do what he wanted it to. Finally they settled on Johnny, who stood there wearing his Sunday pants on a Friday. "Go buy you some blue jeans," he snapped.

"But…" Johnny said.

Floyd didn't hear him. He was busy storming out the back door.

Chapter 45
THE ROSA PARKS LEAGUE

Hazel angle-parked in front of the two-story redbrick building that sat across the square from the courthouse. Not wanting to draw any unnecessary attention, Vida willingly occupied her customary spot in the backseat. Today they were making a visit to the Hopalachie County Jail.

Vida slowly got out of the car, dreading the encounter with the sheriff. When she looked up, she froze. Through the bars of a second-story window, she saw her father, his body swaying from side to side, the way he used to do in the heat of his sermons. He seemed to be gazing down upon her, his face vacant, but his mouth moving to form words she could not make out. Vida felt Hazel's hand touch her shoulder.

"You all right?" she heard Hazel ask.

Vida nodded, still looking up at her father.

"Still want to do this?"

Vida nodded again, but Hazel could feel a tremble under her hand. "Well, then, let's go on ahead, OK?" Hazel said tenderly, and then guided Vida toward the jail.

It had been Vida's idea for Hazel to go along with her to see Levi. That morning after breakfast, Vida had explained, "Daddy been there for two days and the sheriff ain't let me in. And even if I do get in, probly won't let me out agin. I need me a white woman there."

"Vida, maybe you're exaggerating," Hazel said. "After all, he's the law, now. Maybe he's changed since before." Hazel had always been partial to the sheriff and never forgot how he had pulled her out of many a tight spot, not once laughing at her or scolding her or making her feel stupid.

"Miss Hazel, I'm tellin you. You seen the letter."

"But she didn't say Billy Dean was going to kill her."

"He got to be the one who killed Miss Delia." Vida was annoyed at having to explain this again. "She was blackmailin him, Miss Hazel."

Hazel looked doubtful.

"Well, what would you call telling him to leave Miss Hertha and run away with her and be the daddy to her baby, and if he didn't she would tell him on the Senator? Now the sheriff I remembers ain't gone stand for that. No ma'am, he ain't changed." Then she said fervently, "He tole me personal he would kill before losin what he got. He be the kind that takes matters in his own hand. Believe me, I knows."

"Well, Vida," Hazel said sadly, "You know I got my own opinions about this Delia."

"Yes'm. I know."

"And if you ask me, she can't be trusted to be dead. I don't believe a word she wrote."

Even though she still wasn't convinced, Hazel had agreed to go. Maybe she could show Vida how Billy Dean Brister was nobody to be afraid of.

When they walked through the door of the jailhouse, Hazel first and Vida close behind, hugging a bag with a change of clothes for her father, they entered a large open area with several wooden desks scattered about. A couple of deputies were standing in the center of the room talking. Behind them were barred gun racks filled with fierce-looking weapons. Over in the corner was a closed door with a frosted glass pane that read "SHERIFF" in big black letters.

The only desk occupied at the moment was a shabby one just outside a low wood railing, running across the front of the room for no other apparent purpose than to give the inner area more of an official status. Sitting there at the desk-in-exile was a plain young blonde, who was eyeing the two women curiously.

"Yes, ma'am?" she said to Hazel, talking over the crackling of a dispatch radio that took up most of the desk.

"I'm Hazel Graham and I—"

Just then the corner office door swung open and Billy Dean Brister stuck his head out, his mouth already fixed to yell something at the blonde. When he saw the two women, he smiled instead and sauntered up to where they stood by the blonde's desk. "Miss Hazel," he said, nodding like he was happy to see her. "How can I help you today?"

Vida glowered at Hazel. The woman was blushing like a schoolgirl.

"Well, Sheriff. We—me and Vida—are here to visit with Levi Snow. If you don't mind."

The sheriff looked as if the request amused him, and then he glanced back at the blonde, who was also smiling. "Any reason I should mind, Rose?" he asked the blonde.

Rose shrugged her shoulders at the sheriff's question. Billy Dean looked back at Hazel. "No, I don't mind. It ain't like he's under arrest or anything."

"What!" Vida and Hazel gasped at the same time.

"I ain't charged him with nothing. Not yet, anyway. He's in what we call protective custody. I hear there might be those who want to do him bodily harm."

Billy Dean shook his head at the thought of such a thing, and then sat down on the railing and crossed his arms. "I don't even keep the door locked. No call to. That old man don't wont to be nowhere in the world but in that cell. Don't that beat all?"

"See, Vida," Hazel said. "Things aren't as bad as you think. He ain't even arrested. Ain't we been stupid!" Turning to the sheriff, she gushed, "I sure am glad you looking out for him."

Vida tried her best to scald Hazel with her look.

"Well, Miss Hazel, since we swappin compliments," the sheriff said, "I think it's real generous for you to take a interest in somebody everbody else is out to hang." At the mention of hanging, he smiled big at Vida, acknowledging her presence for the first time. She looked down, horrified.

To Hazel he said, "But I guess you've heard all the talk."

"It's terrible, ain't it?" Hazel exclaimed. "That's why I was so pleased to hear them say you were going to get him to Jackson. That's real gracious of you to go to so much trouble."

Vida clenched her teeth. The woman was talking as if she were on a date with the man!

"We tryin our best. But it ain't done yet. Our illustrious head of the city council, Hayes Alcorn, don't agree with me on it. Wants to keep him close by. Might be out of my hands." He shrugged and said with a smile, "But that's enough shop talk. We do what we can, don't we, Miss Hazel?"

When Vida saw Hazel blushing again, her eyes all starry, she blurted, "Can I see my daddy?"

Even Vida seemed surprised at her own abruptness. She dropped her eyes again and mumbled, "Please, sir."

"Right to the point, ain't she?" he said to Hazel. "I see your generosity also extends to his family. That's mighty brave of you."

Hazel smiled stupidly and started to say, "We do what we can," like he had done, but she came to her senses and asked, "What do you mean, Sheriff? Brave?"

Billy Dean grinned. "Oh, nothing really. Except maybe to keep that girl on as your maid and all. The daughter of the nigger suspected by most people of murderin a white woman. I'd call that brave. Or something."

Hazel was red again, but it wasn't from puppy love. She looked down at Vida, uncertain, and again at the sheriff. In a trembling voice she said, "Now, I don't much like you calling Vida a nigger, Sheriff Brister. That ain't good manners."

"Well, Miss Hazel. You could be right about my manners," the sheriff said loud enough for the deputies in the back to overhear. "But if you are, I suspect in your case it would be a lucky guess. Where I come from, it ain't mannered for a white woman to drive around jookin it up with a carload of niggers."

Hazel stood there with her mouth agape. She heard snickering coming from somewhere in the office but she was too ashamed to look.

"Well, if that's all," the sheriff said, rising from his perch. "I'll get my deputy to take you and your *friend* here upstairs to see our guest. Enjoy your visit." The sheriff turned and as he headed back toward his office, he shouted, "Lampkin! See if you can't help the girls, here. And check the nigger's paper sack. Make sure Miss Hazel ain't planning on serving no illegal beverages while she's up there." There was outright laughing this time.

⚜

"Daddy!" Vida cried when they opened his cell door. "You all right? They hurt you any?" She ran into his arms. His beard had grown and his suit was stale, but he seemed unharmed. He looked happy to see her.

Levi smiled at Hazel and nodded, but she didn't notice. Numb with shame, Hazel walked into the cell with them, but edged over into the corner, between the bars and the cot. She stood there silent, her eyes on the cement floor.

Looking back at Vida, Levi said, "I'm fine, daughter. I took that first step and the next move is His. Like the Good Book says, It ain't meant for man to direct his own footsteps."

"Oh, Daddy. Can't you leave that alone? It ain't gettin you nowhere but in trouble."

Levi's face seemed to glow. "It ain't trouble. They finally listenin to me, Vida. That's because the Lord give me a story to live. The people always need a story to look to. When the people don't have no vision, the Lord say they shall perish."

"Daddy, you got to stop it! Don't you know what story they tellin about you? It ain't the one about you standin up to the white man and askin for the vote. They sayin' you went crazy and killed a white girl." Grasping him by the arms, she cried, "Daddy, they sayin you drowned Miss Delia."

He looked down at Vida. There was a glint of remembering in his eyes. "Miss Delia. I knew her since the day she was born. The Senator named her after his momma. Pretty little baby. Willful, too."

"They say they can prove it. They found yo watch chain down by that whirlpool, Daddy."

"My chain?" Levi touched his vest. "I ain't got my chain, Vida. Couldn't find it nowhere. Remember how Nate used to love that chain? How he wouldn't nod off till he could take a holt of it in that little hand of his? He'd grip it till daylight, wouldn't he?"

Vida shook her father and began shouting at him. "Daddy! Don't go off on me now. Listen! What you think it mean the sheriff puts you in here with the door unlocked? Don't you understand? Anybody can get at you. Maybe kill you. Daddy, I'm scared."

But Levi's face was serene. He whispered to his daughter, "I tole you, Vida, don't be scared of the darkness."

"Daddy, the sheriff say you ain't under arrest. Let's go home. Maybe Willie can find a way to get you out of Delphi."

"Vida, God done set everythin in motion. I got to stay and keep my promises. He's sho keepin His." He beamed at his daughter. "Look here!" He walked over to touch the back wall of his cell. "See. A church of rock." And then he reached for the barred window from which she had spied him earlier. "A pulpit of iron."

Vida slumped down to the cot, her eyes staring disbelieving at her father. "Oh, my Lord, Miss Hazel. What we gone do?"

There was no answer. Vida looked over to see Hazel still standing there in the corner, wooden. "Miss Hazel, don't you go mindless on me, too. Somebody need to get aholt of this thing. It's liable to throw us all off in the creek."

Hazel looked down at Vida. "Let's go home, Vida. Please?"

In Hazel's kitchen, Vida fixed a pot of coffee and the two sat down at the table, neither speaking. They were well into their second cup when Vida broke the silence. "If my daddy bound and determined to die," she announced, "at least I wont them tellin the right story at his grave. I got to let people know."

"How you gonna do that?" Hazel said sullenly, still smarting from her rough treatment at the jailhouse. "You said yourself nobody was gonna listen to a colored woman."

"Well," Vida said carefully, "maybe you could help."

"Me?" Hazel checked to see if she was joking. When she saw Vida was serious, Hazel dropped her eyes to her cup. "I guess you could tell today how much weight I carry around here."

"So you givin up? Just cause you got treated like a nigger one day of yo life, you gone quit?"

"You don't need me," Hazel said. "I'll just get in the way. Can't you see? I'm the town joke."

Vida reached for Hazel's hand. "Miss Hazel, what I *sees* is a woman who tole the baddest man in this here county not to call her friend a nigger. Ain't nobody else I know gone do that. What I *sees* is a woman who got so much dignity that she willin to share some with a friend."

Hazel began to mist up, but before she could get too far, Vida pulled her hand back. "And the fact of business is, I need yo help."

"To do what?" Hazel asked. "To get yourself killed?"

Vida gave Hazel a determined look. "It's what I *got* to do."

"It's what you gotta do, huh?"

They were both quiet for a while, avoiding each other's eyes. A few moments later, as she studied her coffee cup, Hazel smiled to herself. "Vida," she said, "you gonna be like that turtle, ain't you?"

Vida looked at her blankly. "What turtle?"

Grinning slyly, like she was teasing a child, Hazel said, "I know somebody who's gonna cross that road somehow or the other, even if it means getting run over."

That made Vida laugh. "How's yo little saying go again, Miss Hazel?"

With a stern look, Hazel said in her deepest voice, "Like I always say, Vida, you can only help a thing in the direction it's headed."

Vida laughed again. "I believe you right. That's as good as anythin Mr. Floyd ever come up with."

All the maids were game for the idea, except for Missouri of course, whom they knew better than to ask. Her allegiances were no secret. But the next day when they met in Hazel's kitchen, they were stumped over just how to go about getting the true story out.

"Can't go to the preachers," Sweet Pea said, rubbing her chin. "They carry it back to the sheriff like a dog totin a bone,"

"Can't take out an ad in *The Jackson Daily News*," Hazel said. "That's for sure."

"Maybe we do like the white folks does," Creola suggested. "The ones that be tryin to get elected. Take the word door to door and talks to the peoples."

"Take a year," Vida said, her tone harsh. "Daddy ain't got a year."

"It's somethin," Creola said. Then she grumbled to herself, "Ain't heard nothin better comin from nobody else."

"Now if we had the vote—" Sweet Pea began.

"We ain't," Vida said, cutting her off.

Sweet Pea looked over at Creola and lifted her brows. Creola gave her a "welcome to the club" look. Maggie shifted her weight and opened her mouth to speak, looked around the group, and closed it again.

After a spell of silence, Creola asked offhandedly, "What do it take to get the vote? When I was in school they razor-bladed them words out of my book."

"Three things," Vida growled, lifting her fingers for the count. "One, you got to pass they readin and writin test. Two, you got to pay they poll tax. Three, you got to be white. Any more questions?" she asked scornfully.

All four women stared at Vida with hard, sharp looks. Finally she dropped her head and shook it. "I'm sorry for it," she said. "I'm as ill as a hornet today. Guess it's gettin to me. It was my idea and now it's me who don't see no hope in it."

Creola waved it off. "I just thought you was bound and determined to carry the load yoself."

"We just wonts to help," Sweet Pea said. "This thang be everbody's problem."

"Well, maybe so," Vida conceded. "But I can't think of no idea ain't gone end up gettin us all killed. I don't wont that on my head."

Creola spoke up. "I had an ol' uncle used to say the way to get supper is to aim at one rabbit at a time. And the way to go hungry is to aim at all of em at once."

"I like it," Hazel said. "What's it mean?"

"Well, I always suspicioned the reason the sheriff never have no trouble with the colored is he keeps his aim to one person at a time. Picks us off easy that way. But supposin we gets together like they did in Montgomery. Crowd the courthouse with rabbits. Get a bunch of colored people to take that test and show him we can vote him out of office next time if we take a mind to. Let him know we all is watchin him. Sheriff

won't know where to aim first less he hits some white man's favorite nigger in broad daylight. What he gone do then?" Creola hooted at the
thought. "He be staggerin round like a blind dog in a meathouse."

"You think it would really work?" Hazel asked.

"Well, all I know, it sho be Mr. Hayes's worst nightmare come true.
Coloreds linin up to vote. Must be somethin to it."

"You right there!" Sweet Pea cried out. "If the white man is so fraid of
us gettin the vote, then I magine we closer to it than we think. Anyways,
it'd sho make the sheriff think twiced about hurtin Rev'run Snow. Just
can't go pushin our people round no mo."

Creola slammed her mighty foot on the floor, making everybody
jump. "Sho it'll work! I bet you a fat man that it do. Specially if we get some
upstandin colored folks to show up with us."

For a while everyone was silent, like they were testing the weight of the
idea. Vida began mulling it over aloud. "It'd sho nuf need to be a mob of
us. Even then it ain't gone be safe."

"He'd probably go for the ringleaders after dark," Creola said.

"And the timin's real bad," Sweet Pea added. "Pickin season about over
and they don't have no use for coloreds till spring. What's a few dead ones
now?"

Creola frowned. "Kill a nigger hire a new one. Kill a mule buy a new
one. That's sho what they say."

Then Vida began nodding to herself. "How be ever, it sho would be a
way to start gettin the truth out about who killed Miss Delia for real." Vida
nodded faster, like she was pumping up her conviction from a deep well.

But Creola had already caught fire, so excited she was visibly shaking.
"We oughta get ever thang writ down on some handbills like them politicians do, splainin bout the vote and the test and the poll tax and about
what kind of sheriff we got and how we can throw his sorry butt out next
time if we all stick together. We tell em bout Rosie and them buses and
bout bein 'too tired to move'!" Creola said it again, louder, "Too tired to
move!"

"Tell it to Jesus!" Maggie sang out.

"We need us a mimeograph machine," Hazel suggested, sounding so smart she felt the need to explain herself. "I used to get the circulars done for the Tupelo Drugstore. Now who in Delphi got one we can borry?"

"Oh, won't Rev'run Snow be so proud!" Sweet Pea squealed. "Look like he started somethin after all. He some kind of special man." She had stars in her eyes.

Vida scanned the joyous faces in the kitchen and then shook her head. "Y'all know this is crazy, don't y'all? Crazy as any thang Daddy ever did. Chances are we gone end up dead." But her comments didn't seem to dampen the growing enthusiasm in the room.

"I feel funny bout it myself," Creola said. "I know it be dangerous. I know we liable to get blowed up. And I sho is scared. But it's a good kind of scared. Like my belly tryin to tickle up against my backbone. So scared make me wont to rise up and dance it out. What is that, you reckon?"

"I know exactly what it is," Hazel said, smiling big, again feeling the expert. "It's hope, Creola. Pure-dee, one hundred proof hope."

Chapter 46
DELIA'S LAST REQUEST

The sheriff opened the door of his cruiser and stepped out onto the pavement. The stabbing pain was about to split his skull clean open. He quickly scanned the courthouse square. It was empty except for the old men sitting on the benches under the pecan trees, as stone-still as the Confederate soldier. Like old cats they were soaking up the weak November sun. He closed his eyes for a moment against the afternoon glare. Then he zipped his leather jacket, lit up a cigarette, and stepped across the street to the jailhouse.

As the sheriff walked up to her desk to collect his messages, Rose said, "Hayes Alcorn is in your office."

"Where's he been?" he asked, shuffling through the papers in the wire basket. "I ain't seen him but six times today already."

Rose pulled out an envelope from her drawer and purred, "Another letter came today, Billy Dean, you old dog." She winked and held the lavender envelope with swirls of cream up to her nose. "Smells nice, too. Expensive."

"Shut up, Rose, will you do that for me?" Billy Dean snatched the letter from her hand and quickly tucked it away in his jacket pocket. Then grinning at her like he didn't mean it, he said, "Go buy me another pack of BCs, would you, honey? I'm almost out again and my brain's commitin suicide against my skull."

He walked into his office to find Hayes pacing back and forth across the floor in quick, energetic steps. His stride was barely long enough to take two tiles at a time.

"Hello, Hayes. Long time no see. What's it been, ten minutes?"

"It ain't funny, Billy Dean. I just talked to Jackson. I told them we don't need any help tending to our problems. We can handle things nicely here."

"You shouldn't ought to have done that, Hayes. Now I might have to go over your head." The sheriff had to smile at that.

Hayes planted his hands on his hips. Billy Dean thought he looked like a little loving cup and couldn't help but smile again. "Billy Dean, you obviously see some humor in the situation, but just you listen. I'm gonna have your job for this. You hear me?"

"I been hearin you all week, Hayes. I just think it's best if we get the nigger out of town."

Billy Dean dropped his cigarette to the floor and crushed it under the toe of his boot. "We ain't got the manpower to protect him night and day. No tellin what could happen if he stayed here. I don't want to be the one's responsible."

"I told you, you won't be. If anything happens, it's the people of Mississippi who will take credit."

"That sounds good and all, but—"

"What's got into you, Billy Dean? You the last one I would expect holding back popular justice. And you not even charging the man yet. That's not sitting well with folks. I got to tell you."

"Well, sometimes this is not a popular job."

"Not a popular job! Don't give me that crap!" Hayes let out a derisive laugh. "If it meant keeping this job, you'd be out there throwing up the rope yourself. What's your angle?"

"Well, Hayes. We don't have a body. We don't have a witness to the killing. We don't know for sure she's even dead. And you know what I just heard? That's the same place the old man used to go to and shout to Jesus! Could of lost his chain then. Too much circumstantial and not enough meat. I ain't gone kill the Senator's boyhood nigger and have it come up that somebody else did the deed." What he didn't say was that his worst fear was for Levi to get lynched and then Delia decide to show up. He might as well climb up in the tree with Levi.

Hayes wasn't buying it. "Bullshit, Billy Dean! You are bullshittin me and I know it. I can smell it from here. You got something else going on the side."

"Yeah right, Hayes. You found me out. I just love gettin calls from sawed-off little fuckers like you twenty times a day tellin me my business so they can go out and get elected governor. It just tickles me seeing my name in the paper, callin me soft on the niggers. It does my heart good to tell Delia's daddy that he's just gonna have to hold off on his revenge a little longer. You onto me, Hayes. It's a laugh a minute."

"Goddammit, Billy Dean, I'm telling you. If you send that nigger to Jackson, I'm gonna—"

"I know, Hayes, you gonna have my job. Well, stand in line. Ever damned body wants my job this week." Billy Dean patted Hayes on the head and smiled. "And I got to tell you Hayes, they's bigger boys in line ahead of you."

At that Hayes just sputtered something incoherent and spun on his heels.

"Governor my ass," Billy Dean growled and kicked the door shut, rattling the glass. He stood dead still waiting for the vibrations from the banging door to finish ricocheting against his skull. Now the pain was like a hot poker behind his eyes. He reached up and switched on the air conditioner that stuck out of a hole in the wall above his desk. It shuddered for a moment like a wounded beast before it settled into a dull, deadening roar. Billy Dean tore open the envelope and read the letter.

"Shit," he said. He wadded it up and threw it against the wall. Shutting his eyes tight, he dropped back into his chair, and held his head, which was now exploding from the sudden burst of rage. After a few moments, he sighed and said out loud. "You ain't leaving me much wiggle room, are you, girl?"

He thought Hertha had been conniving. What'd the Senator do, raise em both on rattlesnake milk? Delia had it thought through and through, down to putting the tail on the z. She knew when she staged her drowning, with the horse and scarf and the whole show, her daddy would assume the worst like he always did, and then, just like he always did, put the screws to Billy Dean. She had it figured just right. There would have to be a body and a killer or he was out of a job. But the kicker was, he couldn't kill the killer. Not even a nigger. Couldn't even charge him.

As soon as he brought the poor slob to trial, Delia would jump out of the bushes yelling, "Perjury!" Her and her daddy would see to it he was picking cotton, chained ankle to ankle with the same niggers Billy Dean himself had sent off to prison.

She hadn't left him one single hole to crawl out of. Had him right by the short ones. Any false move on his part and she shows up a wronged woman, pointing fingers. Delia was bound and determined not to have this baby without his name stamped on its forehead.

"I'm being generous," she had told him. "I could force your hand now, Billy Dean. But I'm giving you some time to put your affairs in order. This way you can ask for a divorce like a man. I'd hate for people to think you were marrying me because I was holding a gun to your head."

Yeah, right, he thought.

That's when he threatened to kill her. Probably wasn't the wisest thing to do. Knowing Delia, it only made her want him more. His only stroke of luck so far in this whole deal was when that crazy nigger came along, begging to go to jail. It was like he was sent by God. Didn't even have to arrest him. Loves it there. Acts like he wants Hayes Alcorn to take him out and lynch him. Serve Hayes right if he strung the preacher up. When Delia showed up alive, it would be Hayes's ass the Senator would be after. Make Billy Dean Brister look like the god-damned voice of reason!

The sheriff picked up the letter and smoothed it out on his desk. You cocky little bitch. Sending it right through the United States Mail. Directly into the Sheriff's Office of Hopalachie County. With his thumbs he rubbed his throbbing temples. The screws they are a-tightening.

He read the letter again. The final screw in the lid.

Dear Billy Dean,

I hear an old friend of mine is lodging with you. Tell Levi I send my love. You know how I feel about that dear old man, don't you, Billy Dean?

Anyway, I'm sure you're anxious to know the latest. I just got back from the doctor. All is well. December 1 is your drop-dead date. A new year. A new life and a new wife. Have you asked H. for the D. yet?

It's an easy decision, darling, even for you. Come to me or we'll come to
you.

   See how simple?
   Love and devotion,
   Delia

She would do it, too, crying about how ashamed she was and how she had to run away because ol' Billy Dean had done her wrong. Woman loved to shock her daddy. And boy did she hate her sister. Delia would get all three of them with that one shot. The woman could have fought the whole Civil War and never reloaded twice.

   But by god that's what he liked about Delia. Jesus she's a sight.

   December 1. That gave him less than three weeks. Maybe in that time he could put some added pressure on the jooks and bootleggers and slot machine operators. Put a little heat under folks owing back taxes. Get some money stashed. Never again would Billy Dean Brister find himself beholden to one of the Senator's girls for his upkeep. Maybe he could even do a few of those one-shot deals he had his eye on. Siphon off the tax receipts. Pocket a few pieces of his wife's fancy jewelry. Clear out her bank account. Get into her safe deposit box.

   He wondered if he could keep the Senator in line for a little longer, especially with him getting crazier every day, yelling to high heaven for a body like he was. "Lord!" Billy Dean had told him just last night, "I ain't saying that she's dead, Senator, but Lord! Do you know what it would look like if she was to wash up after all this time?"

   Didn't make any difference. "You keep dragging, boy. Throw a net over the Port of New Orleans if you have to."

   Staring at the letter he grumbled, "Right, Delia. Simple as Simon shit." Billy Dean took a headache powder dry.

Chapter 47

A GAME OF CATCH

Floyd was in his office going over the books, preparing for his meeting with Hayes on his loan extension. Even though he had lost a few customers for not firing Vida, the year hadn't been all that bad. But he definitely needed to expand his inventory to compete with those dealers from Memphis and Jackson. It was only a matter of time before they would advertise him right out of business. Maybe he should pick up the whole Ford line, he thought. He had it on good word that next fall they were going to announce a sure-fire winner. They were so confident, they were naming it after Henry Ford's poor dead boy, Edsel.

That sure wouldn't hurt. The Mercurys were turning out to be slow movers. He looked out his back window and saw the red Montclair parked on the side lot. It still hadn't sold. Just sitting there looking at him, serving up a daily reminder of Delia.

Floyd slammed the ledger shut and grabbed another from the stack. Get a holt, he told himself. No need to go all sentimental. Get your mind on business. Remember, it's attitude that determines altitude.

"1954," he sighed opening the ledger. Now that was a good year. Everything under control. Back when he took his own good advice. Floyd had always told himself to stay focused on his own business and don't get caught up in other people's craziness. "Play the game you're in, not the one you ain't," he liked to say. "You make the best time by staying the course." That was just it. Lately he had felt so adrift. There was all this Citizens' Council stuff. He was up to his neck in something that he didn't under-stand. It just wasn't his game, he reckoned. Gave him a queasy feeling. Like seeing Billy Dean with that chain the day before he was supposed to have found one just like it. Now Hayes was lathering at the mouth about a hanging. Boy! They say hill people are nigger-crazy. It was nothing like this in the hills. If it wouldn't kill his business deader than a doornail, he would drop out of that council business. No, this was not his calling at all. Need to stick to your fastball. That's what Floyd always said.

It wasn't just the council. It was his family, too. Hazel driving and drinking like the old days. It was a guaranteed time bomb ready to go off in his face. People were starting to talk again. Why couldn't she drink and sew? Or drink and read? Why did she have to be going ninety to do it? Then there was Johnny. Hell, they got him playing with dolls now! The boy doesn't even have a pair of jeans to get dirty in. Insists on wearing his dress pants to school.

Yep. It was time Floyd stepped in and took that bull by the horns. Let the rest of the world go to hell in a hand bag, but maybe he could at least get back at the head of his own family again. Before it turned and stampeded over him. Floyd figured he was in need of a success on at least some front. "Little successes breed big successes." On his way home, Floyd stopped by the Western Auto.

Floyd walked into Johnny's room and found his son down on the floor. He had about ten homemade dolls with their backs against the wall and another ten facing those. Floyd's spirits lifted a little. "You playin war?"

"It's a square dance," Johnny answered.

Floyd shook his head. He didn't want to know anymore.

Looking up at his dad and seeing the bag in his hand, Johnny jumped to his feet and ran to Floyd, grabbing hold of his leg. "What you bring me in the bag! You get me a present?"

Floyd pulled out his purchases. "Look at this!"

Johnny looked curiously at the fielder's glove and back at his father. "It's a football mitten."

"Close. Want to play a little catch? It ain't the season, but maybe if you like it, one day you can try out for Little League. You never know until you give it a shot. Everything takes practice. Like I always say, a goal without action ain't nothing more than a wish. Hey! I could even coach your team.

How about that?"

Johnny had no idea what Floyd was talking about, but the prospect of playing a game with his daddy delighted him.

"Let's go outside and toss a few," Floyd chirped. Johnny grabbed the glove and ran to the backyard.

Floyd lobbed the first few balls to Johnny and he tried catching them in his ungloved hand. He used the glove as a kind of lid to keep the ball from bouncing out again. Johnny thought he was doing pretty good until his father said, "Catch the ball in the glove, son. That's what it's for."

On that advice, Johnny took off the glove and held it out in front of him with both hands like a net. But the ball kept dropping between his arms.

"Put it on your left hand." His father held up his own. "This one. And then just let the ball drop into the pocket. Where those stitches are."

That didn't seem to help much either. Johnny thought it worked a lot better his way. And he could tell that it wasn't going very well for his daddy by the way he would sigh heavily and draw a little closer after each missed throw. Finally they were only inches apart and his father was merely dropping the balls into Johnny's outstretched glove. They were close enough to talk without breaking out of a whisper.

"How you doing in school?" Floyd asked.

"I like it."

"That's good. That's real good. Your ABCs coming along OK?"

"That's for babies! I can make words. And I can add up apples. And I told the class a story about a turtle that crawled all the way Uptomemphis without getting runned over."

"Where to?"

"Uptomemphis."

"Now that's fine. But don't get the big head. Remember, you don't own success, you only rent it out one day at time."

"Yes, sir," Johnny said, wondering if his daddy had just said something good to him.

Floyd held the ball for a moment. Without looking at Johnny, he asked, "How's your momma doing, son?"

"Huh? Sir?"

His father studied the ball in his hand like he had just found a message stitched in the horsehide. "I mean, you're with her all afternoon. At least I reckon you are. Like when you go on them little drives of hers."

Johnny just stood frozen, the glove still in place to catch the ball that didn't seem to be coming. Finally he looked up guiltily at his father.

"Don't worry. I ain't mad about that no more. It's just that I need some help. We got to watch her, you know, and it would be a great comfort if I knew I could count on you. Are you daddy's boy?"

Cautiously, Johnny nodded his head and waited to see what the answer entitled him to.

"You remember what whiskey smells like, don't you?"

"Medicine," he said without thinking.

Floyd raised his brows. "That what she got you calling it?"

Johnny's face colored up.

"What I want is if you would pay attention to how your momma acts. Anytime she starts talking funny or walking like she's got the blind staggers—you know, like how she used to get—I want you to go up and hug her. If you ever catch that medicine smell again, call me. That way I can come home and help her. Remember when you did that for me before?"

"Uh-huh." Johnny said.

"Well, you saved her life, didn't you?"

"Yes, sir."

"You never can tell about your momma. We got to keep close watch so she don't get herself in trouble again. She's walking close to the edge." Floyd tossed the ball from hand to hand for a minute, mulling something in his mind. Then he said, "I need you to tell me something else." Reaching into his pants pocket, he pulled out one of Hazel's blue bottles. "I found this in her hat box. It's got whiskey in it. Do you know where it come from?"

Johnny dropped his eyes. "I don't know."

"Son, this stuff is illegal in Mississippi. Now we can't have her breaking the law and going to jail, can we? You gonna help me?"

Johnny didn't look up. There was a scuff on his dress shoe that he became obsessed with.

"Well?" his father said. "Look at me when I'm talking to you."

Johnny did look at his father, but remained mute, and the longer he went without speaking, the bigger the cords were becoming in his father's neck. After a while, Floyd cleared his throat and then he kicked at something invisible on the ground, embarrassed. Without a word, he turned away and headed back toward the house, taking the ball with him. Halfway there, he turned back around. His face was wooden.

"I thought I told you to get you some jeans."

"But, I—"

"No buts. Saturday I want you to go to Gooseberry's and tell Sid to fit you in a pair." Floyd tossed the ball in the air once and then snatched it hard. "Some sneakers, too."

"I don't want no jeans," Johnny said firmly, bringing his glove down to his side.

"You need you something to get dirty in."

"I don't want to get dirty."

"All boys like to get dirty," Floyd said flatly. "Don't argue. Just do what I say." Floyd headed back to the house, having to settle for a smaller success than he had planned.

Chapter 48
THE INFORMER

"Rose! Get me a Coke," Billy Dean yelled from his office. "Bout to choke on my BC." When she didn't answer immediately, he stuck his head out the door. "You hear me?"

Rose was talking to a colored man dressed up in a preacher's suit.

"Rose!" he shouted, dry-mouthed, "I'm waitin on my Coke."

Aggravated, she cocked her head toward the man. "Been waiting to see you. Said it was important." She got up and headed for the soft drink box.

Billy Dean studied the colored man as he squished his mouth around mightily to make the headache powder to go down. The man stood there with his hat in his hand, eyes on the floor, waiting to be spoken to. Billy Dean didn't have time for this. He only had a few days left to plan his departure, and he was way behind in amassing his traveling money.

"What you want, preacher? I'm up to my ass in gators today."

The man looked up, unblinking, through steel-rimmed spectacles. His eyelids remained raised up like he was using toothpicks.

"Well, what is it, I said." Billy Dean found himself wondering just what kind of jolt it would take to make the man blink. He took the Coke from Rose.

The man mumbled, "Can I have a word with you, Sheriff? It's o'ficial."

Billy Dean almost spit out his Coke, laughing. "*Oh*—ficial, huh? Whachoo know about official?" Billy Dean shook his head. "Hear that, Rose? It's *oh*—ficial."

"Yessuh," the man said. "It's about Miss Delia."

The smile dropped from Billy Dean's face, and he quickly looked away from Rose. "Yeah? Well, get on in here, I reckon."

Despite the air conditioner pumping a steady breeze into the sheriff's office, big drops of sweat ran down the man's face. Holding his hat in his lap, the man shifted in his seat, waiting for the sheriff to tell him it was OK to start talking. But Billy Dean knew he couldn't act like he was in any big hurry. These preachers were slippery as eels. You had to handle them just so, like a june bug on a string, or they would take off in just the opposite direction of what you needed to know. He told the man he could have a cigarette if he wanted one.

"Now, I don't as a custom, Sheriff Brister, but since you so generous to be offering."

The sheriff nudged the pack just a couple of inches toward the preacher, indicating that it was OK for him to cover the rest of the distance himself.

He rose up in a crouch, and leaned over the desk. Then he fumbled with the red-and-white package, finally wrestling one out. The man sat back down and placed the cigarette ridiculously in the exact center of his mouth, so that it stuck out like a peashooter. He sat there, paralyzed, his look as fixed as a mounted deer. Billy Dean sneered at him. Too scared to even ask for a light.

The sheriff pulled out the nickel-plated lighter from his khakis and sent it sliding across the desk. Visibly trembling, the man held the lighter with both hands, and flicked it three times before he struck fire. He squeezed his eyes shut like he expected an explosion and blindly brought the flame to the cigarette. He pulled weakly and coughed once.

"Real diehard smoker, ain't you?" the sheriff said.

The man rose up out from his chair, and bowing over the desk again, held the lighter out to the sheriff. But Billy Dean just nodded toward the desktop, telling him with his eyes where to lay it.

"You the preacher over on the Senator's place, ain't you? Used to be Levi Snow's church?"

"Yessuh, that's right," but added quickly, "now I never knew the man. Nossuh. Not personal like."

"That's right healthy of you, I reckon." Billy Dean lit a cigarette for himself. "You mentioned you got something for me."

"Yessuh." He carefully pulled a folded paper from his inside coat pocket. "I been hearin some things. We got some folks tryin to stir up trouble twix the races." He held the flier out to the sheriff.

As the paper shivered in the man's outstretched hand, Billy Dean leaned forward and read the headline out loud. "WE MUST VOTE NOW." He snatched the paper. "Where'd you get this?"

"Somebody…one of my congregation give it to me," the preacher stammered. "She tole me they been showin up all over her settlement."

"It says down here it's put out by the Rosa Parks League. What's that?"

"I don't know a thang about that….It's the Lord's mystery to me. If I knowed, I'd sure tell." Pinching his cigarette between his thumb and index finger, the preacher squinched up his face and pulled, straining with all his might. He coughed again.

Billy Dean eyed him suspiciously. "You ain't got no idea at all?"

"Well, now," the man said, shuffling his shoes on the floor, "I can't name no names, but I can say for sure they are not from my congregation. I suspect they town coloreds."

"How many of them?"

"Only two showed up to Sister Raynelle Johnson's door. They both women."

The man timidly looked around for a place to drop his ashes, and finding no ashtray within reach, balanced his hat on his knee and flicked the cigarette in the palm of his hand.

"And they were colored, you say?"

"Yessuh. That's what I was told. Mostly." The man dropped his eyes to the floor.

"Mostly. What the hell does 'mostly' mean?"

"Well, now. I been told all this, remember. I ain't seen nothin my own self."

The sheriff took a slow breath, trying to keep from grabbing the man by the throat. It was like pulling teeth. Why couldn't these preachers just come out and say a thing without beating all around the stump? "Yeah. I know," the sheriff said wearily. "You ain't seen shit. Go on. Were they all colored or not?"

"I heard there was one waitin in the car. Now they say that one could a been white. Or maybe just light."

"What kind of car."

"Big car. Big nice car. Blue or green or gray or somethin like that."

"Out-of-state tag?" he asked.

"I don't recall bein told about that, now."

"Man driving?"

"Don't know that neither."

Billy Dean looked down at the flier again. It told all about everybody's right to vote—electing a sheriff to serve all the people, how and where to register, what a poll tax was and when the next sheriff's primary was going to be held. Sheriff was the only office it mentioned. No, this wasn't the work of no town niggers, Billy Dean thought. Too slick. Like Hayes said, it had to be some Jew-Communist outfit from up North messing around in his county. But why were they singling out the sheriff's office? Did they know he might be a tad vulnerable? Billy Dean said, "I don't see anything here about Miss Delia. That *is* what you said you came about, weren't it?"

The man swallowed hard. "That's right. Yessuh."

"Well?"

"Now you got to understand. I don't believe a word—"

"Damn it, preacher! Just say it. I ain't going to hold it against you."

"Well," the man said, talking to the tiles, "these two women was sayin as how.... Well, what they tellin everbody is, you was the one killed Miss Delia." The man quickly looked up, but then averted his eyes.

"And?" Billy Dean said, somehow knowing this wasn't the worst of it.

The smoke from the man's cigarette was curling into his eyes. Even though he was starting to tear up, he didn't shift either his hand or his head. "And they say you killed her because she was...you got her in the family way."

At that the sheriff's head almost exploded. "Jesus H. Christ," he said through his clenched teeth.

Wisely, the man wasn't looking up to catch Billy Dean's expression. "Not that I like to tell on folkses as a custom," he said, "but you the sheriff and needs to know bout these things or chaos is gone reign."

They sat in silence for a few moments, Billy Dean deep in thought, staring blankly toward the preacher, and the preacher studying his own shoes, the cigarette now burning dangerously close to his fingers. Still not looking up, the man said barely loud enough to be heard, "Well, suh. That's about the big of it I reckon."

The sheriff's attention snapped back into the room. "Who else you told?"

The preacher looked up and for the first time he blinked. "Who all I tole?"

It was the sheriff now who looked away. "I mean white people, that is."

"I brung it straight to you, Sheriff."

"Well, keep it quiet for now. Till we can find who's been spreading these lies."

Billy Dean stood up, letting the preacher know his time had run out. He watched the man with contempt as he struggled with the doorknob, holding his hat and his cigarette in one hand, and the ashes in the palm of the other.

When he had finally managed the door and before he walked into the outer office, the sheriff called after him. "I need to know names. You hear?" Then Billy Dean pressed his thumbs to his temples again, the sound of his own words now like the firing of cannons.

Chapter 49
ALL IS WELL

"Congratulations, boys." Floyd pushed the papers across the desk on an imaginary axis between the Gooseberry twins, not knowing which one would want to take charge of the signing. "Y'all got a real good deal out of me. That Mercury Montclair is quite a car. Put all the miles on her myself." Floyd sighed. "All easy miles." He wistfully looked out the window, bidding a silent farewell to the last evidence of Delia in his life. The perfume had dried up weeks ago.

Taking their cue from Floyd, the brothers each reached under the identical tape measures draped around their necks and retrieved the silver Cross pens from their shirt pockets. First Lou scanned the agreement carefully, moving the pen along the paper as he read. Then he slid the paper across the desk to Sid, who signed without reading it.

So that's how it works, thought Floyd, finding the whole thing fascinating. Anybody else would have missed a little incident like that. But Floyd figured that was why he was so successful in business. He strove to understand the psychology behind things that most people took for granted. After all, that's all sales was, psychology and attitude. The study of human behavior.

"How's the family, Floyd?" Sid asked, stoking up a cigar and then handing the lighter to his brother.

"Fine. Real fine. Never been better." Floyd said it like he meant it. Because he did mean it for a change. It had been touch and go there for a while, but now everything was under control. Floyd had amazed even himself at how fast he was able to whip his family into shape. It just proved to him that his instincts for the psychology of people were sharper than ever.

There was a thousand percent improvement in Hazel. Talk about a turnaround! After all the wisdom he had tried to impart to her over the years, and after all the hardheadedness she had paid him back with, who knew the thing she would latch on to was his suggestion for her to do church work? The idea was hardly out of his mouth and then lickety-split, she off and gets a near-about-full-time job volunteering in the church office, putting her bookkeeping skills to good use. She was Brother Dear's right-hand girl. Besides that, visiting sick folks and delivering food to the needy at night, becoming a regular pillar of the community. He hadn't smelled liquor on her in weeks. Something inside Floyd must have instinctively known what to say, even if it was in the heat of anger. Instinct. That's what it was. Pure-dee unadulterated instinct.

"Yep. Real fine," Floyd said proudly. "And Johnny's becoming a baseball fanatic. Just the other day we were out tossing the ol' horsehide around. He's gonna be a real sports nut, I can tell." He winked at Lou. "You know how boys are." Floyd had always wanted to say that.

"That's mighty fine," said Lou.

"He's a real boy, ain't he?" said his brother. They both lifted their large bulks from the chairs.

"Now I'll have that car gassed up and sent right over to y'all's house. Be there before you get home for supper."

"You tell Miss Hazel Happy Thanksgiving," Lou said.

"And that boy of yours, too," added Sid. "Johnny Graham. Gonna be reading about him in the sports pages."

"I'll sure tell the family y'all asked after em."

At that, the twins proceeded one after the other through the office door, like a pair of freighters through the Panama Canal. Floyd followed in their wake.

"Proud y'all came by," he called out to them as they headed down the sidewalk to their store, the smoke from their cigars curling above them into a single column. Floyd stood there for a moment, watching traffic, counting the cars and trucks he himself had put on the road. He thought about the many lives he had touched. No man is an island, that's for sure. With her charity work, he knew Hazel was finding out about that, too. A sense of pride welled up in Floyd's chest, and his eyes filled with tears.

Things really were fine.

Hazel parked her Lincoln behind an old abandoned filling station on the edge of town. It was a half-hour before first dark, and the temperature had begun to drop. She got out and opened the trunk, loaded with turkey hens for the needy. When she found the wires, she disconnected the lights that illuminated the license plate and then got back in the car and waited.

A few minutes later, a battered pickup truck came grumbling down the two-lane highway, braked to a complete stop right in the center of the road, and then died. After starting it up again, the driver turned and came lurching onto the broken apron of concrete, torturing the gears. The truck was soon followed by a red-and-white Chevy. Both automobiles joined the Lincoln in the rear of the cinder-block building.

The doors opened, the cars emptied and the women fell into their work without speaking. Hazel removed a cardboard box from among the turkeys and took it to the hood of the Lincoln. There she and Creola began sorting the circulars, hot off the Baptist Church mimeograph machine, into three stacks.

Sweet Pea went to the trunk of Willie's car and lifted out a box of blank paper and a couple of gallons of mimeograph ink he had donated to the women for their next run. Then she transferred it all to Hazel's trunk alongside the birds.

Vida was crouched over a county map spread on the fender of Creola's husband's truck. Holding a flashlight with her one good arm, Hannah stood over Vida's shoulder aiming at the map, even though it wasn't dark enough to need it yet.

Maggie remained in the back seat of the Chevy gazing out the window with her single eye, admiring the darkening blood-red sky, humming serenely to herself.

As they completed their tasks, the women gathered around Vida. The energy of the group was charged tonight. A current of constrained panic seemed to hum about their heads.

"You hear from that NdoubleACP yet?" Sweet Pea asked, "We need to get some help. It's gettin scary. I'm startin to feel eyes all over me in the dark."

"You ought to be used to that, girl." Creola giggled and jokingly clapped her hand over her mouth.

"I talked to em all right," Vida said bitterly. "They gone be as helpful as tits on a boar hog. They say all they leaders is bein blowed up and run out of the state. Tole us we might better slow down and let them catch up. Say we done jumped the gun a couple of years. They ain't got no organization yet in Hopalachie County." Vida sounded disgusted. "Sides, when they found out we didn't have no man up over us, that's when they almost hung up. Thought I was devilin em."

"What about Rosie?" Creola protested. "You tell them bout her? She a woman."

Vida laughed darkly. "They say this ain't Alabama. Things is worser in Mis'sippi."

"Glad it ain't just my magination," Creola said with a weak chuckle.

"They tole me in Alabama the Law is bad to stand around and let you get kilt. But in Mis'sippi the Law be the ones tryin to kill you. Don't matter if you is a woman. Say less we get some upstandin colored man to speak out for us, we ain't gone make it out of no jail alive like Rosie done. Probly won't even make it to the jailhouse. Least not breathin."

The women exchanged nervous looks and anxious smiles. They knew what Vida was saying was true.

"So," Vida concluded, "if people gone hear the word about bein a first-class citizen and gettin the vote in Hopalachie County, it still gone have to come from us womens, I reckon."

Sweet Pea shook her head. "I knows they need to hear it and I hate to be no doubtin Thomas, but we been talkin up the vote for weeks. Not one soul say they gonna go down to the courthouse with us. The sheriff got everybody scared to get off they porch."

"Ain't just the sheriff," Creola added bitterly. "It's them white niggers like Misery admirin over the white man. Makes my blood boil. And them chicken-eatin preachers. Tellin everbody to wait for the sweet bye-and-bye. 'Don't stand up in the boat,' they all say. They ain't noticed but they's the only ones got a boat. The rest of us is in the swamp fightin with the gators."

"Y'all wont to quit, y'all go ahead," Vida said glumly. "I can't blame you. I only come to it recent. Ain't been but a few weeks since I tole daddy he was wrong for doin what he did."

At the mention of Levi Snow, the women got quiet for a spell. The only sound was Maggie's humming.

Sweet Pea broke the silence. "Awright. Show us where to go."

Vida sighed with relief. Taking the flashlight from Hannah, Vida clicked it off and used the skinny end to point at the map. "Now Hannah you and Maggie take Willie's car and head on out to the Piggtown settlement tonight. Take the old Carrollton Road. Sheriff's people hardly ever patrols it."

"Let that sumbitch come ahead on," Hannah said angrily, lifting her clenched fist in the air. "Sheriff gone pay for doublin his take on me. I can't hardly afford to stay in business no mo'. Let him come ahead on and pick a fight with ol' Hannah! I'll beat his ass till his nose bleeds." Hannah was so agitated she was flapping her stump now. "Let him come on ahead! is what I says."

While everyone else laughed, Vida put her hand on Hannah's shoulder, trying to calm the woman down. "Don't get so worked up, Hannah. You got to be careful. Willie skin me alive if you scratch his new car."

"Don't you worry none," Hannah said. "I know how to handle that boy and his car both."

Vida grinned at Hannah. "Other way around if you ask me. Willie got you wrapped around his little finger."

"Where is that boy?" asked Sweet Pea. "Why ain't that little brother of yours helpin us?"

Hannah answered for Vida. "Willie say don't bother him till the shootin starts. He say, that's the onliest way thangs gone change in this county."

"I hope he wrong," Vida said. "That's how come we got to try Rosie's way first." Then she went on with the business of the evening. "Creola, how's yo drivin comin along?"

"I got here, didn't I?" Creola answered a little defensively.

"Just barely!" Sweet Pea declared. "Thought I was gone have to stand in the middle of the road so Creola would have somethin to aim at."

"Hush! I didn't come close to no ditches this time out. I gettin good as Miss Hazel." She smiled admiringly at Hazel, who beamed at the compliment. The women thought she was the best driver in the whole state of Mississippi, better than any moonshine runner they had heard of.

"Miss Hazel been givin me lessons," Creola said proudly.

"Well, Creola," Vida said, "If you think you up to it, why don't you and Sweet Pea head on out toward Grierville and hit the Nile community."

Creola nodded. "Sho. Ain't no problem long as I don't have to back up. I ain't took my backin-up lesson yet."

As the sun slowly disappeared behind the trees, the little group remained silent for a few moments, their eyes shifting from face to face, gathering their courage and looking for reassurance.

"Well," Sweet Pea said finally, "I guess we best be goin."

"Now y'all remember to unhook your back lights so nobody can get your tag number," Hazel called out as they dispersed. "And cut off your headlights when you moving from house to house. Somebody might be watching."

Hazel was right, somebody was. As they all headed out, no one noticed the car sitting across the road behind a copse of trees. It pulled out shortly after Hazel, and took off in the same direction as the Lincoln.

Vida and Hazel were heading west down Redeemer's Hill and deep into the chilled Delta evening with the windows down and the heat up. The wind was to keep them alert, but as Hazel picked up speed, the breeze lifted several circulars off the back seat and whirled them around the car. Without speaking they both rolled up their windows.

The hill gave out and the Lincoln rolled onto a tabletop landscape of straight lines and perfect right angles, a twilight world uninterrupted by hills or curves or contours. Endless rows of stalks, recently picked over and streaked with white scraps of cotton, with no visible point of origin, ran up to the side of the road, paused as if to let the Lincoln pass through, and then picked up again on the other side, heading off into the rose-tinted distance.

Hazel laughed softly to herself and said, "I remember the first time I saw this Delta. I was standing in them bluffs behind us. Looking down on it all at once."

"Humph," Vida snorted. "I was probly out here underneath you with a hoe in my hand, looking up at you and cussin."

Hazel's voice had a far-off sound to it, as if part of her were still up there with Floyd. "It took my breath away, scared me so. Us looking over the flat-floor of the world. Me gripping on to him for dear life." She chuckled softly to herself. "Him and me was so excited. It was a brand-new world. Nothing but hope in front of us. Stretching as far as from here to China."

Vida looked over at Hazel. "I remembers the first time I seen you. If you ask me, hope done fled the coop."

"I already give up by then." Hazel shrugged her shoulders and smiled. "I just couldn't get the hang of being somebody's wife and momma. Some folks just fall into it, I reckon. Me, well, I just couldn't see it to save my life."

"And I can't see myself bein one of the lovely Lennon Sisters," Vida said. "Everbody don't take to things the same way. Daddy says we each got our own story callin out to us."

Hazel laughed. "I guess the trick is to get everbody else to shut up long enough to hear what it's tellin us to do."

"Maybe so," Vida said

"Of course there's a lot of things I'd do different," Hazel confessed. "Floyd can take care of hisself. God knows I ain't worried about him. Long as he has his little sayings, he can yank his world around anyway he wants it. But Johnny. He's in for some hard times, I can tell. You know how he is. He's..." Hazel looked over at Vida for the word and then said, "I don't know. Special maybe. It's like the world don't fit him right. And he's trying so hard to make it fit. I just hope he don't have to give up too much. It's always the best parts they want to take away from you. I hope they don't take his story away."

Vida smiled. "Johnny too much like you. He gone have to find his own way, but he'll do it. I know that boy. When the time comes, he got a heap of fight in him. A heap of fight." She laughed, remembering. "One time he near about poked my eye out with his little fist. Now that don't change. I know. It's the fight what gets you through. It'll be there when he need it. It was you give him that."

Sniffling, Hazel said, "You're a good friend to me, Vida."

"Don't do that!" she fussed. "You know I can't stand it when you get all boo-hooey."

As the Lincoln sailed smoothly along the blacktop, Vida began singing softly.

Drivin a big black car
For a big white man.

Then she repeated the same lines again.

"What's the rest of the words?" Hazel asked.

"Wisht I knew. If I did, I might coulda found my baby. It was the last thread I got."

"Nice sounding tune," Hazel said, humming the melody.

"I made that part up. All I was told was the words."

"Kinda sad though. Like maybe he's got second thoughts about drivin that big car."

"I change it up now and then, dependin on how I feel," Vida explained. "How be ever, I know I ain't givin Rezel his due." Vida laughed and then squealed like Sweet Pea. "Ooooweee! That boy was some kinda blues-singing guitar-playin scound. To be so young and all. Women use to faint dead out and men would yell at him, 'go on and beat that box, son' and toss pennies at his feet. Rezel could sho loud up a place. I used to think he maybe be famous one day."

She said wistfully, "Still, sometimes I listen to the radio, hopin they put on his song. Then I magine me callin up that radio station and yellin 'tell me where that man is who be sangin that music!'" Vida laughed at herself, and then turned to Hazel. "You ain't never heard it on the radio, has you, Miss Hazel?"

"No, I don't believe so, Vida."

Vida looked back out the window. "No, I ain't neither."

Hazel reached down and turned on the radio real low. They hummed together for a while until the announcer came on to reel off the Thanksgiving Day specials at the Jitney Jungle. Hazel asked, "How's your daddy doing?"

"Still alive. That's somethin for a colored man sittin in a Mis'sippi jail accused of murdering a white woman. Two weeks must be a all-time record."

"You see him?"

"Deputy Butts is good about lettin me in when the sheriff ain't there." Vida worried with the toggle on the electric window. "He about the same I reckon. Sittin in that cell waitin on the Lord. I tole him Mr. Hayes was the one he ought to be lookin out for, the way he talkin it up all over town," she said, avoiding the word "lynch." "But Daddy think as long as he's in that jail, he's somehow preachin to the people. Sometime I don't know if he's been touched in the head or touched by the Lord."

"I onced knowed somebody like that," Hazel said, thinking of Maud. "Turned out it was one hundred proof meanness she was touched with. Plumb knocked upside the head with it!"

"Yessum," Vida replied, but still thinking her own thoughts. "I ask Daddy if he was afraid of dyin. Know what he said? He said, nobody really dies if they somebody left behind to tell the story. How bout that? There's you a sayin, ain't it?"

"That's a good 'un."

"I reckon. Like I tole you, to my Daddy the story is the thang." There was a catch in her voice. Then she fussed again. "You gone get us all weepy-eyed and we be done missed our turn up here."

After Hazel took the next right off the pavement and onto a gravel road, she saw another car making the turn also. It was coming up fast. "Uh-oh. Vida, hold on." Hazel wasted no time. She flattened the gas pedal to the floor and the tires bit down hard on the gravel. The car seemed airborne.

Behind them, in the white Buick, two men urged the driver to speed up. "That's him all right. Just like Billy Dean said. Look at that car go. Can you catch him?"

"Who you talkin to?" the driver scoffed. "I got a 445 V-8 under my hood. Watch this baby strut her stuff."

Hazel was going sixty now, and even though she couldn't see the car through the cloud of dust gushing from her rear, she was sure it was back there somewhere.

"They's a wide place in the road up here," she told Vida. "I'm gonna mash the brakes hard and spin this thing around. Mind your head."

"Jesus Lord, Miss Hazel!" cried Vida.

But Hazel was as cool as a riverboat gambler. "Don't you worry, Vida. I'm gonna take care of you. I can do this."

"I knows you can, Miss Hazel," Vida said as she covered her face with one hand and braced herself against the dash with the other. "I got faith in you."

Hazel hit the brakes hard. The Lincoln skidded forward a few yards, and the other car kept coming, and then swerved trying to miss her. As Hazel continued to skid, the rear swung around. The car spun once and then twice, each time veering farther to the left side of the road, until when it finally stopped, Hazel had the car sitting off on a sandy shoulder aimed in the opposite direction. The other car skidded off the road through a barbed wire fence and came to a stop in an empty field.

Waving good-bye through the blanket of dust, Hazel took off and sped back toward the paved road. But by the time she began to slow for the turn, she saw the other car coming up on her again. She turned hard and swung onto the blacktop, heading the Lincoln back toward town. As she powered the big car into the advancing twilight and the distance between her and her pursuers increased, Hazel began to breathe easier. They would be safely home in less than twenty minutes.

"I don't mind telling you now," Hazel said. "That was close."

Vida was holding her chest, unable to speak. When she turned back to look, there came a loud series of pops, followed by a dreadful pounding noise. The car started to shake. It was as if the Lincoln had a mind of its own. The rear of the car began fishtailing crazily, fighting Hazel. She gripped the wheel with both hands and struggled mightily against the wild sway.

"I think they shot out a tire," Hazel said, trying to remain calm. "Anyways, we sure got a flat."

"Can we make it to town?"

Hazel looked up into the rearview mirror. "Not ahead of them." The car was almost on her again.

The passenger in the back of the other car yelled, "He's swerving all over the road. Flat tire. I'll be damned. You're one lucky shot."

"Luck hell," the man with the gun said, "It was my good shootin how come we be catching him. That ol' boy might be the best driver in the whole damned county."

The driver sulled up. "Shut your mouth and get ready. Remember, he said just to scare em. I'll pull up even and you fire off a couple of rounds. Aim over the roof."

The man readied himself at the window with his .38. "Damn. Be careful. He's all over the road now. He's liable ram into us."

There was little daylight left. As the car pulled up next to the Lincoln the man with the gun stared into Hazel's window. She glanced at him. For a second, their eyes locked.

"It's a woman," he shouted at the driver. "A goddammed white woman. Did he say it was a woman we was after?"

"What difference does it make? Shoot!"

He looked again. "Jesus, she's got a nigger right up in the front seat with her! Goddamn. Could even be a nigger man."

"Hurry up and shoot," yelled the driver. "Let's get out of here before she hits us."

"But it's a goddammed white woman. Makes me sick to my stomach. White women out looking for niggers to fuck." He lifted the gun and fired twice, shattering Hazel's window. The driver sped up, leaving the car behind him. In his rearview mirror he saw the Lincoln veer sharply and fly off the road without slowing.

"Damn. What'd you do? You hit her?"

"But it was a goddammed nigger-fuckin white woman!"

Hazel managed to jump a ditch, negotiate her way through a roadside stand of pines, over a cattle gap, and finally set the car safely in a field of soft winter rye.

"Lord, Miss Hazel! Is you OK? Let's get out of here before they come back."

But Hazel didn't answer. She sat erect, looking out over the steering wheel into the distance.

"Miss Hazel, you hearin me?" Vida's voice was trembling.

"How'd I do, Vida?" Hazel said, her voice small, with an unfamiliar gurgle to it.

"Miss Hazel, you done real good. You showed em up."

Hazel turned and smiled at Vida, pleased, and then she slumped over the wheel, still smiling. She knew she had done well. Except for the shattered window and the stream of blood slowly seeping into the fabric, the car was miraculously unharmed. And, as promised, so was Vida.

Chapter 50
MAGGIE'S DIME

Floyd carefully set the phone back into its cradle. For a moment, he stood stone-still in the darkened stairhall, not even breathing, and not knowing he wasn't breathing. He reached out into the dark to no one, but wanting it to be Hazel. Wanting her to take his hand, stroke the scars on his fingers and tell him she loved him.

Still not breathing he found himself gasping for air. He threw his hands out behind him and staggered backward, suddenly needing the wall, and finding it, he slid himself slowly to the floor. He put his head in his hands and began to sob violently.

Not aware of how long he had been crying or when the persistent knocking had begun, Floyd managed to get to his feet but then felt himself reeling toward the door. Outside, glowing under the porch light, was Brother Dear. He smiled tenderly at Floyd, letting him know that he also knew and that Floyd was not alone. The love that radiated from the preacher's face provoked a new round of tears. Right there in the stairhall, Brother Dear and Floyd knelt down together while the preacher prayed for Hazel and Floyd wept.

After his prayer, Brother Dear insisted on driving Floyd to the hospital. "Mrs. Dear is waiting in the car. She'll be here in case Johnny wakes up. My wife is real good with children at times like this. Knows every Mother Goose there is."

"Johnny would like that," Floyd sniffled, grateful to have the confidence of the preacher to lean on. "He sure likes a good story. Him and Hazel…" Again Floyd was leveled by the void left by Hazel, by the pure necessity of her. He let the preacher guide him out to his car.

"Why did this happen, Brother Dear?" Floyd sobbed, as the preacher drove.

"That's the way Satan operates. He sees a soul leaning toward Christ and he wages full-out war. Hazel was wounded in the line of duty to our Lord. You can take comfort in that, Floyd."

"I do, Brother Dear, I do," Floyd said, trying to smile in a courageous way. "The hospital said she was out ministering to the sick and needy when somebody…" Floyd burst into tears again.

Brother Dear reached over and put his hand on Floyd's shoulder. "Your wife is a real inspiration to the whole community, Floyd. Why, the way she's come around, her life is a sermon. A sermon I am not a good enough man to preach." He removed his hand from Floyd's shoulder to brush a tear from his own eye.

All of a sudden Floyd blurted, "Get me to her quick, Brother Dear. She needs to know."

Brother Dear was calm. "What does she need to know, Floyd?"

"Everything. She needs to know it all."

"No," Brother Dear said carefully. "She doesn't. I don't know what it is you got to confess. But right now she only needs to hear you say one thing. And don't let me catch you telling her anything but that. Do you understand me? Man to man?"

Floyd nodded.

"And are you ready to tell her that one thing?"

"With all my heart," Floyd sobbed.

"That's good, Floyd. That's real good."

The cabin was growing heavy with stale air. Mattresses had been dragged across the floor and positioned over the windows. Even though it was a chilly November night, the maids were drenched in sweat as they huddled together in Vida's darkened house, sitting around a sputtering coal oil lamp. They kept the light turned low, expecting any moment white folks to race down into Tarbottom shooting off shotguns and tossing sticks of dynamite from car windows. This was going to be a nightly ritual, the maids had decided—taking turns staying together in each other's homes, while Hannah and Willie sat up, guarding the jook.

"Y'all know this is crazy," Sweet Pea fussed. "If they gone get us, we just makin it easy for them peckerwoods. Us sitting here together like fish in a barrel. All we doin is keepin down they dynamite bill."

Creola shifted her weight in her chair. "Don't matter to me none," she said, undaunted. "Rufus done got scared and snuck out of town in the truck. I don't aim to die alone and y'all is all I got."

"Rufus lef you?" Sweet Pea asked.

"Never thought I see the day. Not if he had to get up out his chair to do it." Creola managed a weak laugh. "He was some scared. But he be back when things ease up. Or he gets hongry first." She tried to smile again.

But the fear was as thick as smoke in the room. "Y'all, maybe they ain't even after us," Vida said, trying to sound upbeat. "After I finally got Miss Hazel's car to the hospital, they acted like they believed what I tole em. That she been out visitin the poor and sickly when she got shot. I even had the turkeys to prove it."

Sweet Pea gave out a harsh laugh. "Who in they right mind gone believe that story? Fishier than Friday night in a fry house." She dabbed her neck with a handkerchief. "He know bout us. He know everthing. He'll make his move in his own sweet time. When it best suits him. Our gooses is cooked."

"If that what you thinkin, then how come we be sittin around on our hands for?" Vida snapped. "We just gone wait till he come for us?"

"We could get out of the county!" Creola blurted. "Might even leave the state. Get a train up to Memphis and never look back."

"Leave?" Vida was surprised Creola had suggested it. "What happens to Miss Hazel if she can't never speak for herself? Answer me that?" The maids could hear the sadness rising in her throat.

"No, I ain't gone leave her here all wrapped in lies. Bout how she done finally learned to behave herself and do like she was tole. Bout how she got broke to saddle like ever woman oughta."

"And Daddy," she said, "Who gone finish the story he started? I can't go off and let him be just another crazy nigger who killed a white woman."

The maids dropped their heads and studied their hands. They were too ashamed to look at Vida now.

"Y'all go on if you wont, but I'm sure about my place. Somebody got to stay behind and tell the story." Vida searched for their eyes, her voice trembling. "Don't y'all see, if we don't tell it, the white folks will. But it ain't theirs to tell. It ain't..." She couldn't finish, her voice was so choked with tears.

Sweet Pea reached over and placed her hand on Vida's shoulder. "No. It ain't theirs to tell," she echoed tenderly.

"Praise the Lamb," Maggie said softly, seeming especially peaceful tonight. For a moment everybody's eyes rested on her toad-like figure, as if trying to soak up some of her calm. They watched her as she rocked her ancient body gently to and fro, her leathery hands folded serenely in her lap.

After a while, Vida looked up, still with tears in her eyes, but in a clear, certain voice said, "You know, we could go to the courthouse and ask to take that votin test. We could do that."

Sweet Pea snatched her hand away from Vida's shoulder like her compassion had just drained through the cracks in the floor. "You gone crazy in the head?" she yelled. "I thought we was talkin bout how to stay alive! They put yo name and address in the paper when you register to vote. And since it be us, might even draw a map."

"But weren't that the plan?" Vida asked. "Ain't that what we was askin everybody else to do?"

"The plan was to get a hundred of us to march on the courthouse," Sweet Pea shot back. "Not four maids and a jooker."

"But we the Rosie Parks League, 'member?" Creola asked. "What would Rosie do?"

"In Hopalachie County? I don't know," Sweet Pea said. "She had Luther Kang on her side in Montgomery."

"But he weren't on that bus with her, was he?" Vida reminded them. "She faced em down all by her lonesome. Besides, we got each other."

For a long time no one said another word, as the idea hung heavy in the room. Maggie began to hum softly again. Vida smiled gently at her and asked, "What you think bout it, Maggie?"

Maggie sighed heavily and began moving her gums at three-quarter time. Then she lifted her eye. "When I was a little girl, Momma Nell and me always come to town on Saditty." Maggie spoke in a low, quivery voice, like old people do when they're remembering in front of late-night fires. "I loved comin to town with my Momma Nell. We get all dressed up. Momma Nell'd iron my hair and put a ribbon in it. It was good as Santa Claus time."

Maggie stopped there, as if she were trying to remember the color of the ribbon. The maids silently watched her through the flickering of the lamplight, not knowing if she was finished with her story or not. For a long time she didn't move.

Then her chest heaved mightily, as if she had just remembered to breathe, and she said, "One Saditty we come up on a crowd of white mens lisnin to anothern talk about wontin they votes for guvner. This little sawed-off man say if he was to get lected he gone put all the colored folks on a boat and send us back to Aferca. Then he see me standin there watchin and say, 'Hey there, little girl!' and I thought he was talking to me cause Mamma Nell dressed me up so purty."

Maggie stopped again to remember, smiling.

"Then he say, 'Little girl, you gone like it over there in Aferca.' Say 'Collard greens grow ten feet tall and they's a possum in every stalk.' He had a big laugh for a little sawed-off man. And everbody laugh right along with him. He petted me on my haid and then reached in his pocket and give me a shiny new dime. Then he turns back to the peoples and say how much better Mis'sippi be without the niggers stankin up ever thang. Everbody clap and yell real loud."

Maggie stopped again for a moment and looked down at her hands, still folded in her lap. "All I really knowed was I got me a dime out of it."

She raised her head and placed the back of her hand against the scarred flap of skin, like she might be shielding it from the sun. "But I looked up at Momma Nell and big ol' tears was fallin down her face. 'Why you cryin for?' I ax her. Momma Nell tole me, 'Girl, don't you go spendin that dime.' She say, 'Keep it and let it mind you of today. Don't never for-get who owns this here country. When you forget, you is dead.' She tole me to hold on to that dime till the day I can come to town and spend it free and proud."

Some of the maids were beginning to sniffle.

Maggie reached her stiffened fingers into the pocket of her dress. Out came a worn leather coin purse. She unsnapped it, reached into a little inside pocket, and brought out a tissue. Unfolding the paper in her hand, she held out a blackened coin in the lamplight. The maids all leaned in, staring wide-eyed, as if it were a hoodoo charm, pulsating in the dark.

"Many the time I got weak-willed and wont to spend this here dime." Maggie chuckled at herself. "Wontin me some candy. Or the fair come to town. Or a pretty boy. Dime burned a hole in my pocket. But I didn't spend it," she said proudly. "No ma'am. I held on to it just like Momma Nell tole me to."

The maids were stone-silent, still studying the dime in Maggie's old hand.

"Y'all know sumpin?" Maggie asked, her eye circling the little group. "Befo' I dies, I wont to spend this here dime."

The next day four maids plus a one-armed jook proprietor, with little ceremony and not much notice from the square, wearing their best dresses and, in Sweet Pea's case, a sassy red scarf, marched up to the courthouse steps, through the vestibule, and past an oil portrait of the Senator looking like he had everything under control. Not until they turned into the circuit clerk's office did anybody take heed. Nellie Grindle looked up from her desk behind the counter, smile at the ready. Then she saw who it was. "What y'all girls want?" she asked sharply.

Vida hauled back her shoulders and opened her mouth, but it was Maggie who said, "I here to reddish for the vote."

Nellie reached for her pointy-framed glasses that hung around her neck and studied the group for a moment before letting the glasses drop back to her chest. She managed to get herself to her feet. "Y'all wait right here!" she said, befuddled, and then fled the office.

"We in for it now," Creola whispered.

"She gone for the sheriff, I just knows it," Sweet Pea whispered back. "Our gooses is hanging on a spit and near bout well done."

Hannah patted her bosoms, "I got my razor if he tries messin with me. I'll skin 'im like a catfish."

Sweet Pea said, "It ain't too late. We can hightail it out that door."

It was too late. Nellie had found Billy Dean across the hall in the chancery clerk's office double-checking the tax rolls and returned with him in tow. Billy Dean took a few moments to study the group. His eyes would light on a woman, then he would shake his head and move to the next.

"Now ain't this a proud delegation from the colored community," he said. "We got the county whore. A one-armed bootlegger. Two tubs of lard with three eyes between em."

He glared at Vida. "And last but not least, the proud daughter of the local murderin reverend." He smirked at his own cleverness. "This all them Yankee Jew agitators could scrape up?" He paused like he was waiting for some kind of response, but the women had no idea what he was talking about. He homed in on Vida again. "So, you wont to follow in your daddy's footsteps, I see."

Vida tried her hardest to hold his stare. "I proud to. I ain't ashamed for my daddy." After the words left Vida's mouth, the sheriff's eyes bucked her off like a wild horse. She dropped her gaze and studied his star instead.

A world of silence was cram-packed into the next few moments. The sheriff stood there, his jaw muscles bulging and the forked vein in his forehead ready to pop. The hush was so complete and so long that the women even dared to shift their eyes questioningly to one another. Just what life-and-death matters were being considered here?

All of a sudden, Deputy Butts stepped into the office and the tension snapped like a cable. Everybody jerked their heads in his direction. The sudden jolt of attention caught the deputy off guard and he fell back a step. For a moment his eyes bobbled back and forth, trying to get a handle on things. He stammered, "What's going on here, Sheriff? You got trouble?"

Billy Dean heaved a breath. "No," he said wearily, reaching his thumb up to his temple "Nothin more than usual. Bunch of niggers doing their damnedest to ruin my day."

Nellie was indignant. "It's a sight more than that! They say they want to register to vote. Sheriff, this is getting out of hand."

Billy Dean exploded. "Shut up, woman! I decide when things are out of hand or not. You understand that?"

Nellie couldn't answer. Scarlet-faced with her mouth gaping, she stood there frozen, humiliated in front of a bunch of coloreds.

Vida watched him carefully, waiting like everybody else to see what he was going to do now, after yelling at a white woman. The sheriff's gaze fell on her. Again Vida looked back, directly into his eyes, but this time she did not waver. For the first time in her life, Vida was holding a stare with a white man.

It was as if the world around her was hurtling out of control, yet she herself was balanced at its absolute center, enveloped in an eerie calm. Her thoughts were focused and sharp. Things were revealed to her. First she saw that the sheriff's eyes were not gray-black like Nate's. They were the deep, dark blue of the night. Nothing at all like Nate's.

Then she saw another thing. Something she had never seen before in a white man's eyes, burrowing there in the corners and squirming under the lids. She understood why the colored were never supposed to look there in the first place, lest they see it, too. It was fear. The sheriff was afraid, and she knew it had to do with her. The idea was so ludicrous, Vida almost laughed right out loud. Her whole life she had been at this man's mercy, and now she saw that he was afraid of her. Why on earth?

The answer to that question was the final thing that was revealed in this flash of a moment that seemed to have no bottom. She understood deep in her bones what her father had meant. Even though she was a colored woman and maybe nobody would believe her, a story is made to be told and passed on. If it is picked up and touched and handled enough times, the truth will at last shine through the telling, and the world will finally see. What she was doing, now, this very second, would set Nate free and all those like him free. That's why those bad men in the Bible always tried to kill the story, no matter how lowly the teller. That's why her father put all his faith in the story. And Vida knew this man's story. It was forever intertwined with her own. She could recite it loud and clear this very minute. Every jot and tittle. And he knew that she could.

The sheriff dropped his eyes. "Give em the test," he said.

"What?" Nellie gasped.

Billy Dean looked at the old woman again, but the fury was gone. Only tired was left. "Just give it to em, Nellie. They ain't gonna pass it no way."

She opened her mouth to speak, but Billy Dean wouldn't have it.

"Nellie," he said, his finger aimed at the woman, marking off his words. "Not. Another. God. Damned. Word." He spun around and left the office.

Nellie and Lampkin looked at each other in astonishment. As if the women were not there, straining at every thought, spoken and unspoken, Nellie said indignantly, "Well, Lampkin, I reckon you're going to be in for a promotion soon."

The deputy grinned but didn't comment.

Nellie stared sullenly at the door. "Billy Dean Brister couldn't win another election if the Senator voted every dead man in the history of Hopalachie County."

The women left the office and walked through the courthouse doors. They stopped when they stepped out onto the gallery overlooking the square. All the town's coloreds had already cleared out, and a small crowd of whites had gathered around the stone soldier, staring back at them.

The women, terrified, started down the steps. As they did people began to line both sides of the walk. The crowd was eerily silent, like the woods after a shotgun blast. Vida hoped it was because the women had taken the town by surprise and they hadn't had time to plan their courage. So maybe instead of a mob, they were just a confused mess of white people waiting for a leader.

The women moved in a tight little knot across the square while the whites stared opened-mouthed. Though Vida didn't look around to check, she figured they were still watching as they headed down the road to Tarbottom.

Chapter 51
SWEATING IT OUT IN TARBOTTOM

"That's one test I done flunked," Creola grumbled as she came out of her kitchen carrying an iced tea in each hand. "How I supposed to know how many hairs on hog's back?"

Sweet Pea took a jelly glass from Creola, adding, "And how many bubbles in a bar of soap? What's that got to do with electin a sheriff?"

"Got a lot to do with it," Vida said. "You know they don't ask white folks them questions."

"But least we done it!" Creola said, deciding to be proud regardless. "And nobody can't say we didn't. Ain't that right, Maggie?"

Her eye shining in the dark, Maggie sang out, "Yes, Jesus!"

"Well, before y'all go pinnin flowers on yoselves," Sweet Pea warned, "come tomorrow we gone have to decide what to do. Y'all know quick as our white ladies get wind of this, we good as lost our jobs."

Creola eased herself down on her chair. "And that'll be the least of it," she said. "You done forgot who my boss is? If I shows up for work or don't, either way Mr. Hayes gone be chasin me round town with a rope." Realizing what she had said, Creola gave Vida a pained look of regret.

"Guess we could all move in together and live like them nuns I heard about in New Orleans," Sweet Pea said, making a disgusted face. "I don't reckon they's a man in this county wonts my comp'ny bad enough to get blowed up for it."

"How be ever," Creola said hopefully, "I bet when the word gets out, they be people all over the state come in and help us." She raised up her glass like she was making a toast. "Maybe even Martin Luther Kang show up in Delphi. Law! Won't that be somethin!"

"Maybe so," Vida said doubtfully. "But just in case he don't, Willie say he give us some money to git away. I'm stayin but y'all can go."

"And Hannah say she can hide us out at her place if we wonts," Creola reminded them. "But I reckon it ain't no safer there. Sheriff probly already shut her down."

"Or blowed her up," Sweet Pea added darkly.

Sweet Pea had just got the words out of her mouth when the sound came from out on the porch. Footsteps, slow, creeping, but heavy like a man's. Everybody held her breath as each step came nearer. Vida reached out for Creola's hand. A whimper came from Sweet Pea. Maggie rocked her body gently.

Then there came the firm knock on the door. No one in the room moved a muscle.

"Y'all in there?" came the familiar voice. "Vida?"

"It's Mr. Floyd!" Vida said in a loud whisper.

There was a combined sigh of relief around the room. Creola was holding both hands over her immense bosom, like she was trying to keep her heart in her chest. "Like to give me the thumps."

"What he wont I wonder?" Sweet Pea asked. "Think he gone bless us out cause of Miss Hazel?"

"I just glad it be him and ain't you-know-who," Creola said as she hoisted herself out of her chair and scuffed her feet across the bare floor. After lifting up the crossbar and pulling back the door, she saw Floyd Graham, looking little and lost. "Come on in, Mr. Floyd," Creola said gently. "Don't mind the dark. Let me show you to someplace to sit down."

Creola led Floyd into the house, but he stopped after a few steps. "No, I'll stand if it's just the same with you."

"No, Mr. Floyd. Ever how it feels right for you to do. You sho welcome to stand there long as you wonts." Still, Creola left her chair vacant, and went to stand by the foot of her bed in the corner of the room.

Floyd appeared exhausted. He slowly looked around Creola's cabin, until he was able to make out his maid through the dark. "Hello, Vida."

"Mr. Floyd," Vida answered sheepishly, looking up out at him through the tops of her eyes.

"I went over to your place first. I been walking from house to house.

Y'all was the first one that answered."

"Yessuh. I ain't surprised. I spect everbody pulled up they covers early tonight."

"Well, I guess," Floyd said, not understanding. "I'm just glad y'all are up. Hazel wanted me to be sure and find you."

All around the room, a chorus of voices went up. "Miss Hazel!"

The intensity was such that Floyd took a step back. "That's right. Hazel," he said, baffled at the response. "She wanted you to know she's gonna be all right. Bullet went clean threw her neck. Only thing is it took her voice for a while. Writes ever thing down."

Vida burst out crying. "Miss Hazel alive!" she said through her sobs, reaching out for Sweet Pea's hand. "She gone be all right!"

Floyd watched the maids, bewildered, as the rest of them began clapping their hands and stomping their feet and generally whooped up a storm. "I'm proud y'all feel so strong about it," was all he could say to the sight.

"Yessuh, we do!" Vida said, laughing through her tears. "That we do."

Floyd stood silent for a moment considering the maids' joy, but not understanding much in his world tonight. He released a heavy sigh, his shoulders dropping, as if under some invisible weight. "Vida?" he said in a little boy's voice.

"Yessuh, Mr. Floyd."

"Was that really where she was? Delivering a Thanksgiving turkey to poor folks?"

The smile dropped from Vida's face. "Why you ask, Mr. Floyd?"

"I don't know. I hope that's where she was and all," he said uncertainly.

Considerable time passed without Vida answering his question. Floyd, clearly embarrassed, averted his eyes and began rubbing his fingers. He looked up carefully, "Can I ask you another question? Personal?"

"Yessuh," she said carefully. "What is it you wontin to know?"

"Hazel waddent...I mean..." Floyd glanced up quickly at Vida, his eyes pleading with her, and then looked down at his hand again. "What I'm asking is she didn't get hurt doing something she shouldn't of been doing, did she?"

Nervously, Vida ran her finger along the rim of her glass and without answering took a sip. When she looked back up at Floyd, he was still worrying with his hand, rubbing his fingers like he was trying his best to get at those purple marks.

"I mean," Floyd said, struggling with his words, "what I'm asking is, she waddent seeing another fella, was she?"

With a mouthful of tea, Vida let go a loud, gurgling, "Haaah!?"

Floyd glanced up from his hand with a wounded look, but he said nothing. Having worked so hard to get the question out, he decided to silently endure the ridicule until he had his answer.

Vida coughed and wiped her mouth with a handkerchief, but Floyd still thought he heard her giggling. The other maids hid their expressions behind their hands, and nobody would look at him.

Finally, having gathered herself together, Vida said with studied sympathy, "That what you thinkin, Mr. Floyd?" She shook her head adamantly. "No sir! Ain't no other man ceptin you. I swear to it. You the one she loves."

On hearing that, he drew up his shoulders again. "Yep. You right. Course I am," he said, but even his restored self-assurance couldn't hide the relief in his voice.

Smiling at him Vida said, "I spect when she gets her voice back, she'll have some stories to tell us. Won't she, Mr. Floyd?"

Floyd nodded. "I reckon. It's been a long time since we swapped stories."

He dropped his hands to his sides and looked around the room at the maids again, his face having grown serious once more. "I hear y'all had quite a big day."

"Yessuh," they all mumbled.

"Can't of helped your daddy much, Vida."

"Nossuh, I reckon not. Doubt if it hurt him much neither."

"Maybe you right. Like I always say…"

"Yessuh, Mr. Floyd?"

He smiled. "Funny, I forgot what it was I always said. Must be tired. Ain't been to bed for a couple of nights."

"You best get on back and get you some sleep, Mr. Floyd. You can rest easy now."

Almost out the door, Floyd turned back around and stood for a moment in the doorway. "Vida," he said, "I'm sorry, I mean real sorry, if anything I done caused you or yours any harm."

"Yessuh, Mr. Floyd. I believes you."

"And I'll talk to Hayes myself about Levi. See if we can't get things calmed down a bit." Floyd nodded his head up and down like he was seconding his own motion.

"And Vida," he said again, "I know tomorrow's Thanksgiving and all, but if you can, try and come on early. The boy's been asking for you. And with his momma in the hospital again and all...."

"Yessuh, Mr. Floyd," Vida said. "I'd be proud to."

Chapter 52

THE HOSPITALITY STATE

The Trois Arts League had just wrapped up their annual awards meeting and were filing out the door in high spirits when Hayes Alcorn scuttled by them, displaying the requisite charm and courtesies, but at the same time making a beeline for the liquor cabinet. After Pearl had said her last good-bye, she joined Hayes in the library, where she found him muttering to himself as he paced before the fireplace, consuming a portion of bourbon that would have put a stagger in the step of a normal-sized man.

"My people are dropping like flies all around me," he said when he saw his wife enter the room. "Floyd Graham—that hillbilly—just came to the bank and flat-out told me that I was being too hard on Levi Snow. Then in the very next breath he had the nerve to ask for a business loan." Hayes crinkled up his brow, and shook his head incredulously. "And get this!" he cried. "He came libelously close to accusing the sheriff of planting evidence."

Pearl, in high heels, stooped a little so Hayes could interrupt his tirade and give her a welcome-home peck on the cheek.

"Where was I? Oh, yeah. Imagine! Too hard on Levi Snow. That damned murdering nigruh sitting up in that jail as pretty as you please. And Hopalachie County catering to his every need! Well, that's it. Time to put a stop to it."

Pearl took a seat on the sofa, knowing how Hayes hated for her to look down on him when he was working up a steam. Touching her handkerchief to the dimple in her chin, she said, "I'm sorry, Hayes. What does all this mean? Will you explain it to me?"

"Gladly. Means I finally found me some boys willing to do what's got to be done." After taking a greedy swallow from his glass, Hayes continued. "Levi Snow's been sitting in that cell, paid for by the taxpayers, laughing at us, while he's got his people carrying out acts of insurrection. If *your* brother hadn't run the Klan out of the county this wouldn't be happening."

Hayes smiled a satisfied little smile and swirled the bourbon in his glass. "Well, by tomorrow night, that situation will be remedied. There's going to be an example set. People will see Hayes Alcorn as a man of action."

Pearl frowned. "What are these boys going to do for you, Hayes?"

"I'll tell you what!" He was close to snarling now. "They going to take care of that nigruh once and for all. Before he provokes any more public acts of defiance." Hayes took another gulp and then shook his head. "That must have been a sight. A vicious mob of nigruh women storming the courthouse." A hint of a smile crossed his face as he noted the political bounce to the words.

He started his pacing again. "I swear! With Billy Dean Brister as sheriff, that gang of coloreds might be in charge of the county jail soon. Turn it into a jook joint and dance the Sassy Wiggle." He threw back the rest of his drink, leaving Pearl to wonder how he knew about such a thing as the Sassy Wiggle.

"And quite frankly, I'm surprised at you, Pearl. That you aren't any more concerned." Hayes put out his arm to the mantel, which was about shoulder-high, and leaned against it.

"Concerned, dear?"

"Can't you see what's been going on under your nose? Your very own maid tried to vote." His hand was now patting around on the mantle for something, but he kept an eye on his wife. "The fact that every maid in the neighborhood suddenly got a wild hair to participate in the democratic process? All on the same day? Ain't that the least bit suspicious? Even to you, Pearl?"

"Well, yes," Pearl said, "now that you mention it, Hayes. I am concerned."

"Yes, I thought you might be when I explained it to you."

"About these 'boys' you mentioned," Pearl continued. "Are you saying you have a plan to have Levi harmed?" The handkerchief traveled to her throat.

"That's the idea, dear," Hayes said sarcastically. He began to sidle along the mantel, groping among the figurines and picture frames adorning the shelf behind him.

"Hayes, dear, I really believe you should reconsider this idea of yours," Pearl suggested, still smiling pleasantly.

"I don't need any more advice, thank you, *dear*. Action is what is needed." Hayes's eyebrows vaulted as he found what he had been searching for. He pulled out a silver cigar case that had been pushed up behind a photograph of the Senator and Pearl as children. For the first time it hit him that the colored boy in the background of the photograph must be Levi.

Pearl waited until Hayes had selected one of the Havanas before she raised the handkerchief to her nose. "Please, Hayes, don't smoke in the house. I've asked you before."

Testily, Hayes flung the cigar back in the box and snapped the lid shut. As he stood there, sullen, he noticed the handkerchiefed hand had stopped flitting about, and had finally lighted on the arm of the sofa. From where he stood it reminded him of a prehistoric reptilian claw.

"Now about Levi," Pearl said, "this is what I would like you to do, dear. I want you to leave him alone and stop stirring up all these disagreeable feelings toward him."

"But he killed Delia!" he exclaimed. "Your own niece!"

"Pooh," she said, "Levi wouldn't hurt a fly and anybody with a modicum of sense would know that. That's why no one has touched him. Goodness, Hayes, I'm surprised at you."

"But—"

"I've known Levi since he and I were children. The gentlest of God's creatures. And he adored Delia. I know. I saw it."

"But the Senator—"

"Isn't himself," she said. "Hayes, he doesn't know what to think now. My brother is crazy with grief. And for you to take advantage of his state... Well, I don't think that's very considerate of you."

Not able to muster the words to counter such lunacy, Hayes just stood there blowing like a horse after a hard race,

"And what's more. About the maids. Creola has been with me for over twenty years. Don't you think I know everything she thinks and feels? She's no troublemaker, Hayes."

"But she tried to vote! The whole town saw it. You can't just dismiss…" He stopped and looked at his wife, dumbfounded. Her face hadn't changed, it was still pleasantly vacant, completely unheeding of the desperateness of the situation.

"Pearl, listen, honey, let me explain. There was a gang of them. All out to overturn the system. A Communist-backed insurrection."

"Hayes, really! I know every one of them. Creola? Well, that really is unthinkable. And Levi's daughter, she's just full of grief after the way you've been treating her father. The colored do have feelings, Hayes."

Hayes slumped down into the fireplace armchair.

"Then there's Sweet Pea. Now, I myself have taken that poor wayward girl under my wing and turned her around with good literature. And Maggie. Really, Hayes, Maggie? Out to overthrow the system?" Pearl was overcome by laughter so hysterical and unbecoming that Hayes had to shut his eyes against the ugly snorts. "Oh, dear!" she cried, laughter still coursing through her words. "Maggie! What could you have been thinking?" She started howling again.

Hayes sat through it all, seething.

"Now, dear," she said, drying her eyes with her handkerchief, "I want you to be governor as badly as you do. But believe me, this isn't the way to go about it." Pearl dismissed his silliness with a wave of lace.

"Listen to me, Hayes. If you want to win, I don't believe this race issue is going to serve you well. I think everyone is tired to death of it, myself. It's the 1950s, for goodness sakes. The colored question was settled in Mississippi long ago. It's old hat. We all know our places here. And if the only evidence you have to prove this conspiracy of yours is poor old Levi and a few colored maids, why…why…" she bit her lip, just barely able to suppress another fit of hilarity. "Why, I'm afraid you are certain to make a laughingstock of yourself. We've got to think of your stature…" she said, unable to stifle a tiny, leftover giggle, "as a statesman."

"Yes, Pearl," Hayes said, now in a deep sulk.

Pearl watched for a moment and then said, "Oh, Hayes, you just never understood how it was with us, did you?"

"Us?"

"Yes, us. My family. The Columns. The land. Everything and every-body on it. That 'us.' We are all part of that whole. Don't you see? You can't, never could touch Levi, because he is part of us, too. He's been a part of us for three hundred years."

Hayes looked up at the picture on the mantel of Pearl, the Senator, and Levi as children. He was repulsed. "You talking blood?"

"Blood?" Pearl scoffed. "Blood, indeed! Hayes, blood is the least of it."

"What do you mean? Blood is everything."

"Blood is mostly incidental," she said, dismissing Hayes with a flour-ish of her handkerchief. "History is everything. Through the years his peo-ple have schemed to kill us in our sleep. Our people have sold, hung, and bred his people. Levi's great-grandmother burned down the house on the Virginia plantation. We hung his grandfather for trying to start a slave uprising. Levi's father died saving the Senator from drowning in the river when he was only a three-year-old child. Hayes, we have hated and loved and killed and saved each other for almost three centuries, before this country was founded."

"Blood!" Pearl laughed. "For all that time we've taken care of each other. Looked to each other. Not to the government, not to the communi-ty, not to the church. You can't divide us anymore than you can divide air. The Senator may not be talking to Levi, but they will never be able to sep-arate themselves. They—we all breathe through one another's history. Levi almost raised Delia and Hertha. He was a second brother to me. The Senator was in love with Levi's wife before Levi was. That's the way it is. And it will never change. It's not about the weak loyalty of blood. It's fiercer and more stubborn than that. We are grafted to each other through our histories. We are fated to one another, for good or for evil. We may kill each other, or we may save each other, but it is up to *us* to do it."

Pearl gave Hayes a stern look. "And nobody—and I mean nobody—better try doing it for us. Can you understand that, Hayes?"

Hayes just looked at her like a pouting child.

"I thought not," Pearl said with a sigh.

She rose up from the sofa and walked over to him. Putting her hand gently on his shoulder, she said, "Hayes, I've been giving your future a lot of thought. If I'm going to finance your campaign I would prefer that you focus on something pleasant and uplifting. Like a statewide beautification program. Or tourism. That would be wonderful, wouldn't it? Get the true story out there about Mississippi. The Hospitality State."

"Yes. Wonderful."

"Oh, Hayes, don't be so morose! I'm sure I'm right. I've always been good with my hunches. Like when I told my brother to name you president of the bank. That's worked out well, hasn't it?"

"Yes, Pearl. I'm sure I can never thank you enough."

The handkerchief flew into the air. "Hayes! I've just had another inspiration. I think you should get down on your knees and beg that Hazel Graham to campaign for you. Why, just before you walked in the Trois Arts League named her unanimously as the Hopalachie County Woman of the Year."

Pearl touched the handkerchief to her heart and breathed deeply. "She's a saint, Hayes," she said, her words deeply felt. "A genuine saint has been living in our midst all this time. I knew there was something special about that woman." With her handkerchief, Pearl blotted away a little tear.

Chapter 53

THE RESURRECTION

Billy Dean pulled out of the old bootlegger's lair set deep in a hollow. His police radio was all static, exploding like fireworks in his head. Not helping matters, the sun was out again, sending the temperature soaring into the seventies once more. As he wound along the dirt track, leaving the heavy canopy of trees, the inside of the car began to heat up.

Billy Dean rolled up his window and turned the air conditioner on high. He had it put in just last week special. Cold was the only thing that seemed to make his headaches ease off some, that and keeping the radio quiet. The only dispatches he ever got were the constant updates on the four-month-old countywide search for Delia's body, which was now the longest in Mississippi history. He could guaran-damn-tee there wouldn't be any news breaking on that front. Not by a long sight.

Why should he care? Today was the first day of his retirement from the honorable profession of law enforcement. He reached down and clicked off the radio.

He stopped the car before he hit the blacktop and dug into his jacket for the wad of cash. After counting it a second time, he crammed it in the car pocket with the rest of the day's receipts. He stomped on the gas, tires squealing onto the pavement. In spite of his headache, Billy Dean felt pleased with himself. Nice day for collections so far. It was to be his final one. As promised, Delia had sent word. Tomorrow, December 1, he was to drive up to Memphis and meet her at the Peabody. This nightmare was coming to an end.

And not a minute too soon. While he was cleaning out his desk drawer at the house that morning, he discovered it unlocked and he could have sworn there had been a letter from Delia in there. One he hadn't got around to burning. Hertha was bound to be the one to have found it. Or Missouri. Either way, that meant she was on to him. He had no idea for how long, but knowing her she was probably setting some kind of trap. Probably already told the Senator. Anyway, after one last collection he was on his way out of the state for good. He'd worry about a divorce later.

The sky was beginning to cloud up again. It had been doing this all day. Big black clouds, fat with rain, would roll in on a cold wind, darkening everything around. But then they would move out again, without shedding a drop, temperatures shooting immediately to almost summertime levels. Maybe him and Delia could live someplace where it stayed cold all the time. Snowed even. That would suit him fine. By now Billy Dean had pretty much talked himself into looking forward to a new life with Delia. After all, she was a good-looking woman. Probably meant the child would be good-looking, too. That would be a nice change. Wouldn't feel like he was part of a circus act every time he took the family out in public. And them treating him like *he* was the freak.

His old uncle had been wrong when he said the Brister blood always won out when it came to looks. The Bristers had lost a couple of rounds bad in Hertha's case. Besides being unsightly, his daughters were turning out as cold and calculating as the rest of their women kin. There was something mighty scary that came in on that side of the family.

Twenty minutes later, the sun shining in his face, Billy Dean crested Redeemer's Hill. He cut on his siren and floored it, careening down into the Delta. They had blacktopped the road since the days he used to scare his uncle Furman shitless, sailing down the hill and slinging gravel to kingdom come in that bone-rattling Ford. Not near as much fun now. Still Billy Dean would miss it all when he had to give it up.

No turning back now. Soon things would begin to show up missing. Like tax receipts and the contents of Hertha's safe deposit box. Family bonds he had cashed in. Even if he changed his mind and stayed, he wouldn't be able to keep his job. Not with the niggers trying to vote and Levi sitting up in jail, still alive and uncharged. There was already strong talk of impeachment. What a joke! Billy Dean Brister thrown out of office for being a nigger-lover. His daddy would roll in his grave laughing at him.

About a mile before Hannah's, the rain began to fall, pelting the windshield with small, hard drops. He had to make one more collection before the day was done, and he figured that would push his private pension fund up to about fifty-five thousand dollars.

Billy Dean cut off his siren and swung onto the dirt path that led up to Hannah's. It had held together so far. Just barely. Hazel Graham had been one close call. Jesus, those idiots! Taking that fool woman for some kind of Yankee civil rights ringleader. And then shooting her while she was delivering food to the goddamned poor, for Christ's sakes.

"God almighty!" he had told them boys, "Helen Keller lives just over the state line in Alabama. Y'all can probly go whack her and be back by suppertime." Right there was another high-profile crime that would have to go unsolved by Billy Dean Brister. Just add it to the bill of impeachment.

The sheriff slipped out of the cruiser, leaving the door wide open, and eased up the plank steps without a creak. But he didn't surprise anybody. Willie and Hannah had been waiting for him ever since Willie returned from Delphi with the news. For the first time ever, they were delighted to see the sheriff. His showing up at Hannah's instead of heading straight out to the Columns meant he *hadn't* heard the news. Finally they had something on Billy Dean Brister.

When Billy Dean stalked through the door, he found the two standing behind the bar, side by side, just as they had rehearsed it. The sheriff asked for his whiskey like he always did.

Hannah reached under the bar and pulled out the fifth of Evan Williams she kept just for the sheriff and set it down before him. He drank right out of the bottle, refusing to ever use one of her glasses. As the rain pecked at the tin roof, neither Willie nor Hannah spoke. They were biding their time.

"You know why I'm here, Hannah," the sheriff said. "Let's have it."

"Sheriff, this is yo third run this week. I ain't got no more to give. Can't get blood outta no turnip."

"Then don't bother taking out my cut. Just hand me the whole damned tin."

"That's a good idea," she said. "I'll shows you what nothin looks like."

As Hannah reached behind her, she nodded at Willie.

"Sheriff, if you stop by this way when you get back from the Columns, I spect we'll have a little somethin for you then." Willie smiled his smoothest smile.

The sheriff narrowed his eyes at him. "What makes you think I'm going out that way? I never said."

"No, suh! I reckon you didn't. I just figured with all the commotion and all, you be headin out that way first thang."

"Commotion," the sheriff repeated almost to himself. He studied Willie close.

Setting the cash box down on the counter, Hannah jumped in. "Don't mind him none, Sheriff. He ain't meanin to be tellin you yo business. Why you was probably the first one to know bout it. A big thing like that."

Billy Dean's eyes kept shifting between the two, desperately trying to snag the piece he was missing.

"No, suh!" Hannah exclaimed. "I bet you knew befo' she hit the state line." She smiled brightly at him. "Big thang like Miss Delia comin home alive."

The sheriff went cold inside. "What'd you say?" he sputtered, gaping at Hannah.

But it was Willie's turn to go. "I sorry for misspeakin like that, Sheriff, suh. Hannah's sho right. Nobody knows the goins-on in this county like you. Nossuh!"

Hannah went next. "But when we heard what she brung back with her, well, we figured you'd sholy head on out there first thang."

Hannah flipped the cash box in her hand and shook it. "That's why we ain't got nothin here for you yet. Thought we had a little time to scrape somethin together."

"What she brought back with her?" Billy Dean was sick at his stomach. She couldn't have had the baby already, could she? No, not for a couple of months. At least that's what she said.

"Yessuh," Willie said with a laugh. "What she brung this time sho beat them Yankee husbands to hell and back." Willie looked up at the sheriff with an innocent grin. "I hope you don't mind me sayin so, Sheriff."

"Why should I...I mean...no." The sheriff was so tangled in what he was supposed to know and what he wasn't, his tongue knotted on him. Damn, how could Delia ever keep it all straight? At last he could only shout, "Mind your own god-damned business," and almost as an after-thought, "You nigger!" Then he fled through the door.

As the sheriff tore away in his car, Hannah and Willie turned to each other and then, delighted with themselves, started yelling, "You nigger! You nigger!" until they fell out laughing.

Billy Dean figured there was only one thing to do. He had to go straight out there and get in the middle of it. Shoot his way out if he had to.

When he pulled up into the circular drive, everything seemed peace-ful enough. The only disturbing detail being the little foreign car with the New Jersey tag. However, as he climbed the steps up to the gallery, he could hear shouting, loud enough to pierce the cypress door. It was the Senator's voice. "I'm gonna kill that sumbitch. Gimme my gun. Where the hell is my gun!"

The sheriff unsnapped his holster, eased the door open, and stuck his head inside. The first thing he saw was the Senator, jabbing wildly toward the top of the stairs with his favorite hickory cane, the one with the Confederate flag burned into the handle. From somewhere in the house he heard Delia crying, "Leave him alone, Daddy, I love him. If you kill him you're going to have to kill me, too."

With his head still poked through the doorframe, Billy Dean won-dered if this was the right time to be there after all. Maybe after things cooled down a bit. As he pulled the door to, the hinge creaked and the Senator whipped around and saw him.

"There you are!" The Senator came at him still waving the cane. Billy Dean drew his gun and aimed it.

"It's about time you done somethin right," the Senator said.

"Wha...?"

"Billy Dean, take that gun and shoot the both of them. I'll take full responsibility."

Shoot Delia and my baby? Billy Dean thought, trying to reason this out fast. That don't make any sense. And why in the hell is he acting so glad to see me? Now that he knows about Delia and me.

"Billy Dean!" came a cry from upstairs, "Is that Billy Dean Brister?"

Delia came down the stairs carefully, one hand on the railing and the other holding her very prominent belly. "Oh, Billy Dean! You've got to help us. Daddy's gone berserk." Once down the stairs, she scurried over to his side.

"Help...us?" Billy Dean asked, confused. He motioned with his gun to Delia's belly, and asked haltingly, "You mean...us?"

She quickly turned her face away from her father. "No, Billy Dean," she said in a low, scolding whisper. "Not *that* us." Then her face went all soft and innocent and she cried out, "Oh, Billy Dean, I'm so sorry for not writing, but it just happened so fast."

"Why should you be writing him?" the Senator asked, scowling. "What's going on here?"

Delia gave Billy Dean a quick little wink. Yep, he thought, she's enjoying the shit out of this. Whatever it was.

"No, Daddy, all I meant was I should have at least sent the sheriff proof that I was still alive so he wouldn't go to all the trouble of searching."

The Senator laughed bitterly. "That would have been most considerate of the sheriff's feelings." He stamped his cane on the floor. "What about the feelings of your god-damned father?"

Delia tossed back her golden hair. "Well, you can probably deduce from this recent display of insanity why I might have had my hesitations."

God, she's smooth, thought Billy Dean. She had everything so off-kilter, he didn't know where even he fit into her little play.

The Senator aimed his cane at Delia. "Arrest her, Sheriff. Right now. Don't listen to any of her fancy talk. I want her taken to jail and then hung. That's what I want. Give her Levi's cell. Looks like he won't be needing it now that my daughter's been resurrected."

The sheriff grinned at the Senator, feeling a little relief that it was Delia he was furious with and not him. Whatever game she was playing, Billy Dean seemed to be totally in the clear. He watched her with growing admiration. She was a better schemer than he had ever dreamed. More beautiful than he remembered. He wanted her now more than ever.

"What's the charge?" the sheriff said, playing along with the Senator.

"Miscegenation!"

The sheriff hesitated, trying to recollect the word. "Ain't that…?"

"Yep, Delia done gone and married a nigger!"

"Daddy," Delia whispered angrily, cutting her eyes upstairs. "I told you not to call him that."

The Senator jabbed his cane toward the stairs again. "Drove him right through Delphi in broad daylight in a foreign convertible. And a *Yankee* nigger at that. Delia, you've really gone and done it this time."

Delia poked her bottom lip out. "Jeffery's never going to come down now, Daddy."

"Jeffery?" Billy Dean said weakly. "Delia, you gone and married a…and the baby, but I…"

Once more Delia shot Billy Dean a look of severe warning, and then, seeing it had been received, immediately brightened, singing out sweetly, "Yes, the baby!" She laid her hand on her stomach. "You noticed! It must be impossible to miss now. How precious of you to concern yourself."

"Concern myself?" he stammered. "But…"

"Now don't you worry, neither of you. Jeffery will be a wonderful father. Daddy, did I tell you he owns twelve filling stations in New Jersey alone?" Delia raised her voice to the top of the stair. "Don't you, honey?"

There was only silence from upstairs. "See there, Daddy. Are you happy now? Jeffery's too scared to even speak."

"He oughta be. I'm gonna shoot his black ass the minute he hauls it down those stairs. Better yet, you go shoot him, Billy Dean. You already got your gun out. Go do it for me, son, as a personal favor."

Billy Dean didn't move. Things were happening too fast. He desperately needed time to regroup.

"It's too late to ever get you elected sheriff again, but if you do this little thing for me, I promise I'll find something for you. Go on and shoot 'im."

All Billy Dean knew was that he had better find a place to sit down fast. His head was about to bust and his stomach was going queasy. Collapsing on the settee against the entryway wall, Billy Dean took off his Stetson and dropped it on the floor. He sat hunched with his head in his hands, the room spinning, and the gun pointing at the ceiling.

"I'm hearing some pretty brave talk down there," came a booming Yankee voice from up above. "Who's got the guts to back it up?"

Billy Dean raised his eyes to see a giant of a black man, barrel-chested and immaculately dressed in a New York–tailored suit, come stomping down the stairs. He was carrying a .45 of his own.

"There he is Billy Dean!" The Senator was almost squealing. "You got a clean shot! What you waiting for, boy?"

Delia ran to Jeffery and flung her arms around him. "Leave him alone, Daddy. You're talking about the man who's going to be the father of your grandchild."

The Senator looked down at the sheriff. "I changed my mind. After you shoot him and lock Delia away, put Levi in the cell with my daughter. He's the only one that could ever talk any sense into that girl. Where is he when you need him, anyway?"

Billy Dean's head was swaying in his hands, his gun pointing upward at nothing in particular as he desperately tried to figure his next move. Maybe I should just go ahead and shoot the nigger—Jeffery—he thought. No, then I'd have to probably shoot Delia, too. Maybe I could yell out, "That's *my* baby we talkin about here!" but then I'd have to shoot the Senator.

No, she's got me. She's got me good. There ain't a thing I can say. Not a thing I can do. He cast a longing eye toward Delia, who stood there looking pure as the driven snow. Unwed, nearly seven months pregnant, and her arms around a—Jeffery.

The craziest thing was, Billy Dean thought, I don't even hate her for it. How does she do that? he wondered. Hell, he thought as he watched them there, holding each other, I can't even hate Jeffery for it.

"Boy," the Senator said, "are you all right? You don't look too good."

Billy Dean didn't say a word. There wasn't a word he could say. Not a move he could make. Delia had out-checkered him good. Jumped all his men and wiped the board clean.

Chapter 54
LOSS FOR WORDS

The bell rang from upstairs for the third time in twenty minutes, and again Vida, who was busy at the sink, sent Johnny up to see what she wanted. Two minutes later, he had returned. "She wrote, *I want Vida*. I think she's lonely again and needs you to tell her a story."

Vida shook her head. "Yo momma is the beatinest white woman alive. Didn't you tell her yo stories?"

"I told her all my good ones twice. I can't think of no more."

"Two hours before Mr. Floyd gets home and I ain't had the first thought about supper." Vida wiped her hands on the dishtowel and then flung it down on the countertop. "I knows what it is she's wontin. Might as well go give it to her."

She unplugged the coffeepot and placed it on the tray, along with two cups, a glass of grape Kool-Aid, and a slice of fruitcake. Then she stomped up the stairs as loud as she could, trying to stave off any more bell ringing. But before she got to the door it started again. "Put that thang down, fo' I hang it around yo neck like a bell cow!" Vida yelled. "We here already!"

Johnny got the door and Vida entered the room with Hazel propped up on a bank of pillows, her neck wrapped in bandages, scribbling furiously on one of Johnny's tablets. She handed it to him, and he in turn held it out to Vida.

Vida dropped the tray on the foot of the bed and snatched the pad. "News flash," Vida said, not looking down at the paper, but at Hazel, "They's a spoiled rotten white woman in this very room who startin to take 'vantage of her piteous situation."

Not thinking her funny, Hazel pointed her finger at the pad.

Vida read the note and frowned. "Well, I tell you why I ain't been up sooner. I been cleanin up after my friends as you know good and well. Can't we have our coffee and fruitcake and swap Santy Claus, without you gettin yo tail bent?"

Hazel took the pad from Vida and wrote, "WELL?"

"Weeellll," Vida said as she poured the coffee, "Well is a mighty deep subject." Both she and Johnny laughed at that, but Hazel flicked the pencil impatiently against the tablet like a drumstick.

After handing Hazel a cup and taking away her pencil, Vida sat down on the edge of the bed, took a deep breath, and began to recount the day's gossip. "Creola say she done changed her mind about Miss Pearl. Creola done decided that Miss Pearl ain't so much nice as she is stupid."

Hazel narrowed her eyes and looked at Vida scornfully.

"Just because you done switched yo mind on Miss Pearl, don't mean I can't have my own thoughts on the matter."

Hazel shrugged.

"Well, Creola say Miss Pearl tole her next time she gets the fool idea to go vote, she should come talk it out with her first. Miss Pearl say she been doin some readin on the nature of colored people and how they can't think too good for theyselves cause they backed up with feelings left over from Africa and slave times. Miss Pearl say she gone do a better job of lookin out for Creola, so she don't get herself in any mo trouble." Vida and Hazel both shook their heads at that.

"Well, you know Creola was fit to be tied. She say next time she was gone pass that test, just to show Miss Pearl who was backed up and with what."

Vida handed Hazel Maggie's fruitcake. "Course when Creola said that about votin, Sweet Pea right away rared back and say..." Vida looked down at Johnny, who was sitting on the floor, taking in every word. "Cover yo ears, chile,"

Johnny did as he was told. Carefully he watched Vida's lips.

"Sweet Pea say, 'Next time hell! If I go around tryin to vote ever week, I ain't never gone get no man in my house.'"

Hazel rolled her eyes and smiled.

When Vida handed Johnny his Kool-Aid, he dropped his hands from his ears. He had heard it all the first time anyway.

"I don't know who she be foolin. It's my daddy Sweet Pea got her sights on," Vida grumbled. "Merciful Jesus, that's one woman I ain't never callin 'Momma.'" Vida shook her head, disgusted.

"Course Sweet Pea gone have a swolled-up head now, gettin that big reward like she did. I tell you how that come about?"

Hazel shook her head, even though she had heard it twice. "She say she was listenin to Miss Hertha bein real ugly to our new sheriff. Carryin on bout her priceless rangs and cameos and thangs. Say if they can drag ever mud hole in Mis'sippi lookin for her sister who ain't even dead yet, then they sho nuf can sic one damned hound dog on Billy Dean." Vida laughed.

"That's when Sweet Pea took em to where he probly be hidin. Caught him red-handed. Speck he's busy as a man can be hashin over old times with his friends up at the State Prison."

Hazel waved her fork with satisfaction.

"I thought for sho, spite of the roadblocks, he would have got clear up to Chicargo, or some such place." Vida was quiet for a moment, nodding her head, thinking. Chicago, for her, had come to symbolize the very heart of the unknown world.

"Anyway, that where he was all right. I reckon I can see why he went back there. One time I figured it had to be his prayin ground. The last place he seen the face of God."

Hazel nodded as if she could understand such a thing.

"Ashes to ashes," Vida said.

Hazel raised her eyebrows.

"Ashes to ashes. It what he kept sayin when they took him in. Said he was drunk as Cooter Brown. Cryin like a baby."

Vida shook her head. "Ashes to ashes."

Then she looked up again. "And now we got us a Sheriff Butts to fret about. Course we don't know much about him, yet. We ain't got nobody in his house, but we workin on it. Creola got a cousin." Vida winked at Hazel and they both smiled.

"And that ol' Misery! Well, you know how she be. She say, 'All that trouble y'all got into and didn't change nothin. Still can't vote yet.'" Vida winked at Hazel. "You hear that? Even got ol' Misery sayin 'yet.' Now that be a mighty change right there. A mountain done moved. Like Daddy said, 'You caint turn back a step once it's been took.' He say you might can turn back the person what took it. Kill him even. But that step is out there for good. Waitin on the next person to come along."

Hazel nodded appreciatively, like that was a really good saying. Seeing that Hazel liked it, Vida repeated it proudly, "Yep, that's exactly what he said, 'You can't turn back a step once it's been took.'"

Vida went on for another several minutes, keeping an eye on Hazel, whose lids got heavier and heavier until she finally drifted off to sleep. Johnny and Vida quietly loaded up the tray. Vida turned out the lights and the boy carefully pulled the door closed.

Downstairs in the kitchen, as Vida set the tray on the counter, Johnny said, "Santa Claus coming tonight. Ain't he, Vida?"

"Sho is and don't say ain't."

"He coming to your house, too?"

"I speck he'll drop in. Along with all my other friends. And Willie and Daddy."

Vida ran a little more hot water into the sink and then she swished the dishwater with her hand to build a few suds. "And tomorrow," she said, "I be back here. Me and you can show off our presents."

Vida placed the last dishes in the sink and as she washed, she began to sing. This time the tune sounded more like a carol. As she sang, she thought about Nate. What would he be getting for Christmas? He was ten tonight. Clothes maybe? A football? Books? He could probably read real good by now.

She looked up out of the window. The weak December sun was nearly done for the day. Did he remember? she wondered, as she did every day.

After she repeated the two lines several more times, Johnny said, "You always singing them same words, Vida. Ain't you got no more?"

"Don't say ain't. Them's the only ones I know of." She continued singing what she knew.

Thinking Vida had sounded sad about that, Johnny said, "I'll make you some more for your Christmas present."

She smiled into her dishwater. "That would make me proud."

As Vida washed, and Johnny hunched over his tablet at the table, they sang the words together.

Drivin a big black car
For a big white man.

Chapter 55
UP NORTH

He stood at the window, watching the snow. It fell like a lacy curtain across the skyline, its folds covering the streets and gathering up over the sidewalk. Headlights and taillights and streetlights and traffic lights and neon winked and blinked and flashed through the snowy curtain like decorations on some immense tree.

The man never tired of watching the snow, seeing the seasons change with such force. Maybe because in this place, like the seasons, a man could make himself over, too. Here he could change into something more than anybody had ever told him was possible

He wouldn't have believed it, if he had been told. Anymore than if somebody had told him about snow spilling from the sky like freshly ginned cotton and piling deep and soft on the surface of frozen lakes. Crazy, he would have called them, back in the days when getting out was the only thing he knew about change. Getting out of Mississippi and singing the blues. He smiled at himself, at the way he had been.

"One more time," the boy called out, bouncing on the bed behind him. "I want to watch your fingers. I bet I can learn to play as good as you in a week."

He turned away from the window and the snow. "It's past your bedtime. They going to be back any minute."

"Just once more. Please? It's Christmas Eve." The boy looked at him expectantly, knowing that in the end he would get exactly what he wanted.

"Nearly Christmas. It's late."

Even as he said it the man was returning to the chair by the bed. He gently lifted the guitar from its case. The boy leaned in as the man showed him how to make the chord. He began the song once more, slowly this time, so the boy could study the fingering:

Vida, wear yo white shoes to the station
and yo cotton stockins too
But don't tell me that you love me,
Couldn't leave here if you do.

Sheriff had me on the rock pile,
Almost bust my back.
Tomorrow I'll be bustin through the gears
Of a rich man's Cadillac.

I got me a real meal ticket,
A solid gold plan
Drivin a big black car,
For a big white man.

Vida, wear yo white dress to the station
Bring yo parasol too
But don't tell me that you want me,
I got some travelin to do.

You got my motor running hot,
My shaft bout to blow
But I'm gonna be a driverman, baby,
I really got to go.

"*Caaaaause…*" holding the note, he nodded to the boy, signaling him to come in on the final verse:

I got me a real meal ticket,
A solid gold plan
Drivin a big black car,
 For a big white MAN!

The boy let out a whoop and then clapped his hands. For the first time ever, they were able to finish up on the exact same note. "I want you to teach me that one first." Trying to imitate his favorite deejay, he announced, "That's my number one, all-time fave on the Uptown Hit Parade."

The man laughed. "That right?" He plucked a high C and then bent the string, making the note rise up like a question. "Why you suppose that is?"

"Two reasons."

"And I bet they both long ones." The man frowned at the clock on the nightstand. It was hours past the boy's bedtime. "OK. Count em down."

"One. Because you put my father in it." He hopped up on his knees and held a fist to his mouth, singing into it very badly, "A big white man in a big black car."

"Yep. You right about that." The man strummed the final chord of the song again. "OK, two. And make it quick."

"Two." The boy grinned at the man, his dark chocolate eyes twinkling, and almost whispering said, "Because I think it's dirty. Is it? Did you write a dirty song?"

"Don't tell nobody."

"Ha! I thought so." He dropped down to the mattress and propped his chin up on both fists. "Why'd you write a song about him?"

The man shook his head. "It's not going to work. I told you that story a million and one times already. You know it better than me. I think you're stalling."

"Aw, we've got time. Tell me again."

"I know you're stalling." Carefully he laid the new guitar back in the case. He got up, then crossed the bedroom to the window, this time pulling the drapes shut. "They get back and find you still up, we'll both be in hot water."

"Come on, be a sport. Pleeeease? Mom and Dad won't care."

He turned back to the boy. "You take the blame this time."

"Deal!" The boy jumped under the covers. "Tell it."

Sitting down by the boy's bed again, he said, in the slightly bored, rushed manner of someone telling a fairy tale everybody already knew by heart, "I wrote that song because your daddy found a way to get me out of trouble, when nobody else would bother with a Mississippi hick, cotton lint still in his hair. But he did. A big-shot lawyer like him, standing out for a eighteen-year-old punk."

"You!" the boy laughed. "A Mississippi hick!"

"Yeah. Me," he said, laughing also.

"That's when he asked you to come live with us."

"Yep. When he got me out of prison. I started drivin for him. And he gave me a room in his very own home to stay in."

"But we didn't have a Cadillac."

"It rhymed better."

"How old was I?"

The man gave the boy a suspecting look. "When I got out you were almost four. Like you know for yourself. You tryin to stretch this out."

"I think I remember you showing up that day," the boy said, grinning. "Come to think of it, you did look like a hick."

"That why you wanted me to tell it? So you could turn it on me?"

"I'll be good." He held up two fingers, promising. "And now you're going to be a lawyer like him."

"One day. If he's a good enough teacher. End of story. Get to sleep now."

"And he kept your valuables while you were in prison."

"How's that?" the man asked.

"You know. Like in that song you used to sing to me when I was little. About giving my father your valuables to keep for you while you were in jail. He kept them safe until he could get you out."

"That's right. That old lullaby. You remember that?"

"What did you have valuable? You said you were poor."

"Five-dollar guitar." Then, half-smiling, he studied the boy, remembering the night he fled on the night train to Memphis, one step ahead of trouble, trying to quiet the sobbing baby in his arms. "And some other things," he said. "Little no-count things I brought up from Mississippi."

The boy yawned. "Are you ever going to write one about me?"

"When you can carry a tune to sing it with. Time for you to go to bed. Let's cut the light out."

The boy laughed. "You can't *cut* a light! Why do you say that?"

"It was the way they said it when I was coming up. Never you mind. You know what I mean. It's already Christmas. You'll be wontin to roust everbody at dawn."

"I don't do that anymore. I'm a teen rebel. Almost. All grown-up and looking for trouble."

Wide-awake again, the boy threw his arm up in the air. "Indian wrestle! I can take you three out of three."

Considering the boy for a moment, he wondered if it were true what he had said. "No, you're right. You too big now. You'll shame this old man for sure." He reached over for the chain on the bedside lamp.

"Just tell me again," the boy said.

"You still stalling." But he lowered his hand from the lamp. "Tell you what?"

"How white it was."

"Oh, that. Get back under the covers."

The boy moved fast. "Done!"

The man began in a low, bluesy baritone, *"That cotton was white as sugar,"*

"But not as sweet," the boy answered in turn with his breaking alto.

"As white as the snow on a mountain top,"

"But not as cool."

"As white as the white man's smile,"

"But not as cruel."

The boy smiled, but his eyes were heavy. Reaching for the chain again, the man said, "Time to cut off the lights. This time for true."

"Just one more."

"No."

"The story about the hands," he said and yawned again.

The man thought for a moment, and then shook his head. "Don't ring a bell."

"You know. When I was little. The one you told about the golden hands on a golden thread." The boy rubbed an eye with the back of his fist. "I remember you telling me."

"No, I never told it," said the man. "You must have imagined that one on your own. Maybe you got your own song to write."

The boy looked up sleepily at the man, "Can white people sing the blues?"

The man laughed, and then, realizing the boy was serious, said, "In your case they might make an exception."

The boy nodded, too sleepy to know if he was being kidded. Closing his eyes, he said with a yawn, "Thanks for the guitar."

"You're welcome." He clicked off the light. "Merry Christmas."

The boy, on his way to sleep, said softly, "I want to go there one day. Go see the big river and the alligator swamps. Cotton fields. That woman all dressed in white."

The man pulled the covers up over the boy's shoulders. "They just songs. Believe me, you got everything worth wanting right here." He stood over the bed, studying the boy, his face illuminated by a wedge of light from the doorway. He reached down, intending to stroke him lightly on the cheek, but drew his hand back. The boy had been right. He was growing up. Soon he would be too old for bedtime stories and lullabies. Time to give up childish things.

As he stood there, watching, having his thoughts, the boy began to snore softly. But still, he decided, only little boy snores. He had his whole life in front of him. With no history to get over. No past to drag him down. His future was locked up safe and secure like money in the bank. The man told himself for the millionth time that it was the right thing. The best thing.

He was about to pull the door when he noticed the boy's fist. It was clenched on the pillow, next to his head, as if holding on tightly to something as he slumbered.

Finally he whispered, "Good-night, little man," and carefully closed the door on the boy's dreaming.

ACKNOWLEGMENTS

The joy of writing this book was not in concocting, but in discovering, and I was blessed to have generous guides to point out the way. I want to thank John Thew for believing that I could write, novelist Mary Gardner for showing me how, and the late writer John Paul Lee for telling me that I was crazy if I didn't.

I want to thank my parents, aunts, and uncles, and grandparents for submitting to an endless onslaught of questions—from "what is a turn row?' to "how do you dress a squirrel?" to "how do you make a cats head biscuit?" and for burrowing into their pasts for those memories.

I came to rely on several authors to help me explore Jim Crow Mississippi from both sides of the color line. I am especially indebted to Alan Lomax, *The Land Where the Blues Began* (1993); James C. Cobb, *The Most Southern Place on Earth* (1992); John Dittmer, *Local People* (1994); John Dollard, *Caste and Class in a Southern Town* (1937); Neil R. McMillen, *Dark Journey* (1990).

But I am mostly grateful to the African American witnesses to that age, those unlikely memoirists—sharecroppers, maids, midwives, yardmen, preachers, teachers, schoolchildren, and Saturday night brawlers—who shared their precious recollections to help this author discover the true measure of heroism.